April 1906

The clear autumn sunlight lent a hint of gold to the rich green of the grass. Flowers glowed where the light caught them: daisies growing wild in the grass, neat posies in earthenware pots, and a whole basketful of blooms carried by a slight figure dressed all in black.

She carried the basket over one arm, her other arm looped through that of the tall woman who walked at her side. Her hat with its black veil barely reached her companion's shoulder, and a casual observer might have taken them for a woman in charge of a young girl. But closer inspection would reveal fine lines around the eyes of the black-clad woman, and a few threads of silver in her dark hair; while her companion's face was smooth and unlined, and her hair glossy black wings under her white straw hat.

They stopped in front of a small slab of pale grey marble, the woman in black releasing her hold on the other with a hesitation that spoke of how precious the contact was. She crouched before the slab and placed a posy of pink roses in the vase that stood there.

'This is where Granny's buried—your great-grandmother,' she said.

The younger woman crouched beside her, and traced the words on the stone with her fingers. 'Her name was Amy, too. You were named after her.'

'Yes, I was.' Amy stroked the blue silk of the younger woman's skirt. 'And I named you after Mama.'

She rose and went the few steps to where another, larger, slab marked a double plot. 'Come and see Mama and Pa's stone,' she said, looking over her shoulder. The younger woman joined her.

'"In Loving Memory of Ann Leith,"' Amy read aloud. '"Dearly Beloved Wife of Jack Leith".' She fell silent for a moment. 'She was beloved, too. I don't think Pa ever really got over losing her.'

'So young,' her companion murmured, studying the stone. 'Only twenty-seven.'

'I can just remember her,' Amy said. 'She was lovely—that's why I gave you her name.' She smiled wistfully. 'It hides Mama's name, having Sarah in front of it. I know they wanted to give you a new name, but I can call you Sarah Ann when it's just us two, can't I?'

'Of course,' said Sarah. 'I'm not ashamed of the name you gave me.'

Amy placed more of her roses before the stone. '"And of the above Jack Leith",' she read. 'See how new the writing looks compared to

3

Mama's? It's six years since Pa passed away, though. I wish you could have met him.'

'I doubt if we would have been friends,' Sarah said, a tightness creeping into her voice.

'I think you—' A look at Sarah's set expression silenced Amy. 'I hope you would have,' she murmured.

'I found one of these red roses this morning,' she went on more brightly. 'Pa always liked these ones best—Mama planted the bush, and I took a cutting from it. They don't usually have flowers this late, I was lucky to find one.' She held the rose out. 'Would you put it on Pa's grave for me? Please?'

Sarah hesitated only a moment. 'I think not,' she said crisply. 'I can't see that my attentions would make my grandfather rest easier in his grave.' She put a hand on Amy's arm. 'Whenever I think of him, I can't get past the knowledge that he made you marry that dreadful man. That he made you give me away.'

Amy shook her head. 'It wasn't like that. Pa was only trying to do the right thing for me.'

'If that's the case, he had an odd way of going about it.'

'He did his best.' Amy slipped the red rose back into her basket and walked a short distance with Sarah, to a small plot marked by a low white stone. 'This was your baby brother.'

' "Alexander John Stewart",' Sarah read aloud. 'Such a little grave it is.'

'They told me he was tiny. He was born much too early, and he only lived a few hours. I wasn't allowed to see him.' Amy took a small spray of jasmine from her basket and placed it in front of the stone. 'I used to think I'd like to have some of that iron that looks like a cradle around Alexander's grave. They do that with babies' graves sometimes—there's one over there, see? Alexander never had a real cradle.'

'Why didn't you have his grave done like that, then?' Sarah asked.

Amy gave a small shrug. 'Charlie didn't seem to think of it, and I didn't like to ask. I suppose it would have cost a lot of money.'

'I'll see that it's done.'

'Oh, it doesn't matter now, Sarah, not after all this time.'

'Yes, it does,' Sarah said. 'He was my baby brother, after all. Half-brother, anyway. There's no need to discuss it, the thing's settled.'

Amy squeezed her hand in silent gratitude, and kept hold of the hand to lead Sarah over to a tall, imposing monument. 'There's a wonderful stone for Mal, anyway. The whole town put in money to have this put up. Mal was the only boy from here that went to the war.'

'He must have been well thought of,' Sarah remarked, studying the inscription.

'He… people thought well of him after he died, anyway. I suppose that's how it usually goes. He wasn't a bad boy, not really.'

'I had them put Charlie as near Mal's memorial as I could.' Amy shook her head as a rush of memories crowded in on her. 'It tore the heart out of him when Mal died, I think.'

'Are you sure he ever had one?' Sarah said acidly.

'Oh, yes. Especially for Mal. Charlie was never the same again after that.' She gazed up at the monument. 'But he wouldn't ever talk about it—not till right at the end, anyway. He never even saw this memorial.'

She turned aside to the last of her dead. 'And now he's just about alongside it. That was the best I could do for him.' She reached into her basket for the final bunch of roses.

'I hope you're not going to ask me to put flowers on *his* grave,' Sarah said, with the familiar sharpness that edged her voice whenever she spoke of Charlie.

Amy shook her head. 'No, I don't expect you to take any notice of Charlie. He wasn't anything to you.' She placed the roses on the still-bare mound of earth.

There was only one flower left in her basket now: the single red rose. Amy took it up and turned it over in her hand, careful of the thorns. 'I suppose I'd better put this on Pa's grave myself, then,' she said, doing her best to keep the disappointment out of her voice.

'Amy, you are the most soft-hearted creature I've ever met,' Sarah scolded. She plucked the rose from Amy's hand, strode back to the double grave, and crouched before the stone.

'Amy thinks that you and I would have been friends, Grandfather,' she said. 'I've my doubts about that. But Amy loved you, and I'm prepared to believe you cared for her, too. So that will have to suffice for me. Here you are, then.' She placed the rose in front of the stone.

Amy came up behind her and slipped her arm around Sarah's waist as the younger woman stood up. 'Are you happy now?' Sarah asked.

'Oh, yes. I think I'm the happiest woman in the world.'

'Good.' Sarah slid her own arm around Amy's waist. 'I'd do a good deal to make you happy, Amy.'

Her solemn expression melted into a smile, and she lowered her face to Amy's. Her breath tickled delightfully against Amy's skin as Sarah whispered the secret that, in all the world, only the two of them shared:

'Mama.' The word slipped almost soundlessly into Amy's ear. 'Little Mama.'

1

David yawned hugely. He belatedly remembered his manners and covered the last part of the yawn with his hand.

'I'm off to bed, Ma,' he told Amy, standing up to punctuate his words. 'I'm just about asleep already.' He stooped to kiss Amy good night.

She twined her arms around his neck to return the embrace. 'Good night, Davie.'

'I suppose you two are going to sit up half the night talking again,' David said, casting a grin in Sarah's direction.

Amy smiled up at her son, noting with fresh pleasure the subtle likeness between Sarah and him. 'We'll sit up a bit longer, won't we, Sarah? We won't talk loud, though.'

'You must've just about talked yourselves out by now,' David said. 'I don't know what you keep finding to talk about.'

'Why, you, of course,' Sarah said at once, allowing herself a small smile. 'I'm surprised your ears don't burn with it.'

'Well, maybe they would if I didn't sleep so sound.' He yawned again, this time managing to catch the whole of the yawn with his hand. 'Night, Ma. Night, Miss Millish.'

'Dave doesn't quite know what to make of us,' Sarah remarked when David had closed his bedroom door behind him. 'Whatever is his sensible mother doing, spending all her time talking to that odd woman from Auckland?'

'Davie doesn't think you're odd.' Amy spoke in a whisper, all too aware of how thin the wall was between the parlour and David's room. 'He's just not used to seeing me sit up so late.' She reached out and took Sarah's hand. 'He doesn't know I'm trying to catch up on twenty years without you.'

Sarah squeezed her hand in answer. Amy stared into her face, still struggling to take in the wonder of it: that the baby she had only been allowed to keep for a precious few weeks should have found her; should have come back to her as an assured young woman, with all the gifts Amy had ever prayed her child might have. And the greatest joy of all was that Sarah was as ready to return her love as Amy was to offer it. No wonder that Amy resented even the hours spent sleeping, when they meant time spent away from her daughter.

'Let's go and sit in my funny little bedroom,' Sarah said. 'I haven't the patience to be whispering all the time.'

Amy followed Sarah out through the front door of the cottage and into the room that had been formed from a closed-in portion of the verandah. It held a bed and a low chest of drawers, and the floor boasted a small rag rug that stopped a few of the draughts that nudged through the floorboards on winter nights. For years it had been 'the boys' room', then 'Dave's room' when Malcolm had gone. Now David slept in the bedroom that had been his father's, and the verandah room had been empty since Charlie's death. Until three days before, when Amy had miraculously acquired a full-grown child to put in this room.

Sarah propped the pillow against the wall as a back rest and patted the space beside her on the bed. 'Sit here next to me. We can both use the pillow if we sit close—though you can't help but sit close in here, can you? However did you fit two big boys in this room?'

Amy joined her on the bed. 'We managed somehow. My boys didn't know any different, so I don't suppose they ever thought they should have a bigger room.'

Sarah had touched on the one thing that troubled Amy about having her under their roof: the plainness of the lodging. 'I'm sorry it's not very flash here—I know it's not what you're used to.'

'For goodness' sake, Amy, I didn't come for the sake of the accommodation! And you're not to apologise for the fact that that man couldn't provide you with a decent house to live in.'

'It's not as bad as all that. Anyway, I'm used to it.'

'Then it's high time you grew used to something better.' Sarah took Amy's hand and looked straight into her eyes with that disconcertingly direct gaze of hers. 'I want you to come to Auckland with me.'

Amy had been expecting the words for days. 'I can't, Sarah. I just don't see how I can be away from the farm.'

'But you *must* come. You know I can't stay here for long, don't you?'

'No, I don't suppose you can,' Amy said. 'You've got your business to look after and everything.'

'And you surely don't want us to part again so soon? Not when we've so much catching up to do.'

'I... well, I hoped you could stay for a bit longer. I knew it couldn't be as long as all that, though.'

'And after my "bit longer"? What did you expect us to do after that? Make do with letters?'

'I don't know. I've been trying not to think about you going away again.'

'Well, you must think about it,' Sarah said. 'I've got to go home within the next few days—by the end of the week at the latest, I've a meeting on Monday that can't be put off. But I don't want to go without you.'

'I wish I could, honestly I do. But how can I go away and leave Davie?

Who'd look after him?'

Sarah gripped her hand hard, then abruptly let it drop. 'Must David's convenience govern your entire existence? Haven't you spent enough of your life running around after him?'

'It's not like that, Sarah. Dave works hard, and he's got to have someone to get his meals on and everything. You do see that, don't you? He needs me.'

'Dave's had you for twenty years. Isn't it time I had my chance with you?'

'Not twenty,' Amy murmured.

'What did you say? Don't whisper so,' Sarah said, irritation clear in her voice although she kept it low.

'It's not twenty years. Dave's only eighteen.'

'Oh, for Heaven's sake, are you going to turn pedantic on me now?' Sarah's mouth twisted in annoyance. 'Eighteen years, then, if we must be precise. That's long enough, isn't it?'

Her face hardened, and she stared at the bedroom wall; directing her disapproval towards the oblivious David, Amy knew. 'And for all your fussing over him, David didn't concern himself over you, did he? Not when he went wandering off for years and left you alone with that man. I don't see that he thought beyond his own comfort.'

Amy sighed, and wished silently that things did not have to be quite so complicated. 'It wasn't like that. Dave didn't want to go away.'

'Why did he go, then?' Sarah asked, making no attempt to hide her scepticism.

'He...' Amy hesitated. Sarah felt enough bitterness towards Charlie without Amy's giving her more cause. 'Maybe you should ask Dave yourself.'

'Perhaps I will,' said Sarah. 'Leaving you with that man! How could he?' She shook her head in perplexity. 'However did you cope, Amy? Living all those years with that coarse, brutish creature! No, don't you go scolding me, you know well enough what I thought of him, and I'm not going to pretend otherwise'

Amy stared at the opposite wall, aware of Sarah's careful scrutiny. She tried to keep her expression calm as memories washed over her.

Twenty-one years since she had come to live in this house. She had been barely sixteen, haunted by nameless fears that lurked in the shadows of her awareness. She had learned soon enough to give names to those fears; learned that this house held things more substantial than shadows to be afraid of. The worst Sarah had known of Charlie was his lack of social graces. His coarse way of speaking had been the last vestige of the terrifying husband Amy had once known; it had roused more pity than distress in her.

'Amy.' Sarah's voice dragged Amy back to the present. Sarah was studying her, a slight frown creasing her forehead. 'Do you know, I can see the thoughts writing words over your face. I almost feel I could read you as clearly as a book if only I knew the language a little better. What is it, Amy? What are those thoughts of yours saying?'

Amy gave a rueful smile. 'Oh, nothing much. Just things that happened years and years ago. I suppose… well, it's a good thing you didn't meet Charlie earlier. You only met him once he'd got easy to get along with.'

'I find that hard to believe,' Sarah muttered. 'Oh, never mind him. Don't you want to come with me, Amy?'

'Of course I do. But I've got to try and do the right thing by everyone—you as well as Dave. That's what's so hard.'

'Don't worry about trying to please other people—me included, come to that. Just do what you want.'

'But… but that's what I do want,' Amy said helplessly. 'I want to try and make everyone happy.'

'Then you may just be doomed to failure,' said Sarah. 'Dave's interests and mine seem to be directly opposed. I suppose expecting him to consider your wishes is not to be hoped for? Ah, now you're going to scold me for criticising your precious Davie, aren't you?'

Amy felt tears of frustration pricking at her eyes. 'Don't talk like that, Sarah, please don't. I wish you could—'

'Oh, Lord, now you're going to cry, and it's my doing,' Sarah interrupted. 'Come here, my silly Mama, and let your dreadful daughter try and put things right. No, not a word from you until I've finished.'

She drew Amy within the circle of her arm. 'Let me finish your sentence for you. "I wish you could get to know Dave better. I wish you'd make an effort." There, it's said now. But we'll have no more talk tonight about Auckland or husbands or brothers, or anything else difficult.'

Sarah was unused to the early hours Amy and David kept. She emerged for breakfast the next morning some time after David had finished his meal and gone off about his work, while Amy was making a batch of scones.

'Late for breakfast again,' Sarah said cheerfully. She kissed Amy on the cheek and gathered up a plate and knife for herself. 'No, don't you go waiting on me, I'm quite capable of getting myself some bread and jam.'

'It wouldn't take me long to make you a proper breakfast,' Amy tried. 'You're sure you wouldn't like one?'

'Quite sure, thank you. Unlike you and Dave, I'm doing very little useful work at the moment. I've no need for bacon and eggs. Is that tea fresh?'

'Fairly. It's still hot, anyway.'

'Good. Sit down and I'll pour us both a cup.'

Amy wiped her dough-covered hands on her apron and took a seat at the table. 'You seem very bright this morning, Sarah.'

'Mmm. I took advantage of the still of the night to think things through. I see now that I've allowed myself to lose sight of the issues of real import.' She smiled as she toyed with her cup. 'Father would have scolded me for that. "Muster your facts, Sarah," he used to say. "You can't expect to convince others if you've only the woolliest notion of what you're talking about." Well, I've mustered them now.'

'Have you?' Amy said, struggling to make sense of Sarah's words.

'Yes, I have. The facts, then. First: I want you to come to Auckland with me for a good, long visit—I'll expect you to stay three months at least. Preferably four. Next fact, you want to come as much as I want you to. Are we agreed thus far?'

'Yes, but—'

'No buts. They can come later. Now, it seems that the only thing standing in the way of our getting what we want is what's to be done with Dave while you're away.'

'Yes, that's right. There's his meals to get on, and washing and everything. That's why I can't go away.'

Sarah pounced on Amy's words. 'Ah, but it's not quite that simple. That's something Father taught me later—the facts are not always as clear as they might seem. We've looked at the obvious ones, now let's probe a little deeper.'

She raised her cup from its saucer and studied Amy over the rim. 'It's not difficult to see what needs doing about Dave. There are other people in this valley besides yourself who are capable of cooking meals and washing clothes and goodness knows what else.'

'But I couldn't expect...' Under the pressure of Sarah's steady gaze, Amy heard her voice trailing away. 'I just couldn't.'

'The real problem,' Sarah went on relentlessly, 'is that you don't want to upset Dave. Now, that's getting closer to the truth, isn't it? You're reluctant to tell him you want to go away for a while. You've spent so long trying to please everyone, trying to keep everybody happy, that taking the risk of upsetting Dave for so trivial a reason as doing something *you* want is quite beyond you.'

'It's not like that,' Amy protested feebly.

'Ah, but it is. And as if that weren't enough, you've me to cope with.' Sarah replaced her cup on the saucer and reached out to stroke Amy's hand. 'Whenever you dare mention Dave to me, I bristle with indignation and start finding excuses to criticise your darling boy. No wonder you hardly know what you want, let alone how to go about getting it.

'So it's time I helped you along,' Sarah announced. 'Where's Dave?'

'Down at the potato paddock, I think. What do you want him for?'

'Well, you've hinted to me often enough that I couldn't help but like Dave if I'd only make the effort to get to know him better. I'm not saying I'm completely convinced yet, mind. But we shall see.' Sarah stood and leaned over to place a kiss on Amy's cheek. 'I'm going to make an effort,' she said over her shoulder as she headed for the back door.

She found David easily enough; he was in the potato paddock as Amy had said, checking on the mound of potatoes that were to be stored for the winter. He looked up as she approached, and Sarah saw his smile of welcome replaced by a somewhat apprehensive expression.

'I thought you were Ma for a minute,' he said, not quite meeting her eyes. 'Is it time for morning tea already?'

'No, not just yet. I left Amy making a batch of the largest scones I've ever seen, so I expect they'll take a while to cook. May I join you for a little? I feel the need of some fresh air.'

'If you want. I don't know if there's anywhere clean enough for you to sit, though.' David looked about for a suitable spot, then snatched up the jacket he had put to one side. 'Here, you can have this if you like,' he said, spreading it over a dry patch of ground.

'How chivalrous.' Sarah lowered herself onto the makeshift seat. 'Thank you, Mr Stewart. Don't let me interrupt your work, though.'

'I wouldn't mind getting on with it,' David said, casting a glance at his potatoes. 'I've just about finished, anyway.'

Sarah attempted a dispassionate study of David as she watched him spread a final layer of fern fronds over the potatoes. A handsome man; that was undeniable. He was one of the few men Sarah had ever met who topped her own height by several inches, and the well-muscled frame that went with it gave him an impressive stature. His father had bequeathed his height and build to David, but that was the limit of David's resemblance to Charlie. He had Amy's dark hair, in David's case just long enough to betray a hint of curl, and Amy's large, blue eyes. Disguised by a bonnet, his face would have been pretty enough for a woman's. Sarah briefly indulged in the mental exercise of surrounding that face with lace and ribbons, completing the picture with a froth of dark curls.

Yes, he would have made a very pretty woman; prettier than she was herself. He certainly resembled Amy more strikingly than she did. Was that why she felt so jealous of him?

Her musings brought her up short. Jealous? Of David? How could she be jealous of a man who had spent his life in a rough cottage, apart from three years in a mining camp? His entire possessions consisted of this little farm, the earnings of which, Sarah suspected, would barely be noticed on one of her own balance sheets. Amy had assured her that David had done well at his lessons; be that as it might, his father had taken him out of school as soon as the law allowed, wanting the use of his labour full-time.

But he had had Amy. All his life she had been there; he had not had to track her down through vague hints and dusty certificates. And it took no great powers of observation to see that Amy loved him with all the depths of affection she was capable of. How could he have valued that so little as to have left her alone when he had gone to the mine?

She realised that David had stopped working, and was aware of her scrutiny.

'Am I doing something silly?' he said.

'I don't believe so. Why do you ask?'

'It's just the way you were looking at me. I thought you were laughing at something a minute ago—something about me. Then you looked as though you wanted to tell me off. S'pose that's not anything out of the ordinary, though.'

'Whatever do you mean?' Sarah asked, genuinely startled.

'Well, you often do look as though you'd like to go crook at me.' He lowered his eyes and looked away. 'Sorry, I shouldn't have said that.'

'Oh, please do speak freely, Mr Stewart. This is your property, after all. And you and I will never learn to know one another better if we continually stand on ceremony.' She saw the quick twist of his mouth that betrayed his thoughts. 'Now you're wondering why on earth we should want to get to know one another better, aren't you?'

'Sort of,' David admitted. 'I mean, Ma likes you and all that, and I'm really happy for her. Ma hasn't had it too easy, you know.'

'Yes, I do know,' Sarah agreed feelingly. 'That's what I particularly wanted to talk to you about. Sit down, why don't you? Come along, I don't often bite. There's probably room on this jacket of yours.'

'No, over here'll do. I don't want to get your fancy dress dirty.' David squatted down on his heels opposite her.

It was Amy she wanted to talk about, but David's odd manner intrigued Sarah. 'I almost think you're frightened of me, Mr Stewart,' she mused aloud. 'Now, what have I done to deserve that?'

'I'm not really. Well, I suppose I… well, Ma said you were a teacher.'

'Yes, I was. I gave it up last year, when my other obligations grew more demanding. Why does that trouble you particularly?'

'Well, you sort of remind me of this teacher I used to have.'

'Really? Aren't you a little beyond being afraid of school teachers?'

'You never knew Miss Metcalf. You're not really like her,' he added uncomfortably. 'You sure don't look like her. It's just the way you always look as if you want to tell me off. I can just see you with a strap in your hand.'

'I do know how to use one. I don't think you need worry on that account, though. If for no other reason than that Amy would evict me from the house if I tried it.'

She saw the warmth of his smile at the mention of Amy. There was no doubting David's fondness for his mother, though there still remained the mystery of why he had left her alone for so long.

'Amy works terribly hard, doesn't she?' said Sarah.

'Yes, she's always doing something. It's not like when Pa was alive, though. He took a lot of looking after once he'd got sick.'

'And a lot of putting up with, I imagine.' She saw David shoot a rapid glance at her, then look away. 'Don't you agree?' Still no reply. 'Oh, come now, Mr Stewart, it's a simple enough question. Your father was not a particularly easy man to get along with, was he?'

David chewed at his lip, opened his mouth and closed it again. Sarah waited, drumming her fingers lightly on her lap. 'There's no good dragging up all that old stuff,' David blurted out at last. 'It'd only upset Ma, anyway.'

'But she's not here at the moment,' Sarah pointed out in her most reasonable voice. 'And *I* want to know one or two things. Why did you go to Waihi, Mr Stewart?'

She saw him shift uncomfortably. It was clear that he did not want to discuss the matter, but Sarah held his gaze coolly. 'Well?' she pressed.

'There's not many jobs I know how to do, 'cept farming. I wanted to go somewhere I could make a bit of money. I thought the mines would pay pretty well.'

'Yes, yes, I don't mean why you specifically chose Waihi. *Why* did you leave the farm? Why did you leave Amy alone with your father? How did you expect her to cope?'

'Do you think I wanted to?' David startled her with his sudden fierceness. 'Do you think I was happy, leaving her with the old man?'

As if his outburst had alarmed him, too, he fell silent for a moment, and lowered his voice when he went on. 'I tried to make her come with me, but she wouldn't. She said there wouldn't be anywhere for her to stay in Waihi—she was right, too, I couldn't have had her staying in the bunkhouse. I was going to send for her as soon as I could get enough money to rent a house or something. I kept thinking I'd be able to soon. I never did, though.'

'And why were you there yourself, Mr Stewart?' Sarah asked, relentless. 'Why did you leave the farm?'

David's reluctance to answer was almost palpable. 'Ma says you shouldn't speak ill of the dead,' he said under his breath.

'I've always thought that of all people the dead were least likely to be harmed by harsh words,' Sarah mused. 'Why did you go away, Mr Stewart?'

David slumped in defeat. 'I didn't have much choice. The old man told me to clear out.'

Sarah nodded. 'I suppose that shouldn't surprise me, really. I saw enough of your father to know he was capable of that. But you surely could have made some effort to get on with him, couldn't you? For Amy's sake, at least.' She steadfastly ignored the weak flutterings of her conscience as it reminded her that she had found herself incapable of tolerating Charlie in polite silence for more than a few minutes. 'Why did you have to go squabbling with him?'

'I did try and get on with him,' David said in a low voice. 'I put up with him for years and years so's not to make it harder for Ma. I didn't care what he said to me—I didn't!' he insisted, as if Sarah had contradicted him. 'But I wasn't going to let him talk to Ma like that any more.'

'Talk to her like what?' Sarah prompted, her interest stirred.

David made a noise of disgust; for a moment Sarah thought he might be going to spit on the ground. 'Dirty talk. I wouldn't repeat it in front of you.' His forehead creased in a frown that seemed to hold as much puzzlement as anger. 'Awful, awful things he used to say to her. I don't know why. He used to talk as if she was… well, never mind that. You wouldn't want to hear it.'

'No, I wouldn't. Though I rather think I can guess some of it well enough.'

'Maybe,' David said doubtfully. 'Anyway, this last time I was fed up with him. He'd been more of an old so-and-so than ever since Mal died, I was just about sick to death of him. And then he started carrying on with his dirty talk to Ma—it was the worst he'd ever been with it. I told him to shut up, but he just kept going on and on. So I made him shut up. I knocked him down.'

He heard Sarah's sharp intake of breath. 'Pa wasn't old and sick then like when you met him,' he said quickly. 'I wouldn't have done it if he'd been like that.'

'Oh, please don't apologise. I think all the better of you for it.' And it was true. As Sarah pictured David's fists slamming into Charlie's face, silencing the filthy words with a crunch of bone on bone, it was as if they were her own fists cramming Charlie's filth back in on himself. 'It probably wasn't particularly sensible, but one can't always be sensible. Tell me—I can see you're not comfortable with the subject, but bear with me a little longer—did he often talk to Amy like that?'

'Yes,' David said grimly. 'As far back as I can remember. He did more than just talk when I was little, too.' He saw Sarah's expression; she sensed that he had not meant to let slip that particular information.

'Do you mean,' Sarah said in a tightly controlled voice, 'that he used violence against Amy?'

'He used to thump her, yes. That was only when I was little, though,' David added quickly. 'He stopped years and years ago—I don't know how Ma made him stop, but she did it somehow. I'd never have left her with him if he'd still been carrying on like that.'

'I'm pleased to hear it.' Sarah was aware of the tremble in her voice. How could she have been so naive? she berated herself. How could she not have guessed what Charlie had been capable of?

'And I told him he'd better not try it again, too. The day I cleared out of here, I told him if I ever heard he'd laid a hand on Ma I'd come back and I'd kill him.'

'I see.' Her response sounded hopelessly inadequate in her own ears, but it was the best she could summon. They both fell silent, David staring at the ground while Sarah studied him.

'Yes, I do think better of you,' she said at last. 'And I think perhaps I understand things a little better now. Thank you for that.'

David shrugged. 'I don't know. Ma doesn't like people bringing up that old stuff. And he got so sick and everything... well, you couldn't help but feel sorry for the old beggar.'

'I'll take your word for that. It wasn't quite my experience. Mr Stewart... oh, that sounds ridiculous! It makes me think of your father,

16

too. May I call you Dave?'

'I wish you would. It sounds like you're going to tell me off or something when you keep saying "Mr Stewart" all the time.'

'Does it? I hadn't intended that. And I won't tell you off unless you give me good reason to. Dave, then. Will you call me Sarah?'

'All right,' David agreed readily. 'It'd make you not seem like a teacher so much.'

'Perhaps it would make it easier for us to be... well, friends, I suppose. I think we should be friends, don't you?'

'If you want.' David looked somewhat puzzled by her overture.

'Yes, I do want to—for Amy's sake, if nothing else.' Sarah smiled thoughtfully. 'You and I have quite a lot in common, you know.'

'Do we?'

'Yes, we do. Well, we've Amy in common, anyway—I mean, we're both fond of Amy. Perhaps I didn't realise before just how fond of her you are.'

'Yes, I am.' David's attention seemed suddenly absorbed by a roughness on one of his fingers; he picked vigorously at it rather than meet Sarah's eyes. She sensed the deep feeling behind his words, for all their plainness.

'And that fondness we share should be reason enough for us to make an effort to get on. For Amy's sake.' She paused, trying to guess the reaction she might get to her next words. 'I want to take Amy to Auckland with me.'

David's head jerked upright. 'Eh? What do you want to do that for?'

'Because I want to look after her. Because I think it would make her happy. You don't grudge her that, do you?'

'But...' She saw David swallow with difficulty. 'You mean take her up there for good?' His voice was tight with emotion, and Sarah was struck by how young he suddenly looked. For a moment she feared he might cry.

'No, no, of course not—you surely don't think I'd be able to talk Amy into that, do you? No, I'm only trying to persuade her into staying a few months.' No need to tell David just yet that she was thinking beyond a single visit to a time when Amy might divide her year between the two of them. And not necessarily on the basis of six months spent in each place; nine months in Auckland and three on the farm Sarah considered might be a reasonable balance. 'I think Amy deserves a holiday. Don't you?'

'I don't know,' David said, clearly taken aback. 'I suppose she does. She works hard, all right. Especially all that time she was trying to run the place on her own.'

'So a trip to Auckland would be just the thing for her, wouldn't it?' Sarah went on briskly. 'She wouldn't have to lift a finger in my house. And I could take her out and about to all manner of interesting places. I'm sure she'd enjoy herself immensely.'

'It sounds pretty good. I think Ma would like that.'

'Yes. And I know she wants to come, she admitted as much. So what a pity it is that she won't.'

'Won't she? Why not?'

'Can't you guess? Because of you, of course. Oh, don't look so startled, you know Amy well enough. She won't come because she thinks she has to stay here to look after you. That seems a little hard, doesn't it?'

'She hasn't said anything.'

'No, of course she hasn't. She'd rather keep quiet and do without her holiday than risk upsetting you.' She studied David, gauging his reaction. Mainly bewilderment, she decided.

'But I wouldn't mind her going,' he said, shaking his head in confusion. 'I wouldn't make a fuss or anything. I'd *like* her to have a holiday.'

Sarah snatched hold of the advantage offered her. 'Good. You can help me tell her she's to come. She won't try arguing against both of us if we band together. *And* you can tell me who should be roped in to look after you while Amy's away.'

'I suppose I could do for myself.'

'Have a little sense!' Sarah snapped. 'We're hardly going to persuade Amy that you're fit to be left to your own devices if you talk such nonsense.'

She had the satisfaction of seeing David sit bolt upright, his eyes studying her nervously. Sarah let her face relax into a smile. 'Goodness me, I almost thought you were going to hold your hand out for me to strap it. Now, come along, be sensible. Would I be wrong in assuming that making a cup of tea is about the limit of your culinary abilities?'

'I can do a sandwich. I don't suppose I'd be much use at getting dinner on, though,' he admitted.

'No, I'd guessed as much. So, what shall we tell Amy you'll do about your meals?'

'Well, next door's closest,' David said after a moment's consideration. 'I could go over to Uncle John's or Uncle Harry's, maybe. But Aunt Lizzie's the best one for organising things. I mean, even if I was to say I'd go to Uncle John's, she'd probably think of something else and tell me I was to do that instead.'

'Just as I thought,' said Sarah. 'Perhaps I'd better pay your Aunt Lizzie a visit this afternoon. Then we'll have it all settled.'

David went back to his work. Sarah rested on her elbows, enjoying the feel of the sun through her dress, and watched him finish off covering the potatoes. A movement caught her attention; she looked up towards the house, shading her eyes against the light.

Yes, that was Amy approaching, taking quick little steps across the paddock. As she grew nearer, Sarah could see her anxious expression.

'Amy's worried I've been upsetting you,' she remarked. 'Now, you're not going to let me down, are you?'

David shook his head. Sarah stood up, and they walked over to Amy.

'Don't look so worried, darling,' Sarah said, slipping her arm through Amy's. 'Dave and I have discussed the business of your holiday, and we're in complete agreement. You're to come to Auckland with me. Isn't that right, Dave?'

'Yes, I reckon it's a good idea. A trip to Auckland would be just the thing for you.'

Sarah smiled at being quoted so carefully. 'And we've thought out how to manage looking after Dave while you're away. I'm going to talk to Mrs Kelly—perhaps this afternoon, there's no point leaving things. Dave and I are quite sure she'll take on the organising.'

Amy stared from each of them to the other, her face a picture of mingled delight and disbelief. 'I... you don't mind, Davie? You don't mind if I go away for a while?'

'I want you to go, Ma. You deserve a holiday.'

'But—'

'Oh, what excuse are you going to come up with now?' Sarah raised her eyebrows in pretended exasperation.

'Well, there's one more thing,' Amy said. 'It's the headstone— Charlie's headstone. I can't go away till it's arrived, it wouldn't seem right.'

Trust that man to make things awkward one last time, Sarah thought to herself. 'When's it to come?'

'Another three weeks yet, I'm afraid. They said it'd be here around the end of the month.'

Sarah considered the matter. 'I can't stay here that long myself. It'll mean you'll have to travel up to Auckland alone. Do you think you could do that?'

'Oh, yes, of course I could.'

'Very well, then, you're to come up as soon as it's arrived. And I'll be trusting you to see that she's on that boat in three weeks' time, David.'

'I'll have her on the boat all right,' David said stoutly. He took Amy's free arm and tucked it through his. 'I'm starving, Ma. Is it morning tea yet?'

'I was coming down to call you in for it.' Amy caught Sarah's amused expression, and gave a rueful smile. 'Well, I suppose it was mainly an excuse to see if you two were getting on all right.'

'Of course we are,' said Sarah. 'We're the best of friends.' She planted a kiss on Amy's cheek. 'Let's go and check on these scones of yours. I want to see if they really are as big as I remembered.'

Amy walked between them, revelling in the closeness to both. Sarah and David were chatting easily, but Amy's heart was too full for words as she looked up at first one animated face, then the other, while she tried to match their long strides.

'Hey, I can smell those scones now,' David said when they neared the house. 'Hurry up, Ma, they smell good.'

'I can't keep up with you two. You go on ahead,' Amy said, attempting to slip her arms out of theirs.

She saw Sarah catch David's eye over the top of her head, a mischievous expression on her face. Sarah gripped her arm more tightly. 'Let's make her run.'

'I can't!' Amy protested. She struggled to match their fresh pace, laughing helplessly. 'I can't,' she panted out. 'I'm too old to run.'

'Then we'll have to help you,' Sarah said, her smile more mischievous than ever. 'Ready, Dave?'

He nodded, and took a firmer hold on Amy's arm.

'One, two, three, *up!*' Sarah cried.

They hoisted her aloft, the three of them giggling like children. Amy wanted to shout the news to the world, but she made do with a wordless cry of delight. It was decided; it was settled. She was going to Auckland.

2

There was one task Amy dissuaded Sarah from attempting.

'I'll ask Lizzie about looking after Dave,' she said. 'I'd rather do it myself. Not today, either, there's no need to rush. And I'd like to… Sarah, would you mind if I told Lizzie about you? Who you really are, I mean. I won't if you don't want me to.'

'Tell the world if you want,' Sarah said easily. 'I'm not ashamed of you, dearest.'

'No, not the world. Only Lizzie, I think.'

'You're not going to tell Dave?'

'I… I don't think so,' Amy said after a pause. 'Not yet, anyway. I might one day. Do you think I should?' she asked anxiously.

Sarah gave a small shrug. 'It's your decision, not mine. I'll admit to a little idle curiosity as to how he might react. I'd be able to tell him it's my right to order him about, since I'm his big sister.'

It was more than idle curiosity that Amy felt; it was something akin to fear. How would David take the knowledge that she had borne a child before her marriage? Could he ever think of her in the same way again? And the darkest question of all whispered from a deep recess of her mind: would he still love her? Why search for the answer when it was so easy to avoid the question?

Letting Sarah go was a wrench for Amy. But she had her trip to Auckland to look forward to, and before then she had a job to do. It was time to go and see Lizzie.

Few enough of Amy's family had even known of the existence of her first child; of those few, Lizzie was the only one who had ever let her talk about the baby. The joy of her new knowledge bubbled inside Amy, making her step light as she walked along the track down the valley.

Frank and Lizzie were lingering over a morning cup of tea when Amy entered the warm kitchen. Frank had prevailed on Lizzie to let him hold Benjy; the baby waved his arms and chortled a greeting at Amy. Beth and Maisie hurried to fetch a cup of tea for her, and when she had fussed over Benjy and kissed Lizzie she took the seat Lizzie indicated.

'Well, you look bright as a button,' Lizzie remarked. 'I thought you might be a bit down in the dumps, with your visitor going.'

'It did seem a bit flat last night—I missed Sarah straight away. But do you know what's happened?' Amy put her hand on Lizzie's arm, wanting to be sure she had her cousin's full attention for her momentous announcement. 'Sarah's asked me to go and stay with her in Auckland.'

21

'Oh, the silly girl. I hope she didn't make a fuss when you said you wouldn't.'

'But I didn't say that. I've said I'll go.'

'Don't talk rot, Amy! Honestly, fancy that girl getting you to say such a thing. You couldn't go all that way by yourself—and to Auckland, of all places. Frank says it's an awful place, isn't it, Frank?'

'Well, it can be a bit wearying, with the size of it,' Frank allowed. 'It's a bit of a beggar finding your way around, anyway.'

'There you are, then,' Lizzie said, as if her case had been proven beyond question. 'You probably wouldn't be able to find her house, even if you did go up there. You just write her a nice letter and say it was good of her to ask, but you don't want to go after all. She won't mind.'

'I do want to go, though,' Amy said quietly.

'You don't really. That Miss Millish has got you all excited, but once you've settled down and had a little think about it, you'll see for yourself it's a silly idea. Going all that way on your own, and you don't even know her all that well. I know she's sort of Lily's cousin, but she's not anything to you.'

'She *is*, Lizzie. Sarah's special. She's as special as she could be. She…' Amy glanced around the room, taking in their interested audience. 'I need to talk to you. Please?'

She met Lizzie's eyes, and was relieved to see her catch the message that this talk was not for all ears.

'Come up to the bedroom for a minute,' Lizzie said. 'Frank, mind you don't go spilling your tea on Benjy—sit him up properly.'

'Yes, I'm not too good with babies yet,' Frank said, trying to assume a suitably humble expression. 'We've only had the eight of them, after all.'

'I'm just telling you to be careful, there's no need to talk silly. Mama won't be long, sweetie,' Lizzie cooed to the baby. 'Let him suck on a biscuit, Frank, he might be a bit hungry.'

She ushered Amy ahead of her, up the passage and into the bedroom. As soon as she had closed the bedroom door behind them, she turned to Amy with a mixture of curiosity and concern in her face.

'Now, what's going on? Whatever's got you so excited?'

Amy took hold of both Lizzie's hands in hers. 'It's Sarah.' She took a deep breath to calm herself as, for a moment, the wonder of it all threatened to overwhelm her. 'Sarah's my little girl. She's Ann come back to me. She's my daughter.' She savoured the delicious feel of the words as her mouth formed them. 'My daughter.'

Lizzie stood as if frozen and stared at her, not with the delight Amy had hoped to see, but with deep concern. 'Oh, dear,' she said faintly.

'You poor love.'

She took hold of Amy's hand and steered her over to the bed, waving aside Amy's attempts to explain further. 'You just sit down quietly. I'll—now, don't you worry, we'll have a little talk and sort it all—I'll just…' She stared around the room with an air of desperation. 'I'll get Frank!'

Lizzie flung the bedroom door open and leaned out into the passage. 'Frank!' she called. 'Come and help me!'

Frank appeared within seconds, Benjy tucked under one arm. The baby stared around with an air of mild surprise at having been so rapidly moved from one room to another, while Frank's face was all concern. 'What's wrong? Are you all right, Lizzie?'

'What do you think you're doing, carrying Benjy like that!' Lizzie said indignantly. 'Give him here.'

She retrieved the baby and made soothing noises, rendered quite unnecessary by Benjy's beaming smile at the sight of his mother. 'It's Amy, not me,' Lizzie said when she managed to drag her attention away from Benjy. 'She's not well.'

'Yes I *am!*' Amy managed to make herself heard at last. 'I don't think I've been so well in ages!'

'She looks all right to me,' Frank said, taking in Amy's radiant face.

'Well, she's not, the poor thing. It's all got too much for you, hasn't it, Amy?' Lizzie hurried on, giving Amy no chance to reply. 'Having to be brave all these years, with *him* being such a trial. And then the strain of him getting so sick. Now she's finally able to take things a bit easier, and it's got on top of her at last. Having that Miss Millish to stay, too, that's been the last straw.' She paused for breath, then announced solemnly, 'Amy's got a bit muddled in the head.'

'I'm not muddled, I'm not!' Amy protested. 'It's true!'

Lizzie nodded sagely, as if Amy's insistence was further evidence. 'You see what I mean? She thinks Miss Millish is the little girl they took off her.'

'Oh, heck!' Frank said, clearly sharing Lizzie's alarm. 'You'd better get her to lie down, take things quiet. Shall I get her some water? Or laudanum or something.'

Amy looked up at their worried faces, and it was only gratitude for their concern that stopped her from laughing aloud. 'Does Frank know about Ann?'

'Yes, he does,' Lizzie admitted. 'I had to tell him once—oh, years and years ago—when he'd gone upsetting you, mentioning seeing the other fellow in Auckland.'

'I've wondered once or twice if you did know, Frank. I'm glad you do, it makes things simpler—'

'Never mind talking about it now,' Lizzie cut in. 'You sit there quietly. Frank's right, you ought to have a lie down. Yes, that's a good idea, Frank, get some laudanum.'

'No,' Amy said, quietly but firmly. 'I don't want to lie down, and I don't want any laudanum. No, stay here, Frank, I won't take any medicine, so it's no good you fetching it.' She smiled at their anxious expressions. 'And I haven't gone funny in the head, either.'

'Now, Amy, you should just—'

'Lizzie,' Amy interrupted. 'I want to talk. Will you both be quiet and listen for a minute? Please?'

Lizzie's worried expression did not ease. She sat down on the bed close to Amy, while Frank took the chair beside the bed.

'It's all right,' Amy said. 'I know it sounds like I've gone silly, but it's all right. Really it is.'

She paused to gather her thoughts and arrange them in some sort of order, fit to be shared with others.

'Sarah told me herself,' she began. 'Those people, the ones she calls Mother and Father, they weren't really her parents at all. They adopted her when she was just a little baby. When I had to give her away.'

She had thought she could say it calmly, but the sudden rush of painful memories took her by surprise. She bit on her lip and stared unseeing at the bedroom window, and felt the warmth of Lizzie's hand as it took hold of hers.

'Lily mentioned once that Miss Millish wasn't really her cousin,' Lizzie said. 'Her aunt couldn't have any more babies, so they adopted a little girl for her. I didn't think anything of it at the time.'

'It doesn't mean she...' Frank lapsed into silence, but Amy could finish the sentence easily enough.

'It doesn't mean she's my little girl. You're right, Frank, it wouldn't mean anything by itself. But there's something else.' She closed her eyes for a moment and smiled at the memory of the heavy piece of gold lying in her palm, still warm from being worn against Sarah's body. 'There's the brooch.'

'What brooch?' Lizzie asked.

'I never told you about it, did I?' Amy mused. 'It was all secrets and hiding things. The brooch was my Christmas present. He...' She stopped, then made herself say the name. 'Jimmy gave it to me.'

After all those years, the word was so unfamiliar in her mouth that it almost seemed to burn its way out. But it would have been foolish to think she could share with them the wonder of Sarah and at the same time hide from the memory of Sarah's father. She had said the name aloud, and felt she had passed a test.

'It was made in the shape of an "A". A for Amy. It was gold, too, it must've been quite valuable. I thought it was the most wonderful thing anyone had ever given me.' And she had worn it every day, hidden under her dress as it hung on its chain between her breasts. She had thought it was a sign of his love.

'I didn't want it… afterwards. It didn't feel like it belonged to me any more. So I gave it to the baby. I asked the woman who took the baby if she'd look after the brooch for me, and give it to Ann's…' *New mother.* 'To the people who were going to have Ann. A for Amy and A for Ann, too. I wanted to give her something, and that was the best thing I had. And it seemed like it belonged to her. I didn't know if they'd even let Ann have the brooch, but I hoped they would.'

She smiled at Frank and Lizzie. 'And they did let her have it. They told her it had been mine, and that I'd given it to her. She's still got it— she showed it to me. That's how I know she's my little girl.'

There was a long silence when she had finished speaking. Amy watched their faces as Frank and Lizzie weighed up what she had told them. It was Frank who spoke first.

'Well, it sounds true enough to me. Don't you reckon, Lizzie?'

'It's… yes, I suppose it does,' Lizzie said, still looking mildly stunned. 'Yes, it must be.'

Amy laughed aloud at their serious expressions. 'Look at you two! You'd think I'd told you there was going to be a war or something. Aren't you pleased for me?'

They both appeared to give the matter solemn consideration. 'It's a lot to take in, all at once,' Frank said. 'But… well, it's about time you had things come right for you, Amy. Yes, we're pleased all right. Aren't we, Lizzie?'

'I'll say it's a lot to take in,' Lizzie said. 'I suppose it's like getting someone new in the family. It'll take me a while to get used to the idea. I used to think she was a bit odd,' she said, with the air of one being scrupulously honest. 'She's got some funny ways about her. But she was that sensible about letting me know I should get Dave back home for you. I said then that the girl had a good head on her shoulders. It must've been being brought up by those people in Auckland that made her a bit funny.'

Lizzie nodded sagely, pleased to have found so clear a reason for Sarah's supposed strange ways. 'Yes, that'll be it. But there's plenty of you in her too, Amy. That's reason enough to be pleased.'

She enfolded Amy in a hug, careful not to crush Benjy in the process, and Frank leaned across to put an arm around Amy's shoulders. The three of them sat locked in a shared embrace, Amy basking in the warmth of their affection.

Lizzie detached herself first, and Frank returned to his chair. 'Now, about this going to Auckland,' Lizzie said. 'It's a different story, with her being family and all. It's only natural you want to go up there and see her. You'd better get on with it before the weather gets bad, I know Frank's said the boat can be awful in the rough weather.'

'I'd like to go soon,' Amy said. 'I promised Sarah I'd go as soon as I'd got Charlie's headstone organised, and it's meant to come by the end of the month. But there's Dave to see to, that's the only thing.'

Now Lizzie was on ground she felt firmly in command of. 'Don't you worry about that—I'll see to all that business. Beth'll be the best one to look after him, I think. Now, let's see, getting his meals on, that'll be the main thing.'

'Are you sure you can spare Beth?' Frank said doubtfully. 'I want you to have your trip and all, Amy, I just don't want Lizzie to go wearing herself out, trying to do too much.'

'Oh, don't start fussing,' said Lizzie. 'Don't take any notice of him, Amy, you know what he's like for worrying over me. I'll still have Maisie, and Beth won't be up there all the time. Anyway, it'd do no harm for me to take more notice of what those girls get up to with the work, I've been leaving them to their own devices a bit much since Benjy came along.

'Beth can go up there of a morning, after we've got the breakfast things sorted out here,' she went on. 'That'll give her plenty of time to tidy things up at your place before she gets Dave's lunch on. She might as well have her lunch up there with him. Then she can do a few more jobs and get his dinner on before she comes home, and Dave'll be able to dish it up for himself. I'll tell Beth to make things she can just leave on the range for him, stews and suchlike. She can do roasts and chops for their lunch. Yes, that'll be no bother at all.'

'It's very good of you,' said Amy. 'I couldn't really go otherwise.'

'Well, we're family, aren't we?' Lizzie said. 'Now, you just get on with thinking about your trip. We'll see that Dave's well looked after while you're away. There's no need for you to worry about anything.'

David carried Amy's luggage, which consisted of a case borrowed from Frank and a hat box that Maudie had lent her, onto the *Waiotahi* and stowed it in the ladies' cabin.

Packing had not taken Amy long. She was wearing her only warm mourning dress, covered by a blue cloak that was dark enough to do service as mourning, and the other clothes that had seemed worth bringing had not filled the case.

The one garment she owned that she considered truly elegant was more than twenty years old; she had worn it as a wedding dress, but before that she had worn it the night she had lain under the stars with Jimmy. It was old, and suffused with painful memories, but the fabric was of such quality and she had looked after the dress so carefully that the years rested lightly on it. She could not wear the blue silk as mourning, but it would at least allow her to be well-dressed within Sarah's house if the need arose. For outings beyond the house, her warm black dress would have to do. A plain work dress and the small amount of underwear she possessed made up the remaining contents of the case.

She and David rejoined the little group assembled on the wharf to see her off. John had appeared unexpectedly, arriving in his usual quiet, unobtrusive way. He had muttered vaguely about having to be in town that morning anyway, but Amy suspected that he had come in specially to farewell her.

Frank and Lizzie were there, Lizzie clutching Benjy to her and casting an occasional suspicious glance at the sailors as they finished loading goods onto the *Waiotahi*, as if she half suspected they might steal the baby if she did not watch him closely. But this claim on her attention did not hinder her from giving Amy the benefit of her advice.

'Now, you be sure and take care of yourself on that boat. Don't go standing too near the edge if it's rough. And watch those fellows,' she added in a lower voice, plainly still none too impressed by the sailors. 'Oh, and make sure you don't get off at Tauranga by mistake. Frank, how will she know it's Tauranga and not Auckland?'

'She'll know. Anyway, you've got to change boats at Tauranga. Someone will point out the right boat to you, Amy, don't worry.'

'I'm not a bit worried,' Amy assured him. And it was true; she faced the voyage with bright anticipation. 'Don't worry about me, Lizzie, I won't get lost.'

'Well, you just be careful who you talk to,' Lizzie said, clearly unconvinced. 'Especially once you get to Auckland. All those people there,' she said, shaking her head disapprovingly. 'There'll be thieves and goodness knows what sort of rogues, keep eye on your things. The roads, too,' she said, seizing on a fresh idea. 'They'll be busy as anything—didn't you say the roads get busy there, Frank?'

'There's a lot more carts and buggies and things than we're used to in

Ruatane,' Frank agreed.

'You see?' said Lizzie. 'So watch yourself crossing the roads. Oh, and have you got Miss Millish's address written down? You never know, if you get lost when you're up there and have to ask someone the way, they mightn't even know where she lives with Auckland being such a big place.'

'I know the address by heart.'

'You should write it down anyway. It'd be a terrible place to get lost in.'

Amy suspected that, at least for the moment, Lizzie had completely forgotten that Amy had made one other trip to Auckland, long ago. Though there had been little enough chance for her to get lost during that stay, confined as she had been to first boarding house then nursing home.

'You stick close to Miss Millish, anyway,' said Lizzie. 'She'll see you don't get lost.'

'Oh, I'll stick close to her, all right,' Amy said, and smiled. That, she knew, would be an easy promise to keep.

The sailors seemed to be making their final preparations; it would not be long before the boat sailed. Amy was thinking of boarding when her younger brother appeared.

'Tommy!' she said in delight, taking hold of his arm and standing on tiptoe to plant a kiss on his cheek. 'I didn't expect to see you here!'

'I sneaked off for a minute.' Seeing her look of alarm, Thomas grinned and squeezed her arm. 'I didn't really. Mr Callaghan said it was all right for me to come and see you off. I thought I'd better wait till it got a bit quiet, though, then everyone seemed to come into the bank at once. I thought I might have missed you.'

'You nearly did,' Amy said, glancing at the boat. 'I'm glad you came, though. I was just thinking about you.' Thinking about that other trip to Auckland, with all its dark memories. Thomas had been with her on that voyage, though Amy was unsure whether he remembered it. As a little boy of two years old he had been more like her own child than a brother, and he had cried miserably when Amy was left at the boarding house, while Thomas and his baby brother were swept off by their mother to stay with her parents. Looking back, Amy found it hard to believe that she had actually been upset at parting from Susannah. Only the fear of being left alone among strangers could have roused such a feeling in her.

'Mother said she'd try and come along too, to see you off,' Thomas said.

Amy gave a guilty start at having Susannah mentioned aloud when she had just been recalling unpleasant memories of her stepmother.

'Oh, there's no need for her to put herself out.' Amy wished her lack of any desire to see Susannah did not sound out quite so clearly.

'Well, she did say she felt as if one of her headaches might be coming on. You know how she gets those. But she sent her best wishes.'

'Did she really, Tommy?'

'Yes, she did.'

Amy studied the firm set of his expression and decided that, surprising though it was, it must be true. Susannah wished her well. Perhaps she had been thinking of that other trip, too. Amy stored away the unexpected well-wishing as a good omen for the journey.

Just as Lizzie had begun interrogating Amy as to whether she had enough clean handkerchiefs with her, the *Waiotahi*'s captain approached them.

'Excuse me, ma'am, we'll be sailing shortly,' he told Amy. 'If you wouldn't mind coming aboard, I'd be most obliged.' He tipped his hat to Amy and Lizzie and went back to the boat.

Amy found herself enfolded in a hug and kissed by each of her well-wishers in turn. David had hung back till last, and he hugged her more tightly than any of the others, almost squeezing the breath out of her. Now, when the time for reconsidering was long past, for a brief, painful moment Amy wondered if she was doing right to leave him alone.

'Take care, Davie. I hope you'll be all right on your own.'

'Of course I will, Ma. Don't you go worrying—you just get on with having a good time.'

'Don't worry about Dave, he'll be quite all right,' Lizzie put in. 'Beth and I will see to that.'

Amy held on to David's arm, only releasing him when she reached the gangplank. She stood on the deck, clutching the handrail with one hand and waving as the boat slipped away from the wharf. Lizzie shook her head at her and gestured that she should move back from the edge of the deck, but Amy pretended not to understand.

When her arm grew tired she gave up waving, but made no move to leave her place. She stared back at the wharf as it shrank in on itself. Even when it was no more than a shapeless grey smudge in the distance she still imagined she could make out the figures standing there.

The boat crossed the bar, mercifully smooth this morning. A tongue of land cut the wharf off from Amy's view, and there was no longer any use peering back towards Ruatane.

She carefully picked her way around to the starboard side, her steps made clumsy by the unfamiliar motion of the boat. The ocean opened out before her, an unruffled grey-blue, the distant outline of White Island diamond-sharp in the morning light. Amy shaded her eyes and stared out towards the horizon and the island floating on it, and blinked against the brightness. In the east, the sun was shining.

Beth had learned early in life that the noblest creature in creation was a mother; more specifically, her own one. As she had grown up, her imagination had broadened until she could conceive of a person of more consequence than her mother, but she had certainly never met one.

So it was not surprising that she should have approached the task of keeping house for David with enthusiasm. This was an opportunity, albeit temporary, to run a house in her own way and to her own standards. Lizzie had said that she would check up on her daughter's work occasionally, but Beth knew that, to all intents and purposes, for the first time in her life she would be in charge.

Her mother, of course, was her model. Beth took it for granted that no one knew how to run a household as well as Lizzie did; it was a notion she had drunk in at her mother's breast. And if she was to play the role of a truly excellent housewife, she was determined that David would also play his part correctly.

On her first day at Amy's, David came up to the house within minutes of her arrival, attracted by the promise of a morning tea.

Beth stood in the doorway to meet him. 'Take those boots off before you come in here,' she said sternly.

'I always take my boots off before I come inside,' David said, startled.

'Well, I don't want you forgetting,' Beth said, quite unrepentant.

She made a great show of setting the tea things out nicely and making sure she gave David the largest cup the kitchen held. They lingered over their tea and biscuits, chatting about the happenings of the day and what they each intended to do for the remainder of the morning, just as Beth had seen her parents chat almost every day of her life.

When she judged it was time for her to get on with her work, Beth shooed David unceremoniously from the table.

'You'd better get out from under my feet,' she said, standing up to begin stacking their dishes. 'I've got a lot to do this morning.'

'All right. I've got a fair bit to do myself.' David rose from his chair and started towards the door.

'Wait a minute!' Beth said before he was halfway there. 'You have to kiss me goodbye first.'

'Do I? Why?'

'Well, you just do,' Beth said, stating the fact as one not to be questioned. 'Pa always kisses Ma when he goes outside. So you have to kiss me.'

'I suppose I kiss Ma goodbye sometimes. When I'm going to town or down to the factory, anyway.'

'Come on, then.' She tilted her face to receive his kiss, which he placed very carefully and respectfully on her mouth, somewhat awed by this new, unexpectedly self-confident Beth.

'All right, off you go, then.' She spoiled the effect with a sudden giggle.

'What's so funny?' David asked.

'Oh, I was just thinking about Ma and Pa when they say goodbye.' She giggled again at the mental picture of her father giving her mother's bottom a pat. 'Pa does something else sometimes, when he thinks none of us are watching.'

'What does he do? Do I have to do it, too?'

'You'd better not,' Beth said, trying to appear stern. 'And I'm not going to tell you what it is, either.' She smiled at his look of confusion. 'I might tell you another day—if you promise not to tell Ma I said it. Kiss me again,' she ordered, enjoying the sense of power.

'All right.' David obliged, with perhaps a little less reserve this time.

Beth stood in the doorway to watch him move away. She went back into the kitchen and contemplated the pleasant notion that it was completely in her power, limited only by the contents of kitchen and safe, to decide what they would have for lunch. This, she reflected, was going to be fun.

The boat did not leave Tauranga till well on in the evening. Amy tried to will herself to sleep, wanting to be as fresh as possible when she arrived in Auckland.

But sleep eluded her, and not just because a swell off the coast of the Coromandel Peninsula sent her scrabbling for the bucket thoughtfully placed near her bed by the stewardess. Even when the sea grew calm again, she lay on the mattress staring up towards the invisible ceiling of the cabin.

There were too many reminders. The smell of the boat was the same; she had made it even more familiar now, by adding the odour of her own vomit to the mix. The noises of the engine, of sailors moving about on deck, of voices in other parts of the boat, all seemed the same as on that other voyage.

Her hands slid down to rest on her belly, smooth and flat beneath the flannel of her outer petticoat. Then it had been hard and rounded, full of child. She had been violently ill for much of the voyage, hidden away out of sight, shut below decks even during the daytime to try and disguise her shameful condition, with no relief from the stale smells of the engines, her vomit, and the bodies of her fellow passengers.

The voyage had been bad enough, but it paled in memory against what had come after. The journey had been made for the sole purpose of being rid of her child.

Her fingers were digging into the flesh of her belly, the pain throwing her memories into sharper relief. Amy made herself uncurl her fingers and let her hands fall to her sides. Her eyes ached from their futile staring into the darkness. She closed them, and tried to make her body go limp.

As she lay in her berth, the sounds of the boat faded; even the smells grew fainter. Now it seemed that she was lying in another bed, on a hard mattress, looking about her at cold, white walls. There was a cradle on the floor, creaking as it rocked, but bare and empty. A faint sound came from just outside the door. Amy was sure it was a baby crying.

She tried to sit up, but she seemed tethered to the bed by a wide band of cloth that went across her breasts. The only sound she could make was a muffled sob. The sobs grew stronger until they seemed to rack her body, and then abruptly she was awake and retching, and scrambling for the bucket.

When she had recovered enough to look around the cabin, she saw that the darkness had lessened. Whatever sleep she had snatched had done nothing to refresh her, but she had no wish to drift back into that dream of an empty cradle.

She waited until the cabin grew light enough for her to see the opposite wall, then she rose and dressed herself, moving as quietly as she could. She retrieved her hat from under the bed, slipped on her cloak and went out onto the deck.

The sun was up, but in the west the sky was still pale. They were passing close to a large island. Amy tried without success to recall its name. They must be close to Auckland now, but all she felt was weariness and an aching sense of loss.

She found a seat where she could be unobserved, and pulled her cloak more closely around herself as she felt the pinch of a chilly breeze. Islands slid past, teasing her with tugs at her memory. She should know their names. Her father had named them for her. But that was on her journey home. On the voyage to Auckland she had had no names for the islands glimpsed through the porthole of the cabin where she had been shut away.

Her stomach was aching, but there was nothing left to bring up, just a grinding emptiness. She could see the wharves of Auckland now, jutting into the harbour. A few more minutes and some of the larger buildings were visible. There would be cabs waiting at the wharves, eager to pick up their share of the disembarking passengers. Susannah had hailed a cab, and it had taken Amy to the boarding house. Amy was not sure that she knew how to hail a cab. How would she get to the boarding house this time?

No, that wasn't right. She lifted the veil of her hat to let the cold wind sting her face, trying to clear her head. She would not need to hail a cab for herself. She was not going back to that lonely room in the boarding house.

How could it be so sharp in her memory, after so long? She could see the empty cradle, and the nurse carrying it from the room. She could see the mark the cradle had left on the floor. She let the veil drop again, to hide the redness of her eyes from any prying gaze.

The jolt as the boat bumped against the wharf took her by surprise; she had been too lost in her thoughts to be aware of the final approach. The blurring of her eyes and the black net of her veil made the shapes around her seem insubstantial, and she was startled when some of them began to move: her fellow passengers, eager to be off the boat.

She should be gathering her things and getting ready to disembark. She rose and took a few steps towards the ladies' cabin, but there was such a crush now that she was unsure whether she would be able to force her way against the tide of people. A man shouldered past, muttered an apology and hurried on his way. Amy found herself standing by the handrail. She backed against it, trying to retreat further from the crowd, until she felt the metal of the rail pressing into her spine.

Before her, people pushed and shoved against each other. Behind her she sensed the city, its buildings brooding over her. The crush began to subside, and she managed to turn around without being pushed more than once or twice. The veil still made it difficult to make out the details of what she saw. A tall, straight figure stood at the head of the steps leading from the wharf to the street, its concentration obviously directed at the boat. A tall woman in a dark blue dress.

Amy pushed back her veil, and as if that one small gesture had caught the observer's attention, the woman's eyes were suddenly on her. Even from her distance, Amy could see the smile that lit up the woman's face, and the mouth shaping her name.

Sarah swept onto the boat in a whirl of blue silk, the rustling of her taffeta skirts audible above the voices around her. A lively-looking boy of about twelve was close at her heels. She made no visible attempt to push her way through, but people seemed to stand back to let her pass. She reached Amy and enfolded her in an embrace so strong that it was like being hugged by David.

'You're here,' Sarah said, almost breathless with elation.

Amy rested against her, weak from the buffeting of emotions, and too happy to squander energy on inadequate words.

Sarah sent the boy to collect the baggage. With her arm still encircling Amy, she led her towards the gangplank, and in a shorter time than Amy would have thought possible the boy had joined them on the wharf with her luggage safely under his arms.

There was a carriage waiting, close to the top of the steps. A man tipped his hat to Amy and helped her in. Sarah got in beside her, while the luggage was stowed away in the back. The boy scrambled up beside the driver, so like the man that Amy was sure they must be father and son. Sarah took Amy's hand in both of hers and squeezed it, then glanced forward to the coachman.

'Home, Jenson,' she called.

After what seemed only a few minutes, Amy found herself stepping down from the carriage and standing before Sarah's house.

The building was two storeys high, with a broad, curved entrance porch and a balcony above that. Used as she was to the unpainted wood of the cottage, the white plaster seemed almost dazzling to Amy. Large-paned windows patterned with lace curtains softened the rigid lines of the house.

Their approach must have been heard by those inside, for by the time Sarah led Amy up to the entrance the staff had assembled below the front steps, ready to be introduced.

Sarah's household staff consisted of a cook-housekeeper (the wife of Mr Jenson), two housemaids and a kitchen maid, with the outside work being taken care of by Mr Jenson, who acted as gardener as well as coachman, assisted by his son.

'Mrs Stewart will be staying with me for some months,' Sarah told the staff when they had been presented. 'And I'd like it understood that any instructions from Mrs Stewart are to be treated as if they had come from myself.'

Amy was aware that she was being studied, discreetly but carefully, and she sensed a deeper interest being taken in her after these words. Sarah had mentioned having house guests from time to time, but Amy suspected that the guests were not usually accorded the status Sarah had just conferred on her. She was grateful for the gesture, though it was difficult for her to imagine herself giving orders to any of the staff.

One of the maids took charge of Amy's luggage, while Sarah ushered her into a large entrance hall, where the other maid helped Amy and Sarah off with their cloaks. A chandelier hung from the ceiling, a gorgeous thing of sparkling crystal catching the light from the open front door. Amy had little time to take in more details before Sarah led her to the foot of the broad staircase that dominated the hall.

'I'll show you your room straight away,' she told Amy. 'You'll want to change, I expect. And you'll need to freshen up after that boat trip. Alice, some hot water to Mrs Stewart's room, please.'

'The jug's filled and ready on the wash stand, Miss Sarah,' the maid who had taken the cloaks said promptly.

'Good. That will be all for the moment.'

The staff dispersed to their various tasks, and Sarah ushered Amy up the stairs and down a short passage to where a door stood open.

Amy followed her into the bedroom, then stood stock still, staring around open-mouthed. The cottage's parlour and David's room together would not have filled this room. An ornate brass bedstead stood against one wall, with a pretty dressing table opposite it. There was a tiled washstand with pink-embroidered towels and patterned china, and a wooden chair with a carved back. Amy had never lived in a house with any sort of wallpaper at all, let alone such beautiful paper as this room had, intricately patterned with a design of birds and flowers. The *chaise longue*, something Amy had heard of but never before seen, was upholstered in a fabric similar in pattern to the wallpaper.

'Sarah, you mustn't give me your room!' she said when she had recovered her voice.

'My room?' Sarah looked startled, then she laughed. 'Don't worry, Amy, this isn't my bedroom. Mine's a good deal larger—yes, such a thing is possible, don't look so doubtful. I'll show it to you later. No, dear, this room is all yours.'

She turned to the maid, who was unpacking Amy's meagre luggage and hanging the dresses in a wardrobe. 'Nellie, you can finish Mrs Stewart's things later, thank you.'

The maid bobbed a curtsy and left the room, and Sarah turned her attention back to Amy.

'Now, there are a few things here you won't be quite familiar with. The electric light, for one. Here, let me show you.' She demonstrated how pulling on a cord made the light come on, while a second pull made it go off again. When Sarah told Amy to try it for herself she stared in fascination at the light that flicked on, off, on, off in obedience to a sharp tug, until Sarah prised her fingers gently from the cord.

'That's enough for now. You'll wear out the bulb if you play with it like that—no, don't worry,' she said, forestalling Amy's guilty apology. 'I remember playing with the light myself for hours when we first had it put in.

'The bathroom is down the passage,' Sarah went on. 'I'll show it to you in a moment, though there's no need for a tour of the entire house just yet. You've your own washstand, of course, and if you need any hot water—or anything at all, come to that—just pull this rope, and one of the maids will come.'

Her gaze travelled the room, clearly searching for anything else that might be unfamiliar to Amy. 'Oh, yes,' she said when her eyes lighted on what appeared to be a small, wooden cabinet. 'I'm sure you won't have seen one of these before. If you're inconvenienced in the night, there's no need for you to brave the passage in your nightgown.' She lifted the top of the cabinet to reveal a porcelain bowl of unmistakable shape.

'Oh, it's a chamber pot!' Amy said, amazed to see such a thing appearing in a cupboard.

'It's called a commode. Use it as you need. The maid will empty it.'

'There's no need—'

'The maid,' Sarah cut in firmly, 'will empty it. Now, let's go and see the bathroom.'

Amy had heard of bathrooms, but found it difficult to imagine so much space devoted to the purpose of washing oneself. She followed Sarah into a room dominated by an enamelled cast iron bath.

'What a beautiful thing!' she exclaimed. She crouched in front of the bath to examine it more closely, and found its supports were moulded into the shape of lion paws. 'And it's so big,' she said, awed by the thought of how much water would have to be carried up the stairs to fill such a huge tub. A bath every week would seem a dreadful extravagance. Then she noticed the metal pipes resting on the edge.

'You've got running water! Can I try it out? Oh, not if it's a bother,' she added hastily.

Sarah smiled indulgently. 'Try it as much as you like, as long as you don't flood the bathroom. I expect you'll want a bath this evening, after that dreadful boat. I'll tell the maids.'

'No, I had a bath on Saturday,' Amy assured her. She looked up from trying out the fascinating tap, and saw a smile fluttering on Sarah's lips; there was a brief, barely perceptible struggle, then the smile won.

'I usually have a bath a little more often than once a week, Amy,' Sarah said gently. 'I do understand it hasn't been possible for you on the farm, with having to carry water up from that well, but I hope you'll take full advantage of the facilities here. Please feel free to ask the maids to run a bath for you whenever you want. Every night, if you wish.'

Despite Sarah's careful effort not to demean her, Amy felt chastened at the revelation that her standards of cleanliness might be wanting. She hoped fervently that she would not cause Sarah embarrassment by any social graces she might lack.

She was distracted from her uncomfortable thoughts by the next wonder revealed to her. Beside the bathroom was a smaller room that held a large, wooden-topped porcelain bowl with a tank suspended above it. A chain dangled from the tank, with a decorated porcelain handle at its end.

'Pull the chain,' Sarah invited. 'Pull it hard.'

Amy did, then let go of it with a startled squeal and took a step backwards when a rush of water was released into the bowl.

'A flush toilet,' she said, plucking up her courage to lean forward and peer in. 'So that's what one looks like.' She frowned, not quite comfortable with the idea of a lavatory inside the house. It seemed a rather unhygienic arrangement, though the room certainly smelt more of carbolic than anything else. The novelty of the flush toilet appealed to Amy; it also made her realise that she had a need of the lavatory beyond mere curiosity.

'Try it out properly,' Sarah suggested when she saw Amy's expression. 'I'll call Nellie back, she can finish your unpacking.'

She closed the door after her, and Amy sampled the delights of the flush toilet in all its glory. The squares of white paper fastened neatly to the wall were the final touch of luxury; no re-used pages of the *Weekly News*, these, but paper obviously intended solely for the lavatory.

Sarah was waiting in the passage, and she led the way back to Amy's room. 'That's enough surprises for your first morning, I think. I really should leave you in peace to freshen up.' Her hand rested lightly on Amy's shoulder. 'The trouble is,' she murmured, 'now that I have you here at last, I'm reluctant to let you out of my sight.'

'Stay if you want—I'd like you to.'

Sarah's hand travelled up to brush Amy's cheek. 'Look at those circles under your eyes! I've hardly taken any notice of how tired you look. Was it dreadful on the boat?'

'It wasn't specially rough or anything. I'm not very good about boats, though.'

'Neither am I, on the steamships. I must get that from you. Yachts are quite different, of course. I don't suppose you got much sleep?'

'Not really. Not proper sleep, anyway.'

'Would you like to have a nap before lunch?'

Amy felt she did not want to waste a moment of her time with Sarah, but the thought of lying down on that soft bed was inviting. 'I think perhaps I would. I'm not going to be very good company if I keep yawning.'

'Very well, I'll just have to do without you for a little while.' Sarah glanced around the room. 'Now, where might your nightdress be?'

'I think that girl—Nellie, is that her name? I think she put it in the top drawer. I'll get it, Sarah, don't you bother.'

Sarah retrieved the nightdress from its drawer and placed it on the bed. 'You must let me fuss over you, I'm afraid I'll insist on that. Sit down here, please.' She indicated the chair in front of the dressing table, and Amy did as she asked.

'Let me be ladies' maid, this once at least,' Sarah said. She removed Amy's veiled black hat and set it to one side, then carefully removed the hairpins.

'There,' she said when Amy's hair, released, tumbled over her shoulders and down her back. 'I won't attempt to help you undress, though. I'm not really a very good ladies' maid.'

Sarah folded back the coverlet and made a show of smoothing the pillows. 'You should be quite comfortable. Now, if you want anything at all, just pull the cord for the maid. There's no hurry for you to get up, I want you to rest till lunch-time at least.'

She drew the heavy drapes together, leaving the room pleasantly dim, and pulled the door closed as she went out.

Amy undressed and washed herself, handling the beautiful china of the wash set with reverence. She put on her nightdress, then slid gratefully into the bed. It was even softer than it looked; the mattress was what she imagined a cloud might be to lie on. She rubbed her cheek against the top sheet. It smelt faintly of lavender, and the linen was fine enough to have been made into the daintiest of underwear.

Despite the meagre amount of sleep she had had the night before, drowsiness refused to turn into slumber. Her reluctance to close her eyes did not help; the room was beautiful, even in the dim light. The ceiling was particularly lovely, with its intricate plaster moulding and the etched glass light fitting at its centre. Being deserted by sleep was no hardship when it was delightful just to lie in the big, soft bed in this enchanting room.

When she reckoned that at least two hours had passed, Amy got out of bed. The black dress was marked with the dust of travelling; she left it draped over the back of a chair and put on her work dress. She opened the drapes and studied the angle of the sun; well after midday, she judged.

The maid came in while Amy was brushing her hair.

'Begging your pardon, ma'am, but Miss Sarah told me to see if you were awake yet, in case you were wanting anything.'

'Yes, I'm quite awake, I've had a lovely rest,' Amy said. 'Do you know what the time is, Nellie?'

'Just about one o'clock, ma'am.'

'As late as that? What time will lunch be on?'

Nellie looked at her in evident surprise. 'Why, lunch will be whenever you want it, Mrs Stewart. Can I help you with anything?'

'Well, if it's not too much trouble, could you get me a clothes brush? This dress could do with a good brushing.'

Nellie looked more surprised than before. She frowned slightly, as if not sure that she had understood correctly. 'I'll see to it at once, Mrs

Stewart.' She picked the dress up and left the room before Amy had time to protest.

She thought of hurrying after Nellie to tell her that she had not meant the maid to clean the dress for her, but she was not sure whether she would be able to find the girl. Instead she finished putting her hair in order, and when that was done she explored her wonderful bedroom, opening every drawer, examining the lace curtains, and studying the wallpaper until she had comprehended how the pattern repeated itself every foot or so.

When Nellie returned, the mourning dress impeccably brushed, Amy asked the maid to take her to Sarah. She followed Nellie down the stairs, along a passage, and into a room slightly larger than Amy's bedroom. It was a pleasant, sunny room, with pretty lace curtains filtering the light and soft-looking sofas, but the room's greatest importance in Amy's eyes was that it held Sarah.

Sarah took Amy's hand and drew her down to sit beside her on one of the sofas. 'A tray of tea in here, please, Nellie. And tell Mrs Jenson we'll have luncheon in half an hour.'

'What a pretty parlour,' Amy said, looking around the room from her new vantage point.

'Yes, it's a pleasant room, though it's usually called the morning room.' Sarah studied Amy's face with evident satisfaction. 'Oh, yes, you look better now—and that dress is more cheerful.' She brushed a fold of the pink-striped woollen gown, and her fingers went unerringly to a worn area near one seam. 'Though it's a little... plain,' she said, frowning. 'Did you wear this one on the farm while I was there?'

'Most days, I think.' Amy moved her fingers surreptitiously, trying to hide an even more worn patch on the other side of the dress.

'Really? It didn't catch my attention down there.'

Amy could guess why easily enough. On the farm, in the plainness of the cottage, the worn, simple dress could hardly have stood out the way it must in this elegant house.

Sarah studied the dress a moment longer. She gave a small, thoughtful nod, then seemed to put Amy's dress out of her mind. There were distractions enough from so dull a subject, in the enjoyment of each other's company.

After what Sarah called a simple lunch, soup followed by fish, with an apple sponge to finish, taken in the dining room, she took Amy on a tour of the ground floor rooms. 'Though I won't bother showing you the kitchen or the scullery,' Sarah said. 'You've seen enough of kitchens in your life. And I prefer to leave Mrs Jenson in peace, to get on with what she does so well.'

As well as the morning and dining rooms, there was what Sarah called a drawing room, more grandly decorated than the others. The most elaborate porcelain was kept here, and the plaster ceiling was more ornate than elsewhere in the house, while the wallpaper had its embossed pattern picked out in gold. The chairs and sofas were upholstered in deep red velvet, the same colour as the room's heavy drapes.

What arrested Amy's attention the moment she entered the drawing room was the large portrait above the marble mantelpiece. She could see that the painting had been done several years before, but the subject was immediately recognisable as Sarah. She wore a blue silk gown and held a posy of white roses. There were matching rosebuds in her hair, part of which was pinned up while the rest fell in waves over her shoulders. Her mouth was curved in a soft smile, though the artist had captured the disconcertingly direct gaze that Sarah's eyes so often held.

'Rather too flattering, isn't it?' Sarah said, seeing where Amy's interest was centred.

'No, not a bit—it's beautiful. How old were you?'

'Sixteen. That was my first long dress.' Sarah gazed pensively at the painting. 'Mother had always said they'd have my portrait painted when I was eighteen, but when I was coming up to sixteen Father announced he wanted it done for my birthday. By then we all knew that Father mightn't be with us if we waited till I was eighteen. And he wasn't,' she added quietly.

Staring up at the portrait was making Amy's neck ache. She lowered her gaze to the mantelpiece, and her attention was caught by a photograph in a silver frame. A grey-haired woman in a dark dress held a baby of about six months old on her lap; instead of facing the camera, the woman's whole attention was on the child. She held the baby's tiny hand in her own and gazed at the little face, her eyes deep pools of love.

'Mother and I,' Sarah murmured from close behind Amy. Her hand rested lightly on Amy's shoulder. 'She told me she'd always been grateful to you. I'd like to think she'd be happy that I've found you.'

The final room on this floor, apart from the servants' domain, was Sarah's study. This was decorated more soberly than the other rooms, though with no less elegance. The chairs were of dark brown leather, with the one behind the large, walnut desk being particularly imposing. Wood panelling came halfway up the walls, with a dark red wallpaper above it, but there was little enough of panelling or paper visible. The walls were lined along most of their length with tall bookcases crammed with leather-bound volumes.

'Books,' Amy said faintly, clutching at the back of a chair for support. 'Look at all your books!'

Sarah gazed around the room with a satisfied smile. 'Yes, I've quite a good collection. Though I must warn you that some of them are exceedingly dull legal texts and the like. And I didn't share Father's interest in military history, so some of his books tend never to leave their shelves.' She ran her fingers lightly over the spines of the books nearest her. 'But most of them are extremely precious to me. I hope you'll enjoy them as much as I do. Treat them as your own, Amy.' Her smile broadened, and she gave Amy a mischievous look. 'Perhaps I should make you stay with me until you've gone through the entire collection. That would be one way of keeping you here.'

'I don't think I could read all these if I lived to be ninety,' Amy said, still awed. 'I'd like to try, though.' She reached out a hand towards the nearest shelf, then let it drop. 'However will I know where to start?'

'There's an order to how they're set out. Novels are on these shelves, poetry's there, and plays on the top—there's a stool, so even you should be able to reach them. The rest are generally by subject. I'll guide you through it, don't worry. I often just browse them at random till something catches my eye, I suggest you try that approach, too.'

'I'll have a go,' Amy said, eyes darting around the shelves as she took in Sarah's explanation.

'Perhaps I'll choose you one to start with. But let's leave it for the moment—I want to plan the next few days with you.'

They sat down near a low table that Amy had not noticed before. It held a collection of lead soldiers arranged in a complex formation. Sarah followed her gaze; she leaned over to pick up one of the soldiers and passed it to Amy.

'An English officer from the battle of Waterloo, I believe. Maurice apparently used to sit at this table when he was small, playing with the soldiers while Father was working. That was before I was born, of course. My turn came later.' Sarah smiled, her eyes staring into the invisible distance. 'Father had a special chair by this desk, a nice, tall one so that I could sit near him. I used to spend hours here, I think—Mother suffered from migraines occasionally, and I'd always come to Father when she had to take to her bed with them. He'd let me put my dolls on the desk—I had my own corner of it where I'd dress and undress them.'

'He must have been very patient,' Amy said, moved by the description of the man who had shared his desk with a little girl.

'Yes, he was. I've photographs of him, see? That's Maurice with him in the earlier one.'

She fetched two photographs from the desk. One was of a man with a boy of around five years old; the other showed the same man, clearly many years later, sitting in an armchair with Sarah standing beside him, her hand on his shoulder. Sarah was wearing the same dress as in her portrait. The man's hair and moustache were white, but his eyes were surprisingly bright, and, Amy thought, full of gentleness.

'His nature shows in his face, don't you think?' said Sarah. 'Not that I knew it was anything out of the ordinary. I just took it for granted that Father wanted me sitting at his desk. I remember trying to use this once, though.' She gestured at the low table. 'Father didn't scold me, but he had an odd look on his face when I put my doll there. Even at that age I could tell he didn't want me to disturb the soldiers. They reminded him of Maurice, of course.'

'They're beautifully made,' Amy said, noting the delicate paintwork on the toy soldier's uniform. 'They look so real. Even the horses look like they might gallop off any time.' She turned the toy around to admire it from all sides. 'Mal would've loved them, especially the horses.'

'Didn't he have toy soldiers? I rather thought all boys did.'

Amy shook her head. 'No. My boys never had any toys, really. Not proper ones from shops.'

She handed the soldier to Sarah, who restored it carefully to its place.

'Something of a waste, I suppose you might say,' Sarah mused, studying the toys. 'Your Mal who would have loved my soldiers but probably never dreamed such things existed, and me with armies of them that hardly get touched except when the maids dust them. But Father kept them in memory of Maurice, and I keep them in memory of Father. That's reason enough to treasure them.'

She turned her attention back to Amy. 'Well, what shall we do, then? There are things Auckland offers that Ruatane doesn't.' She smiled at her own understatement. 'I want to take you out, to something special. A concert, perhaps. Would you like that?'

The sudden swell of excitement briefly robbed Amy of breath. 'Oh, yes!' she said when she managed to find words. 'I'd love it.'

'We'll have our first outing this very week, then—why, we could go out tonight if you wish.' Sarah's smile broadened when she saw Amy's eyes widen. 'Well, why not? There's sure to be something on, this is Auckland, after all. Yes, tonight it's to be.'

She pulled the cord that summoned the maids. Alice appeared, and was asked to fetch the newspaper, which she returned with moments later. Sarah scanned the paper, then passed it to Amy, pointing to the paragraphs that dealt with entertainments.

'We've a choice. Two plays, and a choir. Which would you prefer?'

'Oh, whatever you want, Sarah. I'm sure I'd like anything you picked.'

'No,' Sarah said firmly. 'The choice is up to you.'

Amy did not protest; she already knew that set expression of Sarah's too well for that. She studied the newspaper carefully, trying to decide which outing Sarah might prefer, though she had known her own preference the moment she saw the titles of the plays.

'Would it be all right if we went to this one?' she asked, her finger marking her choice. 'Only if you want to—I'm sure I'd like any of them.'

'What I want is for you to choose whatever you'd like best, and for me to have the pleasure of taking you to it. Yes, I'm sure this will be very pleasant,' Sarah said, glancing at Amy's chosen outing. 'I'll send out for tickets. What made you pick this one, dearest?'

'It's Shakespeare,' Amy said, convinced that that explained all. 'I've wanted to see a Shakespeare play… oh, all my life, I think.'

'Well, tonight you shall have your wish.' Sarah's expression turned thoughtful. 'Ah, what exactly were you thinking of wearing?' she asked delicately.

'It'll have to be my black dress, that's my only good one for outings.' Seeing Sarah's dubious expression, Amy added quickly, 'It's looking much better than it did this morning, Nellie made a lovely job of brushing it for me. It's looking quite smart now.'

'But that's a mourning dress,' Sarah said, her voice sounding carefully controlled. 'Quite apart from any other shortcomings it might have.'

'Yes, Sarah,' Amy said quietly. 'You know I'm in mourning.'

'In Ruatane you might be. In Auckland there's no need to pretend.'

Amy closed her eyes for a moment, not relishing the prospect of arguing with Sarah. 'It's not pretending, it's showing respect. I owe—no, I don't owe it to Charlie, I want to do it. It just seems the right thing to do.'

'It's dishonest,' Sarah said, her face hardening. 'It's pretending you're sorry he's dead.'

Amy shook her head. 'No, it's not. I don't go around crying or anything. I just dress respectfully. That's not so much to ask.'

'But why? He's dead, and no one's sorry about that. You of all people—you should be celebrating. After the way he treated you, scarlet satin would be more appropriate than black wool.' Her eyes flashed as she spoke.

'It was just the way he talked,' Amy said, taken aback by Sarah's ferocity. 'It didn't mean anything.'

'The way he talked? That would have been enough on its own, wouldn't it? But what about the rest of it, Amy? What about the beatings?'

Amy was briefly startled into silence. 'Who told you that?' she asked when speech returned.

'Dave told me—well, I dragged it out of him, I should say. It's like drawing teeth, getting you or Dave to tell me anything about that man. Just the bald statement that his father used to... thump you, I think was the expression he used. Amy, it's not right for you to wear mourning for a man like that.'

Amy looked away from Sarah's dark frown and gazed around the room; at the toy soldiers, and at the desk where a man had made space for a little girl's dolls. No wonder that Sarah could find no room in her heart to pity Charlie. 'That was all a long, long time ago, Sarah. I don't even think about it. It does no good, dragging up those old things.'

'You can't just forget something like that,' Sarah protested. 'It's not possible.'

'No, I haven't forgotten. I just don't think about it. Charlie was sorry for it in the end,' she added softly.

That seemed to bring Sarah up sharply. 'Was he? It's difficult to believe of the man.'

'Yes, he was.' Amy was surprised to find tears pricking at her eyes. 'He was very sorry. He told me he was, the night he died.' In his own awkward way he had told her; clumsily, and not making an overt apology of it, but it had been an expression of remorse none the less clear for that.

'And so he jolly well should have been sorry,' Sarah said, but the force had gone out of her censure. 'Perhaps he wouldn't even have wanted you to wear mourning,' she tried half-heartedly.

'Oh, I think he would have.' Amy watched Sarah, noting the firm set of her mouth and the slight movement of her fingers on the arm of her chair. That meant Sarah was carefully thinking the matter through, Amy knew; "mustering the facts", as Sarah put it.

'You don't wear mourning on the farm,' Sarah said after a few moments of this reflection. 'Only when you go out. Why is that?'

'Well, I can't wear my good black dress for working, and I haven't got any plain ones warm enough for winter. I made a cotton one, and I wore that the first few months—I suppose I could make one out of wool, but it seems a waste. Mourning's to show respect, and there's no one around to see what I wear when I'm on the farm—well, except Dave, and he knows how I feel about respect.'

'Exactly,' Sarah pounced. 'And in Auckland there's no one in the entire city who even knew the wretched man, so no one to notice whether you're in mourning or not. Except me, and I, too, know only too well how obstinate you are about this respect nonsense. So it's just like being on the farm, isn't it? There's absolutely no need for you to wear mourning. You do see that, don't you?'

Amy smiled at Sarah's expression, a mix of settled conviction and anxiousness. Pleasing her seemed more important than a gesture to a dead husband. 'I expect you're right, Sarah. It doesn't really matter what I wear up here, with not knowing anyone. Except for church—I'll still wear mourning to church. I wouldn't feel right otherwise.'

'Thank Heaven for that,' Sarah said with exaggerated relief. 'You really can be very stubborn. And I'll let you have your way regarding church.' She smiled. 'I do know how to recognise an unwinnable argument.

'But *not* out to the play,' she added firmly. 'Your first outing definitely demands something more cheerful than black wool. So what do you think you'll wear?'

Amy's heart sank; cold reality made a nonsense of the whole discussion. 'The trouble is, that black dress is the only good one I've got. Well, except my blue silk, but I think that's a bit old, really.'

Sarah nodded thoughtfully, and stood up. 'I think we had better check your wardrobe.'

Amy followed her up the stairs. Sarah set a pace Amy could not match, and when Amy went into the bedroom she found Sarah standing before the open wardrobe, staring at its scanty contents.

'This is all?' Sarah asked. 'This is everything you brought with you?'

'Except for the underwear and things, that's in one of the drawers. Yes, that's everything.'

Sarah shook her head, and turned to Amy. 'You've only brought three dresses,' she said, speaking slowly and deliberately.

'I know,' Amy said, feeling that she had unwittingly committed an offence against decency. 'But I haven't really got any others—not ones that were good enough to bring, anyway.'

'I see. Yes, I suppose I should have thought of that before. Well, I'd better see this blue silk dress, then. If nothing else, it's not mourning.'

Amy lifted the dress out of the wardrobe, handling it with the care she felt the fine fabric deserved. 'It's quite old,' she said, trying to excuse the dress in advance. 'But it's not worn out or anything.' She held it up against herself, flattening the bodice over her chest with one hand while with the other she spread the skirt wide.

Sarah stared at the dress. 'Goodness, this must be almost as old as I am.' She took her chin in her hand, tilted her head to one side and smiled, clearly amused.

Something in Sarah's eyes, the odd mixture of affection and amusement, gave Amy a jolt. She found herself unexpectedly and painfully reminded of Jimmy; the way he had gazed in admiration when she had appeared before him in this dress for the first time. His admiration had been unfeigned, certainly; but when she called to mind his face it was the hint of amusement she remembered most clearly. Had she ever been more to him than a pleasant diversion in an otherwise boring summer?

But Sarah's amusement was too thoroughly suffused with kindness for her resemblance to her father to give Amy more than a moment's discomfort. 'It's a little bit older than you,' Amy said, and saw Sarah's eyebrows lift in surprise. 'I got it before you were born.' She stroked the dress reverently. 'It was my first silk dress—it's the only dressmaker dress I've ever had.'

'It's… ahh… well, yes,' Sarah said uncertainly. 'Yes, I'm sure it was very nice in its day.' Her attention shifted to the top shelf of the wardrobe. 'And what do you have in there?' she asked, pointing to the hat box.

Amy replaced the dress in the wardrobe and lifted down the box she had borrowed from Maudie. She would not have dared bring the hat at all without the protection the box gave it. 'This is my special hat.' She held her breath as she opened the box and lifted the hat out, relieved to see that it had survived the journey unscathed. She held it out for Sarah's inspection, the blue feather bobbing jauntily at the movement. 'Isn't it lovely?'

Sarah gazed at the hat in silence. Her shoulders gave a small, jerking movement, and Amy realised that she was trying hard not to laugh. 'It's…' Sarah stopped, gave a little cough to hide the awkwardness, then let herself smile. 'Yes, I suppose it is lovely, in its way. I'm sure it was the talk of Ruatane once. It's surely contemporary with the dress?'

Amy stroked her precious hat. 'It's the same age you are. Just the same age.'

Sarah looked at her quizzically. 'Now, why does that sound so momentous?' she murmured, more to herself than to Amy. 'May I?' she asked, reaching out for the hat.

She handled it with almost as much care as Amy had, turning it round in her hands and studying it. 'You've a story in you, haven't you?' she said, addressing the hat. She turned her attention back to Amy. 'But it's you who'll have to tell it to me, Amy.'

Could it really have been twenty-one years ago? Amy remembered it so clearly: the dragging weakness and the dull ache of loss that had made her dissolve into tears at the sight of another woman's baby in the park; the wonderful treasure trove of a store that her father had taken her into, the beautiful hat that seemed made for a fairy-tale princess, and her father's insistence on buying it for her.

'Amy?' Sarah's voice broke into her reverie. 'Are you all right, dear? Don't talk about it if you don't want to.'

'No, I don't mind. I was just remembering old things.' Amy managed a smile with difficulty. 'Pa bought me that hat. It was just after you were born. He came to fetch me—he came up from Ruatane on one of the sailing boats, he had to sleep down in the hold with the cargo, I think. And he took me home on the steamer that same day. Poor Pa, he must have been worn out.'

'It's not a journey I'd relish,' Sarah remarked.

'He didn't complain or anything. He was so kind to me. That's why he bought me the hat—he thought it would cheer me up. I was… upset. They'd taken you away. I woke up and you weren't there any more. Then the nurse took the cradle away.' Her shoulders heaved with the effort of holding back a sob. 'I wanted to go home. Pa came all that way to fetch me. We saw that lovely hat in Milne and Choyce—it cost an awful lot of money, but Pa bought it for me. It was to make up for not having you any more. He thought it would make me happy, you see. Pa only wanted me to be happy. That's all he wanted.'

Sarah put the hat down on Amy's dressing table, slipped an arm around her and drew her close. 'I see,' she said softly. 'Well, I think I do, anyway. Sit down, sweetheart, you've overreached yourself today.' She guided Amy to the bed and they sat down on its edge, Sarah still keeping one arm firmly around her.

'I know what I'll do with you tomorrow, at any rate,' Sarah said, her voice determinedly light. 'I'm going to take you to my dressmaker—she has a milliner working for her, too, we'll need the services of both. I should have thought of it before you came, but never mind. Mrs Stevenson can produce dresses remarkably quickly when there's a need. But no plays tonight, I don't think. Your wardrobe's not quite up to it.'

'Oh. I see.' Amy bit her lip to hold back treacherous tears, annoyed at the childishness of her reaction, but feeling too weak to fight it. 'Yes, you're quite right, Sarah.'

She tried to stare fixedly at the floor, but Sarah put a finger under her chin and lifted it to look into her face.

Sarah sighed, and released her. 'Well, perhaps we could. Yes, I suppose the black dress will do—there won't be many people there in any case, with it being so early in the week. Very well, Amy, we'll go out tonight.' She smiled at the look on Amy's face. 'You're easily pleased, aren't you?'

'But first thing tomorrow, we're going to the dressmaker,' Sarah announced. 'It's a good thing I made sure I wouldn't be caught up in meetings the first few days you're here, we'll need the time to set your wardrobe in order. Goodness me, Amy, my maids on their days off dress better than you're able to, and not just when I give them my cast-offs. However, we'll see to all that tomorrow. Tonight you're to enjoy yourself.'

And enjoy herself she did, though the word was too feeble for the delight Amy felt at her first ever visit to the theatre. She sat perched on the edge of her seat through most of the performance, only vaguely aware of the beautifully dressed people all around her. *It's like a dream*, she caught herself thinking. But whenever the play released its hold on her attention for a moment, the warmth of Sarah's hand resting lightly on her arm made the evening more full of joy than any dream could be.

She was still bursting with the excitement of it all when they were back at Sarah's house. 'And the actors—it was as if they really were those people, wasn't it? I mean, they must be ordinary people in real life—just people like you'd see on the street—but you'd really believe they were dukes and soldiers and things. They put such *feeling* into it. "Good night, good night! Parting is such sweet sorrow, that I shall say good night till it be morrow."'

Sarah smiled indulgently. 'Yes, it was a good performance,' she allowed. 'Don't let your milk get cold.'

Amy looked at the mug in front of her in mild surprise; she had forgotten its existence for the moment. She took a sip, and cradled the mug in her hands. 'It's still quite warm,' she assured Sarah. 'I've nearly finished it, anyway.'

They were sitting in Sarah's room; as she had said, it was even larger than the one she had given Amy. The fire was burning low, but the room was cosy. They sat in two deep armchairs within the wide bay window that, in daylight, gave a view over the surrounding houses and a glimpse of the park, but the room's blue velvet drapes were closed against the night chill. The bed was an elaborate brass affair, with a quilted coverlet and a lace bedspread over that. A small shelf on a table beside the bed held a few books, Sarah's current favourites.

'Speaking of saying goodnight, it's really quite late,' Sarah said, glancing at a clock on her mantel. 'Do you feel ready for bed once you've finished that milk? Take one of those books with you, if you like.'

'I'm not very sleepy.' Amy took a last mouthful of warm milk and placed the empty mug on a dainty table at her side. 'Weren't all the lights at the theatre pretty? And so bright! That electric light's just wonderful.'

'You'll be sleepy soon enough, after the day you've had. I know I always was after going back and forth to Ruatane. Let me choose you something nice and soothing.'

Sarah went over to the books, and came back with a slim volume bound in blue leather. 'Here you are. Not as soothing as all that, perhaps—and a little improper in places, I suspect—but truly beautiful language.' She opened the book at a marked place and read aloud:

> ' "Twice or thrice had I loved thee,
> Before I knew thy face or name.
> So in a voice, so in a shapeless flame,
> Angels affect us oft, and worshipped be." '

She closed the book and smiled. 'Let John Donne sing you to sleep, but dream of me.' She placed the book on Amy's lap. 'Now, come along to bed.'

Amy followed her. When she tried to start talking about the play again, Sarah put a finger on Amy's lips to silence her.

'Not another word till tomorrow morning. It's after eleven o'clock.'

The bed looked inviting, and the room was warmed by its own fireplace. Sarah sat Amy down in front of the dressing table and once again removed the pins from her hair.

'You really should go straight to bed,' Sarah said when she had finished. 'I intend to. Don't read for too long, either. Good night, dearest.'

She planted a soft kiss on Amy's cheek, and rose to leave. In the doorway she paused and turned back. 'Thank you for coming to me, Amy,' she said softly, then pulled the door closed after her.

Amy was undressed and in bed within minutes. She read a few pages of the poems, but soon a pleasant drowsiness crept over her limbs. She got up to turn off the light, enjoying the novelty of having electricity at her command, then slipped between those delightfully soft sheets.

The room did not have the pitch blackness of nights on the farm; a faint glimmer from the street lights crept through the drapes, and the damped-down fire still gave out a dim glow. She had thought the light might keep her awake, but it only made the room seem more warm and comforting. Amy closed her eyes and fell into a sleep that held only comforting dreams.

4

Sarah's dressmaker, Mrs Stevenson, was a tall, grey-haired woman in her late fifties, with bright eyes and a pleasant smile. When an assistant ushered Amy and Sarah into a comfortable sitting room, Mrs Stevenson greeted Sarah with an enthusiasm that suggested Sarah was one of her more valued customers.

The young girl assistant was despatched to fetch morning tea, and Sarah explained that it was Amy rather than herself who was to be outfitted.

'Mrs Stewart was unable to bring a great deal of luggage on the boat,' she said. 'And as she'll be staying in Auckland for some months, she'll need a range of outfits.'

'Just a few things,' Amy put in timidly, but the other two women ignored her for the moment.

'So we'll need to look at day wear as well as evening, of course,' Mrs Stevenson said, clearly delighted at the thought of producing a complete wardrobe of garments. 'Tea gowns as well as costumes for visiting?'

'Oh, certainly,' Sarah agreed. 'One or two cloaks, as well.'

Mrs Stevenson opened a notebook and began writing. 'Two evening outfits, would you say?'

'Three,' Sarah said decisively. Amy gave a gasp, and was about to protest, but Sarah raised a finger to silence her. 'Let me,' she said, smiling at Amy's stunned expression.

'Three evening outfits,' Mrs Stevenson repeated as she wrote in her notebook. 'Tea gowns?'

'Two should be enough for now,' Sarah said. 'And two walking costumes. Two for afternoon visits, as well. We'll talk about hats when we've the dresses organised. Oh, and one other thing,' she added, giving Amy a brief, sidelong glance. 'Two sets of lingerie.'

Amy felt herself redden, and wondered if Sarah had inspected the contents of her underwear drawer. Her second-best chemise had a small patch, while her spare corset cover was frayed around the neckline.

She was rescued from her embarrassment by the distraction of the girl's returning with tea and a plate of dainty biscuits on a tray.

Mrs Stevenson produced a tape measure from her pocket and placed it on a small table by her chair. 'I'll take down your measurements when we've had some refreshments. Then we'll look at fabrics, so you can decide what you might prefer. Ah, I must just ask,' she said delicately, eyeing Amy's black dress, 'are you in mourning, Mrs Stewart? It makes a difference to what fabrics I should show you, of course.'

Sarah cut in smoothly before Amy had a chance to answer. 'Mrs Stewart was in mourning earlier in the year—light mourning, that is. She's in the process of returning to dressing normally.'

'Ah, I see,' Mrs Stevenson said, clearly relieved. 'That does make things simpler.'

'Except I don't think I could wear bright colours,' said Amy. 'I'd rather not—it wouldn't seem right.'

Sarah made a small grimace, but she nodded. 'If that's what you want, dear.'

'Hmm,' said Mrs Stevenson. 'Well, of course if that's the case... it's rather a pity, when... ah well, it can't be helped.'

Sarah pounced on the dressmaker's hints. 'What were you about to say, Mrs Stevenson?'

'Oh, it's just that with your pretty colouring, Mrs Stewart, there's a lovely red velvet that suggests itself to me. Now, you have the same colouring, Miss Millish, but with your statuesque build red could be rather overpowering. But for Mrs Stewart with her neat little figure, it would be just right.'

'Not red,' Amy said, steadfastly thrusting the tempting image from her mind. 'I couldn't wear that.'

'Perhaps not,' Sarah said.

Mrs Stevenson noted down Amy's measurements, then ushered her and Sarah along a passage and into a larger room, one wall of which was lined with bolts of fabric. The fabrics were arranged according to some system that Amy could not grasp, though Mrs Stevenson seemed able to go straight to the bolts she wanted without the least difficulty.

'Now, what shall we start with? Day dresses or evening wear?'

'Day, I think,' Sarah said. 'We might have trouble coming back down to earth if we start with evening dresses. Do you have any special preferences, Amy?'

Amy shook her head, too awed by the sight of so much satin and velvet, braid and lace, crowded into one room. 'I'm sure any of these things would be lovely. You decide for me, Sarah.'

'I have every faith in your taste, Mrs Stevenson,' said Sarah. 'What would you recommend?'

Mrs Stevenson was very willing to offer suggestions. She held up different fabrics against Amy, frowning at the effect of some, which were then returned to their places, while others received an approving nod. She sought both Amy's and Sarah's opinions of each of her selections, sometimes offering a choice between two or three fabrics; when this happened, Amy insisted that Sarah choose for her, not trusting herself to make a proper job of it. If she had been able to find a price tag on any of the fabrics her choice would have been made easy, but none of them seemed to carry any indication of their cost. Amy decided that they must all be worryingly expensive.

Even her so-called tea gowns, which, as Sarah had to explain to her, were intended for casual wear around the house, were to be silk; one in pale mauve, and the other a light green with white flowers. The fabrics chosen for the walking costumes were both of wool, but it was woollen fabric of a finer quality than Amy had ever worn, one rust-coloured and the other pale grey. Her gowns for visiting were to be silk as well, a heavy bronze satin for one and a dark green taffeta for the other. A silvery-grey woollen cloak would go with the walking costumes as well as the visiting gowns.

Mrs Stevenson spread out engravings from magazines on a table for Amy to study the dresses illustrated. 'Which styles appeal most?' she asked, but Amy shook her head helplessly.

'They're all lovely. My head just goes round and round when I try and pick one. I don't know which ones would go with which material,' she added, casting an awed glance at the growing pile of fabrics chosen for her.

'It's up to you again, Mrs Stevenson,' said Sarah. 'What do you suggest?'

'Well, I do think that simple styles might be best, with Mrs Stewart not being very tall. What about something like this for the mauve?' she asked, turning unerringly to the correct page of a particular magazine.

They went through the whole range of Amy's day dresses, and Amy gradually gained the confidence to make some selections of her own when offered a choice of styles.

'Those should all be most satisfactory,' Sarah said when they had decided on the last of them. 'Shall we go on to the evening dresses now?'

'We do need to choose the trims for these dresses as well,' said Mrs Stevenson. 'Perhaps we should do that first? I thought this lace would be perfect with the green and white gown.'

Amy felt pleasantly wearied from helping choose the styles, and she let the trims be chosen for her, taking pleasure enough in handling the frothy laces placed before her and admiring the soft colours of the braids. The room seemed something a genie had conjured up in answer to a girl's wish for magically beautiful clothes, and Amy would not have been completely astonished if the whole scene had vanished to be replaced by her own plain little parlour.

'Oh, Amy, you must show Mrs Stevenson your blue dress,' Sarah said.

'I suggested to Mrs Stewart that she might like to have one of her dresses remodelled,' she explained to the dressmaker. 'It's several years old, but perhaps worth keeping.'

'It's too good to throw away,' Amy said, carefully unwrapping the neat parcel of tissue paper the maids had fashioned around the dress. 'I know it's old-fashioned, though.'

Mrs Stevenson spread the dress out on a table and examined it. 'It's good quality fabric. Quite well made, too. Yes, I think I could make something of this. Does it fit you comfortably, Mrs Stewart? It's a very close-fitting style.'

'I let it out a little bit a few years ago. I've had it since I was fifteen, and it was snug on me even then.'

'Yes, the styles were tighter in the bodice when this was made. Now, perhaps if I were to add a panel in the front, and side panels to the skirt… here, I'll show you what I mean.'

She took up a sheet of paper and sketched rapidly, showing a full-bodiced dress with a patterned panel down the centre of the bodice, and matching panels on either side of the skirt. 'This pale blue silk overlaid with this lace would be rather pretty,' she said, placing the fabric and lace beside Amy's dress. 'I'll have to alter the neckline, of course, but if I add a wide frill like this, in the same lace, it would look as though it had been intended that way. I'd remove this organdie frill at the hem—in fact I could change the lower edge completely, if I add a row of tiny pleats and a scooped frill. Like this, perhaps.'

She sketched more details, showing a transformed hemline. 'The sleeves aren't quite right, being so narrow, but the neckline frill will conceal that fairly well, and I'll add these frills at the cuffs.' Her pencil again moved rapidly. 'Yes, that should look rather nice,' she said in evident satisfaction, passing the drawing over to Amy.

'That's beautiful,' Amy said, awed by the woman's skill. 'That'll be the nicest dress I've ever had.'

Sarah squeezed her arm. 'They all will be, dear.'

Amy had thought the day dresses wonderful enough; when they came to her evening gowns, it was harder than ever to believe that such dresses could really be intended for her. A selection of the finest of all Mrs Stevenson's fabrics was spread out for Amy's consideration; silks and velvets and laces, and the most elaborate of trims.

'Black?' Sarah said, frowning in surprise at the first of Mrs Stevenson's suggestions, a heavy black satin that slid like water through Amy's fingers. Where the light caught it, the fabric gave back the impression of a shimmer of moonlight on a midnight ocean. 'I'm not sure about the colour.'

'Well, it's up to you, Miss Millish—and you, of course, Mrs Stewart. But for a mature woman there's no colour more elegant than black. It's certainly not confined to mourning clothes. Especially when decorated—like this, say.' She scattered a handful of tiny, silvery beads over the black fabric, and Amy gasped at the effect they made. 'Imagine the bodice embroidered all over with these. Hardly sombre, is it?' Mrs Stevenson asked, the barest hint of a challenge in her voice.

Sarah studied Amy's expression at the sight of the beads sparkling against the fabric, and she smiled. 'How can I possibly say no? Very well, Mrs Stevenson, it seems that you're the best judge.'

Amy was coaxed away from the black satin to give her opinion on a midnight blue velvet.

'This drapes beautifully.' Mrs Stevenson illustrated her point by draping the fabric around Amy. It fell in soft folds, seeming to want to mould itself to Amy's form, and the silver lace Mrs Stevenson held against it enhanced the graceful effect. 'Do you think it's suitable?'

'Quite definitely,' said Sarah. 'It's just right.'

Mrs Stevenson looked over at her bolts of fabric. 'We were thinking of three evening gowns, weren't we?'

Amy dragged herself away from wide-eyed study of her dress fabrics to snatch at the chance of sparing Sarah some expense. 'Two's enough—really it is, Sarah, I can hardly imagine even having one lovely dress like this. Anyway, I think I'd just about faint if Mrs Stevenson shows me any more lovely materials like these.'

'Well, I suppose we could leave the third till another day,' Sarah allowed. 'It might be more fun for you that way.'

'Just as you wish, of course,' said Mrs Stevenson. 'And we definitely don't want any bright colours?' she added, an oddly cautious tone to her voice.

'No, I really don't,' said Amy.

Sarah was studying Mrs Stevenson's expression with interest. 'Why do you ask, Mrs Stevenson?'

'Oh, it's just the fabric I was speaking of earlier. I'm certain it would look quite stunning on Mrs Stewart. It would do no harm just to look, would it?'

'No harm at all,' Sarah said, the hint of a smile hovering around her mouth.

Mrs Stevenson picked up a bolt of fabric and unrolled a long length, which she draped around Amy. It was velvet, a little heavier than Amy's midnight blue, but still soft enough to fall beautifully into folds.

The colour was a red so rich that Amy could not find a name for it; 'crimson' seemed woefully inadequate for a shade that seemed to pulse with life. It was the red of a fruit so tempting that the sternest of ascetics would scarcely have found strength to refuse it. The velvet cried out to be stroked, and when Amy gave in to its cry she found it as soft as kitten's fur. It looked beautiful enough from where Amy stood, looking down at the fabric enveloping her body; if she had been able to see herself, pale skin and dark hair set off to perfection by the jewel-like richness, she would not have wondered at the expressions of the two women staring at her.

'That really is lovely,' said Mrs Stevenson.

'Oh, yes,' Sarah agreed softly. 'That's perfect.'

Amy felt that she was breaking a spell when she freed herself from the fabric. 'No, I'm sorry, I really couldn't. Not red.'

Sarah said nothing, but Amy had a fleeting impression of the two taller women exchanging a nod over her head. And the red velvet, though Mrs Stevenson put it to one side, was not returned to its shelf.

'Mrs Stewart will need several hats to go with the outfits we've planned today, of course,' Sarah said when styles for Amy's two evening gowns had been chosen. 'I've always found your milliners quite satisfactory, Mrs Stevenson. Do you have any particular ideas, Amy?'

Amy knew it would be pointless to try and say that she really did not need more than one or two hats. She was equally sure that her own grasp of what was fashionable was vague at best. 'Not really. Except… well, I know those great big hats are in the fashion, I've seen lots of women wearing them. But I don't know if I could. I mean, I'm so little, I think I'd look like a mushroom in a hat like that.'

Sarah laughed aloud at the notion. 'A very pretty mushroom you'd make, too! But you're probably right, dear, you are a bit small for those hats. A gust of wind might carry you away.'

'Hats should be in proportion to the wearer,' Mrs Stevenson said. 'And it's perfectly possible to have fashionable hats that aren't particularly large. It's simply a matter of style and trimmings. I'll show you a few to give you some ideas.'

Mrs Stevenson rang for her assistant, and sent the girl off to fetch a selection of hats. Amy was relieved to be shown a dozen, all of them pretty, and none of them frighteningly large. 'Oh, yes, I could wear any of these. They're all lovely.'

'I'm sure Mrs Stevenson's milliners will produce a nice collection,' said Sarah. 'Now, Amy, do you want to show Mrs Stevenson your hat? Don't if you'd rather not,' she added gently.

Amy's hand reached out to rest protectively on the hat box at her feet. 'I know it's old,' she said, aware of the defensive note in her voice. 'But it was a really smart hat, I know it was. It cost an awful lot of money, too.' She hesitated, then decided to be brave. 'I'll show it to you.'

'This is a rather special hat,' Sarah explained while Amy got it out of the box. 'Mrs Stewart's late father bought it for her many years ago. I suggested she might like to consider having it remodelled, so that she could get a little more use out of it.'

Amy clutched at the hat. 'But I don't want it cut up or anything. I'd sooner not wear it if it's too old-fashioned. I'd rather just keep it how it is.'

'May I?' Mrs Stevenson reached out a hand. 'I'd like to see it.'

Amy made herself hold the hat out, and tried to take some relief from the obvious respect with which Mrs Stevenson handled it.

'Oh, yes,' Mrs Stevenson said as she examined the hat. 'Yes, this is a fine piece of workmanship—it's extremely well-made, and of the best quality materials, too.' She looked up, and smiled at Amy. 'I don't think there's any need to be cutting into it, Mrs Stewart. I could simply add some extra trimmings. Some pretty blue chiffon around the edge, perhaps, to give it more width—that would give the hat a more up-to-date appearance without damaging it. A little veiling, too, that's always flattering. You want to keep the feather trim, I presume?'

'Yes,' Amy said. 'I want to keep everything.'

'But do you think those alterations would be all right, dear?' Sarah asked. 'It would be nice if you could actually wear the hat, wouldn't it?'

Amy paused to consider the matter properly. She was aware that to the other two women her attachment to the hat might seem foolish, but she was not going to let that sway her. The hat was a link with her father, and she could not bear to have it mutilated. 'I think that sounds quite nice,' she said at last. 'As long as you only add those things to it. Don't take anything away.'

Mrs Stevenson assured Amy that she would, indeed, take nothing away from the hat, and on the strength of that Amy agreed to leave it behind for the proposed retrimming.

'That was rather a marathon, wasn't it?' Sarah said when the two of them were on the footpath outside Mrs Stevenson's. The coachman was moving the carriage from a short distance down the road where he had been allowing the horses to graze a grassy verge. 'I'd better take you straight home, you must be exhausted.'

Now that she was away from them, the spell of the gorgeous fabrics was relaxing its grip on Amy, allowing something of cold reality to take its place. 'Sarah, all those dresses!' she said in sudden alarm. 'They must be going to cost an awful lot of money. I really don't need all those, you know. You could tell Mrs Stevenson not to make so many, couldn't you?'

'There's no need for that.'

'But all that material! It looked so expensive. Perhaps you'd better—'

'Amy,' Sarah interrupted. 'Walk over here a little, I want to show you something. We'll be with you in a moment, Jenson,' she called to the patiently waiting coachman, who tipped his hat in acknowledgment. Now, Amy, do you see that building over there?' She indicated a busier part of the street.

'That grey one?' Amy asked, trying to follow Sarah's pointing finger.

'No, darling, that's the Bank of New Zealand. I mean that brick building—the two-storeyed one. It has several shops in it. Do you see it now?'

'Yes, I see the one you mean,' Amy said, wondering what the building's significance might be.

'Well, my dear, I happen to own that building. It brings in reasonable rents. And it's only one of… actually, I'm not sure that I could tell you the grand total off the top of my head. A good number, at any rate.'

She took Amy's arm and led her towards the waiting carriage. 'I think I can afford a few dresses for you.'

'Where did you leave that other cake tin, Dave?' Beth asked when she had unsuccessfully sought the tin on the kitchen shelf where it usually lived.

'In the parlour, I think. Yes, that's right, it's in there.'

Beth retrieved the tin from the other room. She was surprised to find it so light, and when she lifted the lid the mystery was revealed.

'Have you eaten all those biscuits?' she asked in amazement.

'Well, I get hungry,' David said, a little guiltily.

'You must do! Ma always says there's nothing hungrier than boys, but you're even worse than my lot. When did you eat all those? That tin was just about full when I went home yesterday.'

David frowned in thought. 'I don't know. I suppose it must've been last night. You know, it's that dull and quiet at night, I just sort of eat to pass the time.'

'Well, never mind, there's a couple of these plain ones left.' Beth put a biscuit on each of their plates and sat down beside him. 'Do you get lonely at night?'

'I suppose I do, a bit. It's all right in the day time, with you here. I've got my work to do, anyway, so I don't go thinking about a lot of stuff. But in the evening it's… well, it's sort of funny with Ma not here.'

Beth felt a pang of sympathy at the sight of David's wistful face. 'It's a shame Biff died.' David's old dog had been found dead one January morning, when David had gone to call him. 'Animals are good company. It must be awful, being here all on your own.' She reached out and put her small hand over David's broad one.

David turned his hand palm upwards to take hold of hers. 'It's all right, I suppose. Hey, I got a letter from Ma, I picked it up this morning.'

'Another one? She must be writing just about every day.'

'She said before she went away that she'd write a lot. It sounds like she's having a good time.' He used his free hand to fish the letter from his jacket pocket and spread it out in front of him. 'She says she went to a play—a Shakespeare one. It was really good, she reckons.'

'I wonder what it was like,' Beth mused. 'Richard's been to plays and things. I suppose Aunt Lily might have, too. What else does Aunt Amy say?'

'There's some stuff about dresses. Sarah's getting her some new dresses. She sounds pretty excited about that, too.'

'Oh, *Sarah*, is it?' Beth said tartly, her sharp reaction taking her by surprise. 'I didn't know you were such good friends with her. What happened to "Miss Millish"?'

'Well, she said to call her that,' David said, clearly unsure just how he had earned such an attack. 'And she's the sort of person that you just do what she says, you know. Like with your ma.'

'She's a lot younger than Ma,' Beth said, wondering as she did so why she felt the need to argue the point. 'I heard Ma say she's twenty-one. She's really pretty, too.'

'Is she only twenty-one? She sort of seems older than that.'

'Do you think she's pretty?' Beth pressed.

I suppose so. Not as pretty as Ma, though.' He grinned at Beth. 'Not as pretty as you, either.'

Beth knew she was being teased, but that did not prevent her taking a secret pleasure in the compliment. She would not let David see it, though. 'What a lot of rot! Miss Millish has got such pretty dresses and things. She looks much nicer than I do.' Failing to raise the hoped-for contradiction, she returned to more straightforward conversation. 'She must be really well-off, eh?'

'Mmm. Ma says it's a neat house she's got, too. I bet it is. I don't suppose she misses this place.'

He looked wistful again, and Beth resorted to a method that never failed to cheer her if she found herself as low in spirits as David seemed to be. 'I'd better get on and do some work, or I'll never get through it all,' she said, extricating her hand from his. 'You look after the kitten for a bit.'

She fetched a tiny bundle of fur from a box she had placed close to the range. The bundle stirred, and unfolded itself into a small black kitten that stared around the room with bright eyes and gave a tiny squeak of surprise at being moved.

The kitten was the runt of the latest litter born at Beth's home, and she had soon realised that the little creature had no prospect of fighting its siblings for a fair share of its mother's milk. Turning down her father's well-meant offer to put the kitten out of its supposed misery, Beth had taken it upon herself to rear the waif.

As was usually the case with Beth's waifs and strays, the kitten showed every sign of thriving. But Beth was taking no chances; rather than leave the kitten at home where she could not be sure anyone would remember to feed it as often as it needed, she brought it to David's farm every day, balancing the kitten in a small box on her lap as she rode.

'It's all right, kitty,' Beth soothed. 'Davie will give you some milk.' She placed the kitten on David's lap, poured a little milk into a saucer and put it on the table. 'Get kitty to lick it off your finger if you can,' she told David. 'It's a bit like teaching calves, only you've got to be ever so gentle.'

The kitten licked David's finger with surprising energy for so tiny a creature. 'It's got a tickly tongue,' David said, smiling at the gentle rasping. 'Shall I try him with the saucer?'

'Have a go. Mind he doesn't fall right in, though.'

David balanced the saucer on his knee and carefully persuaded the kitten to transfer its attentions from his finger to the saucer. Beth had already had some success with the same lesson, so she was not surprised when the kitten began lapping greedily. 'He's doing it,' David said, his face lighting up. 'Gee, look at him go for that milk!'

The kitten lapped busily for a few seconds while Beth stacked dishes on the bench, then it abandoned the milk to wash its face with its paw. 'He didn't have very much,' David said.

'He's only got a tiny tummy. He's growing fast, though—he was like a baby rat a couple of weeks ago.' Beth paused in her work to run a finger gently down the kitten's back. 'Kitty's going to be all right, I'm sure he is. I think I might call him Pip—he's little and black, like an apple pip.'

The kitten curled into a tight ball on David's lap. David lowered his head to catch the tiny rumbling noise emerging from the warm bundle. 'He's purring. You can only just hear it, but he's purring all right. You're good with animals, you know.'

'So are you. See how the kitten likes you? He's scared of most people, especially boys. Animals can tell when you like them—I think they know when they can trust someone.'

Beth carried a handful of washed carrots to the table and sat down beside David. 'You know what you said about Aunt Amy before?' she said, slicing the carrots as she spoke. 'About how she probably isn't missing the farm or anything, because she's having such a good time?'

'I don't mind if she's not missing it,' David said quickly. 'I want her to have a good time. She deserves to have something nice happen to her.'

'Of course she does. She must like Miss Millish an awful lot, too, to go all that way. But it made me think of when Maudie got married. I cried when she went away, but she wasn't upset to be leaving. It sort of seemed funny, you know? I mean, she was really lucky to get Richard, but I still thought she'd be sad to be going away from home. I know I would be, even if I did get someone like Richard. I won't, though,' she added, not bitterly but with the calm resignation of one who had lived her whole life in the shadow of a self-assured older sister. 'Not like Maudie did.

'I suppose it made a bit more room, anyway, with Maudie going,' she said, determinedly bright. 'Except then Maisie came to live, and then we got Benjy. It's always full of kids at our place, eh? It's a shame you can't come and stay with us, you know—you can't get lonely there. I don't know where we'd put you, though.'

'No, there's enough people at your place without me turning up. Maybe you should stay here of an evening instead.'

He spoke lightly, but Beth frowned, pondering just why the notion seemed so unlikely. 'I don't think I could,' she said slowly. 'Not at night. Not on my own.'

David's grin faded, to be replaced by a thoughtful expression. 'No, I suppose not.' His eyes met hers, and they exchanged a look that sent an unfamiliar fluttering through Beth.

She broke the moment by returning her attention to the carrots, finishing the job with a few rapid slices. 'That's the vegies done—I should have time for a bit of baking if I get on with it. I think I'd better make some more biscuits, with you gobbling the last lot up like that.' She stood and piled the sliced carrots on to a plate.

'Mmm, make some of those ones with coconut in them again,' David said, apparently as relieved as she was to have the discomforting moment passed. As Beth walked by him on her way to the range, he took the opportunity to pat her bottom.

Beth had shared this particular item from her knowledge of things marital within her first three days of housekeeping for him. The first time he had tried it for himself, he had earned a scolding by being too energetic, and giving Beth a much harder slap than he had intended or she had hoped for. He had the way of it just nicely now, Beth thought. In fact it was really quite pleasant. Spending every day with David, as she was lately, was very pleasant indeed.

She ruffled his hair as if he had been one of her little brothers, and leaned down to plant a light kiss on his cheek. 'I wish I could stay here at night, too,' she said, the words taking her by surprise. To make a joke of it, she added, 'It'd be better than Rosie and Kate whispering and fighting and things, like they do at night. At least it must be quiet here.'

'Yes, it's quiet.' David managed another bottom pat before she moved out of reach. 'Except when you're here.'

5

The first hint of daylight sliding into her bedroom woke Amy. Used as she was to having her days ruled by sunrise and sunset, she had not yet been able to persuade her body to adopt the much later hours Sarah kept.

But it was no hardship to have a little time on her hands; not when she had such delightful new toys to play with. Amy opened the drapes to take full advantage of the pale early morning light, then crossed the room to her wardrobe and opened the doors wide.

Her new dresses had been delivered the previous evening. Although Amy had had two fittings in the interim, she had not seen the completed costumes until they arrived at Sarah's. The fabrics had been beautiful enough when they were simply lengths of silk and wool; now that they had been made up into dresses, they seemed the stuff of dreams.

Amy still found it difficult to believe that she could possibly own such garments, but when she opened her wardrobe she found that, dreamlike as they might be, the dresses were real, and were hanging there just as the maid had left them the evening before.

She took them out one by one and held them up in front of her, from the walking dresses that she could actually imagine wearing, to the startlingly beautiful evening gowns. She stared at herself in the mirror, her own face almost unfamiliar with such finery below it.

There was one dress Amy had not had any fittings for, though its arrival had not greatly surprised her. She had no idea when she might be able to wear the red velvet, but it gave her pleasure enough just to know such a beautiful thing lived in her wardrobe.

She drew it carefully from its hanger, held it against herself and studied the effect in the mirror. The rich colour of the dress appeared to heighten Amy's own colouring, as though the red velvet were drawing her blood closer to the skin in a kind of sympathetic magic. Even her heart seemed to beat a little faster. The dress cried out to be touched. She rubbed her face against the velvet, its soft pile caressing her cheek, and the scent of the fabric an elusive hint of roses.

Amy replaced the red dress in the wardrobe and searched for something more serviceable to put on. On the farm, her dresses were divided into those for working and the one or two suitable for church and visiting. Only since her first visit to the dressmaker had Amy learned that there were so many categories of clothing, and she was far from confident that she had a firm grasp of what type of dress was suitable for particular times of day or social occasions.

The most likely candidates seemed to be her two tea gowns, though wearing a silk dress as an ordinary house dress seemed almost sinful. She chose the pale mauve, its colour so subtle that it could in some lights be taken for a soft grey. She laid the dress on her bed and opened the second drawer of the chest, which had been devoted to underwear.

Lingerie, Sarah had taught her to call it, and these garments were certainly too refined for any name less elegant. There were two full sets, one in the finest of cotton lawns while the other was silk. Every item was white, of course; Amy had never heard of such a notion as coloured underwear for any item worn closer to the skin than an outer petticoat, and would have thought it slightly improper if she had. But the ribbon trims that had been used so extravagantly on all the garments were in palest pink, making the white fabrics look even fresher by contrast.

Yards and yards of lace must have gone into trimming the lingerie, Amy calculated, and it was lace of the finest kind, not the coarser ones more familiar in Ruatane. She dreaded the thought of having to wash such delicate items, though she would not have to face that task while she lived in Sarah's house; Sarah had assured her that her staff were more than capable of taking suitable care of Amy's lingerie.

Her tea gowns might be silk, but wearing silk underwear for a quiet day spent inside the house was too great an indulgence for Amy to contemplate. The cotton lawn was distant enough from her previous experience of underwear.

The lawn was so soft that it was almost as if she was wearing no underwear at all. The sight of her body in the mirror startled Amy. Deep flounces of lace topped with pink ribbon bows floated against the whiteness of her legs where they emerged from her drawers, and rows of tiny pintucks patterned her camisole. The narrow band of lace that formed the top edge of the camisole, only visible where the hair tumbling down over her shoulders divided itself into separate locks, sat low on her chest, emphasising the slight swell of her breasts. She saw a flush creep upwards from her bosom to her cheeks.

The mauve silk gown hid all traces of sensuous flesh, and when Amy had brushed and pinned her hair into submission she had assumed a duly respectable outward appearance. Now would be a suitable time for her to make herself useful; except that there were so few ways in which she could be useful in this house. She made her bed and slipped her nightdress under the pillows, and made a pretence of tidying her already pristine dressing table. Her fireplace needed cleaning, of course, but she could not possibly contemplate so grubby a task in her finery, and even if she put on one of her old dresses she would have to summon one of the undoubtedly busy maids to ask for a dust pan and shovel.

If there was nothing useful for her to do, she might as well indulge herself. The new clothes had in no way lost their novelty. Amy rearranged the dresses in the wardrobe, and went through the pleasant exercise of matching hats to outfits. There were cloaks, too; an evening cloak in heavy satin, trimmed with fur, and a day one of wool, lined in satin. She draped each cloak against one of the dresses it was intended to cover, and placed hats on the shelf above to form pleasing ensembles. Then the silk underwear cried out silently to be included in the entertainment, and Amy released it from the chest of drawers and spread each item on the bed.

The finest of the silk petticoats was more than beautiful enough to have been worn as an outer garment. It had deep, scalloped edges over a triple-pleated flounce, each scallop trimmed with layers of lace and topped with knotted ribbons. Amy lifted it from the bed, held it against herself and twirled round and round, the petticoat making delicious swishing noises as she moved.

'Yes, your frou-frous are as fine as any Frenchwoman's.'

Amy gave a start; she had been so absorbed that she had not noticed Sarah coming into the room.

'This petticoat makes such a lovely swish-swish noise,' Amy said. 'Is that what that word means?'

'Frou-frou? Yes, exactly that. The sound is perhaps a little more subtle when the petticoat's worn under a dress instead of outside it. But I'm delighted to have caught you out in such mischief.'

Amy put the petticoat back on the bed. 'It seems too good to wear— all these things do.' A wave of her hand took in her new outfits. 'Is this dress all right to wear in the morning?' she asked, seeing Sarah's eyes on the mauve silk.

'Perfect. Don't worry, I'll see that you get the chance to wear them all—including your silk petticoat. Now, come along to breakfast, you must have worked up quite an appetite playing with all your new finery.'

'I'd better tidy these away first,' Amy said, guiltily aware of the underwear strewn over the bed. 'I've made a bit of a mess.'

'No, leave it. That's not for you to worry yourself about.'

They were lingering over toast and a second cup of tea when the morning mail was brought in to Sarah.

'One for you.' She passed an envelope across to Amy.

'It's from Dave,' Amy said, so eager to get at the letter that she had torn the envelope open before she noticed the paper knife Sarah was holding out to her. 'Oh, I hope he's all right.'

She scanned the letter quickly, then allowed herself to relax and re-read it at a more leisurely pace. 'He sounds happy—he's really quite cheerful, from the way he writes.'

'I should think he would be,' Sarah said. 'I'm sure he's being well looked after.'

'Yes, he will be, Beth's a lovely girl. And it's so good of Lizzie to spare her for me.' She smiled at a paragraph towards the end of David's letter. 'Beth's got a kitten she's taking up there every day—a runty one she's rearing. Beth and her waifs!'

'I seem to remember she had an injured bird when I visited the Kelly's.'

'Oh, Beth's always got some creature or other she's looking after. Dave's been helping her patch up hurt animals since the two of them were only babies, really. Frank says she's got a wonderful touch with any of the cows that are sickly, too.' She folded the letter, replaced it in its envelope and put it beside her plate. 'I'm so pleased Davie's sounding cheerful. I was a little bit worried about him, being there on his own.'

'Well, there's obviously not the least need for you to worry—which is a good thing, as fretting over Dave is forbidden in this house.' Her smile made a joke of it, though Amy suspected she was at least half in earnest.

Sarah tilted her head to one side and studied Amy. 'You do look lovely in that dress. I'll be able to take you on some day outings now that you've nice clothes to wear. I haven't really felt able to till now—I've been rather worried people might think you were my maid.

'But not this morning, I shouldn't think,' she added. 'As it happens, I do have to go out this morning, but I really don't think you'd enjoy the outing. It's purely business, regarding some property I've been looking at. Do you think you'll be all right here by yourself while I'm out?'

'Of course I will,' Amy assured her. 'You mustn't worry about me, you've got enough to think about with that sort of thing. I know what I'd like to do, too—could I have a look at your books?'

'Treat them as your own,' Sarah said. 'I can't think of a better way for you to pass the morning.'

Neither could Amy. And when she stood in the study, walls of books rising around her to well above her head, every one of them at her disposal, it was difficult for her to imagine there could be any pleasanter way of whiling away the hours.

For the moment she determinedly ignored the works of fiction; novels, she decided, would be saved for bedtime reading. What she wanted most was to improve on the scanty education the valley had been able to offer her.

With the thirst for knowledge that had seen Amy doing Standard Six work before she was eleven years old, and had induced her to spend whatever she could spare of her modest annuity on her own tiny collection of books, she made her assault on Sarah's library. It was as if a small army of scholars were arrayed before her, ready and willing to share their wisdom, and awaiting her command.

Surrounded by the works of so many strangers, Amy searched first for a familiar name. She fathomed the arrangement of the books far more easily than she had feared, and it did not take her long to discover the section of shelf devoted to John Stuart Mill. She took down a title that she had not read before, settled herself in one of the study's deep leather chairs, and began reading.

There were occasional references in the book to the works of other authors; Amy was familiar with such references, and had always found them frustrating in the tantalising hints they gave of writings she had no way of accessing. She was several chapters in before it occurred to her that Sarah's library might just possibly be beyond such limitations.

To her delight, she found that references could be a joy instead of a frustration. While the study did not hold books by every one of the authors Mill referred to, in a satisfyingly large number of cases it did. It gave her the most delightful of introductions to authors she had never before heard of, and as she dipped into chapters of these new books at random a hint might be given of another subject, another author. Soon there were sizable piles of books around her chair, among them a dictionary and an atlas to solve the mysteries of the more difficult words and obscure places.

Amy was so absorbed in the delights of the library that she lost all track of the hours passing. A discreet knock on the door intruded on her concentration, and she looked up to see the older of the two housemaids, Alice, standing in the doorway.

'Excuse me disturbing you, Mrs Stewart. Only you haven't rung, see, and I thought the bell might have gone wrong.'

'Rung?' Amy said, vaguely confused at being hauled so abruptly from a discussion of comparative economic systems. 'What would I ring for?'

'Weren't you wanting morning tea, ma'am?'

'Is it time for that already?' Amy glanced at the longcase clock that stood against the far wall, and was startled to see the time. 'Nearly eleven o'clock! How did it get so late?'

'I'll get your morning tea, then, shall I?'

'Oh, don't worry about me. I don't really need anything, I've only been reading. I don't want to be a bother.'

Alice had the composure of a long-experienced servant. She managed to answer as if Amy's behaviour were not at all out of the ordinary from someone whom Alice must assume to be of the same social class as her mistress.

'It's up to you whether you want it or not, ma'am. Miss Sarah usually has morning tea about this time of a morning.'

'Yes, I suppose she does,' Amy said, reassured by the answer. 'Well, if it's really no trouble, I wouldn't mind something.'

'I'll bring it in here, shall I?'

'Would it be a nuisance?' Amy asked anxiously; the study was a little more distant from the kitchen than most of the other ground floor rooms. 'Would you rather I had it somewhere else?'

'It's all one to me, ma'am,' Alice assured Amy, too well schooled in her job for more than the trace of a smile to hover around her mouth.

Amy was on the point of asking if it would be better for her to go into the morning room instead, when she abruptly realised that she was making far more of a nuisance of herself with her fluttering indecision than she would by a simple request for tea and biscuits. Difficult as it was for her to let herself be waited on, it was simply something she would have to get used to.

'Thank you, Alice, that would be very nice. I'll have my tea in here.'

She was careful to move her reading matter out of harm's way before Alice returned with a tray.

After her short break, Amy returned to her reading with renewed vigour, and was soon as absorbed as before. Her piles of books had grown even higher by the time Sarah came home and went to the study to look for her.

'You *have* been making good use of your time.' Sarah picked up a book from the top of the nearest heap and glanced at the title. 'I always find Matthew Arnold rather impenetrable, though I approach him with ever such good intentions,' she remarked, replacing the book. 'His poetry's a good deal easier to digest than his prose. Cast him aside if he's boring, Amy.'

'Part of it was quite interesting. He was talking about some things Mr Darwin had written—did he really say our ancestors were monkeys? I've heard people say he did, but you know how people make things up.'

'Yes, he really did. There have been times when I've almost believed it, too—some people are certainly not far from being animals, at any rate. Mr Darwin's books are here.' Sarah pointed to one of the shelves. 'Choose a day when you feel up to being shocked before you tackle them, though.'

She sank into a chair and leaned against its high back. Her face looked somewhat drawn, but at the same time she was noticeably pleased with herself. 'So you've had a productive morning?'

'It's been lovely,' Amy said. 'I've had a wonderful time with all these books. I read all the newspapers, too—you get more here than we do in Ruatane. Did your meeting go all right? You look a bit tired.'

Sarah sat with her eyes closed for a few moments. She opened them, and flashed a dazzling smile at Amy. 'I, too, have had a productive morning. Yes, it was rather hard work in places, but that did me no harm. I've just acquired a piece of land, and I'll let you in on a secret—I spent somewhat more this morning than I did on your dresses the other day.'

'Did you? Is everything all right? I know those dresses must have cost you an awful lot.'

'I'm already receiving a fine return on the investment in the pleasure of watching you,' Sarah said, indicating Amy's silk dress with a graceful wave of her hand. 'But really, Amy, you must learn to be teased. A few silk dresses are not about to ruin me.

'This morning's work was most satisfactory,' she went on. 'I'd prepared my ground thoroughly, and I was well rewarded. I paid quite a bit less than the original asking price, and I believe the land will be worth a good deal more than that asking price in a few years. It's an area that I expect to flourish—Newmarket, it's called, I'll take you for a drive out there some afternoon.'

'I'd like that. I don't know anything about buying land, but I want to try and understand things.'

'There's nothing amiss with your understanding,' Sarah said. 'Though I rather suspect you're too soft-hearted ever to develop a head for business.' She studied Amy, her satisfaction evident. 'Well, my dear, now we've some decent clothes for you, I'd better do something about showing you off properly. I think I shall arrange a soirée.'

'What's that, Sarah?' Amy asked, completely mystified.

Sarah smiled. 'A soirée, dearest, is distantly related to what Mrs Kelly calls a... a soyree, is it?'

'Oh! I always wondered if Lizzie was saying that properly. How do you say it? Could you teach me?'

'Of course. Say soirée,' she said, sounding it out slowly and clearly.

'Swah-ray,' Amy echoed carefully.

Sarah repeated the lesson several times until they were both satisfied with Amy's pronunciation.

'Very good,' she decreed. 'You'd almost satisfy my old French teacher, and she was not easily pleased. There's an odd way one is supposed to sound the "r", but I never could get my tongue around that. It's a French word, you see. It means "evening".'

'But Lizzie usually has hers in the afternoon. It's more convenient, with everyone having to get up early of a morning.'

'Yes, I know. I never felt it my place to point out her error of translation. And hers are, after all, "soyrees".'

'Let me see,' Sarah went on with growing enthusiasm, 'next week should be notice enough if I organise a guest list straight away. There are one or two people I've been intending to invite. My plans have been rather turned upside down over the last months, of course, due to you, my dear.' She smiled at Amy, and reached over to give her hand a squeeze. 'You've been more than worth it.'

'Soirées are so much simpler than dinner parties. For dinner parties I feel the need to rope in a respectable gentleman of mature years to act as host to my hostess, and presumably to keep the younger men in some semblance of order over the port. I do have the occasional dinner party, of course—apart from social obligation, Mrs Jenson happens to be an excellent cook, and it wouldn't be fair to deny her the opportunity to show off her skills. I'll probably have one later in the year, you'll be well used to society by then. But we'll start with a soirée.'

6

An invitation to a Millish soirée was keenly sought after, but not easily gained. The soirées had been well-known enough under the senior Millishes, but Sarah had put her own particular stamp on them in recent years, with younger guests sprinkled among the influential people of Auckland, and a fair selection of struggling artists only too grateful for Sarah's discreet patronage.

Amy was an interested observer as Sarah drew up a guest list and sent out invitations. The maids moved the drawing room furniture about, and special flower arrangements were set up in the drawing room and hall on the day before the soirée. The piano tuner was called in, his first visit in some time, as Sarah frankly admitted to having neglected her playing for months. Amy admired the way the household staff went about their tasks, with no fluster or bother, simply an impression of well-ordered busyness.

The day of the soirée arrived. Amy was shy at the thought of meeting so many strangers, but eager to observe such interesting people. And she was sure that in her visiting gown of heavy bronze satin she would be as well-dressed as anyone in the room.

Sarah had explained that, along with various acquaintances of hers, there would be two people at the soirée whom she had not yet met.

'A violinist who's moved here from Wellington—he wrote me such a terribly deferential letter, full of apologies for presuming so much, but just wondering if I might *possibly* have any interest in someone to entertain at social functions, and if he could *possibly* be of any use in such a capacity. I thought it would do no harm to offer the fellow a good supper and something to defray his expenses in exchange for his providing us with pleasant music—always assuming his playing *is* pleasant, of course. And we're to have a lady composer, no less! I gather the woman's making a precarious living out of selling her songs, so any sort of exposure can only do her good. It should be an interesting evening.'

The first guest to arrive showed a good deal more nervousness than Amy had felt even at her most anxious. Sarah and Amy were giving the drawing room a final inspection, and were about to go upstairs to add the finishing touches to their costumes for the evening, when one of the maids ushered into the drawing room a young man with a faintly terrified expression, a case under one arm, and a mop of straw-coloured hair that, judging from the convulsive movements of his right hand, seemed to need constant smoothing down.

The maid introduced the new arrival as Mr Vincent, the violinist, then bobbed a curtsy and left the room.

'Ah, how do you do, Mr Vincent,' Sarah said, extending a hand for the new arrival to shake. 'I'm so glad you've arrived a little early.'

'Early?' Mr Vincent echoed anxiously. 'Am I too early? I'm so sorry—it's the trams, you see. I wasn't sure how long they'd take, and I had to change trams, so I made sure I allowed plenty of time, and… oh, dear,' he said when he caught sight of the clock on the mantelpiece. 'I *am* too early. I should have walked about in the park a little—I'm terribly sorry, Miss Millish.'

'Not at all,' Sarah said. 'It's most sensible of you to get here well in time. I'm sure you'll want to check the acoustics of this room and so forth—I know how particular you musicians are.'

'Oh,' the violinist said, his nervousness replaced by confusion, and then by a visible relief. 'Oh, well, I suppose it would be rather good… yes, I wouldn't mind the chance to try out the room first.'

'Very well.' Sarah graced him with a smile. 'Mrs Stewart and I will leave you in peace.'

She and Amy managed to get halfway up the stairs before meeting each other's eyes made them both dissolve in fits of muffled laughter.

'What a terrified little man,' Sarah said when they had gained the comparative safety of the upstairs passage. 'I almost thought he was going to run away when he realised the time.'

'The poor man,' Amy said, sympathy struggling to prevail over mirth. 'He's probably not used to fancy houses like yours. I almost know what he must feel like.'

'Well, no one would know it by looking at you. You look quite in your element, dressed so beautifully. And I think I know just the finishing touch.' She took Amy's arm and steered her towards Sarah's bedroom.

Sarah opened an inlaid wooden box that rested on her dressing table. The box seemed to have numerous compartments, but she reached unhesitatingly towards one of them and drew forth a necklace set with blue stones. She fastened it around Amy's neck, then led her over to a long mirror to see the effect.

She stood behind Amy, hands resting lightly on her shoulders. 'Yes, that's just right.'

'Such a pretty necklace,' Amy said, watching how it caught the light at her slightest movement. 'Especially these lovely blue stones.'

'They're sapphires—the blue matches your eyes beautifully. This was one of Mother's favourites.'

Amy put a tentative hand on the necklace. 'Was it?' she asked, a twinge of guilt threatening to mar her pleasure.

'Yes, it was. And no, Mother wouldn't have minded your wearing it. She would have been delighted.'

Sarah found the necklace's matching bracelet and placed it around Amy's wrist, then chose a heavy gold necklace for herself. The gold brooch Amy had given her so long before was already pinned to Sarah's bodice. She ran an appraising eye over Amy and gave a nod.

'Perfect. Now, come and let me show you off.'

It was still a few minutes before eight o'clock when the next guests arrived, these two showing none of Mr Vincent's nervousness.

Left to her own devices, Amy might have slipped away into a quiet corner and observed the new guests unseen, but Sarah's firm grip on her arm banished any such foolish urges. She steered Amy into the entrance hall, where the new arrivals were being relieved of their cloaks by the maids.

'Amy, may I introduce Mr and Mrs Martin Wells.' Sarah released Amy's arm to exchange a kiss of greeting with the young woman. 'Emily and I were at school together.'

She took Amy's arm again and drew her forward. 'And this is my very dear friend Mrs Stewart, whom I've talked of so much.' Sarah cast the warmest of smiles at Amy. 'Emily happens to be a very fine singer, so we can be sure of some pleasant entertainment, even if Mr Vincent is too terrified to give of his best.'

'Terrified of me?' Emily Wells said, her eyes wide open in mock horror. 'Goodness, I didn't know I had that effect on musicians!' Her serious expression dissolved into a smile, and a small giggle escaped her.

'Your reputation obviously precedes you, my dear,' Martin remarked, and was rewarded by a broader smile from Emily.

'Oh, I think Mr Vincent would be terrified no matter how meek a creature you were,' Sarah said. 'I really must warn you, dear, he's such a frightened little rabbit of a man that if you so much as look at him sharply he may run away.'

Emily laughed merrily. 'I'll be on my best behaviour—I won't frighten him even a tiny bit. Oh, I've so looked forward to meeting you, Mrs Stewart,' she said, taking Amy's hand. 'Sarah's hardly talked of anything else since she knew you were coming to Auckland.'

Sarah led the way into the drawing room and introduced Mr Vincent. At the mention of Emily's name, the violinist looked more nervous than ever.

'Mrs Wells,' he said faintly. 'Such an honour.' His eyes slid away from Emily, and Amy thought she saw him cast a glance at the door of the room, as if measuring the distance in case he should have to make a run for it.

But Emily gave him little opportunity for so foolish a move. As soon as she had been introduced, she hurried up to Mr Vincent, an anxious expression on her face in place of the bright smile of a few moments before.

'Oh, Mr Vincent,' she said, slightly breathless in her haste, 'I do hope you'll be patient with me—I'm afraid my voice is really not quite *in* this evening. I hope you won't find accompanying me too unpleasant.' She allowed herself a hesitant smile.

'Why... why, not at all, Mrs Wells,' Mr Vincent said, looking first puzzled, then a good deal more assured. 'I'll be most honoured to play for you. And I'm sure your voice will be more than satisfactory,' he added with growing courage.

'How kind of you,' Emily said.

Sarah ushered Emily and Amy to seats close to the fire. Amy had warmed immediately to this bright, bubbly woman, and within five minutes of sitting by her Amy knew that Emily had married just before she turned eighteen; that she had two little girls, one aged almost three and a baby of a year old, safely in the care of their nursemaid this evening; that Martin had a senior position in the Customs Department; and that Emily regularly sang at private functions. Amy relaxed quickly in Emily's company, and was grateful to Sarah for providing her with so congenial a companion.

The remaining guests arrived only a few minutes apart. Sarah had sent out her carriage for the lady composer, so that the young woman would not be obliged to walk the streets of Auckland alone at night. Miss Farrell's outpourings of gratitude for the favour were only silenced when Sarah politely suggested she might care to set out her sheet music and acquaint herself with the piano.

Miss Farrell had just begun acting on Sarah's suggestion when the final guest arrived. Her first sight of the man told Amy that, unlike the two musicians, this was no shy, awkward person.

'Mr Lewis, how delightful that you could come,' Sarah greeted the newcomer. 'Mr Lewis has only recently arrived in Auckland,' she told her other guests. 'He's taken up an appointment at our university, lecturing in Classics, I believe—is that correct?'

Mr Lewis smiled his agreement. The smile improved his already handsome face, Amy thought as she studied him discreetly. He looked to be around thirty, with pale skin and fair, almost white, hair. 'Quite correct, Miss Millish,' he said, revealing a pleasant speaking voice. 'I'm still finding my way about the place, but I must say I've been made very welcome since I arrived in the Colony. Although I'm still to adjust to the topsy-turvy seasons!'

The gentlemen took their seats, Emily went to stand close to the musicians, and the musical entertainment began.

Emily had a lovely, rich voice with a wide range, skipping into the higher register without apparent effort. With her engaging manner and animated expression, she was a pleasure to watch as well as listen to.

She began with two songs that seemed familiar to most of her audience; even Amy thought she had heard Lily play similar melodies. Then Miss Farrell started shuffling her sheet music about, casting anxious glances around the room as she did so, and Amy guessed that she was preparing to play some of her own compositions. Emily let her hand rest lightly on Miss Farrell's shoulder for a moment in a gesture of encouragement before the music began.

Amy knew she was no judge of music, but the songs seemed pretty to her. All three were love songs; all with a wistful feel about them. Emily sang beautifully, and there was vigorous applause when she had finished; Amy noticed that Martin was particularly enthusiastic in his.

Emily returned to her seat to rest her voice, and Mr Vincent stood to take his turn. He played several pieces that sounded very clever and complicated to Amy, then he and Miss Farrell played together, which Amy enjoyed rather more. For the final performance, Emily went back to stand in front of the piano and sang another of Miss Farrell's songs. As the last plaintive notes died away, the small audience applauded loudly, the gentlemen rising to show their admiration.

A generous supper had been set out on a table against one wall. In the centre of the table was an elaborate floral arrangement, surrounded by bowls of fruit that seemed intended more for decoration than consumption. Spread around them were plates of dainty sandwiches, sliced meats, and pieces of fish, as well as meringues, fancy pastries, and half a dozen kinds of cakes and biscuits. The musicians stood awkwardly for a moment after Mr Vincent had put his violin in its case and they had tidied away their music, but Sarah gathered them up and led them to the supper table, where the guests were already serving themselves.

There seemed to be nothing to drink but wine. Amy took a glass so as not to stand out, but did no more than moisten her lips with it. People began moving to sit down; Sarah slipped her arm through Amy's and led her to a sofa to sit by Emily, while Sarah took a chair opposite them.

The seats made a rough semi-circle, with some placed closer together than others, designed to encourage conversation among the whole group while also allowing two or three people to talk quietly together. Emily beckoned Miss Farrell to a chair on Amy's other side, and Mr Vincent took the last free seat, which happened to be next to Miss Farrell's.

Emily leaned towards Miss Farrell and asked her opinion of how the concert had gone, managing to imply a certain nervousness on her own part over whether she had done the compositions justice. Miss Farrell, her eyes noticeably brighter, assured her that the songs had been much improved by Emily's performance of them. Martin engaged Mr Vincent and Mr Lewis in conversation, though Mr Vincent seemed too awed to contribute more than a word or two. Sarah shifted her attention from group to group, adding a few words wherever discussion seemed on the point of lagging, and encouraging return visits to the supper table by anyone who cast a glance in its direction.

'I must thank you, Miss Farrell, and you, Mr Vincent, for your fine performances this evening,' Mr Lewis said, nodding to each of the musicians in turn. 'I can assure you that such music would be well-received in any drawing room I've had the honour to visit in London.'

Miss Farrell gave her thanks, accompanied by much nervous fluttering of her hands, while Mr Vincent seemed to have lost the power of speech.

'Do you find Auckland society very different from that you were accustomed to at Home, Mr Lewis?' Sarah asked.

'Well, I arrived rather too recently to have a well-informed opinion on the subject. Of course I've been made aware that one can meet with many cultivated people here in the Colony, and there are opportunities to discuss music and books and the like. I must say I'm relieved not to encounter suffragettes, be it in drawing rooms or on the streets,' he added with a smile. 'There have been some unpleasant episodes at Home.'

'We've no need for suffragettes here,' said Martin. 'Our ladies gained the vote some time ago.'

'And we value it highly,' Sarah said. 'I took great pleasure in casting my vote for the first time last year. I'm sure you vote, Amy?'

It took an effort for Amy to speak to the room at large, but there were only friendly, interested faces turned to her. 'Yes, I do. I voted the very first time women were allowed to.' She smiled at the memory of how she had managed that feat, after Charlie had at first so firmly refused his permission.

'I was *so* annoyed that I couldn't last year,' Emily said, pulling a face. 'It seemed so unfair—I turned twenty-one just after the election.'

'Your politicians are obviously very forward-thinking men, to be so much ahead of ours in England,' said Mr Lewis. 'I've been told Mr Seddon takes great pride in the progress that's been made under his leadership. I understand that the ladies gained the vote without any great difficulty?'

He addressed no one in particular, but Amy was aware of several pairs of eyes on her as the person likely to have the best memory of those days. Sarah was smiling encouragingly; Amy met her eyes for a moment to boost her courage, then turned her attention to Mr Lewis.

'I wouldn't want to say anything against Mr Seddon,' she said, choosing her words with care. 'I know he's done a lot—and he's getting quite old now, I don't think his health's what it was. But I followed it all in the paper, back when they were trying to get it through the Parliament, and... well, Mr Seddon wasn't very keen on women getting the vote. It was the other men, really, like Mr Ballance and Mr Stout, who wanted it to go through.'

It felt a long speech to have made in front of people she had just met, but Sarah beamed her approval, and the other guests looked impressed.

'Mrs Stewart's quite right,' said Martin. 'My uncle was in the House at the time—I'm happy to report he supported the cause himself—and I've often heard him say similar things. According to him, there were remarks made behind closed doors by certain Members that were less than flattering to the ladies in question.'

'How very interesting,' said Mr Lewis. 'Well, no doubt England will catch up with its offspring eventually. There's been talk of perhaps allowing married women the vote—they're already permitted to vote in local elections.'

'That's because they think married women will vote the way their husbands tell them to,' Amy said, emboldened by the respect with which her opinion had been received.

'I do look forward to having you tell me how to vote next time, dear,' Emily told Martin, her eyes twinkling.

'I rather get the impression that colonial ladies have no difficulty forming their own opinions,' Mr Lewis said.

'We certainly don't,' said Sarah. 'We even have the audacity to believe our opinions can be as sound as those of men.' There was a hint of steel in the smile with which she delivered her words.

'I can quite believe it.' Mr Lewis' own smile, while perfectly polite, suggested a certain wariness.

Discussion turned to such innocuous subjects as the weather, and Mr Lewis asked Martin about his work at the Customs Department. The evening was wearing on, and Amy had to make an effort not to show any sign of the sleepiness creeping up on her. She was content to be an interested observer as conversation flowed around her, contributing only an occasional few words when politeness required it.

After sitting in complete silence for so long that the very air seemed heavier in their corner of the room, Miss Farrell and Mr Vincent had at last begun conversing together. It had started as no more than a few polite remarks on each other's performance, but as Amy sat and listened she noticed that they were becoming more animated. She heard words like "modulate" and "first inversion", and decided that they must be speaking of music in a language that, while it appeared on the surface to be English, was all but incomprehensible. As far as Amy could tell, Miss Farrell was describing a musical sequence that was giving her difficulty in a composition she was developing; it made no sense at all to Amy, and she turned her attention to conversations elsewhere in the room.

To her embarrassment, she realised that she would need to use the lavatory. She chose a moment when no one seemed to be looking in her direction, got up as quietly as she could, and slipped from the room.

When she returned, she found that the musicians had taken their discussion over to the piano. Miss Farrell was seated at the keyboard, quietly trying out different combinations of notes, while Mr Vincent stood close to her, leaning forward slightly to catch the sound. As Amy watched, Miss Farrell tried a sequence that clearly pleased her, then looked up at Mr Vincent, her eyes bright. 'That's just right,' she said, bestowing a warm smile on him. 'Thank you so much for suggesting it— I was quite at a loss how to finish that phrase.'

'I was only building on what you do so cleverly in the first few bars,' Mr Vincent said. Amy noticed what a pleasant voice he had when it was not shaking with nerves.

Emily had moved to sit with Sarah, and they were talking quietly. Amy saw Emily glance in the direction of the piano and smile at what she saw there. Emily placed her hand on Sarah's arm, and indicated the two musicians with a flick of her head. Sarah followed her direction, then turned to Emily and raised her eyebrows in mock exasperation.

Tea was brought in; this seemed to be a signal that the soirée was nearing its end. Mr Lewis took his leave soon after finishing his second cup, thanking Sarah with what seemed genuine appreciation. Emily and Martin went soon afterwards; they insisted on taking Miss Farrell, whose boarding house was only a little out of their way, in their carriage. Mr Vincent left immediately after them, staying only long enough to thank Sarah profusely, barely allowing her a moment to thank him in her turn for his performance.

Late though it was by the time their guests had all gone, Amy and Sarah lingered over cups of warm milk in Sarah's room, talking over the events of the evening.

'I kept the guest list short tonight,' Sarah said. 'I didn't want to overwhelm you at your first soirée.'

'Everyone was very nice—and the music was lovely.'

'Yes, Mr Vincent played a good deal better than I feared he might, from the state he was in when he got here. He seemed to come into his own once he was playing. Of course neither he nor Miss Farrell would be able to perform at all if they couldn't control their nerves.'

'It seems a hard way to try and make a living,' said Amy. 'Just hoping people will get you to play at their houses.'

'I wouldn't say either of them shows signs of living particularly well. But I'll do what I can to make the evening worth their while. I'll pay them for their performances, of course, but what's probably worth more to them is the attention they'll receive. I'll see that an appropriate item appears in the newspaper. "A most pleasant evening was had at the home of Miss Sarah Millish lately. Musical performances by Miss Jean Farrell and Mr Alfred Vincent gave much enjoyment to those present, who included", etcetera, etcetera. That should help them become better known around Auckland. I suspect Emily will take Miss Farrell under her wing, too.'

'I liked Emily very much,' said Amy. 'She was so easy to talk to. I felt as if I'd known her for ages.'

'I thought you'd like her. She and I got on well at school—Emily always seemed to have more sense than most of the other girls. Of course then she would go falling in love, but I must say she could have done a good deal worse than Martin. Miss Farrell's songs were rather too sentimental for my taste, but Emily liked them—and she certainly sang them beautifully. She'll praise them to everyone she knows, and that should help Miss Farrell sell her work.'

'I'd never heard of a lady composer before. I hope it turns out all right for her. And for Mr Vincent, too—I thought he looked quite thin.'

'I doubt if he's actually starving, but that suit he was wearing verged on the threadbare. Of course a man living on his own mightn't notice such things. Emily says he needs a wife.' Sarah rolled her eyes. 'I've no doubt she'll be offering subtle guidance to Miss Farrell in that direction—I'm sure you noticed her interest in the two of them this evening? Emily's been like that ever since she got married, thinking it's the answer to any problem.'

Amy nodded. 'Yes, I saw her looking at them when she was talking to you.' She took a sip of her milk, and held the mug between her hands, enjoying the warmth. 'Mr Lewis was nice. He must be very clever, too, to be a teacher at the university. Did you like him?'

'He was pleasant enough. I'd been introduced to him before, of course, but tonight was the first time I'd had any real conversation with him. There's a little too much of the sophisticated gentleman condescending to visit the land of Britain's uncultured offspring about him, but he'll get over that, and be the better for it. I think he was rather startled at how well-informed we colonial ladies are.' She smiled at Amy. 'You certainly helped our cause there.'

'It was nice to meet people who're interested in talking about things like that. So do you think you'll have Mr Lewis around again?'

'Quite possibly. He seemed to mix well enough. Why do you ask?' Sarah's eyes narrowed. 'Amy, are you trying your hand at matchmaking? Because if you are, it's to stop at once. Emily's bad enough without you joining in.'

'I wasn't really. He just seemed like someone who might suit you. I mean, he's clever, and polite, and interested in some of the same things as you.'

'And no doubt expects to run a household as he does a classroom, with him at the head, giving instructions to an admiring wife. I wouldn't suit him, and he certainly wouldn't suit me. Can we agree that there'll be no more talk of such things?' Sarah's mouth curved into a mischievous smile. 'You'd best watch yourself, Amy, or you might find you're on the receiving end. "Have you met that pretty little widow who's staying with Sarah Millish? She's still rather young, you know. She'd be quite a catch." I'm sure there'd be plenty of men capable of appreciating your fine qualities if they were noised abroad.'

'Don't tease, Sarah,' Amy said, smiling in her turn. 'I know you don't mean it. Anyway, I wouldn't marry again whoever asked me.'

'I should think not! And I've no desire to try the experiment even once.'

'You might change your mind later. When I was young, I didn't think I wanted to get married, either. I was a lot younger than you are, though—I'd had four babies by the time I was your age.'

Sarah shuddered. 'I don't think I'll change my mind. I'm quite set in my ways, and comfortably so.' She frowned, puzzled. 'Are you really so eager to recommend marriage? Forgive me, I know you don't like to hear me speak ill of that man, but I would have thought your own experience had done little to endear you to the state.'

Amy looked down for a moment, gathering her thoughts. 'It doesn't have to be like it was for Charlie and me. I'm not trying to interfere, Sarah. I just don't want you to miss out on anything. I want you to be happy.'

'Believe me, my dear, that's exactly what I want for myself. And that's why I don't intend to marry.' Sarah put down her mug and leaned back in her chair. 'Very few women have the luxury of financial independence. I'm fortunate enough to be in that position, so I've no need to put up with the inconvenience of a husband.'

'But lots of women are happy with their husbands.'

'Are they?' Sarah's expression was sceptical. 'It seems to me that most women make a virtue of sheer economic necessity.'

'They really are. I know some women get married because they have to—I suppose you could say that's what I did—but it's not fair to say they all do. Frank's always made Lizzie very happy.'

'Yes, well, he'd hardly dare do otherwise, would he?' Sarah saw Amy's expression, and pulled a face. 'Oh, all right, the Kellys are an exception. And before you throw Emily in my face, I'll admit that she seems happy enough with Martin, and she didn't exactly marry to avoid being destitute.' Her eyes grew wide. 'But that's just what poor Lily did—that's the reason she married.'

'Whatever do you mean, Sarah?'

'Lily as good as told me so herself, when I got her talking. She was struggling to manage on the pittance she was paid, trying to put money away for when she wouldn't be able to work any more—and she knew her health might break down, so she had no idea how long she'd be able to keep working. Teaching really didn't suit Lily, but there are so few choices for a woman in her situation. So when Cousin Bill proposed, she snatched at the chance of a way out.'

'Did Lily really tell you that?' Amy asked, shocked.

Sarah met her eyes, then looked away. 'Well, not exactly. She told me about the difficulty she'd had managing, and how worn out she'd been. I suppose the part about why she accepted Cousin Bill is my inference. I must confess I feel rather guilty about Lily.'

So you should, saying she only married Bill because of money, Amy was tempted to say, but she bit back the retort, contenting herself with, 'Why?'

'Oh, I practically forgot her existence. I was only a child when she left Auckland, but that's a poor excuse, given how ready I was to take advantage of our connection when it came to seeking you out. And then I found what a difficult time of it she'd had over the years, and what she'd had to do to cope. If I'd only taken notice of her earlier… but it's too late for that now. I still wish I could do something to make her life easier.' Sarah turned a questioning gaze on Amy. 'I suppose it would cause offence if I were to offer to buy her a piano?'

'I should think it would,' Amy said, still fighting the urge to say more.

Sarah sighed. 'Yes, I'm afraid so. Poor Lily, with her real musical gift, reduced to snatching at chances to play the Kellys' piano in exchange for teaching their girls to thump away at it. Of course it wouldn't occur to Cousin Bill to buy one for her.'

Sarah picked up her mug and drained the last of its contents, while Amy searched for the right words. It did not come easily to her to contradict Sarah, but she could not allow this to remain unchallenged.

'I don't think that's fair,' she said carefully. Sarah looked up, surprised. 'Just because Bill can't afford to buy Lily a piano, you shouldn't go saying he's never thought of it, or he wouldn't like to. I've known Bill my whole life, and I know the sort of man he is. He thinks the world of Lily.'

Sarah raised her eyebrows. 'Goodness, Amy, from you that's almost a scolding. I'll try to be suitably contrite.'

'He really does, you know. I remember seeing them together when they were courting. I could see straight away how fond he was of Lily. And Lizzie told me about one time an awful boy—it was one of the Feenans—threw ink at Lily and ruined her dress. Lily came home crying over it, she must have been really upset. Bill's not one to lose his temper, but he went down to the school the very next day and gave Des Feenan a seeing-to with his riding crop.'

Sarah gave a startled little laugh. 'How gallant of him! I had no idea Cousin Bill could be so chivalrous.'

'He can when Lily's in it. That was when he proposed to Lily, after he saw how upset she was.'

'This family you've presented me with is full of surprises,' Sarah said, smiling. 'Very well, I'll accept that Cousin Bill is a true gentleman who worships the ground Lily walks on.'

'Now you're being silly,' Amy said, but she smiled in her turn. 'I don't think Lily married Bill because she thought she had to marry someone, either,' she added, emboldened by her success. 'She married him because she wanted to.'

'Enough,' Sarah said, throwing up her hands in a melodramatic gesture. 'I concede defeat. Not of my case in general, I'll have you know, just as regards our immediate circle. But putting that to one side—as is my usual habit when I'm in danger of losing an argument, by the way—I still fail to see any reason why I should consider marriage. What's there to put on the other side of the ledger against the independence and freedom that I'd be sacrificing?'

Amy reached out to stroke Sarah's cheek. 'There's children.'

Sarah took Amy's hand in her own, and drew it down to rest in her lap. 'I'm afraid that seems poor compensation to me, Amy, even with myself as a shining example.' She squeezed Amy's hand. 'I can see I'll have to take more care in drawing up my guest lists in future, if I'm to avoid romantic flights of fancy at my expense,' she said, eyes twinkling. 'From now on, personable, unattached young men will be banned. The only single males allowed will be elderly—and preferably portly—clergymen.'

7

Beth leaned forward to take a biscuit from the plate in front of them, then snuggled back into David's lap. He had a very comfortable lap, she had found.

'I'd better go in a minute,' she said. 'Aunt Lily's coming down later to give Rosie and me our piano lesson, and I'm meant to do some practice first. She could tell last week that I hadn't done any.'

'You're really good at it,' said David, but Beth shook her head.

'I'm not, you know. I can play a couple of things well enough for soyrees, and when Pa wants to hear me play something of an evening, but I'll never be much good. I'm a bit sick of it,' she confessed. 'I don't mind playing those easy ones, especially when it's just the family, but it's so hard to try and learn anything new, when I know I'm never going to get much better.'

'Well, I think you sound pretty good. But you might as well tell Aunt Lily you can't be bothered doing lessons any more.'

'I wish I could, but Ma wants all us girls to learn—even Rosie, and she's hopeless. Aunt Lily just *cringes* sometimes at how she bashes the keys. I don't think she's looking forward to Kate starting when she gets big enough.'

'I suppose it means you can all take turns playing for the soyrees.'

Beth shrugged, nestling more snugly against David in the process. 'I wish we could just have Aunt Lily playing all the time, she's the only one who's any good. But Ma's that keen on us learning. She got the idea with Maudie—she thought if Maudie could play the piano she'd marry someone flash. It worked, too, she got Richard. I suppose that wasn't just about the piano, though,' Beth added thoughtfully. 'But remember how Ma used to make such a fuss at the soyrees when Richard came out? "We're going to listen to *Maudie* play now," she'd say, as if it was ever such a treat.'

'I wasn't around when they were courting,' David reminded her. 'I was still in Waihi when Richard turned up.'

'Oh, of course you were! I was forgetting. You missed the wedding and everything.' She smiled ruefully. 'I was almost as glad as Maudie was when Richard finally proposed.'

'Why?'

Beth pulled a face. 'It was awful before they got engaged—Ma made me hang around with them if they went away from the house. Richard was nice about it and everything, but I felt stupid walking along behind them all the time. I wasn't allowed to get close enough to hear them talking, so I didn't even get to hear any of Richard's stories about castles and things.'

'I didn't know you were keen on castles.'

'I quite like them in stories. I don't think I'd want to go and see them, though. They're all such a long way away.' She pressed more closely against David. 'I like it here in the valley best. It's nice and quiet.'

The kitten had clambered out of its box by the range and tottered across to the table. Beth reached down and scooped it onto her lap. 'Richard's nice, and I like him all right, but he can be a bit funny, you know?'

'How do you mean?'

'Well, I wanted to give Maudie a kitten when she went to live in town—it was a good one, too, it turned out a really good mouser. But Richard said he'd rather not have a cat in the house.'

'Eh? Why not?'

'He said cats aren't very hy-gie-nic,' Beth said, carefully sounding out the unfamiliar word. 'That means they're not clean. Isn't that silly? Cats are always washing themselves.' She stroked the kitten, who had curled into a small ball. 'As soon as Richard said that, Maudie said she didn't want one. She's still like that—"Richard says such and such". Of course she only takes notice of him when it suits her to.'

David gently ran a finger along the kitten's spine. 'Just like your ma and pa, eh?'

'Well, she probably takes a bit more notice than Ma does,' Beth allowed. 'I'm glad, really, the kitten might have got run over by a cart or something if they'd taken it. It can get that busy in town.'

She tilted her head to look up into David's face; he took it as a signal to kiss her. Keeping one hand curved protectively over the kitten, she put her free arm around David's neck and kissed him back.

Kissing with David, once they had moved beyond their first cautious attempts, had been something of a revelation to Beth. It sent a shivery feeling through her that was unsettling, but not at all unpleasant. She now looked at her parents in a whole new light when she saw them exchange a kiss.

'I really have to get going,' she murmured when her lips were free. 'Ma'll go crook if I'm late.'

She moved to disentangle herself from David's embrace. For a moment she thought he was going to keep hold of her; for a moment she thought she might let him. But David released his hold, and Beth considered the consequences of coming home later than her mother had said she should.

'You finish this,' she said, giving him the last remnants of her biscuit. 'I'll see you tomorrow.' With an effort, she resisted the urge to offer a farewell kiss.

Sarah liked to have the newspaper brought into the morning room as soon as she and Amy went in there after breakfast. After scanning the headlines together, they would turn to the pages where the current entertainments were listed, and discuss any that caught their attention. It was a rare day when there was nothing at all worth considering. At least once a week they went out to a play, a musical performance, or a lecture with magic lantern slides presented by some learned gentleman; and occasionally on to a supper afterwards.

Plays were Amy's favourites among such outings, but she found herself with a growing appreciation of musical entertainments, beginning with a lively presentation of "The Gondoliers" soon after her arrival in Auckland. And a performance one evening by a Mr R. G. Knowles offered a real novelty. Mr Knowles, a music hall artiste, presented a series of comical talks, interspersed with songs and dancing, accompanied on the piano by Mrs Knowles, who also performed several items on the banjo. The items were amusing enough, but what truly caught Amy's imagination were the moving pictures, projected by a machine called a Bioscope, with which Mr Knowles illustrated his songs. It was Amy's first experience of moving pictures, and she was fascinated by the images, which included an exciting trip by motorcar and scenes of the King and Queen walking about.

'There's talk of making moving pictures of entire plays eventually,' Sarah remarked when the two of them were discussing the show late that evening. 'Though not being able to actually hear the actors speak would be rather limiting.'

Interesting as the moving pictures had been, Amy agreed with Sarah that such entertainments seemed unlikely to displace live performances.

Going to church each Sunday was an outing in its own right, a far grander affair than Amy was used to. They went by carriage to Evensong at the Cathedral, a lofty building lit by candles as well as electric light, with a large and well-schooled choir accompanied by a skilled organist who sent music soaring to the distant rafters.

Their evenings were spent together, whether on outings or contentedly staying in, but Amy sometimes had the house to herself during the daytime. Sarah had obligations, Amy found, beyond those relating to her business interests. She was on the boards of several charitable institutions, and involved herself less formally in the fund-raising activities of others.

'I more or less inherited the role,' Sarah told Amy. 'As soon as I came of age I felt I should make myself available for the boards that Father had been on. And Mother was often asked to open school fêtes and that sort of thing, so I feel it's only right that I do the same. She always held a garden party in summer, too, to raise funds for the orphanage, and I continue that tradition—it would be nice if you were here to help me host it next year.'

With so many responsibilities, Sarah frequently had meetings that took her out of the house for hours at a time. Amy assured Sarah that she was quite happy to be left to her own devices, and she found no difficulty in keeping herself occupied. There was the wonderful library in Sarah's study, of course; Amy continued her exploration of it, ploughing through weighty tomes crammed with new and often thought-provoking ideas, and then losing herself in novels and poems.

On days when Sarah was out, Amy got into the habit of spending much of the morning in the study. The maids knew to find her there, and brought morning tea through without waiting for her to ask.

And in the afternoons she took herself on outings; at first somewhat nervously, then with growing confidence. She began by going no further than the park a short walk from Sarah's house. It held a weight of memories for Amy: she had sat there with her father, struggling against tears and her own weakness after having her baby taken from her. That loss had now been put wondrously to rights.

In a quiet corner of the park was a statue of a young soldier, a monument to the men who had served in the Boer War. Amy often visited it, and sometimes left flowers at its base. The handsome young man who had served as model bore no resemblance to Malcolm, but Amy was pleased to have what felt like a memorial of her son so near at hand.

With the park conquered, she turned her attentions further afield, and began making expeditions to Queen Street and its immediate surroundings, the city's main commercial area. Sarah had already taken her there, but going to such a bustling place on her own was a very different experience. Amy smiled to herself at how Lizzie would scold her if she knew that Amy was being so reckless as to venture there alone.

It was indeed a busy place for one used to Ruatane's quiet roads. Electric trams ran up and down the street, sharing it with what seemed vast numbers of buggies and carts. Amy even saw an occasional motor car; bizarre contraptions that gave the appearance of buggies pulled by invisible horses. When she wanted to cross the road, she made sure she was surrounded by other people who appeared to know what they were doing. It was not hard to find such people; the pavements were as crowded with pedestrians as the road was with wheeled traffic.

Amy had brought a modest amount of cash with her, along with her bank book in case she needed more, but she found little to tempt her to spend any of it. The book shops were delightful to browse in, but there were more than enough books in Sarah's study to occupy her without buying new ones. Her first visit to one of the large department stores showed her that the outfits Mrs Stevenson's seamstresses had made were superior to anything she saw for sale there. She did not linger in the dress department, but in the drapery she purchased embroidery silks and some fine linen, to give herself something to keep her hands busy during evenings at home with Sarah. Amy was not used to letting her hands rest idle of an evening. She had a project in mind: she would embroider a set of cloths for Sarah's dressing table, using the shades of blue she had noticed Sarah was particularly fond of. The intricate design she was planning seemed likely to take many weeks, especially since they were so often out during the evenings, but there was no need to hurry.

On her third visit to Queen Street, Amy watched the people getting on the electric tram until she was sure she knew what to do; she then climbed aboard, paid over her penny to the conductor, and rode the tram for several blocks. The speed was disconcerting, and the swaying motion made her feel rather dizzy, but it was with a sense of accomplishment that she stepped down at the end of her ride. It would be something interesting to put in her next letter to David; though on reflection she decided it would be best not to tell Lizzie about this particular adventure.

Amy found the busy area bounded by a few blocks around Queen Street was quite far enough to explore on her own when she felt like going further than the park, and interesting though the shops and passers-by were, it was always something of a relief to return to the peace and order of Sarah's house, where she would generally occupy herself with writing letters for what remained of the afternoon.

When Sarah was not otherwise engaged in the daytime, she often took Amy further afield. One afternoon in June, about six weeks after Amy's arrival in Auckland, they paid a visit to Sarah's friend Emily, who lived a short carriage ride away in Parnell. Amy enjoyed fussing over Emily's pretty little daughters, while Sarah visibly made an effort to show some interest in them. When the children became noisy, Emily rang for the nursemaid and returned the little girls into her care.

'I didn't specially care for children before I had my own,' Emily said, with a knowing smile. Sarah chose to ignore her remark.

Before they left, Emily played and sang what she told them was Miss Farrell's latest composition, a lively little piece with a melody that seemed to skip up and down the scale.

'Goodness, that's more cheerful than her earlier efforts,' Sarah remarked. 'I might almost attempt to learn that one myself.'

'Oh, yes, she's a good deal brighter than she was,' Emily said with evident satisfaction. 'One of the music shops is stocking the sheet music for several of her pieces now. And it's early days yet, but things are going rather nicely regarding personal matters.' She said it with the air of one who could be drawn to elaborate on the subject, but Sarah gave her no encouragement.

'If the matters are personal, we had better not pry into them,' she said.

Emily met Amy's eyes, and they exchanged a smile.

Rather than taking the shortest route back home, Sarah directed Mr Jenson to go via Newmarket, so that she could show Amy the property she had recently purchased there. They did not stay long; although the sky was now clear, it had rained that morning, and the bare land was muddy and uninviting.

Their way back from Newmarket took them through a part of Auckland that Amy was sure she had not previously been to with Sarah. She watched idly as the carriage rolled past a line of rather unprepossessing buildings.

They crossed a small side road. Amy cast a glance at the new buildings it revealed, and felt a jolt run through her whole body. Without thinking what she was doing, her hand closed on Sarah's wrist and gripped it convulsively.

'What is it?' Sarah asked. 'What's wrong?'

Amy turned to face her. In a voice barely above a whisper, she said, 'I think I just saw the place you were born.'

It took Sarah barely a moment to react. 'Jenson,' she called. 'Stop the carriage. Mrs Stewart and I are going to walk about a little.'

Amy found herself helped down from the carriage and standing on the footpath almost before she knew what was happening. Sarah looped Amy's arm through hers and looked up the side road. 'Is it this way?' she asked, already walking as she spoke.

'I think so, if I'm remembering properly. Sarah, I didn't mean I wanted—'

Sarah stopped, and turned to face her. 'I'm sorry, I'm letting myself get carried away. It's just that... well, I know so little of my beginnings. I know I was born in Auckland, but I've never known quite where, and it wasn't something I could ask Mother—if she even knew, come to that. I just thought it would be nice to know. But if you don't want to, we'll get straight back in the carriage and go home.'

Sarah sounded calm, but Amy saw the spark of excitement in her eyes. She was aware of the effort Sarah had been making to avoid asking questions Amy might find painful; this inspection of her birthplace seemed a small favour to ask. 'I don't mind having a little look, Sarah. But don't get your hopes up, darling—it was such a long time ago, I mightn't be remembering properly. Somehow the look of the buildings and the way you can just see that windmill up on Symonds Street reminds me of it, but that doesn't mean anything. This probably isn't the right place at all.'

But it was. Amy became more convinced of it as they approached, and when they reached the foot of the steps she was sure. The building looming above her, its windows like dark malevolent eyes, seemed just as it had on the day she had first come here. She had been hurried up those steps as fast as her bulk had allowed, her swollen belly making it impossible to see her feet, but she remembered her slow climb back down them, clutching her father's arm as tightly as she was now clutching Sarah's. The very cracks in the steps, and the chipped paint on the railing beside them, seemed burned into her memory.

With an effort, Amy raised her gaze to the top of the steps. When she saw the door, she felt a rush of relief.

'Oh, I think it's deserted,' said Sarah. 'There's a padlock on the door.'

'It looks as if it's been locked up for a while,' Amy said, noting the signs of rust on the chain attached to the padlock.

Sarah looked at Amy's expression and smiled ruefully. 'I gather you're not exactly disappointed that we won't be able to have a grand tour of the place. Ah, well, it was probably a foolish idea on my part.' She glanced down the road to where Mr Jenson was letting the horses graze the grass verge. 'Let's walk to the far corner and back, since Jenson's gone to the trouble of stopping.'

Sarah looked about her as they strolled, running an appraising eye over the dumpy little houses with their tiny front yards. 'All rented, I'd say. And owned by a landlord who doesn't take a great deal of interest in his property. Most of them are sadly in need of a coat of paint, at the very least. A pity—it's not a bad location.'

'Do you own any houses near here?' Amy asked.

'Good lord, no! No, my rental property's shops and offices, mostly. There are a few tidy little cottages Father rented out very cheaply to people he was told of who'd fallen on hard times, and I keep those up, of course, but otherwise I generally avoid residential property.'

They reached the corner and began walking slowly back towards the carriage. 'Were you here for long?' Sarah asked.

'About three weeks. Before that I was in a boarding house. It can't have been all that far from here, it didn't seem to take long in the cab, but I don't think I'd be able to find it again even if I walked right past it. I was there nearly two months, but I don't really remember what the outside looked like.'

'A boarding house?' Sarah frowned. 'And you were there on your own all that time?'

'It did seem a long time. It wasn't an awful place or anything, but it was lonely with no one to talk to. I mostly remember how boring it was—I didn't have anything to do all day. I think the landlady felt a bit sorry for me towards the end, she started giving me the newspaper to read and the odd magazine. She brought me here in the cab when we knew you were arriving.'

The path had led them back to the old nursing home. Amy glanced at it, then looked away quickly. The windows were thick with grime, and in one of them water had run through a broken pane, leaving lines in the dirt that looked like a face distorted with malice. Amy could picture Sister Prescott lurking behind that window, lying in wait for girls to torment. She could not suppress a small shudder. Sarah, with her hand on Amy's arm, stopped at once.

'Was it so very dreadful?' Sarah asked, concern in her voice.

Amy looked up at her, and remembered looking into those same deep blue eyes when they had belonged to a tiny baby in her arms. 'Not while I had you with me. I didn't care about anything except you.'

She placed her hand over Sarah's. 'You were such a lovely baby. And I knew you were going to be clever, right from when you were born, just about. You took so much notice of everything. I used to talk to you all the time,' she said, smiling at the memory. 'Telling you all sorts of things. I thought maybe you'd remember it somehow when you were older. Silly, wasn't it?'

Sarah answered Amy's smile with one of her own. 'Perhaps you were right. Perhaps that's why when we first met I felt as if I'd known you always.'

She tugged gently on Amy's arm, and they walked on. 'If it wasn't dreadful once you had the benefit of my company, am I to understand that it *was* dreadful before that? I'd like to know just how much of a nuisance I was on my arrival in the world.'

Sarah seemed to be trying to make a joke of it, but Amy was aware of the keen interest behind her light words. She struggled to decide the proper way to respond.

'Please, Amy,' Sarah said softly. 'Don't shut me out as if I were a child. I know it's not something that's usually spoken of in front of unmarried women—Emily wasn't at all forthcoming, although even I could see she was unwell after she had that younger girl of hers—but I can see the very sight of this place troubles you. I suppose I feel responsible for whatever you suffered here.'

'Oh, now you're being silly,' Amy protested. 'Of course it's not your fault.' She looked about her to check that there was not the slightest chance of their being overheard. 'It was a long time ago, and the bad part didn't seem to matter once I had you,' she said, keeping her voice low. 'I was scared, mostly. I didn't know what to expect. And the nurses... well, they weren't very nice. Especially the one in charge. There's ways they can make it easier—you can just go to sleep till it's all over.'

'Like an operation in hospital? Father had one once, when I was very small. I remember being taken to see him when he was just waking up from it.'

'Yes, like that, I expect. They use chloroform to make you sleep. I had it later, with my other babies. But the nurse wouldn't let me have it with you.'

'Why ever not?' Sarah asked, frowning.

Amy stared at the distant windmill, just visible between two buildings. It was easier to speak if she did not have to look at Sarah. 'She said it's meant to be awful for girls like me. She wanted me to be so scared I'd never come back to her nursing home again. She wasn't going to waste chloroform on a whor—on a bad girl.'

She met Sarah's eyes, and saw cold fury there. 'How dare she treat you like that!' Sarah said, her eyes flashing. She halted, released her hold on Amy's arm and half turned back towards the building. 'I wonder if there's any way of tracing the woman,' she murmured. 'I'd like to tell her what I think of such behaviour.'

The idea was so ridiculous that Amy laughed aloud. 'Sarah, it was over twenty years ago! And she wasn't very young—I'm sure she was a lot older than I am now. She'd be an old, old lady now, if she's alive at all.'

She slipped her arm through Sarah's and pressed close against her. Any ghosts of memory lingering in this place seemed banished by Sarah's warm and solid presence. 'The worst part of all was when they took you away. And you've made that come right. Because you came back to me.'

92

Sarah stooped to plant a soft kiss on Amy's cheek. 'Shall we go home now?'

'Yes,' said Amy. 'Let's go home.'

8

Beth was already halfway along the road to David's farm before she realised that she had forgotten to bring a coat. She glanced apprehensively at the iron-grey sky, but decided to risk it rather than ride all the way home again.

She was on the track up to the house when the heavens opened, drenching her in moments. She made no attempt to urge the horse into a faster canter; that would only risk a dangerous stumble, and she could hardly get any wetter than she already was.

When she neared the house she saw David running towards her, carrying a halter and a spare coat. His own coat was flapping open, as he had not taken the time to button it. As Beth slid from the horse, he flung the coat over her shoulders. The two of them got the halter on the horse, took off its tack and turned it in to the nearest paddock. The horse gave them a reproachful stare and shook itself ineffectually.

'I'll put this stuff away,' David called over his shoulder as he ran towards the nearest shed carrying the tack. 'You go inside and get dry.'

Beth was still in the porch, struggling with numb fingers at the laces of her sodden and muddy boots, when David joined her there. He pulled off her boots before removing his own. They hung the streaming coats on two nails, then erupted into the kitchen.

They stood dripping water on the floor and laughing helplessly at the sight of each other. Their hair was plastered to their scalps, and their clothes were so wet they might as well have been swimming in them.

David fetched a towel from his room. Beth rubbed her hair with it, and made a futile attempt at dabbing some of the water out of her clothes. She passed the towel to David, and watched as he gave his hair a quick rub, leaving it tousled but still dripping.

'That hasn't done much good,' she scolded. 'Here, let me. Lean forward so I can reach.'

David obligingly lowered his head, but Beth still had to stand on tiptoe to lift the towel high enough. She rubbed vigorously at his thick, dark mane, ignoring his protests that she was pulling it, then dropped the towel, slipped her fingers through his hair and pulled his face down to hers till their lips met.

When David came up for air, Beth kept her fingers twined in his hair and admired the way the ends were turning up as it dried. 'You and your curls,' she said. 'Ma used to say you were too pretty to be a boy. I wish I had hair like yours—or blonde like Maudie's.'

'I like yours best.' David took a rather damp lock of Beth's fine, light brown hair in his hand and kissed it. She shivered slightly. 'Are you cold? Come in the parlour, I've got the fire going.'

He put his arm around Beth and led her through to the next room. David built up the fire, and they sank onto the rag rug in front of it, leaning against each other.

Beth held out her hands towards the warmth of the fire, but her teeth chattered. 'You're really cold,' David said in concern. 'You need to get some dry clothes on. Do you want to see if Ma left any dresses here?'

'I can't go poking around in Aunt Amy's stuff! Anyway, I don't think her things would fit me, she's so little. I'll be all right.' Despite herself, she shivered again.

'You'd better get out of that wet stuff, anyway.' David got up and went into his room, and was back a few moments later with a blanket, which he held out towards Beth. 'You'll be decent enough in this,' he said with a grin.

'You needn't think I'm getting undressed with you watching me. Go and get changed yourself—your clothes must be nearly as bad as mine.' She took the blanket, and watched as David went into his bedroom. 'Close the door!' she called after him. David made a show of firmly closing it. 'And don't come back out here till I say you can.'

She took off her dress and outer petticoat, only to find that her under-petticoat was damp, too. So she stripped to her chemise and drawers, draped her clothes over a chair and wrapped herself in the blanket. 'You can come out now,' she called.

To her surprise, David emerged wrapped in a blanket and carrying his clothes. 'Why didn't you put some dry clothes on?' she asked.

'I haven't got any clean ones left except my good ones for Sunday.'

'Well, why didn't you put everything in the wash when I collected it the other day?'

'I forgot,' he admitted. 'These'll dry pretty quick.'

'Oh, honestly! I'm going to go all through your drawers, and check under the bed and everything before next wash day.'

She took the trousers and shirt from him and draped them over the room's other chair. She wondered what David was wearing under the blanket; as he pulled both chairs closer to the fire, the blanket gaped a little, and she caught a glimpse of what looked like woollen combinations.

They sat on the rug again. David took off his socks and spread them on the bricks of the hearth. Beth followed his lead and slipped off her stockings under cover of the blanket, and put the stockings with her wet clothes. 'You should make one of those drying racks for Aunt Amy,' she said. 'We use ours all the time in winter.'

'That's a good idea. I'll come and have a look at yours some time to see how to make it.' He looked at Beth, who was hugging her knees under the blanket. 'Are you warm enough yet?'

'Not really. Even my... what I've got on's a bit damp.'

David held out an arm, letting the blanket drop slightly. 'Cuddle up, then. I don't want you getting a chill.'

Beth hesitated a moment; two rather threadbare blankets did not seem much of a barrier between two bodies clad only in underwear. But David's solid form looked invitingly warm in the draughty room that the fire had still not done much to heat. She snuggled into the crook of his arm, and tilted her face for the kiss she was expecting. David obliged.

They twined their arms around each other, kissing more and more enthusiastically. For the first time since the rain had started, Beth began to feel warm.

When her lips were released, she leaned back against David's supporting arms to look into his face, with its dark blue eyes and frame of curls. 'Too pretty to be a boy,' she teased, taking a curl in one hand and tugging it gently. David retrieved her hand and kissed it, then returned his attention to her mouth.

As he pressed against her, she almost lost her balance under his weight, and put out a hand to steady herself. David let go of her just long enough to snatch two cushions from the couch. With the cushions as pillows, they stretched out on the rug to cuddle more easily.

'Mmm, this is nice,' Beth murmured when her mouth was again free. She was vaguely aware that her blanket was no longer wrapped around her; instead both blankets were lying loosely over the two of them. But it was too comfortable in David's arms to take notice of such details.

They pressed together more closely, their legs entwined. Warmth crept through Beth. She could feel her heart pounding, and her breath coming rapidly. She ran her hand down David's arm, feeling the hard muscle moving under her palm.

He was beginning to make moaning noises that struck Beth as comical. She giggled, and tried to free her mouth to tease him about it. David pushed against her; she found herself rolling onto her back with him on top of her.

'Oof! You're too heavy! Get off,' she said, but the only response was more moaning. She was aware of an odd pressure, and then a sudden sharp pain. 'Stop it!' She batted against his arms with both hands. 'You're hurting me! Stop it, Davie!'

David's voice came oddly thick to her ears. 'I can't,' he moaned. 'I can't stop!'

It took David some time to show any reaction to the fact that he was being hit quite hard. He had rolled onto his back, and Beth was crouched over him, punching him without any real skill, but with more strength than her size might have suggested.

'I told you to stop!' she shrieked. 'You *hurt* me!'

David blinked stupidly and said nothing, which maddened Beth all the more. She redoubled her efforts, and he recovered the power of speech.

'I'm sorry, I'm sorry.' He took her hands in his, forestalling her next attempt to hit him. 'I didn't mean to.'

Beth snatched her hands from his grasp and turned her back on him. She looked at herself under the blankets. 'There's blood! You've made me bleed!'

David sat up quickly. 'How did I do that?' He made to lift the edge of the blankets and look, but Beth slapped his hand away.

'You leave me alone! You're horrible!' She swung her hand at him. It made a loud *thwack* as her palm connected with his face.

David made no attempt to hinder the slap, nor the one that followed it. He waited till Beth paused for a moment to catch her breath, then he took her hands and held them too tightly for her to pull away.

'I'm really sorry,' he said. 'I didn't mean to do that. It just sort of happened. How sore is it? Is it really bad?'

The shock was beginning to subside. 'Not really—it's almost come right. And there's only a little bit of blood. But why didn't you stop when I told you to?'

'I tried to, honestly I did. But I couldn't seem to help it.' He cautiously slipped his arm around her, and she allowed him to guide her head onto his shoulder. 'It'll be all right, don't worry. I'll marry you, Beth.'

'Well, of course we're going to get married!' Beth said, almost without thinking.

David looked startled. 'Oh. I didn't know that. I mean, I want to and all, but… when did you decide that?'

Beth frowned in thought. 'I think I've always known. I never exactly thought about it, I just knew we'd get married one day.'

'Well, I'm glad you finally told me,' David said, grinning. He gave her a squeeze. 'Come on, get up on the couch and I'll make you a cup of tea.'

He helped Beth upright, then onto the couch with her feet up. He placed a cushion behind her head and tucked one of the blankets around her before going off to the kitchen with the other blanket wrapped around his waist.

David was soon back with their tea things and a plate of biscuits, which he put on an upturned box. He sat on the floor in front of the couch. 'I didn't eat all the biscuits this time,' he said proudly. 'I didn't find these ones till this morning.'

He took a biscuit and devoured it in two bites. 'So when do you reckon we should get married?'

'As soon as we can. Davie,' Beth said anxiously, 'do you think they'll let us? Ma and Pa, I mean. Aunt Amy too—I suppose she'll have to sign the paper to say you're allowed.'

'Why? Do you think they mightn't want us to?'

'Well, they might think we're a bit young. They *might* let us get engaged—I'll be seventeen in November, and Maudie was allowed to get engaged when she was seventeen. I think she would've been allowed before then, come to that, if Richard had got on with it. They were meant to wait till she was eighteen to get married, but they talked Ma around. But you're only eighteen, they might think that's too young for a boy. Richard was nearly thirty, and he was—' She caught herself just in time to bite back the word "rich". 'He was sort of… settled.'

'I'm settled, too. I've got my own farm.'

'I know, but it's not…' She trailed off, reluctant to risk hurting him. David might have his own farm, and she knew he worked hard on it, but it was far smaller than her father's, and she had seen for herself how rundown its buildings were, and the low quality of his stock. 'Well, we'll just have to ask, and hope for the best.'

She could see that she had made him anxious, too. 'Do you think we should tell them about this?' he asked, waving his hand vaguely in a motion that seemed meant to take in the rug, the blankets, and all that had happened there. 'They'd have to let us then.'

'No!' Beth said, horrified at the thought. 'Ma would give me the worst hiding there's ever been! Maudie used to get hidings just for giving her cheek—I hate to think what I'd get for this lot.'

'It was my fault, really,' David said, but Beth shook her head.

'No, it was both of us. It wouldn't have happened if we hadn't been doing all that cuddling and stuff.'

'I'd just as soon not tell Ma, either,' David admitted. 'She wouldn't go crook or anything, but… you know.'

'I know.' It was hard enough for Beth to imagine discussing such things with her aunt, who always seemed serenely above anything improper; she knew that for David it would be far worse.

They both fell silent, mulling over the problem. 'So you reckon they might make us wait till you're eighteen before we can get married? That's a long time, Beth.'

'Mmm. And after Aunt Amy gets home, we won't be able to see each other nearly as much.' They exchanged a glance. 'No cuddles or anything then.'

After another long pause, David said, 'She won't be home for a while yet.'

'That's true.' Beth let her hand rest on his shoulder for a moment before taking a biscuit.

David was looking down at his hands. 'A year and a half,' he said quietly.

'What?'

'A year and a half till you're eighteen. Till we can get married.'

'I know. It seems like ages.'

'Beth,' he said after a moment, 'do you think it'd hurt you like that every time?'

'You needn't think I'm letting you do *that* again till we're married!'

'No, I know—I meant when we get married.'

Beth considered the question. 'I don't think so. Not from what Maudie said.' She smiled. 'Maudie was funny when she first got married—she'd keep saying she couldn't talk about stuff because I wasn't married, then she'd get annoyed when I said I didn't care if she did or not. So she'd say little bits just to try and get me interested. I think I know what some of them meant now,' she mused. 'Anyway, she said something about Ma had told her not to worry, it was all right after the first time. I think she must have meant about it hurting—maybe it's only the first time it hurts.'

'That's good. I wouldn't want to hurt you. I want to look after you.'

'I know you do, Davie.'

David took another biscuit, then seemed to forget he was holding it. 'A year and a half,' she heard him murmur.

Beth studied his face as he stared at the far wall. His wistful expression gave her heart a wrench. She stroked his hair, and turned away to hide her own expression. She could not have put into words the thoughts that were running through her mind.

9

Sarah opened the morning mail, glancing at each item and setting it to one side until she came to an envelope that contained a thin piece of card. She propped the card against her tea cup and turned to Amy, her eyes alight.

'What a stroke of luck—we've been invited out on *Wanderer*. That's Mr Dewar's yacht—he's a partner at the firm that looks after my business affairs. He wouldn't usually take it out at this time of year, but the weather's so glorious that he's decided to dust it off. I'm so glad this has happened while you're here. I expect you've never been sailing before?'

'Sailing?' Amy echoed. 'You want us to go out on a boat?'

'That's the usual method, yes. What did you think I meant?'

'It's just… well, I'd never really thought about going on a boat for fun. I'm not very good on boats.'

'Oh, it's not like those nasty little steamers. I get ill on them myself. Goodness, I wouldn't drag you out on one of those for a treat. Sailing's completely different. You'll love it, Amy!'

Amy remained unconvinced, but she would not have dreamed of saying no. A day spent being ill was a trivial matter compared to the prospect of pleasing Sarah.

The following Saturday, she and Sarah went down to the harbour and strolled along the water's edge to a dock where a long, sleek yacht was moored.

'Isn't she beautiful?' said Sarah.

Amy saw at once that this was a very different vessel from the stumpy coastal steamers that had been her only experience of boats till now. *Wanderer* had graceful lines, and when Amy had made her way on board she found polished brass, glowing woodwork, and pristine surfaces. This was a gentleman's plaything, not a workhorse vessel designed to transport goods and cattle, human as well as four-footed, as cheaply and quickly as possible.

To her relief, Amy found that the passengers were expected to settle themselves in a quiet spot and stay out of the way of the sailors while the boat got underway. She sat snuggled close to Sarah and watched the men move about, swiftly but with a practised ease. The sails were run up, the wind bellied them out, and the boat began making its way down the harbour.

'He's seeing how fast he can get her,' Sarah said, indicating the yacht's owner, who was urging on the sailors. With a steady wind helping it along, the boat was soon skimming over the waves. 'Not that he'll get her up to full speed today, with all our dead weight.' She gave Amy's arm an affectionate squeeze. 'He takes her out racing in summer. I've never tried to have myself invited for a race, I think that's best left to the experts.'

'I wouldn't like to see you do that,' Amy said, pointing to a sailor who had scrambled up one of the masts.

Sarah shaded her eyes to look aloft. 'He's untangling the halyards. No, I can't quite see myself doing that—skirts aren't designed for such activities. I do usually manage to go sailing a few times during the season, though. We'll make sure you're here over the summer, then you'll be able to come out with me.'

Although Sarah's assurances that Amy would not feel ill had been met, so far at least, the idea of a longer voyage still held no appeal. Sarah saw her expression and smiled. 'Oh, don't worry, it'll be a sedate outing. *Wanderer* can tow a little dinghy, and she anchors off one of the islands. Then we all get rowed ashore and have a picnic. It makes a delightful day—and it'll be all the more so with you there.'

Sarah pointed to various parts of the boat, explaining what was going on. Sailing, Amy found, seemed to have its own language. She heard a variety of strange words like "mizzen" and "bowsprit", and did her best to identify which parts of the yacht were being referred to.

They made their way past several of the gulf islands, the boat's motion smooth thanks to an obliging breeze over a flat sea. The sun was bright, the air clear and with a lively tang of salt. Sarah coaxed her to walk about the deck, and Amy found herself enjoying the adventure. She was surprised to find that the skipper had turned the boat and they were on their way back in.

'I'll make a sailor of you yet,' Sarah said with satisfaction.

The wind had risen somewhat, and it strengthened as they got closer to shore, stirring up small waves that slapped noisily against the hull. It was not rough enough to make Amy queasy, but the pitching of the yacht made her sway and almost stumble. Sarah took her arm and helped her to a bench out of the wind.

'They'll take it more gently going back,' Sarah said.

Amy could see that the sailors had a more relaxed air than on the outward leg, when they had been intent on increasing the boat's speed.

'I suppose I can't persuade you to come up to the prow?' Sarah asked. 'It's much more exciting up there, with the waves and the spray and everything.'

Amy shook her head. 'I'd only get in the way. You go if you want to.'

'You're sure you wouldn't mind being left on your own?'

'Of course not. Go on, off you go,' Amy urged, seeing how keen Sarah was to do so.

Sarah did not need much persuasion. She strode off towards the prow, sure-footed despite the motion of the boat. Amy smiled as she watched.

'Excuse me, do you mind if I sit here?'

Amy turned her attention from Sarah to see a man standing in front of her, waiting politely.

'No, not at all.' She moved along slightly.

The man carefully lowered himself onto the bench, clinging to the rail until he was safely seated. 'I see you're no more enamoured of wild seas than I am,' he said, smiling. 'I'm sorry, I don't think we've been introduced. I'm Henry Kendall. I'm a partner with Dewar Bright and Kendall.'

'I'm Amy Stewart,' Amy said, extending her hand to be shaken. The man looked to be in his middle fifties, with a thick head of greying hair and a fine moustache. His name seemed familiar, though Amy was sure they had not met before. Since he worked at the law firm that handled Sarah's affairs, perhaps Sarah had mentioned him at some point. 'I'm staying with Sarah—with Miss Millish, and she brought me along today.'

'Delighted to meet you, Mrs Stewart. And that's Mrs Kendall up there, attempting to pursue Miss Millish.' He tilted his head towards the prow.

Amy followed the direction of his gaze to see a dark-haired, elegantly dressed woman clambering somewhat awkwardly along the forward deck, some distance behind Sarah.

'I can't say I'd give much for her chances,' Mr Kendall added, with a wry smile. 'Miss Sarah's a good deal more agile.'

Sarah was indeed making easy progress. As Amy watched, she reached the prow and leaned out over the edge. She stood upright again and looked back at Amy, smiling broadly. Tendrils of her hair had been whipped free of their pins by the wind, and they danced around her face. She looked younger and more carefree than Amy was used to seeing her.

The boat hit a wave, and a shower of spray came over the prow. Sarah laughed, but Mrs Kendall turned and began walking slowly and cautiously back in Amy's direction.

'It's a pity our daughter Laura couldn't come today,' Mr Kendall said, reclaiming Amy's attention. 'She's a far better sailor than either of us. But she felt she should stay home and practise her new piano pieces— she's playing at a concert next week. Only a social occasion at the home of one of her friends, but Laura takes such obligations seriously. She's often asked to play at such events.'

'She must be very good,' Amy said.

'Oh, she is indeed. She's very talented, as well as conscientious. And clever, too—she did well at school. I only wish her brothers had applied themselves half so diligently as she did.' He stopped speaking, and smiled ruefully. 'I'm sorry, Mrs Stewart. I'm inclined to run on rather when it comes to Laura.'

'That's all right. It's nice to see a father so fond of his daughter.'

'And I'm fortunate enough to have three of them, as well as two sons. But Laura's always been my little pet. She's somewhat younger than our other children, and she came as rather a pleasant surprise. She's the only one still at home, and she brightens our lives considerably.'

What a nice man he was, Amy thought.

'How do you come to know Miss Sarah, Mrs Stewart?'

Amy had become used to this question, and more able to answer it without feeling uncomfortable. 'I met her when she came to Ruatane— that's where I live, it's in the Bay of Plenty. She was teaching there.'

'Oh, that's the name of the place? I knew she'd gone to some little country place, but I didn't know quite where.' He looked thoughtful. 'Hmm, Ruatane. That sounds familiar, somehow.'

'It's very small. No one in Auckland ever seems to have heard of it.'

'And yet I think I have.' Mrs Kendall had almost reached them; her husband stood to help her over to the bench. 'Mrs Stewart, this is Mrs Kendall. Constance, Mrs Stewart is currently staying with Miss Millish, but she's from Ruatane. Isn't that where Susannah lives?'

Constance. Amy was beginning to realise where she knew the name Kendall from.

'Yes!' Mrs Kendall said, too excited to take her seat. 'But Mrs Stewart, you must know my sister—she's Mrs Susannah Leith.'

The sick feeling in Amy's stomach had nothing to do with the motion of the boat. 'Yes, I know her. She's my stepmother.'

'Oh, my goodness, how wonderful!' Mrs Kendall exclaimed. 'Why, we're almost family. Oh, Mrs Stewart, you and Miss Millish must come and visit us! Mustn't they, Henry?'

Mr Kendall agreed readily enough, though in a more restrained fashion than his wife. Amy found herself with a tall figure standing on either side of her, pressing her to accept an unwanted invitation. She shrank back against the hard wooden back of the bench, wishing she had never agreed to come on this outing.

Sarah suddenly appeared before her, the Kendalls falling back as she reached out a hand to Amy. 'Do excuse me, but I'm going to drag Mrs

103

Stewart up to the prow whether she wants to come or not. You're missing the best part, Amy!'

Amy grasped gratefully at the proffered hand. Holding tightly to the railing with her free hand, she let Sarah lead her to where waves were lashing the prow. She could not see the attraction of being tossed about and splashed with seawater, but it was pleasure enough to see Sarah enjoying herself so much.

'Are you all right?' Sarah asked. 'I know Mrs Kendall can be rather overpowering, but there's no real harm in her. And Mr Kendall's a decent enough fellow.'

'Yes, they were only being friendly. I just got a surprise, that's all. Meeting someone from… from Susannah's family like that.'

'I'm sorry, I should have warned you. I'll confess I'd completely forgotten that Mrs Kendall is Mrs Leith's sister, though your stepmother mentioned it often enough when I was in Ruatane. I know you're not eager to have reminders of her.'

It was not the Kendalls' connection with Susannah that had so unsettled Amy. 'They want us to come and visit, but I'd rather not. Is that all right?'

'Of course it is. It's completely up to you. I've no pressing desire to visit them.'

'They'll probably keep asking,' Amy said, remembering Mrs Kendall's eagerness.

'Don't worry about that—I have an inexhaustible stock of polite excuses. We may encounter them on social occasions like this, but there's no need for any closer acquaintance.'

Amy tried to take comfort from Sarah's assurance. But she had been shaken by the realisation that Auckland, particularly the circles in which Sarah moved, was a much smaller place than she had thought.

Beth propped her head on one hand and looked across the pillows at David. He was lying on his back, eyes half-closed and wearing a contented smile. She trailed a finger down the side of his face. He caught her hand and pulled on it, overbalancing her so that she fell forward onto his chest. Her lips found his, and they met in a long, lingering embrace.

Their resolution to wait until they were married had lasted barely a week, till the next rainy day had reminded them of how pleasant hours trapped indoors could be. Beth could not remember which of them had first suggested using the bed, but as soon as they had tried it they had both agreed that even with its ancient, lumpy mattress it was much to be preferred over a hard floor.

That had been some weeks ago now, and the bedroom had become a familiar place to Beth. They generally went there as soon as she arrived at the house each morning; she teased David that she had at last found something he would choose over eating.

She lifted her head to free her mouth for speech. 'We'd better get up, or we'll never get anything done today.'

'Just a bit longer,' David coaxed. He reached up to stroke her hair. His hand slid onto her shoulder and tugged gently.

'No,' Beth said, steeling herself to be firm. When his hand kept hold of her shoulder, she added, 'What say Ma turns up to check how I'm doing the work?'

She felt a jolt run through him. He looked about guiltily, as if already half expecting his aunt's doom-laden approach. 'Do you think she might?'

Beth took advantage of his distracted state to extricate herself from his grasp. She sat on the edge of the bed and smiled at his anxious expression. 'Not really. Back when I first started coming here, Ma said she'd be along sometime, but she only said it so I'd be careful about doing the work properly. She doesn't really ride any more, not since she had Benjy, and she wouldn't walk this far. I suppose she could always get Pa to bring her.' She smiled more broadly at the look of near-panic on David's face. 'Well, that's one way to get you to think about something else for a minute. Come on, then, lazy.' She leaned over and poked at his arm until he wriggled out of the way.

David got out of bed and began pulling on his clothes. 'I don't know how anyone ever gets anything done, once they find out about this. I just feel like I want to stay in here all the time.'

'Not much chance of that when there're kids around,' Beth said, buttoning up her bodice. 'They'd be banging down the door, wanting to be fed.'

'I suppose. I'm a bit hungry, come to think of it.'

'Trust you! I'd better feed you, though, you need to keep your strength up.'

The kitten was sitting on the floor, looking as disapproving as only a cat can. Beth had a vague recollection that it had been on the bed at some point; perhaps it had been knocked to the floor when matters became vigorous. She scooped it up and kissed it on the top of its head, promising it a saucer of milk as apology.

In the kitchen, she cut thick slices from the fresh loaves she had brought, and spread them generously with butter and jam. 'Ma said to do some baking here today, because she didn't have any to spare,' Beth said as she watched David demolish the bread and jam. 'I'll make scones for our morning tea, and some biscuits to leave with you.'

'Mmm, scones. I haven't had them for ages.' David wolfed down the last piece of bread and stood up. 'It's a good thing you made me get out of bed, I haven't been round the cows yet. A couple of them looked just about ready to drop their calves yesterday.'

'Oh, I'll come with you,' Beth said eagerly. 'Ours haven't started yet, and I might be too busy here to go out with Pa as much as I usually do.' She took off her apron and followed David to the porch, where they both pulled on their boots.

Two of the cows had indeed calved overnight, and both had produced heifers. Beth helped David look over the cows and their offspring. Afterwards they walked around the rest of the herd, checking their health and estimating how long it was likely to be before the remaining calves arrived.

'You should write down about those two calves being born,' Beth told David as they walked back to the house. 'I'll show you how Pa does it, with the names and which cow had which calf and all.'

'Why?'

'Because that way you'll know which cows have the best calves, and which ones turn out to be the best milkers. That's how you know which ones to keep.'

David shrugged. 'They're all about the same, I think. None of them are that flash. Still,' he added more brightly, 'I should get in the way of writing it up like you said. Your pa said I could borrow the bull this year, so I should get a good lot of calves next season. What's so funny?' he asked when he noticed Beth giggling.

'The bull. I remember when I was little I asked Pa what Duke William was doing when he was in with the cows. He just said the bull was playing with them—I suppose that was true enough, really.' She grinned at David. 'You'll be worse than ever if you get watching the bull. Maudie and me heard Ma say that to Pa one time.'

David snorted with laughter. 'Did she really say that?'

'Mmm. They probably thought we couldn't hear them, or we wouldn't know what they were talking about. We figured it out later, though.'

She slipped her arm around David's waist. 'I'm glad you're borrowing the bull. It'll be good if you can get some better bloodlines in your herd.'

'Especially with us getting married.' David put an arm around her shoulder, and planted a kiss on the top of her head. 'Next year with the calves being half Jersey, I'll try and keep plenty of them and see if I can build the herd up a bit.'

'Only keep the best ones, though. I'll help you decide which ones, I know from doing it with Pa.'

When they got back to the house she insisted that David fetch paper and pencil right away. He returned with his accounts book, and they used a blank sheet near the end to record the details of the new calves. 'You're to write this stuff down for every new calf from now on,' Beth told him.

She glanced at the clock, and was startled to see how late in the morning it was. 'Look at the time! I don't think I can make you any scones after all. I don't know when I'm going to get that baking done, either.'

David looked downcast. 'Oh. I was looking forward to scones.'

'I'm sorry, Davie, but I'll have to start getting lunch on as soon as we've had our cup of tea. I'm going to do us a roast today, and there's spuds to do and pudding and all. And then after lunch I need to do some cleaning before I get your dinner on. I shouldn't have spent all that time looking at the cows, and writing it up and everything.'

'I liked doing that with you. It's better than going around on my own.'

'I know, and I like it too, but I can't do that stuff and the cooking and everything as well.' She saw his disappointment, and considered what she might do to relieve it. 'If I'm going to help you with the farm, how about you help me in the kitchen?'

'Me?' David said doubtfully. 'I don't know if I'd be much good at that.'

'Of course you will, with me telling you what to do. I'll just find you nice, easy things.'

Beth found David to be a useful assistant, as long as she told him precisely what she wanted and was not too fussy about how things looked. She kept him well away from the scone dough, knowing that it would be too much to expect him to give it the light touch it required. But when it came to stirring a heavy biscuit batter he came into his own, doing it faster and with a good deal less effort than she would have herself.

'I bet you'd be good at kneading bread dough,' she said, admiring the results of his vigorous work with the wooden spoon. 'Just give it a couple more stirs while I grease the trays.'

The only problem was that when she went to take the bowl from him there was rather less of the mixture ready to be baked than she had expected.

'Ow!' David yelped when Beth snatched up the wooden spoon and rapped him over the knuckles with it. 'What's that for?'

'Don't eat it all before it's cooked. You can lick out the bowl when it's finished, but you mustn't go helping yourself till then.'

'I only had a bit,' David grumbled.

'Well, when you run out of biscuits, just you remember why there aren't many.' But she left a generous amount in the bowl when she handed it to him ready to be licked out, and then spoiled the effect of her scolding by helping herself to a spoonful before passing the spoon over.

She peeled the vegetables herself when she saw David's attempt at it, and she knew that her mother would not have approved of the odd-sized chunks he cut them into, but the tasks went far more quickly with such congenial company.

They paused in their work to have a morning tea of scones hot from the oven and dripping with butter, then David went off to do some outdoor tasks while Beth finished the lunch preparations. After lunch David dried the dishes as she washed them, and swept the kitchen floor while she dusted the other rooms. Later in the afternoon she helped him feed out hay to the cows, then David in turn helped her prepare dinner.

With the stew for David's dinner gently simmering on the range, they kissed goodbye and Beth rode home. It had been even more fun than usual, she reflected. She and David had been able to spend most of the day together, and she had enjoyed being out of the kitchen and working with the animals.

She came into her own kitchen, smiling at the pleasant memories of the day, to find Maisie banging pots on the range and scowling at the world in general.

'What's wrong with you?' Beth asked, surprised that anyone could manage to scowl on such a day.

'I've got the cramps bad,' Maisie grumbled. 'It's the blood rag business.'

'Oh, poor thing. You sit down for a minute, they're always worse if you've got to stand. You can peel those spuds while I get the pots going.'

Maisie pulled out a chair and flopped into it. 'You and me usually get it around the same time. You must be about due to get yours.'

'I suppose so,' Beth agreed absently. 'I seem to be a bit late this month.'

'Lucky you,' Maisie muttered.

As July wore on, Beth found herself busier than ever at David's farm, but enjoying her time there all the more. There were the new calves to tend, and the milking season was beginning. Cooking and cleaning were quickly done with David's help, and she could spend much of her time out on the farm with him. They were barely apart all day, whether in the paddocks, the kitchen, or the bedroom.

It was a delightful routine, and the time slipped away pleasantly. Beth was guiltily aware that, fond as she was of her aunt, she was not greatly looking forward to Amy's return from Auckland.

'Ma said they had about a dozen kinds of cake at some tea party she went to,' David told her one morning as he worked his way through a plate of biscuits he had helped her make. 'I bet there were none of them as good as these ones, though.'

'She goes to a lot of things like that up there, doesn't she?'

'Mmm. Did I tell you she went out on a boat a couple of weeks ago? A big, fancy sailing one. They were out half the day on it.'

'Has Miss Millish got a boat?' Sarah's world seemed so glittering to Beth that she would hardly have been surprised if told she owned a fleet of yachts.

'No, it wasn't hers. Just one of the flash people she knows.'

'Aunt Amy's not going to want to come home, at this rate!'

She said it lightly enough, but when David met her eyes she saw his troubled expression. 'I want her to come home,' he said earnestly. 'But... you know.'

'Mmm.' She moved from her chair to his lap, and laid her head against his chest. 'It'll be nice for you to have company in the evenings again. But I'll miss being here and everything.'

His arms closed around her. 'There's lots of things I'll miss,' he murmured.

'Still,' Beth said, determinedly bright, 'once Aunt Amy's home, maybe we can tell them we want to get engaged. She might help with Ma and Pa—Ma takes a bit of notice of what Aunt Amy says.'

'And we can't ask them till Ma comes home.' David held her more tightly. 'I just hope they say yes.'

'They will sooner or later,' Beth said, trying to sound more confident than she felt. 'And once we're engaged we'll be allowed to be together a lot. They'll let us go for walks and things. We'll be able to see each other every day.'

'It won't be the same as all this, though. There's lots of stuff we won't be able to do any more. Not till we're married.'

'Then we'll just have to keep on at them till they let us get married.' Beth wound her arms around his waist. 'And we should make the most of it till Aunt Amy comes home.'

'Good idea,' David whispered in her ear.

With so much to do and enjoy, Beth was too busy over the next few weeks to wonder at her bleeding's continued absence. It was only when she saw Maisie rinsing out a bundle of cotton rags in the wooden tubs near the copper that Beth realised another month had gone by, and had brought no sign of it. That was unusual enough for her to consider asking her mother's advice, though she would have to wait for a chance to talk to her on her own.

Perhaps it was best not to bother her mother with it, she decided. Maisie, when asked her opinion, did not seem to think it was anything to worry about.

'I was nearly as old as you are before I got mine,' she told Beth. 'The missus says it's because I was so skinny and all before I came here. I used to miss months with it when I was your age.'

That eased Beth's mind somewhat, though her own bleeding had been regular for the past year. If Maudie had still been at home, it might have been more useful to ask her opinion. She would certainly have been ready enough to give it.

Beth remembered Maudie proudly claiming that she was as regular as clockwork herself. Maudie had said that was how she had known at once when…

A shudder went through her. That was how Maudie had known she was going to have a baby.

Without ever considering the matter deeply, Beth had assumed that people had babies because they decided to. She had occasionally wondered why her parents had wanted to have so many of them, but that was a mystery she had wasted little energy on. Now it occurred to her that babies were simply the result of what she and David had been spending so much time doing. And she was going to be in more trouble than she had ever been in her life.

'You look like you're going to be sick,' Maisie said, frowning in concern.

'I think I might.' But she brushed aside Maisie's attempt to feel her forehead. 'No, I'll be all right. I probably just had too many biscuits with Dave.'

'You must be fed up, having to go over there all the time. When's his ma coming home?'

'I don't know,' Beth said distractedly. 'I don't know what's happening about anything.'

She walked towards the house, heedless of the questions Maisie called after her.

It was a long wait until the next morning, when she could see David again. He ran to meet her as she slid from the horse, his broad smile of welcome quickly wiped away when he saw her expression.

'What's wrong? What's happened?'

Beth's words were lost in the helpless sobs that convulsed her. David took her in his arms and held her close, one hand rubbing her back, as she gradually calmed herself enough to speak.

'We're in s-such t-trouble,' she said, her voice shaking. 'I think I'm going to have a baby.'

She looked up at David's face; to her astonishment, the first emotion she saw there was delight.

'A baby!' he repeated in wonderment. Then, as she watched, cold reality sank in. 'We're in trouble, all right.'

But he was clearly less upset than she was herself. He looked after the horse for her, then led her to the house, his arm around her waist. He made her sit at the table while he got a cup of tea ready, then dragged his chair close and held her hand.

'Don't worry. I'll look after you, whatever happens. And they'll have to let us get married now, that's one good thing. We'd better tell them straight away.'

'No!' Beth said in alarm. 'No, let's leave it for a bit.'

'Why?'

'Well… what say I'm wrong?' she said, floundering for an excuse. 'We'd get in all that trouble for nothing.'

David frowned in confusion. 'Can't you tell one way or the other? How do you know if you're having one or not?'

'There's things that happen. And then they don't happen.' She looked down at the floor as she spoke.

'Eh? What do you mean?'

Beth felt herself blushing. 'There's some bleeding every month down *there*. When it stops coming, that's when you know you're having a baby.'

With that said, she felt able to face him. David looked startled. 'I didn't know that. Cows don't have anything like that. How long does it take to have a baby, anyway?'

'I don't know exactly. With Ma, we could always tell she was having one a few months before, but it probably took us a while to notice. It seemed to be ages from when Maudie said she was having a baby till Lucy was born.'

'It takes nine months for a cow,' David said thoughtfully. 'But cows are bigger, so they might take longer. When do you think you'll know for sure?'

'I think I'm just about sure now,' Beth admitted. 'But I don't want to tell them yet, just in case I'm wrong. Ma's going to be so wild with me.'

'We'd better not leave it too long, or they'll go finding out anyway. We'd get in worse trouble then. How long do you want to wait?'

'A month?' Beth said hopefully, but David shook his head.

'We can't leave it that long. You know we can't, Beth.'

'I know.' She took a deep breath, and clutched at his hand for support. 'A week, then. Let's wait a week. If I haven't had the bleeding by then… well, we'll just have to tell them.'

Amy and Sarah dined in, then went upstairs to get dressed for that evening's outing. They were to attend a concert, followed by supper.

'Don't wear anything too grand tonight,' Sarah said. 'It's quite a modest occasion, and several of the orphanage staff will be there—it's something of a treat for them, as well as a fund-raiser for the orphanage. Evening dress wouldn't really be appropriate—one of your visiting gowns will do nicely.'

'I might wear my blue dress,' said Amy. 'It's so pretty now Mrs Stevenson's remodelled it.'

With a light cape over her blue silk gown and a warm cloak over that, Amy was comfortably warm during the carriage ride to the church hall where the function was being held.

'These concerts can be quite dreadful,' Sarah said. 'I think the boys are chosen more for their enthusiasm than any natural ability. But I have hopes of better things this year—the orphanage has acquired a music teacher who comes highly recommended.' She smiled at Amy. 'I recommended him myself.'

'Mr Vincent? Oh, that was nice of you, Sarah.'

Sarah laughed. 'Call it self-interest. I'm obliged to attend their concerts, after all. But really, I did feel it was time the orphanage had a competent teacher for any boys who show a real talent. One or two of the staff members can play the piano, and they've done their best, but I'm sure they'll all be happier with an actual musician taking over the role. He's only engaged there two afternoons a week, but I imagine the steady employment has eased his situation somewhat.'

Several carriages had already pulled up outside the hall when Sarah and Amy arrived, and more people were approaching on foot.

'You'll find a good deal more people attend the supper than the concert,' Sarah murmured as they made their way to the door. 'It's amazing how many of them have commitments that prevent their being here for the musical performances, but leave them free for the more social part of the evening.'

'Do you know many of these people?' Amy asked, looking around her.

'Most of them by sight, at least.' Sarah leaned towards Amy and lowered her voice further. 'I'd say you could divide the guests into two parts—those with an actual interest in the orphanage, and those who feel it might do their reputations some good to be seen at such an event. You'll find the latter group well represented among those who only arrive in time for the supper.'

As Sarah was a generous benefactor to the orphanage, she and Amy were shown to seats in the front row. The boys were energetic performers on a range of instruments, with brass predominating. Despite a higher volume of sound than the hall could comfortably accommodate, their efforts were rather better than Amy had expected.

'Mr Vincent has done wonders,' Sarah murmured in her ear as they applauded a piece. The man himself was there, looking far less nervous, as well as better fed, than Amy had last seen him. He conducted the performances, as well as accompanying most of the pieces on his violin.

The final item was a song. Mr Vincent introduced it, telling the audience that it was a recent composition by the Auckland composer Miss Jean Farrell. Sarah nudged Amy and tilted her head to indicate the far end of the row, where Miss Farrell sat blushing and smiling in acknowledgment of the polite burst of clapping that met Mr Vincent's announcement. It was a cheerful piece about walking in the mountains, and the boys sang it with gusto. When they had finished, the applause was enthusiastic and, as far as Amy could tell, genuine.

The boys were ushered off the stage, and the guests went through to the supper room. As Sarah had predicted, their numbers were soon swollen by people who had timed their arrival to match the end of the concert. After a time the room became quite crowded, and pleasantly warm. Amy excused herself from a small group of guests and went out to the entryway to take off her cape.

She hung it up with her cloak and slipped back into the room. Looking around to find Sarah, she saw her at the far end, at the centre of a knot of conversation. Instead of going straight through the crowd to join her, Amy found a quiet spot near the wall, from where she could study Sarah.

Sarah was talking animatedly, occasionally waving a hand to

emphasise a point she was making. Amy saw her gaze dart about from time to time, and knew Sarah was looking for her. She would join her in a moment; for now she was indulging in the pleasure of watching her daughter.

People moved about, small groups forming and drifting apart. As the group nearest her dissolved, Amy found herself with a clear space before her that extended to the doorway. Through it she saw that even more people had arrived, despite the lateness of the hour. One of the newcomers towered above those around him; as always when she saw a tall man, Amy thought of David. Although she knew it could not be him, she gave the man a second glance.

It was not David, of course. But there was something oddly familiar about this man; something about his easy smile and the set of his head. Something that made her uneasy.

As if aware of her scrutiny, the man glanced over the head of the woman in front of him and looked straight at Amy. His smile wavered, to be replaced by a puzzled expression. His eyes widened, and his mouth opened to shape a single word: 'Amy'.

She saw him exchange a few quick words with the people around him; clearly making his excuses before moving towards her. Amy's mouth was dry. She stared about the room, looking for a means of escape, but before she had taken more than a step or two towards the nearest door he had crossed the space between them and stood before her.

'My God, Amy! It *is* you!' said Jimmy.

10

Amy darted quick glances around the room, trying to see who might be watching them. She did not want to be seen; most of all, she did not want Sarah to see her talking to Jimmy.

'Go away,' she murmured under her breath. 'Just go away.'

'We have to talk,' he said in a low voice. 'Talk properly, I mean—we can't do that here. Where can I see you?'

'Nowhere. Leave me alone.'

'Where are you staying?' Jimmy persisted. 'Are you in a boarding house? I'll come and see you there.'

'No! I don't want to see you. I don't want to talk to you. Go away.'

'Come on, Amy, don't make a fuss. People will notice.' Amy looked around and saw that they were indeed attracting curious stares from the people nearest them. 'Just tell me where I can see you, and I'll leave you alone for now.' He glanced over his shoulder, and turned back grimacing. 'She's spotted us. Hurry up, for God's sake!'

For a moment Amy thought "she" must refer to Sarah. She quickly realised Jimmy could not possibly mean her, but she was shaken by the inference, as well as by the urgency in his voice. 'All right, you can meet me in Albert Park. I can be there tomorrow afternoon.'

'Yes, the park. Good idea.' Jimmy cast another glance over his shoulder. 'Let's meet by the fountain. What time?'

Amy knew that Sarah would be out for much of the afternoon, so it would be easy for her to leave the house without having to explain herself. 'Four o'clock.'

'I'll be there. Amy,' he said, looking intently at her, 'promise me you'll come.'

Amy stared back, stunned that he could say such a thing to her. 'I've said I will. You've no reason to doubt me.'

Before he had a chance to reply, Amy was aware of a woman gliding up to them.

'Why, Jimmy, how engrossed you are,' the woman said. She had a full, rich voice, but there was an unmistakably sharp edge to it. 'Aren't you going to introduce me to your friend?'

Jimmy turned to her, his face abruptly schooled into a bland expression.

'Of course, my dear. Amy,' he said, turning back to her for a moment, 'this is Mrs Taylor. Charlotte, this is… well, actually she's my niece,' he said with a smile. 'This is Miss Leith.'

'Mrs Stewart,' Amy said quickly. She saw Jimmy glance at her, startled.

'I was Miss Leith when I met Mr Taylor, but my late husband's name was Stewart.' Summoning all her self-control, she made herself look into the woman's face with what she hoped was an appearance of calm as she extended her hand. 'How do you do, Mrs Taylor.'

Charlotte Taylor would have turned heads in Ruatane; even in this elegant setting she cut a striking figure. She was tall, with a statuesque build and an impressive bosom that Amy found was uncomfortably near her own eye level. Her gown was of pale green silk, with bands of matching lace draped over the bodice and wound around the skirt in a long spiral down to a wider band at the hem. A row of dusky pink silk blooms edged the low-cut neckline, and a necklace of green stones set in gold rose and fell with each breath. Charlotte had blonde hair done in an elaborate style, features that could have been chiselled in marble, and light blue eyes that were currently narrowed slightly as she studied Amy. She gave Amy's hand the briefest of touches before withdrawing her own.

'Mrs Stewart,' she said coolly, and turned away from Amy. 'Oh, come now, Jimmy, don't be foolish. I can see that this… lady is hardly likely to be your niece.' The brief pause she inserted before "lady" turned the word into a barely veiled insult.

'Nevertheless, it happens to be true,' Jimmy said. 'After a fashion, anyway. Charlotte, dear, this is Susannah's stepdaughter.'

'Oh, really?' Charlotte looked Amy up and down. 'From a farm. I see. And how do you come to be in Auckland, Mrs Stewart?'

'I'm just visiting a—' Amy began, when she felt a hand on her arm.

'Amy, there you are!' Sarah exclaimed. 'I was beginning to think you'd gone home without me!' She turned to look at Amy's companions and her smile faltered, to be quickly replaced with a polite semblance of one. 'It's Mrs Taylor, isn't it? I believe we've met.' She extended her hand, and Charlotte Taylor took it with rather less reluctance than she had shown Amy's. 'And Mr Taylor.' She gave Jimmy a brief nod, but made no move to offer her hand.

'Ah, Miss Millish, how delightful to see you,' Jimmy said, his smile growing broad. The sight of him looking admiringly at Sarah made Amy's stomach turn. Sarah's resemblance to Jimmy, in her height and carriage as well as something in her features, suddenly seemed so striking to Amy that she feared the whole roomful of people must see it. 'And I see you're acquainted with Miss Leith… Mrs Stewart, I should say.' He shot a quizzical glance at Amy; she could see that the name "Stewart" meant nothing to him.

'Yes, Mrs Stewart has been kind enough to come and stay with me.'

'Oh, a lady companion,' said Charlotte. 'I see. How very suitable.' She bestowed a patronising smile on Amy.

Sarah slipped her arm through Amy's. 'You misunderstand me, Mrs Taylor. Mrs Stewart is not a paid companion—she is my very dear friend, who's doing me the favour of staying in my house.' Amy felt Sarah's hand give her arm a squeeze. 'Now, if you'll excuse us, there are some other guests I'd like to introduce to Mrs Stewart before we leave. Good evening to you, Mrs Taylor. Mr Taylor.' Another quick nod, and Sarah was deftly shepherding Amy to a distant part of the room.

Amy did her best to appear unaffected by the encounter, but it was clear that Sarah had noted her discomfort. Sarah spent the next few minutes making polite farewells, then they retrieved their wraps and went out to the waiting carriage.

'I'm so sorry you were exposed to that ill-mannered display,' Sarah said as they rode home. ' "Lady companion" indeed! I've no time for Mr Taylor, but I think he and his wife deserve each other. And the two of them bailing up my little Amy like that!'

'It doesn't matter,' Amy said distractedly. Her mind was full of what she had committed herself to: seeing Jimmy again, and talking to him. Realising that Sarah was genuinely anxious for her, she dragged her attention back to the present. 'She didn't upset me, Sarah. I'm all right. I had a lovely time tonight.'

'Until you were attacked by the terrible Taylors, that is,' Sarah said with a little laugh. She gave Amy a quick hug. 'Don't worry, I won't leave you on your own with either of them again.'

Amy pleaded tiredness when Sarah suggested a late-night chat over warm milk, and she was soon in bed with the lights out. But sleep eluded her for a long time. She lay awake, her mind churning with a confused mixture of old memories and trepidation of the meeting to come. An effort of will stopped her from tossing and turning, but she could not order her thoughts into the stillness she forced on her body.

Amy was careful to appear composed when she met Sarah at the breakfast table next morning. She managed to maintain a calm demeanour into the afternoon, aided by Sarah's preoccupation with preparing for the meeting she was to attend. Amy sat quietly in the study for much of the day, reading while Sarah worked.

Sarah left the house an hour after they had had lunch. 'I'll be gone till after five, I expect,' she said as she pulled on her gloves in the hall. 'I'm sorry to leave you on your own for so long.'

'I'll be all right,' Amy said. 'I might write some letters, then I think I'll go for a walk later.'

'That's a good idea. You're looking rather tired today, an airing will do you good.' She kissed Amy goodbye and went out.

Amy told herself that there was no need to take any particular care with getting dressed to go out. She did have to change; she could hardly appear on the street in one of her tea gowns. But that would only take a few minutes.

So she was mildly surprised to find herself in her room an hour before it was time to leave, with both her walking costumes spread out on the bed along with several hats. She would probably wear the plainest of them, she decided. But it would do no harm to try on the others.

Rather than the grey costume, she chose the rust-coloured one. Sarah had told her she liked the way this dress suited her colouring. That was a good enough reason to choose it, and it seemed only logical to match it with the hat that she knew set it off best. Before donning the hat she let her hair down, brushed it, and pinned it up again carefully. She was not on the farm, she told herself; it was important to look tidy.

The park was only a short walk from Sarah's house. Amy was ready well before she needed to be, but she waited until it was almost four o'clock before she set out. It would do Jimmy no harm to wait a few minutes for her; she had no intention of wasting any more of her life waiting for him.

She saw him before he saw her. He was walking back and forth near the fountain, with the long-legged, restless stride she remembered from so long ago. When he saw her his face lit up. From this distance he could almost have been the twenty-year-old she had known.

He was at her side in a few rapid paces. 'Amy, you came! Let's go over behind those trees, it'll be more private.' He made to take her arm, but Amy took a step out of his reach. She walked beside him to the seat he had indicated, and sat down as far from him as the bench allowed.

It was the first chance she had had to look at Jimmy properly since he had erupted back into her life. He was still easily recognisable, but the years had left more traces on him than the previous evening's hurried encounter had shown her. While he was still trim, he had lost the lean, rangy look of his youth. His complexion had acquired a florid tinge that spoke of a fondness for good living. His hair was thinning a little on top, and there were traces of grey around the temples.

He saw her studying him, and smiled. 'I knew you at once. You haven't changed a bit.'

'Don't talk rubbish,' Amy answered sharply. 'I'm nearly forty. The last time you saw me I was fifteen.' Fifteen when she had found herself frightened and alone and carrying his child. Fifteen, and wondering what she had done to make him abandon her.

'Well, you haven't changed in my eyes. You're still my pretty little Amy.' His smile broadened. 'I remember I could always tell exactly what you were thinking, just by looking at you. Perhaps I can still do it. Shall I tell you what's going through your mind right now? You're thinking about how long we've been apart, and how right it feels to be together again.'

Amy remembered how irresistible she had once found that smile of his; now it struck her as nauseatingly full of self-satisfaction. This was the man she had given herself to. The man she had trusted. 'No,' she said, shaking her head as she spoke. 'I wasn't thinking that. I was wondering how I could have been so stupid.'

His smile faltered. 'Stupid? What do you mean, Amy? It wasn't your fault we couldn't stay together! It's just that we were so young—I had no proper job, no home of my own. It wouldn't have been fair on you to drag you up here away from your family and make you live with Mother and Father—especially not with a baby on the way, and all the fuss there would have been. No, don't blame yourself. If anyone's at fault, I suppose it's me.'

'You suppose it's you,' said Amy. 'Do you know, I think you might be right.' It was hard to imagine having any useful discussion with this man, but there were questions demanding to be aired. 'I want to ask you something. Did you mean those things you said to me? When you asked me to marry you?'

'Oh, yes,' Jimmy said readily. 'You turned my head the moment I saw you. I thought I'd be stuck in a boring little place all summer, with no better company than Susannah, and there you were, just like a princess in a fairy tale—one of those stories where the princess is looking after pigs, or something like that. Of course I thought I'd rescue you and take you away from all the mud and squalor. I didn't think it through, not when I was so busy being happy.'

'And that last day—the day before you left. You helped me pick peaches, do you remember?'

He grinned at her. 'I certainly do. I knew you were a passionate girl, but you outdid yourself that day. You gave me quite a sendoff. I've always found the scent of ripe peaches rather delightful since then.'

Amy pushed down the awkwardness she felt in speaking of such things. 'I want to know when you decided you wouldn't be coming back to me. Was it after you got back home? Or had you already made up your mind that day? When you took something to remember me by?'

His obvious discomfort was answer enough. 'Amy, you have to try and understand the position I was in.' He spoke without meeting her eyes. 'When you told me there was a child on the way, it stopped being a fairy story. It became all too real. I had to think of the future—yours as well as mine. If we could have waited a year or two, till I was properly settled, it would have been quite different. It wouldn't have mattered so much that you… well, that you weren't… your father wasn't…' he trailed off awkwardly.

'That Pa wasn't rich?' Amy finished for him. 'That I wasn't good enough for you?'

'It wasn't a matter of being good enough!' Jimmy protested unconvincingly. 'It's not that simple. I just wasn't in a position to get married right then. Surely you see that?'

'So you just went off and left me thinking you were coming back? You didn't bother telling me?'

He looked somewhat shamefaced. 'It seemed easier like that. I thought you might get upset.'

Amy found herself lost for words. 'And how did you think I was going to manage?' she said at last. 'What did you think I'd do, with a baby on the way and no husband?'

'Well, I thought people mightn't worry so much about that sort of thing in the country,' Jimmy said feebly. 'And I knew you'd be all right, with your father to look after you. Don't you remember me asking you whether he'd beat you? You told me he wouldn't.'

'No, he didn't beat me,' Amy said quietly. 'Pa was always kind. I just about broke his heart, but he still wanted to do his best for me.' For a moment she lost herself in memories of her father.

Jimmy broke into her thoughts. 'I did try to find out what had happened to you. Later, when I'd had time to think about how it all might have turned out differently. When I came back from Melbourne I tried asking Mother about Susannah's family. She didn't seem very interested, though, and I couldn't go on about it or she would have got suspicious. I tried with Constance, too—I had a feeling she knew something about it, just from the odd remark she made about country girls. I didn't get very far with her, either.

'When Father was ill and Susannah came to Auckland, I thought I might have a chance to find out at last.' He shook his head. 'But I couldn't seem to get her on her own. She was in an odd mood the whole time—she kept looking at me as if she wanted something from me, and half the time I was worried she might be going to make a scene, like she did when I was on the farm. She and Charlotte took an instant dislike to one another, then they spent the rest of the time pretending to be fond of each other and making cutting remarks, in that way women have. Well, Charlotte did, anyway,' he amended. 'Susannah didn't say much at all. And Charlotte was hanging about the whole time, so there was no chance to try and draw Susannah out.'

He turned to Amy and smiled. 'I'd almost given up on ever hearing anything about you again, and then last night you suddenly appeared, just like magic. I used to say you were a bit magic, remember? I'd actually been thinking about you earlier in the evening—about that funny little dance we went to at the schoolhouse, and how pretty you were in your blue dress. And I looked across the room and saw you—I could hardly believe my eyes. You were even wearing a dress that looked much the same.'

'It's the same dress,' Amy murmured.

'Really? But it's been more than twenty years!'

Amy shrugged. 'I had to make it last. I couldn't go getting new silk dresses every year.'

'Oh.' He absorbed this revelation in silence for a moment. 'You said you'd wear it to our wedding, remember? Back when we were telling ourselves we'd be able to get married.'

'Yes. And I did get married in it. Just not to you.'

'Who did you marry, Amy? I don't remember meeting anyone called Stewart in Ruatane.'

'Oh, you met him. I doubt if you had much of a conversation, though. He wasn't much for talking. I didn't go far from home when I got married, only next door. I married Charlie.'

She saw his puzzled expression gradually replaced by one of disbelief. 'Charlie?' he echoed. 'You can't mean that bad-tempered old fellow who was always staring at you?'

'I don't suppose he was all that much older than you are now. He seemed old to me then, though. When I was fifteen and I said I'd marry him.'

'But I remember you saying you were frightened of him!'

'Yes, I was. I learned to be a lot more frightened after I married him.'

'But... but why, Amy? Why marry a man like that?'

'Because he asked for me. Because Pa was so happy at the idea of me getting married, and I'd hurt him so much. Because Susannah told me no one else would want a bad girl like me, and if I cared about Pa or the others I should marry Charlie.'

'Susannah!' Jimmy snatched at the word. 'She made you do it. My little Amy! The thought of a girl like you being given to a man like that—it makes me feel quite ill. What was Susannah thinking of?'

Amy waited for his self-righteous tirade to run its course before speaking again. 'Susannah didn't get me with child, Jimmy. That's the reason I ended up with Charlie. Anyway, I don't think Susannah really knew what it would be like with him. She never liked me, and she wanted me out of the way, but she didn't think there was much difference between one farmer and another.'

'You were meant for better things than that. Well, how did it turn out? What sort of father did he make for my child?'

'He didn't. He wanted me, but he didn't want another man's child. That was part of the bargain.'

'Wh-what?' Jimmy's brow furrowed. 'But... what about the child? What happened to it?'

One thought was uppermost in Amy's mind: she had to protect Sarah. She had to do her utmost to prevent Jimmy from finding out just who Sarah was. She would not lie, not even to the man who had betrayed her; but she would do her best to keep the truth from him. 'I gave it away,' she said, her voice flat. 'Susannah found a woman who arranged adoptions, and she took the baby.'

'You gave my child to strangers?' Jimmy said, clearly shocked.

'I gave *my* child to strangers. You hadn't shown any interest in it.'

'How could you do that, Amy? What were you thinking of?'

'Don't you dare tell me what I should or shouldn't have done,' Amy said fiercely. 'You went off and left me! I had to decide what was best for everyone—I had to decide it on my own. If I'd kept the baby, everyone would have been miserable. People would have called it a bastard. I wanted it to have a good home, with people who'd love it. They told me—Susannah and the adoption lady—they said it was best for the baby, and I thought it was the best for Pa and the boys, too. I *wanted* to keep it. I didn't want to marry Charlie. But I had to think of everyone else. I couldn't be selfish.'

'But weren't you worried? Didn't you wonder what had become of it?'

'Of course I did. I fretted and wondered every single day.' She glanced at him to see if he had noticed that she had put her fears in the past tense. 'I found out a little bit years later,' she said carefully. 'Lizzie helped me. I found out the baby had gone to very good people. I didn't know their name or where they lived, but enough to stop worrying so much.'

'I suppose that's something,' Jimmy said doubtfully. 'Amy, I'll admit I didn't really think about my child for quite some time after we parted. I often thought of you, of course, but not of the child. And then when I married, naturally I assumed Charlotte would give me children. I never expected to be let down in that way. Charlotte's barren.'

'I'm sorry for her,' Amy said with all sincerity.

'Oh, she's probably not that bothered. Childbearing would get in the way of all her outings, and she wouldn't be able to wear her fanciest gowns.'

'I don't believe it. No woman would be pleased about that.'

'Well, she has made an awful fuss over it at times,' Jimmy admitted. 'She used to get in floods of tears, years ago. And she must have spent a fortune on quacks and their remedies, after the doctors told her they couldn't do anything. She's even had the cheek to suggest it might be my fault,' he said indignantly. 'As if I've ever shown any lack in that area. There've been times I've almost been tempted to tell her just how I know there's nothing wrong with me.'

He glanced at Amy and pulled a face. 'Ridiculous, isn't it? I lost you because you were just a little too fruitful—you got with child too quickly. And then I go and marry a woman who's barren.'

'What do you mean, you lost me? You make me sound like a parcel you left somewhere. You knew where I was. I didn't go anywhere.'

'Amy, I don't need to be told that I married the wrong woman,' Jimmy said, full of self-pity. 'I realised that many years ago.'

'Well, you *did* marry her. And it's not right for you to complain about her to other people—least of all to me. I won't listen to any more of it.'

'It's not a subject that gives me any pleasure to dwell on. I'd much rather think about you.' He leaned a little closer to Amy, studying her face. 'Do you know, I thought I knew every inch of you—by feel if not by sight.' His smile became close to a leer, and Amy kept her own gaze resolutely aloof. 'But there's a tiny scar on your lip. Now, how did I come to miss that? I certainly saw your lips close up often enough.'

'It wasn't there when you knew me. It's from having a fist split my lip open.' Her discomfort and irritation abruptly overflowed into words. 'Do you want to see anything else? You can look in my mouth if you like, and see where I had teeth knocked out. I've got some good scars, too, especially the one where I had a cracked rib. I can't show you those, though.'

Jimmy was staring at her in horror. 'He did that to you?'

Amy nodded. 'Among other things.'

'Just how bad was it? If you can bear to tell me.'

'It was as bad as… no, that's wrong,' Amy stopped herself. 'I was going to say as bad as you could imagine, but you can't imagine it. It's different when you're a man, and you're so much bigger and stronger. Did you marry in a church?'

'Of course. In Melbourne Cathedral—quite the social highlight, and with Melbourne's finest citizens in attendance.'

'So you promised to love your wife. Do you?'

His face hardened. 'Charlotte doesn't choose to make herself very lovable.'

'Well, I hope you're kind to her. I hope you don't hit her.'

'Oh, one doesn't take liberties with Charlotte,' Jimmy said bitterly. 'There've been times I've wanted nothing more than to give her a good slap. But her dear papa would be sure to hear about it, and there'd be no end of trouble. He soon made it clear to me that as far as he was concerned my only role in life was to make his precious Charlotte happy. Just the odd slap, though,' he added hastily. 'Not the sort of thing you've suffered—and I can't believe you ever deserved it. He used his fists on you?'

'Yes. And he beat me with a stick sometimes, when he thought I'd been specially bad. I've been beaten and kicked and...' She bit back the last word.

'And what?' Jimmy prompted. 'Tell me the worst of it.'

'Yes, it was the worst,' Amy said pensively. 'Even worse than being beaten.' She lifted her gaze to look him straight in the eyes. 'Raped.'

Jimmy gave a start, then his mouth tightened. 'Don't be ridiculous, Amy. A man can't rape his own wife. I think you'll find the law supports that fact.'

'I used to think that, too. I thought a man could do whatever he wanted with his wife, short of killing her. But it's not true. A man doesn't own a woman just because he marries her. A wife has rights of her own.'

'Goodness, you're quite the little suffragist, aren't you?' Jimmy said, his voice full of condescension.

'I've voted every election since women got the vote.'

'Really?' It was clear that he did not find the topic at all interesting. 'I've no idea whether Charlotte does or not. Perhaps she does, just to make sure she cancels out my vote. That would be just like her. Amy, there's a young woman looking at us—do you know her?'

Amy looked in the direction he was indicating, and recognised Alice, who was walking briskly across the grass, taking the shortest route on her way to Sarah's house. 'Good afternoon, Mrs Stewart,' Alice called cheerfully, but she made no move to stop.

'It's one of Sarah's maids,' Amy said, trying to keep her agitation out of her voice. There was a chance that Alice might mention having seen her, and she would prefer Sarah not to hear of this meeting.

'Ah, the lovely Miss Millish. And how do you come to be her guest? She's not someone I'd have expected you to be acquainted with.'

Amy chose her words with care. 'It was through Lily. Oh, you wouldn't have met Lily, she was after your time. She was the schoolteacher, and she married my cousin Bill. Well, Sarah's Lily's cousin, and she came to visit. I met her, and she invited me to Auckland.'

The explanation seemed to satisfy him. 'How gracious of her. You must feel quite honoured.'

'She's been very kind. She thought I needed a holiday, and her and Davie talked me into it.' She smiled at the memory.

'Davie?' Jimmy prompted. 'Who's that?'

'My son,' Amy said proudly. Seeing his sudden eager expression, she added, 'Mine and Charlie's.'

'Oh.' Disappointment was clear in his face. 'You only had the one child to him, then? He was rather elderly, of course.'

'I bore him three children born alive, and I don't know how many miscarriages,' Amy snapped. 'I lost count of them. He wasn't as old as all that, you know. Not when we were first married.'

'I just assumed... what happened to the other children, then? You only mentioned the one.'

'Alexander was born much too early. He only lived a few hours. And Mal...' Her eyes drifted to the statue of the soldier, just visible through the trees. 'Mal went off to the War. He died there.'

'I'm sorry,' said Jimmy. 'That must have been very difficult.'

'Especially for Charlie. It was an awful blow to him.'

'I can understand that. I know what it is to lose a child.'

Amy looked at his self-pitying expression with distaste. 'It's a different matter for someone who actually took an interest in the child in question.' She sighed. 'Charlie never got over losing Mal. He just about turned into an old man overnight.'

'You speak of him very kindly for someone who treated you so abominably. The man was a brute! I hate the very thought of—'

'Then don't think about it,' Amy interrupted in rising irritation. 'It was between me and Charlie, and I forgave him long ago.'

'That's remarkably charitable of you.'

'It's not so hard to forgive people when you know they're sorry for what they've done to you.' She was already regretting having let Jimmy provoke her into saying as much as she had. Charlie was the frail old man who had clung to her for comfort; the harsh memories of those bad times should have been left where she had buried them. 'Anyway, it's none of your business, and I don't want to talk about it any more.' She looked around, noticing how low the sun was. 'I should go.'

'No! Not just yet. Please, Amy—hear me out.'

It was becoming increasingly difficult for her to remain calm in his presence. 'What do you want from me, Jimmy? I don't think we've anything useful to say to each other.'

'Oh, but we do. Seeing you again has made me remember what it was like with you. It's made me realise what I've missed. Amy, I've something to offer you. Would you like to stay on in Auckland?'

'What are you talking about?'

'Live here permanently, I mean. I could do that for you. I could find somewhere for you to live, and then we'd be able to see each other as often as we wanted—well, as often as I could get away, anyway. We wouldn't be able to appear together in public, of course, but there'd be ways around that.'

'What are you suggesting?' Amy asked, unwilling to believe what his words seemed to imply.

'You've no idea how lonely it can be, living with a woman like Charlotte. I've thought for some time about trying to arrange a more pleasant companion. Seeing you again and remembering what it was like being with you—oh, Amy.'

His hungry expression reminded her of the early years with Charlie. Her disgust was so strong she could taste it like bile in her mouth.

'You want me to be your whore? You think I'd do that?'

'Whore's an ugly word,' he protested. 'I want you to be my mistress.'

'That sounds like a fancy name for the same thing.' She felt her heart pounding. It took all her self-control not to scream at him. 'I've been called whore before, Jimmy, but I don't think anyone's ever meant it as much as you seem to.'

'You'd be my wife in all but name. And perhaps... you don't seem very old. Do you think you could still have a child? Just the one, Amy. I just want a child of my own. That's not much to ask, is it? I need an heir—the business isn't going so very well right now, but it's sure to pick up soon. And with a child of my own that I could look forward to passing it on to, it would all be so much more worthwhile. I'd acknowledge it, you wouldn't need to worry about that. The child would have my name. I wouldn't even mind if it was a girl. We could take up where we left off. It would be perfect.'

Amy got unsteadily to her feet. Jimmy stood and made to take her arm, but she slapped his hand away. 'Don't,' she said, managing to get the word out with difficulty. 'Don't touch me. No, don't talk to me. I don't want to hear another word. I'm going.'

'Just think it over. Perhaps I raised it too abruptly, but don't dismiss the idea out of hand. I'll let you go now, but we must meet again—soon, too. In a day or two.'

'No,' Amy said, her voice low. 'I don't want to ever see you again.'

'Oh, come now, Amy, don't be foolish. Think it over, and I believe you'll see what a fine thing it would be for us both. I'll give you a few days, then I'll contact you. I know how to find you.'

Amy turned on him. 'Don't you dare! Don't you come near Sarah's!'

'I'll be discreet, don't worry about that.' He peered at her in sudden concern. 'You look a little unwell. Shall I walk you to Miss Millish's? Here, take my arm.'

She found herself unable to get another word out. She shook her head emphatically, turned, and walked away as briskly as she could. When she risked a backwards glance, she was somewhat relieved to see that Jimmy was not following her.

Alice came into the passage as Amy was opening the front door. 'Miss Sarah's home, Mrs Stewart. She's in her study.'

For the moment, Amy felt incapable of putting on the calm face she wanted to show Sarah. 'Thank you, Alice. Would you tell her I'm going to have a lie-down before dinner? Oh, and could I have some hot water in my room, please?'

'Of course, ma'am. I'll get right on to it.'

Amy went up the stairs, half stumbling in her haste to get out of sight. The churn of her emotions seemed echoed by a churning in her belly; before she had reached her bedroom she changed directions and made a rush for the bathroom.

Vomiting brought some relief. She left the bathroom and almost walked into Alice, who was standing in the passage holding the jug she had used to carry hot water to Amy's room. It was clear from the concern in her face that Alice had heard her.

'Are you all right, Mrs Stewart?' the maid asked. 'Should I fetch Miss Sarah?'

'No, please don't bother her,' Amy said quickly. 'I'll be all right after I've had a lie-down.'

'Well, if you're sure.' Alice sounded doubtful. 'You just ring the bell if you need anything.' She moved towards the stairs, casting an anxious glance over her shoulder at Amy as she went.

Amy turned from the sight of Alice's kind, honest face and entered her room, closing the door behind her. The room was immaculate, as always. Everything in Sarah's house was well-ordered. Everyone went about their business quietly and efficiently; everything was clean and neat and *proper*. The way Jimmy had looked at her and spoken to her, the easy way in which he had assumed she would be willing to become his mistress, had left Amy feeling sullied. She suddenly felt out of place in this house, as if she were tainting it by her presence.

She poured some of the water Alice had brought her into a bowl; stripped, took soap and a cloth, and began washing herself. The water was hot enough for the cloth to be painful against her bare skin, but Amy ignored the discomfort. By the time she had rinsed herself with clean water her skin was red and tingling.

She put on a dressing gown, the silk blessedly cool and smooth. She carefully hung her walking costume in the wardrobe, but her chemise and drawers she flung into the washing hamper. She wanted clean undergarments, not the ones she had worn while listening to Jimmy.

Amy closed the drapes and lay on her bed in the dim room, staring at the ceiling. Her stomach still felt unsettled, and her head had begun to ache. The thought that Jimmy might come to this house! That he might confront Sarah; might learn who Sarah was. And it would be her fault. Her fault for letting herself be persuaded to come to Auckland. Her fault for failing to think of the possibility that in so vast a metropolis as Auckland her path might cross Jimmy's.

When the bell rang for dinner, Amy got up and dressed herself. She splashed her face with cold water, and hoped that her agitation would not be visible.

Sarah was already in the dining room when Amy went downstairs. She looked up, smiling, then her expression changed to concern.

'Goodness, Amy, you don't look at all well. How pale you are! You shouldn't have got up.'

'I'm all right,' Amy said, trying to sound reassuring. 'I've got a bit of a headache, that's all.'

'I kept you out too late last night, didn't I, when we'd been out the night before as well? I'm so sorry—I should remember you're not used to the hours I keep.'

Amy was relieved to have Sarah assume such an innocuous reason for her quietness over dinner. She showed as much interest as she could muster in Sarah's account of her own doings that afternoon, contributing little more than an occasional word or two.

By the time they had gone through to the drawing room, where Alice brought their tea things on a tray, her head was pounding. She wondered how soon she could make her excuses and go upstairs without worrying Sarah.

Sarah poured tea into their cups and handed one to Amy. 'Oh, I almost forgot,' she said, her eyes twinkling. 'I've caught you in some mischief.'

'What do you mean?'

'Don't look so anxious!' Sarah said with a smile. 'I'm only teasing. Alice said she saw you in the park today. And she told me you were sitting with a *gentleman*. I think you'd better tell me just who the fortunate gentleman was.' Amy hesitated, and Sarah's smile faded slightly. 'You did know the man, I hope,' she said carefully. 'Amy, you do realise that politeness doesn't oblige you to talk to complete strangers if they accost you?'

'I knew him,' Amy admitted.

'And who was it?' Sarah prompted, still looking amused.

There was no avoiding it. 'It was that man we were talking to last night. Mr Taylor.'

Sarah pulled a face. 'Ugh. What bad luck for you, running into him. He didn't make himself too unpleasant, did he?' When Amy did not respond, Sarah frowned. 'Amy, has something happened? Did that awful man upset you?'

'It doesn't matter,' Amy said, wishing she sounded more convincing. 'It was nothing, really. I'd rather not have talked to him, that's all. And I'd rather not talk about it now,' she added, but the firm set of Sarah's mouth told her there was little chance of the subject's being allowed to lapse.

'Really, you ought to be able to walk in the park without having to worry about the impertinence of a man like that. What was he doing there at that time of day, anyway? He should have been working, not hanging about the park making a nuisance of himself to ladies. Goodness knows his business could do with having some attention paid it, from what I hear. Did he have any excuse for being there?'

'He…' Amy could think of no safe answer that would not be a lie. 'He wanted to talk to me.'

'What?' Sarah frowned in confusion. 'But how did he know you'd be there?'

Amy was aware of a growing feeling of dread. 'He asked me last night. He said he wanted to meet me, and I thought of the park. We just talked for a little while, then I came back here. Please don't worry about it, Sarah. I won't see him again.'

Sarah studied her with obvious unease. 'Amy,' she said slowly, 'did you not think how inappropriate it was for you to agree to such a meeting with a man you barely know? A married man, at that. I'm aware he's Mrs Leith's brother, and no doubt he played on that association, but the fact remains that he's almost a stranger to you. I realise you don't know his reputation, but even so… it wasn't quite sensible of you, darling.'

'No, I see that. I'm sorry, Sarah. It was just that… it was all so sudden, last night. I thought he was going to make a fuss in front of everyone—people were starting to stare. I thought if I could just see him for a few minutes he'd leave me alone. I hope he will now.'

'I'm afraid you probably encouraged him. You really will have to be more careful, Amy. I hate to think of your exposing yourself to the conduct of such a man. Frankly, there's very little I'd put past him. I could tell you stories about Mr Taylor that would curl your hair even more than it is.'

'Please don't talk about him any more,' Amy said, dimly aware of a renewed feeling of nausea.

Sarah continued to look uneasy. 'No, I think I had better tell you a few things about him—you need to be on your guard. I'm not in the habit of listening to idle gossip, but one can't move in Auckland's business circles without hearing rumours—nor in its social circles without hearing worse ones.'

She paused, and for a moment Amy dared hope that she would let the subject rest with her vague warnings. But Sarah was only mustering her thoughts.

'His business is not at all sound. His father was a competent businessman by all accounts, and as far as I know he had a fair reputation. But the current Mr Taylor has a name for cutting corners, and for sharp practice when he can get away with it. It's well known that small tradesmen—the sort of hardworking men Father always insisted must be paid before anyone else—struggle to get their money out of Taylor. Many of them refuse to have anything to do with him now. And he's reaping the results of his behaviour. It's common knowledge that his wife's money subsidises the business—it would be running down even faster than it is without that prop. His personal expenses, too—he struts about as if he thinks himself quite the gentleman, but I've heard it said more than once that those fine suits of his are bought out of the allowance his wife pays him.'

'That's not really any of my business, Sarah.'

'Perhaps not, but I want you to know as much as possible about the man. I think he's capable of creating a better impression of himself than

130

is justified on closer acquaintance.' Again, Sarah paused; and again, Amy hoped that the subject might be allowed to drop. Hoped in vain.

'I'm only telling you these things so you'll understand how flimsy his façade as a successful man of business is. His business dealings would be enough on their own to mark him as a man to have as little to do with as possible. But as for his personal life—'

'Sarah, *no*,' Amy pleaded. 'Please don't say any more.'

'I'd be quite ready to respect the man's privacy if he hadn't bullied you into meeting him like that. I want you to be properly armed. Let me finish, Amy, then we won't need to speak of him again. Believe me, I take no pleasure in it. You must prepare yourself to hear some rather distasteful things.'

Sarah took a sip of tea before going on. 'I spend much of my time with men, at the meetings that drag me away from you. There's a certain advantage to that—men sometimes forget for a short time that there's a woman in their presence, and they talk as freely as they might among themselves. I've picked up many an interesting piece of information in that way, along with a good deal of gossip. Never let anyone tell you that it's only women who gossip.

'Some of the sillier fellows I've encountered seem to have a sneaking admiration for the likes of Mr Taylor, but I've found that more steady men have little time for him. Especially the ones with daughters to worry about—or perhaps wives that they suspect are not entirely trustworthy. One of the great injustices of our society, Amy, is that a woman's reputation is far more fragile than a man's.'

'I know,' Amy whispered.

'And men like Mr Taylor seem to have no compunction about damaging that reputation. I gather that there have been... incidents. There was one in particular last year that apparently came close to landing a foolish woman in the divorce courts. Fortunately for all parties, Mr Taylor had been *just* cautious enough, and nothing could be proved. He's also known to frequent a certain type of establishment—'

'Stop it, Sarah,' Amy interrupted. 'You mustn't talk like this. It's not right.'

'I'm not going to pretend ignorance, Amy. I would have thought I could talk to you without any such pretence. Why in the world shouldn't I tell you what I know about him? Well?'

Amy's head was pounding harder than ever. It was difficult for her to think straight, but Sarah seemed to want an answer. 'You shouldn't talk about him like that. It's not right. It's not respectful.' The moment the word was out, she knew that she could hardly have chosen a worse one.

'*Respectful?*' Sarah said in disbelief. 'Are you telling me I should show respect to that man? Why? Because he's older than I am? Heaven forbid you think I should because he's a man and I'm *only* a woman. I believe respect is something to be earned, and I'm not aware of anything that man has done to earn mine. He's at best a buffoon, and at worst a scoundrel. Can you give me one good reason I should show him respect? No? In that case I'll tell you—'

'He's your *father*,' Amy cried, the word tearing from her like a scream. Silence flooded the room, so heavy that she could barely breathe through it. 'He's your father,' she whispered.

11

Sarah was staring wide-eyed at her. 'My father?' Her mouth twisted in disgust, as if the very word left a foul taste. '*Him?* Good God, Amy, was that the best you could do? I credited you with more intelligence—more refinement—more basic *decency* than that. How could you have—'

She turned aside, biting off whatever she had been going to add, but she had said enough. No one else would have had the power to wound Amy so bitterly.

'I'd better go home,' Amy said quietly. Sarah said nothing. 'I'll go and see about a passage tomorrow. I'll leave as soon as I can.'

'Yes, perhaps you'd better,' Sarah said, almost spitting the words. She glanced at Amy for a moment, then turned away again.

Amy got up and left the room. She did not say goodnight; still less did she attempt to kiss Sarah.

The flight of stairs had never seemed so steep. Mounting each step meant a deliberate effort to push one foot up to the next level, then drag the other after it. When she had at last reached the top, she walked slowly to her room and closed the door behind her.

She undressed, put on her nightgown and hung the dress in her wardrobe, her limbs leaden. She stood in front of the wardrobe for some time, looking at the beautiful gowns Sarah had bought for her. She would leave them there, Amy decided. There was no point in taking them to Ruatane, where she would have no occasion for such finery. She would return to wearing the mourning she had only set aside for Sarah's sake. If Sarah did not give them away, the dresses would stay here, shut up in the wardrobe and slowly fading. Just like Amy's memories of these precious months she had spent with Sarah.

She was lucky, she told herself. She had never allowed herself to hope that she would ever have so much as a glimpse of her daughter again; beyond hope, she had spent this time living in Sarah's house and seeing her every day. She had a treasure of memories to hoard. She must content herself with them, knowing that after she caught the boat home to Ruatane she would never see Sarah again.

It was too much to expect that Sarah might have understood something of how it had been. How could she? Sarah's life had been spent surrounded by people whose chief care was her comfort and security. A man like Jimmy would never have been allowed to come near her. Even if he had, Sarah would not have been beguiled by soft words and the assurance that she was special. The people who loved her had been telling her such things all her life.

Amy halted her train of thought, aware that she was coming close to blaming Sarah for having reacted with such disgust. The innocence that had produced Sarah's response was something to be thankful for, not resent. And in the whole untidy muddle, Sarah was the one person who was blameless.

She sat down in front of the dressing table and picked up her hairbrush, then put it back. Even running a brush through her hair demanded more energy than she could muster at the moment. Her head throbbed, and she felt bone-achingly weary.

In the morning she would have to brave the commotion of the Auckland wharves. She had no idea where in that confusion of ships and cargoes and sailors and wharf labourers she might find the ticket booking office, but she would have to look for a helpful face among the strangers and ask her way. She hoped there would be a boat leaving soon; her last days with Sarah seemed destined to be an awkward period of trying to keep out of each other's sight. Best to get it over with. She wondered if Sarah would bother saying goodbye to her.

There was a soft knock on the door, and it opened a crack.

'Amy?' came Sarah's voice. 'May I come in?'

Without waiting for a response, Sarah entered the room and walked slowly over to the dressing table. She picked up Amy's discarded hairbrush and turned it to and fro, then walked around the room, still clutching the hairbrush.

'You know,' she said, apparently addressing the far wall, 'Mother very rarely punished me. I suppose that explains a lot. But once or twice when I was small, I managed to exhaust even her patience. Then she used the hairbrush on me.' She crossed to Amy, knelt down and placed the hairbrush in her lap. 'Feel free,' she said in a low voice. 'I've never deserved it more.'

Amy raised her eyes to look into Sarah's, and saw tears brimming there. 'I'm sorry,' Sarah whispered. 'Can you forgive me?'

Amy held out her arms and Sarah sank into them, resting her head in Amy's lap. 'You only said what was true. There's nothing to forgive.'

Sarah raised her head. 'Oh yes, there is. I had no right to speak to you like that. When I think of the abuse you've had to put up with over the years on my account, and now you hear the same sort of language from me! I'm thoroughly ashamed of myself. Please, Amy. Please say you forgive me. I need to hear the words.'

'If there was anything to forgive, it's forgiven. I know you must have got a shock, hearing it like that.'

Sarah got up from the floor and pulled a stool over close to Amy's chair so that she could sit beside her. 'It's ridiculous of me—logically I knew it couldn't have been a man of honour. If my father had been a hero tragically killed saving a hundred people from a shipwreck the week before you were to be married, you'd have told me the moment you found out who I was. Since you were silent on the subject, I knew he must be no one to be proud of.' She smiled ruefully. 'But I find there's a large difference between a conveniently faceless rogue and one who's all too substantial.'

She stroked Amy's cheek. 'Does your head still hurt?'

'A bit,' Amy admitted. 'It doesn't matter.' Nothing mattered, now that she knew Sarah still loved her.

Sarah fetched a pillow and slipped it down the back of Amy's chair. 'Lean back. I used to do this for Mother when she had headaches.' She took a bottle of lavender water from the dressing table, dabbed some on her fingers and gently massaged Amy's temples. 'Is this all right?'

'Mmm. It's lovely.' Amy closed her eyes and gave herself over to the comfort of Sarah's closeness. The scent of lavender and the soft touch of Sarah's hands drove a wave of contentment through her. The pain in her head became no more than a dull ache, powerless to spoil the moment.

'Amy?' Sarah said quietly. 'Do you feel able to tell me a little of how I came to be? I'll understand if you don't want to, but I must confess that I'm curious now. I'm sure he must have been very different back then, to win you over the way he did.'

Amy considered her answer carefully. Sarah had the right to know, however uncomfortable Amy might find recalling those days. 'No, I don't think he was so very different. Not in the ways that really matter. He was much younger, of course. I thought he was very handsome. And he was less... oh, I don't know the right word for it. Less hard, somehow.'

'Cynical?' Sarah suggested.

'Yes, perhaps that's it. He was a lot more cheerful then, too—everyone liked him. Well, everyone except Lizzie. She never did trust him.'

'How wise Mrs Kelly is,' Sarah murmured. She wiped her fingers on a handkerchief to remove the traces of lavender water, took up the hairbrush and began brushing Amy's hair. 'But whatever was he doing in Ruatane?'

'It was because of Susannah. He asked if he could come and visit her.'

'Mrs Leith? Of course, he's her brother. Good Lord, she's my aunt!' The brush stopped moving.

Amy studied Sarah's face. It was twisted oddly, as if she were fighting back tears. Sarah let out a strangled little sound, somewhere between a sob and a laugh, then laughter won out. 'Oh, Amy!' she said when she had caught her breath, 'if these new relations you've given me don't cure me of vanity, nothing will!'

Amy smiled at the sight of Sarah's mirth. She waited patiently till Sarah calmed herself, content to watch that merry face.

'So he decided to try farm life?' Sarah asked at last.

'I think there might have been some trouble up here. He got his mother to write and ask if he could come, and Pa said he could. He was... I don't know if I can explain properly. You know how I wanted to be a teacher? I had such grand ideas—I'd get a job in Auckland, and I'd be able to study things. I thought I'd buy lots of books, and go and see plays. I wanted that as far back as I can remember.

'I had to stop working at the school because I couldn't get all my work done at home. Then when Susannah came, Miss Evans—she was my old teacher—thought maybe I could start again. But Susannah said I wasn't allowed.'

'That doesn't surprise me,' Sarah murmured.

'Well, Pa was never very keen on the idea, anyway. That summer I was fifteen. Susannah was miserable, and she made Pa miserable, too. Her and I would fight, and that'd make Pa even more unhappy. All there seemed to be was cooking and cleaning and helping look after the babies, and everyone seemed to think all I should want was to get married and carry on doing that in a house of my own.'

'And then he arrived.'

'Yes. He was *nice* to me, Sarah. I don't mean everyone else was horrible, but... he made me feel as if I was special. He'd talk to me about books and plays and things. He'd tell me I was pretty, and clever. He bought me nice things.' She hesitated before adding, 'He gave me that brooch.'

'This?' Sarah touched the gold brooch she wore. A brief look of distaste passed over her face, rapidly replaced by a determined expression. 'Well, I've always thought of it as coming from you, and I've valued it for that reason. I'll continue to do so.'

'It was my Christmas present. I had to keep it secret from everyone else, though. Everything had to be secret.' It was becoming more difficult to go on, knowing what she would soon have to speak of, but Amy made herself continue.

'He told me he loved me. I thought he meant it. And he asked me to marry him—I thought we were engaged, Sarah. When... when it

136

happened. I thought we were going to get married. He told me he'd bring me to Auckland as soon as we were married, and he talked about how he'd buy me fancy clothes, and take me to the park, and to the theatre.' She smiled at Sarah. 'All the things you've done for me instead. But he said it had to be a secret engagement, just for a while. I was stupid enough to believe him.'

'You were fifteen,' Sarah said quietly. 'You had a trusting nature, and you fell into the hands of a rogue.'

'I still should have known better. I knew it was wrong, but… well, I kept thinking it would be all right as soon as we got married. He said he'd ask Pa, then he said he'd better write and ask his father first. And somehow it all took so long.'

She fell silent, thinking back to that time, then sighed and went on. 'And then I realised there was going to be a baby. If I'd had any sense I would have known things weren't right from the way he acted then. He'd managed to put off asking Pa or writing to his father for months, but after I told him you were on the way, he was on the boat and out of Ruatane in under a week.' And having indulged himself with a passionate farewell from Amy. That was one detail she would never share with Sarah. 'He told me he'd ask his father and come back soon, and I should keep it secret till then. So I did. I waited and waited. Then after he'd been gone a few weeks, Susannah had a letter from her mother saying he'd gone to Australia. That's when I knew he wasn't coming back. That's when I knew he'd been lying to me.'

Sarah's voice shook a little when she spoke. 'Such men should be flogged through the streets, then put in stocks in front of the courthouse. Instead, we allow them to be respected members of society.' She was silent for a few moments, then continued more calmly. 'Thank you for telling me that, Amy. But why did that man want to see you again today? I don't suppose it was to beg forgiveness.'

Amy smiled faintly. 'No. Mostly he wanted to ask me what had happened to the baby—I didn't tell him about you, Sarah. I didn't even say if it was a girl or a boy. I just told him I gave the baby away, and I knew it had gone to good people.'

'And why the sudden interest on his part after all these years?'

'I suppose it was because of seeing me again. But he's got some idea in his head about wanting an heir.'

'An heir? To that business? Ha!' Sarah said in derision. 'I'm glad you gave him no satisfaction.' She was too observant to have missed a single detail. 'You said it was "mostly" to ask about me. What else did he want?'

'It doesn't matter.'

'It *does* matter, Amy. Whatever he said had you in quite a state this evening. What was it?'

'I'd rather not say. I don't want to talk about it.'

'I'm afraid you don't have a choice in the matter, my darling. You're going to have to tell me exactly what he said to you. Because, you see, I won't leave you in peace until you *have* told me, and I'm quite prepared to sit here all night repeating the question if necessary. I need to know it all. How can I protect you properly if I don't know the complete story?'

'Protect me?' Amy said in confusion. 'What do you mean?'

'He's clearly upset you, and I don't intend to let it happen again. Now, tell me what he said. It can't be any worse than what you've already told me tonight.'

Amy had come to know the futility of arguing with Sarah when her mouth had that particular set to it. 'All right, then, if you must hear it. He... he wanted me to stay on in Auckland. So that he could...' She looked down at her hands. 'He wanted me to be his mistress.' She glanced at Sarah to see whether she had understood the word; the anger on Sarah's face answered her. 'I think he thought I'd be pleased to be asked. Grateful, even. He thinks I'm no better than... a bad sort of woman. He even... he even thought I might want to have another child for him,' she finished in a whisper. 'To give him an heir.'

They sat in silence for some moments, then Sarah said, 'Well, I was wrong. I'd believed I couldn't possibly think any worse of that man. I'm sorry, Amy.'

'What for?'

'For almost letting him come between us. For almost driving you out of my house.'

Amy took Sarah's hand between both of hers, then voiced the thought that was nagging at her. 'I think perhaps I *had* better go home, Sarah. I'm worried he could cause trouble for you.'

'How could he do that?'

'He said he wants to see me again. He knows I'm staying here, and he might come here after me.'

'Don't you worry about that. If he calls, we won't be at home. No, I don't mean we'll stay out all day,' Sarah said, seeing Amy's puzzled expression. 'We simply won't be "at home" to Mr Taylor. I'll instruct the maids accordingly. If he sends you any notes or letters, we'll return them unopened—though I doubt if he'd do that,' she added thoughtfully. 'He wouldn't want to risk such a thing falling into his wife's hands. I don't think you should go out alone any more, though. I don't want him accosting you again. I'll start going with you on some of those walks of yours.'

'I'd like that—if you're not too busy.'

'When I can't get away, you can take one of the maids. And if *they're* both busy, you could always take young Walter. I'm sure he'd be only too pleased to get out of working in the garden to squire you around town.'

'I don't want—' Amy began, but Sarah held up a warning hand.

'Let there be no talk of being a *nuisance*. The function of my staff is to keep the household running smoothly, and to make my life comfortable. I won't be comfortable unless you're happy. So by looking after you they're only doing their job.

'You'll be safe enough at public events, like the theatre,' she went on. 'I'll be sure not to leave you alone at such functions.' She smiled at Amy. 'If I'm to make good his promises, I believe I owe you a few outings yet. As for private functions like dinner parties, I'll ask for a guest list before we accept.'

'Can you do that?' Amy asked in surprise.

'Oh, yes. It's not something I've made a habit of, but I believe I do have the social status to make such a request. Don't look so shocked, dear.'

'It just doesn't seem quite... polite.'

Sarah gripped her hand. 'Believe me, Amy, when it comes to protecting you I'm prepared to take measures a good deal more drastic than requiring a guest list.'

David went out to meet Beth when she arrived at the farm on the day they had agreed must be their deadline. One look at her face told him there had been no last-minute release. 'We'd better go and tell them, then,' he said.

'Now?' Beth said nervously.

'We said we'd do it today. No sense putting it off, Beth. We'll only get more worried if we sit around thinking about it. Come on, let's go right now.'

'Couldn't we have a cup of tea first?' She rested a hand on his arm and looked up into his face, a plea in her eyes. 'I think I'd feel more up to it if we did.'

'Well... all right, then,' David relented. 'Just a quick one, though. Let's just tether Jess here, that'll save time later.'

They walked towards the house, arms around each other's waists. 'I'm glad of the excuse to put it off, myself,' David said. 'I can't say I'm in a rush to tell Uncle Frank about all this.'

'It's all right for you, Pa never gets wild about anything. But Ma'll... well, I don't know what she'll do. But I know it'll be awful.'

'I don't know, he might get a bit wild,' David said doubtfully, but Beth shook her head.

'No, I'm sure he won't. You don't need to worry about that.'

The tea was made and drunk rather more quickly than Beth had hoped, and they set off down the road, riding side by side. She would have preferred to keep their horses to a walk, but David insisted on cantering much of the way. All too soon, they had drawn up to the fence in front of the house.

They dismounted, and tethered their horses. 'Pa'll be looking at the new calves,' Beth said. 'Yes, there he is over by that shed.' She pointed out the direction. 'I suppose I've got to go and see Ma, then.'

Shielded from view by the horses' bodies, they squeezed hands briefly, then went their separate ways.

Beth found Maisie alone in the kitchen. Directed by her, she went through to her parents' room. Her mother had just dressed Benjy, and was encouraging the little boy to take a few steps, holding tightly to his chubby hands so that there was no risk of a fall.

Lizzie looked up at Beth in surprise. 'What are you doing back so soon, love? Did you forget something?'

Beth took a deep breath. 'No. I need to talk to you, Ma.'

'Mmm? What about?' Lizzie scooped Benjy up on to her hip and looked questioningly at Beth.

'I...' Beth looked down at the floor, then around the room. Her father had left one of his belts lying across the back of a chair. Beth's eyes fell on it; she looked away quickly. David was right: best to get it over with.

'It's... it was... I—we—didn't mean to, it just sort of happened...'

'Whatever are you on about, girl?' her mother said, halfway between amusement and irritation. 'What's happened? Did you break something of Aunt Amy's? Is that it?'

'No... I...' Beth gulped down the sob that was tightening her throat. 'I haven't had my bleeding for ages now—I've missed two times. It hasn't come since Dave and I started... I'm really, really sorry, Ma. I think... I think I'm going to have a baby.'

Her mother's mouth dropped open. For a moment she stared at Beth in shock, lost for words. Beth had expected that, and she fully expected to see the shock rapidly succeeded by anger. She cringed, waiting to see what form her mother's wrath would take, and wondering just how painful it would be.

Lizzie reached out blindly, and grasped at the bedpost. She sat down heavily on the bed, easing Benjy onto her lap as she did. She gave her head a small shake, as if to clear her thoughts.

'Well,' she said at last, 'I never thought of that happening. I see now I should have, now it's staring me in the face. Ah well, no sense going on about it. We'd better see how quickly we can get you two married.' She looked at Beth in surprise. 'What are you doing, standing there with your mouth open? Of course you're getting married!'

'I know, we really want to. It's just...' Beth hesitated, studying her mother's expression to assure herself of the astonishing fact that she seemed in no danger of being punished. 'Aren't you wild or anything? I thought you'd give me a hiding.'

'Where's the sense in that? It's not as if it'd make any difference now. Anyway, we need to take things carefully with you having a baby on the way. I'm not saying I wouldn't have given you a good one, mind you, if I'd caught on before things had gone that far. No, it's my fault as much as anyone's, leaving you two alone all that time and never thinking anything of it. I thought you and Dave were like brother and sister.' She frowned. 'Hmm, you're cousins, come to that. Still, that can't be helped now. And it's only second cousins, that doesn't really count.

'Now,' she went on briskly, 'Don't you breathe a word about this to your father. I'll need to go carefully there, it's going to take him a bit of getting used to. I'll have a think about the best way to tell him.'

'Dave's telling him now. He came down with me.'

Lizzie gave a start. 'What? Telling him on his own? You silly girl! What were you thinking of?' She rose and hurried from the room, down the passage and through the kitchen (stopping only to thrust Benjy into the arms of a startled Maisie), and out of the house, Beth following in her wake.

'Dave! Nice to see you here,' Frank said when he saw David approaching. 'How's calving going at your place?'

'Pretty good. I'm getting quite a few heifers. Beth's been helping me decide which ones to keep.'

'Well, you couldn't have anyone better—I tell her she knows more about calves than I do. She's got a real way with animals. You want to have a look at this lot?' He waved a hand to indicate the calves in the paddock.

'Um, maybe a bit later. Uncle Frank, can I have a talk with you?'

There was something in his tone that made Frank look more closely at him. He saw David cast an uncomfortable look around at the boys, who were watching with mild curiosity. So it was something David wanted to speak to him about in private.

Frank was touched that David should come to him for advice, and glad to try and help, if something was troubling him. It was quite a responsibility for a boy of eighteen to be running a farm on his own. And with Charlie as his father, Frank knew that David had not had the easiest of childhoods.

'Let's take a stroll up there,' Frank suggested, pointing to a paddock just above the house. 'I've got a few calves in there, too. No need for you boys to come,' he added. 'I'll just show the calves to Dave, then it'll be just about morning tea time.

'Now,' he said when they were far enough away from the boys to be sure of some privacy, 'what's on your mind, Dave?'

'I… I want to…' David began, then trailed off. He looked at Frank, and quickly looked away.

Something really must be troubling the poor lad, Frank thought. Whatever it was, David was embarrassed about it. 'Is it anything to do with money?' Frank prompted. 'I know it's not always easy keeping that sort of thing straight. I don't mind telling you I got in a muddle that way myself once—when I was a fair bit older than you are, too, so I had a lot less excuse.'

'No, it's nothing like that,' David said, still looking at the ground.

'No? What is it, then? Come on, Dave, don't be shy about asking. We're family, right? If it's anything I can help you with, I'm only too happy to.'

David raised his eyes, and Frank thought he looked a little less anxious. 'I do want to ask you for something, Uncle Frank. Something really big.'

He looked so earnest that Frank had to make an effort not to smile. 'Really big, eh? Well, we'll see what we can do. What is it, then?'

He saw David take a deep breath before speaking. 'I want to marry Beth.'

It was all Frank could do not to laugh out loud. He managed to turn his snort of amusement into a cough. 'I can't say I expected that!' he said, unable to keep the smile out of his voice.

'Now, Dave,' he went on, trying to give the appearance of taking the outrageous suggestion seriously, 'I suppose it's not so surprising, with you spending all this time together lately, and her more or less keeping house for you. And the two of you have always been good mates, right from when you were little kids. But you're both much too young to be thinking about getting married—you especially.'

'We really want to get married,' David said, looking more earnest than ever.

'Well, I'll tell you what,' Frank said easily, 'maybe in two or three years, if you still think that's what you want, we might have a talk about it then.' It was a painless enough offer to make. David and Beth had been playing house together, and that had put this silly notion into their heads. Frank was quite sure they would have all but forgotten it long before two years had passed. And in the meantime, he would see what he could do to help David improve that farm of his, so that when the boy was at a reasonable age to think about getting married, he might be in a position to ask a girl and hope to be accepted. Frank was fond of David, and he hoped it would be a nice girl, who would make him happy. But it would not be one of Frank's daughters. He was comfortably sure of that.

'No!' David said, startling Frank out of his reverie. 'No, Uncle Frank, we need to get married right now—really soon, anyway. You have to let me marry Beth. You *have* to.'

All amusement drained out of Frank as he looked at David's wild-eyed stare. His eyes narrowed. 'What do you mean, I have to let you?' he said slowly. 'You got something to tell me, boy? What's been going on? Eh?'

'I'm really, really sorry.' David looked on the verge of tears, but there was no room in Frank for sympathy. Not with the rage that was flooding through him.

'What have you done to my daughter?' he growled.

'She's… Beth's going to have a baby.'

Almost before he knew what he was doing, Frank had launched himself at David. He grabbed him by the shirt and swung his fist.

If they had not been on sloping ground, with David standing somewhat below him, Frank would have had little chance of reaching higher than David's chest. But the punch slammed into his face, knocking his head to one side. When Frank let go of his shirt front he took a step backwards, and raised his hands in a feeble effort to defend himself, but Frank's next punch got through as easily as the first. Blood began running from David's nose. He made no attempt to fight back or to escape. 'I'm sorry, I'm sorry,' he said helplessly, then closed his eyes against the sight of the fist once again coming at his face.

Frank heard Lizzie's voice, loud enough to carry easily. 'Frank!' she called. 'Don't you kill that boy, he's got to marry Beth!'

He turned aside from David to see Lizzie hurrying towards him, moving faster than she had in years. 'He's bloody not!' he shouted back.

12

'Davie!' Beth screamed at the sight of blood trickling down his face. She made to rush at him, but Lizzie caught her by the arm and took a firm hold.

Frank saw David take a step towards Beth. 'You stay away from her! You get off my farm right now, and don't you ever set foot on it again. If I see you coming here trying to hang around my daughter, I'll knock your bloody head off. Go on, get out.'

David cast a helpless look in Beth's direction and walked slowly to where he had left his horse tethered, looking over his shoulder as he went. 'Stay here,' Lizzie told Beth. She lifted her skirts and scurried off after David.

'Lizzie!' Frank called. 'Don't you go near him!' Lizzie ignored him. 'Lizzie!' he shouted. 'Are you listening to me?'

'I'll just be a minute,' Lizzie called back. She reached David and talked rapidly for a few moments, while Frank fumed. After a quick glance at Beth, who was sobbing, he could not bring himself to meet her eyes. Instead he glared at the back of Lizzie's head, which seemed to him to have a particularly defiant tilt to it.

Beth stood where her mother had left her. She watched Lizzie talking to David, then allowed herself to be led back towards the house. 'Davie's got blood all over his face!' she wailed.

'He'll be all right,' Lizzie said briskly. 'It's just a bleeding nose. I'm sure he got a lot worse from his father.'

'But who'll look after him now? Who'll get his dinner on and everything?'

'He'll have to look after himself for a bit. That won't kill him. Oh, don't get in such a state over it, girl! He can go to his Uncle John's for meals. Anyway, it won't be for long, only a week or so. I told him to write to his ma and tell her to come home. I'll write to her myself as well, to make sure she does. I might need her help to sort this out.'

Beth looked over her shoulder at her father, who was staring grimly at David's retreating form. She had never seen such an expression on his face. 'Y-you always said,' she choked out, gulping back a sob, 'you always said if we were really bad Pa would get wild at us. But he never did. Maudie told me you were just saying it to make us behave. I thought that was right. I thought I'd never see Pa get wild. But now he has. And it's because of *me*.'

She dissolved into fresh sobs. Lizzie stopped in her tracks, took Beth by the shoulders and shook her; not roughly, but effectively. She waited for Beth to calm herself enough to pay attention. 'Of course he's wild,' said Lizzie. 'The one thing that could get him in a state like this is if he thinks someone's done wrong by one of you kids. And that's why you should have left it up to me to tell him about all this, not let Dave go blundering in saying Lord knows what. I'm going to have a beggar of a job with him now.'

Frank's sons were not the most perceptive of boys, but they soon caught on that something was up. They had not witnessed the fight, but had seen how abruptly David had left, and they noticed their father's silence and his uncharacteristically grim expression. They had the sense to keep quiet themselves; there were some jobs on the farm that were a good deal less pleasant than others, and none of them wanted to find himself assigned to digging out drains for the next few days.

Beth was not in the kitchen when Frank and the boys went in for an unusually quiet morning tea. When they had had their tea and biscuits, and Maisie had slipped away to take a cup through to Beth, Frank sent the boys off ahead of him and paused in the doorway. 'I know what you're going to say,' he said before Lizzie had a chance to speak. 'And you'll be wasting your breath. I'm not letting him marry her, and that's that.'

Lizzie opened her mouth, closed it again, then contented herself with, 'We'll see'. Frank went out without waiting to hear if she had anything to add.

For the rest of the day he had no private conversation with Lizzie. He did not see Beth until dinner time, when she sat pale and silent, toying with her food, but he was sure that Lizzie had spent much of the day talking to her.

Only when he and Lizzie were alone in the darkness of their room did she raise the subject again, keeping her voice low so that they could not be heard through the wall. 'Frank, we need to talk about this.'

'She's not marrying him.'

'Frank—'

'No, my mind's made up. He might have thought he could get her by doing that to her, but he's wrong. He's lucky I'm not getting the law on him.'

'Eh? What for?'

'For raping her, of course!' Frank said fiercely.

'Don't talk rot. From what she's told me, she was as keen on it as he was.'

There were things Lizzie could say that Frank would not have

146

permitted from anyone else in the world. This was one of them. That did not mean he wanted to believe it. 'I don't know how you can talk like that about your own daughter.'

'And I don't know how you can talk such nonsense. Of course he didn't rape her! If he'd tried forcing her, she'd have told me straight away. And she certainly wouldn't have wanted to keep going back there.'

Much as he would have liked to dispute it, Frank had to admit the sense in Lizzie's argument. 'Well... if she did go along with it, that's only because she didn't know what she was doing.'

'And what makes you think he did?'

'Because he's older than her! He's a grown man, and she's just a little girl.'

'He's only eighteen, Frank. And I don't seem to remember you knowing all that much about it when you were a good few years older than he is. No one fooled anyone, and no one forced anyone. They want to get married, and the best we can do is let them.'

'No.'

He felt Lizzie roll onto her side, facing him. 'Frank, I'm not saying this is how I'd have wanted things to turn out, any more than you would. Especially with Beth being so young—I'd've rather had her wait till she was eighteen to get married. But it's not so bad. Beth's got all her funny little ways, wanting to look after birds and kittens and all that, and happier out on the farm with you than inside helping me. She's said herself enough times that she'd never want to go and live in town like Maudie did. There's not all that many men would suit a girl like her. But Dave's almost as funny as she is. He's just right for her.'

'No, he's not. He's not right at all.'

'Why not?'

'Isn't it flaming obvious? He's Charlie's son. My daughter's not going to marry Charlie Stewart's son.'

'Frank! Are you blaming the boy for who his father was?'

'It's nothing to do with blaming. I'm just trying to look after my daughter.'

'Of course you are, but have a bit of sense. What are we going to do when the baby arrives? What do you think that'll be like for Beth? Sixteen—no, she'll be seventeen by then—with a baby and no husband. That's not much of a life, is it? Is that what you want for her?'

The baby was an uncomfortable fact Frank would rather have ignored. 'We'll have to make the best of it. We'll... I don't know, we'll probably tell people it's ours. No one'd think twice about you having another one. As long as Dave keeps his mouth shut, no one outside the family'll find out.'

'And how are you going to make him do that? Hit him?'

'If I have to.'

'Humph! You know perfectly well he let you thump him today. If he'd raised a hand to you, you'd've been flat on your back before you knew what had hit you.' Only the fact that this was undeniably true stopped Frank from arguing the point.

'And what about Beth?' Lizzie went on. 'Do you think she'd go along with pretending it's not her baby? Because I don't. You can stop her from marrying Dave, but you can't stop her wanting to see him. What happens when the baby's born, and she wants to take it over to see its father? Will you tell her she can't?'

Frank tried to keep the distaste he felt for such a task out of his voice. 'I'll just have to. She's too young to know her own mind. That's why I have to decide these things myself.'

'Well, you're going to have to watch her every minute. Because *I'm* not going to tell her she can't take her own baby to see its father.'

'Shut up about it!' Frank said, a good deal more sharply than he had meant to. 'I'll do whatever I have to, if it means keeping Beth safe.'

Lizzie somehow contrived a silence that was as eloquent as if she had spoken. Frank rolled over and pretended to go to sleep.

He was on the point of genuinely falling asleep when Lizzie spoke again, dragging him back into consciousness. 'So you'd shut her up in the house?' She sounded annoyingly alert.

'Eh?' Frank said groggily.

'Beth. Is that what you'd do to keep her away from Dave? Keep her shut up in the house?'

'It won't come to that.'

'I don't see why it wouldn't. She's going to want to see him, and you say she's not allowed to. So you'll make her ask your permission every time she wants to leave the farm? And you'll say no if you don't like where she's going? You'll treat her like a child, even when she's got a baby of her own?' Frank was still fumbling for a response when Lizzie went on. 'That's just what Charlie used to do to Amy. I never thought that was right, myself. I didn't think you did, either.'

'That's different.'

'Is it?'

There was another long silence; again Frank was on the point of sleep. 'Well, we'll leave it for now,' Lizzie said.

'We'll leave it for good.' Frank lay awake for a long time, waiting for Lizzie to say aloud what he knew she was thinking.

For much of the following day, Frank saw only glimpses of Beth. She sat with the family for meals, able to disappear in the noise and bustle of ten people at the dinner table, but at other times of the day, if Frank came into a room she would slip quietly out of it. After dinner, she sat in the parlour only long enough after Rosie and Kate had been sent to bed for her to be sure the little girls were asleep. As Maisie, who Frank was sure had been told what was going on, went off to bed with her, and Lizzie seemed not to have much to say during the evening, the parlour was unusually dull.

The little he saw of Beth was enough to show him how unhappy she was. His inability to do anything to help her did not improve his mood.

'Now, about Beth and Dave,' Lizzie began as soon as she had put out the lamp and joined him in bed.

'There's nothing more to say about it—and there's no use going on with the same stuff.'

'Yes, there is. I have to keep on about it, because you won't see what's staring you in the face. You know Beth's miserable, don't you?'

'I'm not blind, Lizzie.'

'Well, the only way you're going to see her happy again is if you let her marry Dave.'

'No. We'll just have to do our best for her here.'

Lizzie's hair tickled his face as she shook her head. 'It can't be done, Frank. We can't make her happy, not with a baby on the way. The only one who can do that is Dave.'

'He could make her pretty miserable, too. He could give her the sort of life his father gave Amy.'

'No, he couldn't—because he's *not* his father. Dave hasn't got it in him to be cruel.'

Frank made a noise of disgust. 'I don't see why not. He's Charlie Stewart's son.'

'He's Amy's son. There's much more of her than Charlie in him.'

'I don't know about that.'

'Well, I do.'

Frank made no answer beyond another disbelieving snort.

Lizzie had a knack of waiting just long enough to catch him on the edge of sleep. 'I don't know why you're so set against it,' she said. 'You've always been fond of Dave.'

'That was before he did this to Beth. I see what he's like now. He's as bad as that Jimmy, taking advantage of a girl and getting her in this state.'

'Of course he's not! Jimmy had his fun then ran off. Dave wants to marry Beth. He wants to do right by her. You're the only one stopping him.'

Her accusation stung all the more for Frank's awareness of the truth behind it. 'He can't do right by her,' he said, uncomfortably aware of the shallowness of his argument. 'That dump of a place, and his mongrel cows. He's no business thinking of getting married at all, let alone to one of my daughters.'

There was a long pause, as if Lizzie could hardly believe what she had heard. 'And do you think you were such a wonderful catch when we first got married? What about when you got in that muddle over Ben's money? No, I don't want to drag up old things,' she went on, too quickly for Frank to protest. 'But it seems pretty mean to say Dave's got no right to marry Beth just because he hasn't got enough money. Frank, you came jolly close to losing the farm back then. But I never for a moment thought I shouldn't have married you because money was tight. I just knuckled down and made ends meet, and did my best to help you through it. Just having you and the kids, that was enough for me. And now you think Dave's not good enough for one of our girls? I never thought you'd turn into a snob.'

'It's not the same thing at all,' Frank said, scrabbling desperately at the moral high ground as he felt it slipping away from him. 'This place was much better than his dump.'

'Is it Dave's fault you had a better father than he did?'

She had no business being so irritatingly right. 'Well… he should have had a go at smartening it up before he thought about getting married. He should have waited a few years.'

He heard Lizzie sigh. 'Frank, I might even agree with you if it wasn't for the baby. He's too young—they both are. But there's no sense thinking like that, not now.'

'And there's no sense going on about this, either. Now, can I get some sleep?'

Sleep was fast becoming an elusive memory. Lizzie contented herself with reproachful looks during the daytime, but she renewed her assault the next night.

'Beth's making herself ill over this, you know,' she began. 'She's hardly eaten a thing these last couple of days. I made her have some dinner, but she sicked it up later.'

'Well, that's just morning sickness, isn't it? You used to get a bit of that.'

'No, it isn't. I think I know more about that than you do. No, it's just from being so miserable. Maisie told me Beth's been crying half the night—crying till she's sick. I'm starting to wonder...'

She trailed off; the uneasiness in her voice gave Frank a jolt. 'You really think she's crook, Lizzie?'

'Yes, I do. I just about wonder if she might lose the baby.'

'That wouldn't be such a bad thing.' Frank said it under his breath, but Lizzie heard him.

'Frank! What an awful thing to say about your own grandchild!'

'Charlie Stewart's grandchild,' Frank muttered.

'Yes, Charlie's grandchild. And my grandchild. And Amy's—the only one she's ever likely to have, if you get your way.'

Frank grunted. 'I don't know about that. He'll get hold of some other girl.'

'No, he won't. There's only Beth for him now—I'm quite sure of that.'

'How do you know?'

'Because I can see he's like you, of course. You'd have been just the same.'

Outrage left Frank speechless for several moments. 'What do you mean by that?' he said at last.

'If things had turned out for us like they have for Beth and Dave, you wouldn't have gone off with some other girl even if Pa had said we couldn't get married.'

'That's just talking rot. I wouldn't have carried on like he has.'

'Are you going to try and tell me you wouldn't have done just the same if I'd let you?'

'Of course I wouldn't!'

Even in the dark, and without saying a word, Lizzie managed to fill the air between them with scepticism.

'Give it up, Lizzie. I'm not changing my mind.'

Lizzie was silent, but Frank knew that would not last. She was simply waiting long enough to be sure of waking him up when she next spoke.

Every night was the same.

'Lizzie, how long are you going to keep this up?' Frank groaned.

'As long at it takes you to see sense.'

'Till I agree with you, you mean. Not this time, Lizzie.'

They seemed to be covering the same ground over and over, and he repeated the same answers over and over: No. I want what's best for her. He's not having her. Not Charlie Stewart's son. The words came without any conscious thought, till he almost felt as if he were talking in his sleep. He wondered how Lizzie could keep it up, since her nights were as broken as his.

That particular mystery was solved one afternoon, when he found her curled up in bed with Benjy in her arms, the two of them fast asleep. Even faced with such evidence that Lizzie was not playing fair, he could not bring himself to disturb her.

Every night he fell asleep to the sound of Lizzie's voice, and woke to the same sound. There was a respite in the daytime, but with the knowledge that it would start again that evening. And all the while as Lizzie repeated her arguments, he would see in his mind's eye the shadowy figure of Beth, who if she was given the chance would slip out of any room he entered.

He missed her. Beth was a quiet girl, especially compared to Lizzie and Maudie, but she had always been the most affectionate of his children. She was the one whose face would light up whenever she saw him; the one he would find curled up in his lap and have no memory of how she had come to be there. He had felt her absence while she had been spending so much time at David's, but even with all the tasks she had had at both houses she had often managed to join him in the late afternoon. She would slip her hand into his as he walked around the herd, giving her opinion on the new calves and giving him the sweetness of her company. That had not happened since her confession and his outburst.

He only wanted her to be happy. He wanted the best for her. The trouble was, it was becoming increasingly difficult to decide just what that might mean.

'Here's the mail, Miss Sarah,' said Nellie. She placed a silver tray with a small pile of envelopes beside Sarah's plate.

'Thank you, Nellie.' Sarah flipped through the envelopes, and removed two. 'These are for you, Amy,' she said, handing them across the table.

'One from Lizzie, and this one's from Dave,' Amy said. 'I had one just the other day, it's nice to get another one so soon.'

She picked up the envelope that bore David's writing and slit it with Sarah's letter opener. The letter was so short that it took only a few moments to read, and left her frowning in thought.

'Dave wants me to come home.'

'Well, he'll just have to wait,' said Sarah. 'We agreed you'd stay four months, and that won't be up for weeks yet.'

'He sounds worried about something. I think I might have to go back.'

'What's he so worried about?'

'He doesn't say.' Amy studied the letter as if it might have some hidden meaning to be teased out of its few lines. 'But I can tell there's something.'

'Oh, nonsense! If he won't even take the trouble to write a sensible letter, he needn't think I'm going to let you rush home to him. What does the letter actually say?'

Amy scanned the single sheet. 'He says, "Please can you come home, Ma. We need you to help sort everything out. Aunt Lizzie says to tell you to come as soon as you can." '

'That's not exactly helpful. It's probably nothing at all, Amy. Perhaps Beth made him a pudding he didn't like, and that's put his nose out of joint. He wants you to fuss over him.'

'No,' Amy said, shaking her head. 'Dave wouldn't have asked if it wasn't important.' She braced herself for the argument she knew was looming. 'I'll have to go home.'

'No! You're not going to be at his beck and call. I won't allow it.'

'Davie needs me, Sarah. I have to go.'

'*I* need you.'

Amy gave a startled laugh. 'No, you don't! You don't need anyone.' Seeing Sarah's hurt expression, Amy reached across the corner of the table to take her hand. 'I'm sorry, I didn't mean it to sound like that. But you're so strong, and you're so sure about things. You never have to ask anyone what you should do, and you never seem to be frightened that you'll do the wrong thing.'

'That doesn't mean I don't need you,' Sarah said, a hint of reproach in her expression.

'I think it does, Sarah,' Amy said gently. She squeezed Sarah's hand. 'I'm so very grateful that you want me to be with you. These last few months have been like a dream for me. And I do want to come up here and stay with you again. But just now I have to go back to the farm. I have to see Davie.'

Sarah continued to look obstinate. 'I won't allow it till he gives a proper account of himself. I'm not buying your ticket before then.' She cast a triumphant look at Amy.

'Then I'll buy it myself. I've got my own money.'

'What?' Sarah said, clearly startled. 'Enough for a passage?'

Amy nodded. 'It's in the bank, but I've got my bank book, and Tom gave me a letter I can show them at the bank up here and get some money out.'

'You have your own bank account?' Sarah looked more astonished than ever.

'Yes. Pa left me an annuity, so I'd always have some money of my own.'

'That was remarkably enlightened of him. More so than I would have expected. Well, since you're so set on it, we'll go into town this afternoon and book a passage for you. I'll pay for it, of course—it was my idea to bring you up here, after all. And just what *do* you think he's supposedly so anxious about?'

'It's something he doesn't want to put in a letter. I'll see if Lizzie says anything about it.'

'Hmm. I'd be a little more inclined to take all this seriously if Mrs Kelly thinks it's important.' Sarah drummed her fingers on the table while Amy opened Lizzie's envelope and quickly read the letter it contained.

Lizzie's letter was almost as short as David's. 'She says more or less the same as Dave,' said Amy. 'Apart from a bit about Benjy getting a new tooth, she just says, "We need you to come back home. Things are in a bit of a muddle." I wonder if it's to do with money,' she said thoughtfully.

'What do you mean, Amy?'

'Well, it's something Dave's embarrassed about, I think. That's why he doesn't want to put it in a letter. And Lizzie always leaves things to do with money up to Frank, so she wouldn't know the ins and outs of it. If Dave's got into a muddle to do with the farm owing money, or something like that, he'd need me to come and look at things.'

'But couldn't someone down there help him, if he's in difficulties of that sort?'

'Yes, Frank would always help him out, he'd be only too glad to. But if there's anything that needs signing, I'd need to be there, because Dave's under age. Charlie left the farm to him, but he made me Davie's guardian, and I'm the...' she struggled to remember the word, 'the trustee of the farm. So I'm the only one who can sign things.'

Sarah raised her eyebrows. 'In the space of an hour, I learn that my grandfather was enlightened enough to leave you an income of your own, and that husband of yours showed more sense than I'd have thought he was capable of. Next you'll tell me something decent Mr Taylor's done, and my view of the world will be turned completely on its head.'

Amy sometimes found Sarah's sense of humour disconcerting, but she

154

smiled and shook her head. 'I can't think of anything just now.'

They booked a passage for later in the week, which gave Amy two days for her packing, a visit to a studio to have her photograph taken with Sarah, and some last-minute shopping.

'I want to buy something for Alice and Nellie,' she told Sarah. 'They've been so nice, running around after me.'

'Well, it is what I pay them for,' said Sarah.

'I know. I still want to give them something, to say thank you.'

Sarah smiled indulgently. She waited while Amy bought two pairs of gloves for the maids, then took her to a tearoom for afternoon tea.

'I've still got some money left from what I brought up,' Amy said, counting her few shillings carefully. 'I'd like to get something for Beth. I couldn't really have stayed so long if she hadn't been looking after Dave for me all this time. I wonder if I've got enough for a bracelet, or something like that.'

'I expect you have,' said Sarah. 'I know just the place.'

When they had finished their tea, she took Amy to a brightly-lit jeweller's store, with displays of rings, bracelets and watches that dazzled her. Amy looked at a tray of gold bangles, then reluctantly turned away from them when she saw that the cheapest cost several shillings more than her purse held.

'What about this?' Sarah asked, pointing to a brooch on display under glass. She nodded to an assistant, who got it out and passed it to her for inspection.

Amy studied the brooch as it lay on Sarah's palm. It was a lovely thing; filigree gold twisted into the shapes of leaves and flowers, the petals of the flowers made of tiny gems. And it was clearly well beyond her means. 'It's beautiful, but—'

'But it's not going to be from you alone. I'm as grateful to Beth as you are for making this visit possible, Amy. So you must allow me to contribute to her gift.' Sarah handed the brooch across the counter to the assistant. 'We'll take this,' she told the young man. 'You may put it on my account.'

While they waited for the brooch to be put back into its box and wrapped, Amy held out the contents of her purse. Sarah took two shillings, and contrived to finish the transaction without allowing Amy to see what the brooch had actually cost.

On the night before her departure, long after Sarah thought she had gone to bed, Amy sat in her room stitching at the dressing table set she had been embroidering for Sarah over the last few months, giving thanks as she worked for the electric light that was so much better for the task than candlelight. It was almost midnight before she put in the last few stitches, then slipped gratefully into the wondrously soft bed.

She gave Sarah the set over breakfast the next morning, and was gratified by her delighted response. Sarah insisted on taking the cloths upstairs then and there, and placing them on her table.

'Though you're not to think of it as a farewell gift,' Sarah told her. 'Because you're coming back, you see. But I'll treasure these in the meantime, and think of you every time I see them.'

They both managed to fight back tears when they said goodbye just before the *Waitangi* sailed, though Amy could see that Sarah's eyes were suspiciously bright. 'It won't be for long,' Sarah insisted. 'I fully expect you back here in a few months. I'll come and fetch you myself if necessary.'

Amy stood on the deck, straining her eyes for the first glimpse of a familiar figure on Ruatane's wharf. As soon as the boat was close enough it was easy to pick out David, towering above everyone around him. When he came onto the boat she rushed to him, put her arms around his waist and hugged him. Then she took a step back to study his face and assure herself that he was well.

He looked healthy enough, but she could see the signs of strain in his face, and guessed that he had not been sleeping soundly. Whatever had made him ask her to come home was clearly preying on his mind.

She tilted her face up for a kiss; after a moment's hesitation, he lowered his head and gave her a peck on the cheek. His uncharacteristic reserve surprised her, but she put it down to shyness with so many people about.

There was no chance of any real conversation while they were busy retrieving Amy's baggage and getting it slowed in the gig. When Amy had made a quick visit to the Post and Telegraph Office to send a cable assuring Sarah of her safe arrival, she settled in beside David and leaned her head against his arm as he coaxed the horse into a trot.

'It's lovely to see you again, Davie.' She sat upright and slipped her arm through his. 'Now, tell me what's worrying you.'

David looked around nervously. 'I don't want to talk about it here.'

After the bustle of Auckland, the streets of Ruatane seemed almost deserted to Amy. But she did not press David; there was no need to embarrass him. 'Is everyone well? Uncle John and Uncle Harry and everyone next door?'

'Mmm, they're all good.'

'I'm looking forward to seeing Beth again, so I can thank her for everything. How is she?'

'I don't know,' David said in a low voice. 'I haven't seen her since last week.'

For a moment, Amy had the foolish thought that perhaps David and Beth had indeed argued over an unsatisfactory pudding. 'Why not?' she asked when she had recovered herself.

David looked over his shoulder again. 'I'll tell you later,' he said, leaving Amy more puzzled than ever.

'But... who's been getting your meals on and everything?'

'I've been going over to Uncle John's for lunch and dinner. I've just had bread and stuff for breakfast. Aunt Sophie's been giving me cakes and things, too, and she did my washing on Monday.'

'I suppose that's all right, then,' Amy said doubtfully.

She waited till they had left the town and were on the beach, out of sight of any prying eyes. 'There's no one to hear us now. What is it? What's happened?' When he still did not speak, she squeezed his arm encouragingly. 'Come on, Davie, it can't be as bad as all that. Whatever it is, I'll help you sort it out.'

David looked at his hands where they held the reins. She heard him take a deep breath. 'Beth and me... we want to get married.'

'Davie!' Amy said, startled. She had always known, in an abstract sort of way, that David would one day marry, but it had seemed so far off in the distant future that it was as if it concerned someone else, not her little boy. 'You're much too young to get married! In a few years, maybe it'll be time to start thinking about that sort of thing, but—'

'We can't wait, Ma,' David interrupted. 'We need to get married right now. We *have* to.' He turned to look at her; she saw him wince at the dawning awareness he must have seen in her face before he quickly turned away again. 'Beth's going to have a baby.'

Beth was a year older than Amy had been when the same thing had happened to her, and David was two years older again. It was foolish to be so astonished. More than that, it was futile. 'Well, it looks like you weren't too young after all,' she said when she could trust her voice to sound calm. 'I expect Uncle Frank's not too happy about it?'

'No, he was really wild. He said we can't get married.'

Amy nodded thoughtfully. 'Did he hit you very hard?'

David shot her a quick glance. 'Not really.' There was no need to ask if David had fought back; she knew her son too well for that.

'He thinks I'm a real ratbag,' David said bleakly. 'That's why he doesn't want me to marry Beth. S'pose you think I'm awful, too.'

'Of course I don't! I'd never think you were awful, Davie. We all do wrong things—goodness knows I've done my share.' David looked at her doubtfully, and she smiled at him. 'But you want to put things right. That's because you're a good boy, really. You're not just going to leave Beth on her own to make the best of it.'

'No, I don't want to do that. I want to look after her, Ma. I want to marry her. I would anyway, even without the baby. But we can't unless Uncle Frank lets us.'

Amy patted his arm. 'Well, we'll just have to see about changing his mind. I expect your Aunt Lizzie's been doing some work on that already. I'll go and see them tomorrow morning.'

'I can only take you as far as the gate. Uncle Frank says I'm not allowed at his place any more.'

'And we'd better do what he says. That's all right, I don't mind walking that little way.'

For the remainder of the journey she coaxed small pieces of news from him, in an attempt to lighten his mood. He told her how things were on the farm, what the weather had been like, and how her brothers' families were, but it was clear that his thoughts were elsewhere. As they passed Frank's farm she saw David staring intently towards the house, obviously hoping to catch a glimpse of Beth. But no one was in sight.

When they drew up to the cottage, David helped her from the gig and lifted down her bags. As well as the case borrowed from Frank, she had a smart new one Sarah had insisted on buying for her.

'I thought you'd have a lot more bags than this,' David said, rousing himself to a show of interest as he carried her baggage up the steps. 'You talked a lot about dresses and stuff in your letters.'

'Oh, I left most of those fancy things at Sarah's—it's not as if I've got anywhere to wear them in Ruatane.' She smiled at the memory. 'Sarah says she's holding them hostage, so I'll have to go and stay with her again.' She had only brought one of her three new evening gowns with her: the black satin dress, which lay at the bottom of her new suitcase carefully wrapped in tissue. Beautiful though it was, it could pass as a mourning gown, and now she hoped to wear it at David's wedding.

While David went back out to see to the horse and gig, Amy changed into a work dress and made afternoon tea for the two of them. The room was tidier than she had expected, given that David had had the house to himself for several days. She found some biscuits in one of the tins, and by the time David came back she had a pot of tea ready.

'I've been so lazy all the time I've been away,' she said. 'I haven't done any cooking or anything. I'm quite looking forward to baking again—I'll make a nice lot of biscuits tomorrow and fill up the tins.'

When they had finished their afternoon tea, Amy used what was left of the hot water to wash their tea things and the dishes from David's breakfast. She was startled when he picked up a towel and begin drying the dishes.

'What are you doing, Dave?'

'Eh? Just helping you.'

'Why?' Amy asked, bewildered.

David looked thoughtful. 'I suppose I didn't use to. Well, Beth's been helping me on the farm, especially with the new calves. Then it was hard for her to get everything done inside before she had to go home, so I've been helping her a bit, too.'

'Well, you've no need to help me, Davie. It's just as fast for me to do it on my own and let you get on with your work.' She retrieved the towel from him and finished doing the dishes.

When David was on his way out soon afterwards to do the milking, Amy took the opportunity to claim another kiss. Again, there was that strange hesitation; and again, he kissed her on the cheek rather than on the mouth. Had he not been so clearly relieved to have her back home, Amy might almost have wondered if she had annoyed him in some way.

She put the puzzle to the back of her mind while she went through the cottage to see what needed doing. The parlour only had to have its fireplace swept out and a new fire laid in the grate; the dust she stirred up could wait another day.

The clothes Sophie had laundered for David were piled on a chair in his room. His bed, with its sheets twisted and blankets flung every which way, had obviously not been made for days. Amy began to make it, then it occurred to her that the bed might have got into such a rumpled state while Beth was still visiting the house every day. These two had not had to make do with furtive couplings in sunlit clearings. She hurriedly stripped the bed and made it up with clean sheets.

The mechanical task of folding David's clothes and putting them away left Amy free to mull over all that had happened since her return. She had been fondly thinking of David as still her little boy; had pictured Beth keeping house for him almost as two children playing together, the way she had seen the two of them playing since the time Beth could first walk. They had shown themselves to have grown up all too quickly. When Amy had set off for Auckland, she had said farewell to a boy who would readily give his mother a child's kiss, full on the lips. Now she would have to make do with the careful kisses of a grown son.

Amy hung up the last shirt and closed the wardrobe door. It was a good thing she already loved Beth, she reflected; because from now on she was going to have to share David. And she was the one who would be taking second place in his life.

She had made her way back to the kitchen and begun getting dinner ready before the wondrous realisation struck her: she was going to have a grandchild. That would go a long way towards making up for having to share David's affections. And it was another reason to do her very best to help coax Frank into allowing this marriage.

After dinner, Amy and David sat talking in the parlour till late. Amy had picked up the habit of keeping later hours from Sarah, and David wanted company. She offered him what encouragement she could, though she could tell from David's account that Frank had set himself firmly against the marriage. Amy took quiet comfort in the knowledge that whenever Frank and Lizzie had disagreed in the past, Lizzie's will had always prevailed.

David kept returning to what was clearly his main concern: Beth's welfare. 'I hope she's all right,' he said, for what seemed at least the dozenth time.

'I'm sure she is. Aunt Lizzie will be looking after her.'

'She was really scared about telling Aunt Lizzie.'

'Well, she's got that over with now. I expect it wasn't as bad as she thought it would be. Aunt Lizzie's not one for making a fuss when it's no use.'

'I wish I could see her, just to see if she's all right.'

'I'll see her tomorrow, and I'll be able to tell you how she is.' She studied David's anxious expression. 'I expect she's just as worried about you.'

'Me?' David said, startled. 'She doesn't need to worry about me! She's the one with... you know, the baby and all.'

'I know. That won't stop her worrying about you, though.'

David yawned, and Amy felt the weariness of her long journey beginning to catch up with her. 'Time we both went to bed,' she said, careful to sound cheerful. 'I've got an important job to do tomorrow.'

She leaned over to kiss him goodnight, and let her hand rest on his arm. 'It'll be all right, Davie. We'll work it out somehow.'

13

There was a chilly wind the next morning. It blew stinging rain into Amy's face as she made her way up the track to Frank's house. It was a relief to find herself being ushered into the warm kitchen, where she was given the seat nearest the range and a pot of tea was soon set brewing. Beth was nowhere to be seen.

'Did you walk over here in this rain?' Lizzie demanded.

'No, only from your gate. Dave brought me that far.' She saw Lizzie cast a meaning look in Frank's direction; he refused to meet her gaze.

Lizzie looked rather tired, but Frank looked exhausted. He managed to rouse himself to give Amy a brief, tired smile before his mouth drooped again. She could see that he could barely keep his eyes open. 'Sorry you had to walk, Amy,' he said.

'That's all right, Frank. The exercise will do me good, with all the sitting around I've done lately.'

They managed a stilted conversation over their cups of tea, with Lizzie asking questions about Auckland that Amy knew she was not particularly interested in the answers to. As soon as they had finished, Frank sent the boys outside, telling them to tidy out some of the sheds while the rain lasted.

'Can I see Beth?' Amy asked.

'Of course you can,' said Lizzie. 'Maisie, go and get her.'

'She won't want to come out here,' Maisie said, glancing at Frank as she spoke.

'Never mind that—you tell her I said she's to come. Hurry up, girl.'

Frank watched as Maisie left the room. 'I don't blame you for this, Amy,' he said.

Amy knew he meant well, but she found it difficult not to jump to her boy's defence. 'Perhaps you should, Frank,' she said carefully. 'I brought him up, after all. So I suppose it's partly my fault.'

'That's just what I've been saying about Beth,' Lizzie said with more than a hint of satisfaction. 'I think I'm as much to blame as anyone. I'm the one who let my daughter spend all day with a boy, with no one to keep an eye on them.'

'All right,' Frank said testily. 'There's no need to go on about blaming.'

'Well, that's what I've been trying to tell you,' said Lizzie. Frank scowled at her; she stared back, unabashed.

Amy looked up at a slight noise, and saw Beth in the doorway, with Maisie standing close behind. Beth looked as if she had just splashed water on her face, but it was still blotched with red, and her eyes were swollen. She came a few steps into the room, then stood as if afraid to come any closer. Amy's heart went out to her. She got up from the table, crossed to Beth, and took the girl in her arms.

Beth clung to her, sobbing. Through the incoherent gulps, Amy could make out 'I'm sorry,' but little else. 'Shh, shh,' she soothed. 'It's all right, Beth. It'll be all right.' It was all she could do to keep from weeping in sympathy.

Beth calmed herself enough to murmur, 'Is Davie all right?'

'Yes, except for being so worried about you,' Amy answered softly. 'We sat up late last night talking about it all. I'll be able to tell him I've seen you, so that's good.'

'Tell him I miss him,' Beth whispered.

'I will.' Amy disengaged herself, took Beth by the hand and led her to the table. 'Come and see what I've got for you,' she said, as if promising a tearful child a treat. 'I brought you something from Auckland.'

She took the small box from her drawstring pouch and handed it to Beth. 'It's to say thank you for...' Amy stopped herself just in time; "Looking after Dave" would be tactless in front of Frank. 'For looking after the house and everything. It's from Sarah as well—she helped me get it.'

Beth sniffed, wiped a hand across her eyes, and took the box. She opened it, saw the brooch, and gasped. 'Oh, Aunt Amy, it's lovely! Thank you.' For a moment she seemed on the verge of smiling, but instead she dissolved into fresh tears.

Lizzie pulled a handkerchief from her sleeve and handed it to Beth. 'Blow your nose, girl, we don't want to hear you sniffing like that. Now, let's see this on you.' She took the brooch and pinned it to the front of Beth's dress. 'Doesn't that look nice?'

Beth looked at Amy, Maisie and Lizzie all smiling encouragingly at her, and again she seemed on the point of smiling herself. Then she caught her father's eye, and looked away quickly. 'Thank you for the lovely present, Aunt Amy.' She turned a pleading face to her mother. 'Can I go now, Ma?'

Lizzie made a noise of irritation. 'All right. Go and do some tidying up in the parlour, I'll call you in a bit to come and help me get lunch on. Maisie, you go with her, I want to talk to Aunt Amy.'

Frank watched the girls go. 'She can't stand the sight of me,' he said morosely.

'It's not that,' said Amy. 'She thinks you can't bear the sight of her. No, I know that's not true,' she said, forestalling the protest she saw on his lips. 'But it's how Beth feels. Don't forget, I know a bit about what this is like for a girl.'

'I'm only thinking of her, you know,' Frank said, the pain clear in his voice. 'I just want the best for her.'

'Of course you do. We all want the best for them.' Amy could see that Frank was about to go outside; she quickly gathered her thoughts and spoke again. 'Frank, I know Dave's not the sort of boy you were thinking of for Beth. He hasn't got a lot of money, and our place isn't very flash—it's not nearly as nice as yours.'

'I'm not too worried about that,' Frank said unconvincingly.

'I'm sure you could have found someone better off than Dave, especially for a lovely girl like Beth. But I don't think you'd ever have found anyone who cares more about her than he does. He loves her, Frank. That counts for something, doesn't it?'

Frank opened his mouth to reply, but closed it again without speaking. He gave a helpless shrug, and went outside.

Frank had not had a good night's sleep for what felt like months, and there was no sign that he was to be allowed one in the near future. His daughter was wretchedly unhappy, and this had somehow become his fault. His sons were increasingly wary of him. He had found himself shouting at Danny for knocking over a bag of oats; the boys were not used to hearing their father's voice raised in anger even when they had done something to deserve it, let alone for a simple accident. Whenever he was unwise enough to let Lizzie catch his eye, her expression ranged between reproachful and exasperated.

He sat in the kitchen, listening to the hum of conversation around him and trying to rouse the energy to decide what to do next. Even putting his thoughts in order seemed to take a huge effort.

Amy was there, as she had been every morning since she had come home. She would share morning tea with the family, then stay on for a short time afterwards, talking with Lizzie. Frank was not part of those discussions, but it was not hard to guess their main subject.

'You going to be here a while yet, Amy?' he asked when there was a lull in the conversation.

Amy looked over at him and smiled. Hers was the only reliably friendly face there seemed to have been in his house since this whole business had started. Before she had the chance to speak, Lizzie answered for her.

'Yes, she is. We might do a spot of baking before she goes home.'

'That's good,' said Frank. 'I just wondered, because I'm going out for a bit. I'll give you a lift home after that if you don't mind waiting.'

He saw a knowing look exchanged between the two women. 'Thank you, Frank,' said Amy. 'I don't mind waiting.'

Frank tethered his horse to the fence and walked up to David's back door, to see David himself standing in the entrance, a half-eaten biscuit clutched in one hand. He filled the entire doorway, even having to stoop slightly to avoid hitting his head.

'Hello, Uncle Frank.' He eyed Frank in evident surprise.

They stood looking at one another for a moment, then Frank said, 'Can I come in, then?'

'Yes,' David said cautiously. He stepped back into the kitchen, making space for Frank to enter.

'Do you want a cup of tea?' he asked when the silence had lasted long enough to become awkward.

'No thanks.' Frank studied David, towering over him in the small room. What had possessed him to take on this young giant? He was uncomfortably aware that he had only emerged unscathed from the encounter because David had made no attempt to defend himself. Lizzie claimed she had seen David bend down to make it easier for Frank to reach him, but Frank felt that was going too far.

'How much do you make off this place, Dave?' he asked abruptly.

'Um… I've been writing up accounts,' David said, a tiny spark of pride in the accomplishment discernible in his voice. 'You want to see them?'

'All right,' Frank said, impressed despite himself. A guilty memory nudged at him, reminding him that he had been close to ten years older than David was before he had started keeping proper accounts.

David shoved what remained of his biscuit into his mouth and went through to the parlour, and from there to his room. Frank followed without being invited. He looked around at the stark little parlour while he waited for David to return.

The walls and floor were bare wood, a faded rag rug the most colourful thing in the room. There was an ancient sofa and two mismatched chairs that he suspected might have been in the cottage even before Charlie had moved into it. An upturned wooden crate served as a side table. The room was spotlessly clean, and crocheted covers disguised some of the places where stuffing showed through the arms of the furniture, but there was little of comfort and nothing of luxury here.

'You ever think about doing this place up?' Frank asked when David

164

emerged from his room with a large accounts book.

David looked startled at the notion. No,' he said simply. He carried the accounts book through to the kitchen and spread it out on the table for Frank's inspection.

Frank took the chair David held out for him. He flicked back a few pages to the beginning of the book while David sat down beside him. The early entries were in a neat writing that looked to be a woman's.

'Ma showed me how to write them up,' David said. 'She used to help Grandpa with his.'

Amy's writing was soon replaced by a clumsier hand that was clearly David's. Frank scanned the columns and found the entries for David's cream cheques. The figures he had so painstakingly entered were pathetically low.

Another hand had written in the last few columns. David saw Frank's eyes go to them. 'Beth did those. I was having trouble getting it all to add up properly, but we figured it out together.' He turned to the back of the book, where a different set of columns had been ruled. 'She showed me how to write all this stuff about the cows, too, see? I've been writing it all down, what cow had which calf and all. Beth says maybe I can improve the herd. And you said… you said I could borrow your bull this year.'

'I suppose I did,' Frank said, mildly surprised. It could only have been a few months since he had made the offer, but it felt like something from the distant past, when life had been a good deal simpler.

David chewed at his lip, obviously working up the courage to say something. 'How's Beth?' he asked.

'Miserable,' Frank said. 'She cries all the time, as far as I can tell. Not that I see much of her.' He studied David's anxious face, and felt himself torn between resentment and dimly remembered fondness for the boy. Resentment was currently the stronger emotion, but stronger still was the memory of Beth's unhappy face. He shook his head, trying unsuccessfully to clear his thoughts. If only he weren't so desperately tired, perhaps he would be able to think straight.

'Listen, Dave. You came barging in the other day, telling me I had to let you marry Beth. A man doesn't like to be told what he has to do with his own daughter. How about you come down tomorrow afternoon and ask me properly—*ask*, I said, mind—and then… well, we'll see.'

He saw David's eyes light up. The boy leaned forward eagerly, hands resting on his knees. Large, strong hands they were. The thought of those hands daring to touch his daughter sent a fresh wave of resentment through Frank. He lifted his gaze back to David's face and was struck by how much it resembled his mother's. Instead of reassuring him, the sweetness of David's expression irritated Frank. The boy had no business sitting there looking as if butter wouldn't melt in his mouth; not after what he had done. The soft, dark curls that brushed against his cheeks seemed the height of impudence.

'Get your ma to give you a haircut first,' Frank snapped. 'A good, short one.'

David flinched. 'I don't need—'

'I haven't said yes, boy,' Frank interrupted. 'I've only said you can come and ask me. You needn't bother asking if you turn up looking like that.'

Amy was grateful to Frank for taking her home, but by the time the short ride had ended, she was almost wishing she had walked. Frank had barely said a word to her, and she had quickly run out of banal remarks to fill the silence.

The awkward trip at least had the advantage of getting her home more quickly. She said a hurried goodbye and rushed into the house to find David.

'What happened?' she asked breathlessly. 'Did Uncle Frank come and see you? What did he say?'

David turned a troubled face to her. 'He said I can come and ask him properly tomorrow. I'm allowed to go to his place and ask to marry Beth.'

'That's good! I'm sure he must mean to say yes, he wouldn't tease you about an important thing like this.' She looked at David's gloomy expression in surprise. 'What have you got such a long face for?'

'He said I have to have a haircut first.'

Amy laughed. 'Is that all? Oh, I'm sorry, Davie, I know you hate having your hair cut. But it's not so much to ask, is it? Not if it means you're going to be allowed to marry Beth.'

'I suppose not.' David did not sound completely convinced.

As soon as they had had their lunch, Amy fetched her scissors and draped an old towel around David's shoulders. She snipped off the first few curls, doing her best to judge when he was about to give a sudden, nervous twitch.

'You'd better...' David began, then trailed off.

Amy paused in her snipping. 'I'd better what?'

David looked down at the floor. 'He said to make it good and short,' he said miserably.

'Then I will.' She moved the scissors closer to his scalp, and halted as he flinched again. 'Davie, if I'm going to cut it short you'll have to try and keep still. Or I really might nick your ear.'

David looked grim and determined, clenched his fists where they lay on his thighs, and managed to keep more or less still.

The scissors sliced off long locks, leaving a pile of hair spread in an arc on the floor and leaving David looking somehow small and vulnerable. When Amy had finished, she brushed the last few loose strands away from his face and stepped back to check her work. 'There. You won't need another one for ages now. I think I might get Beth to do it from now on, she must be used to cutting boys' hair.' She put her arms around his neck and kissed him on the cheek. 'It'll be all right, Davie. You'll see.'

Frank managed with difficulty to avoid satisfying Lizzie's curiosity as to his errand until that evening. Then there was no escape.

'I saw Dave. And he's coming down tomorrow afternoon to ask me.'

Lizzie's expression showed how ridiculous she considered this. 'Why didn't you just tell him then and there? What have you got to have him running around here for?'

'Because I want to be asked properly. And now I want a good night's sleep. I want to be thinking straight tomorrow. I've got some business at the factory in the morning, and then I've got him coming in the afternoon.'

Whether Lizzie would have allowed him to sleep undisturbed remained unanswered, because soon after she had put out the lamp Benjy broke the silence. Frank had to admit that Benjy was normally a good sleeper, but tonight he was fretful and hard to settle. 'It's that new tooth he's getting,' Lizzie said as she paced the floor with him. 'That, and he's sick of you being so grumpy all the time.'

Benjy did not want to be fed, and he did not need his napkin changed. His wails subsided to a fitful sobbing as Lizzie walked with him, but they began anew when she tried to put him back in his cradle. Lizzie gave in readily enough, and took him into bed with her. Snuggled between his parents, Benjy soon returned to his usual cheerful mood, though not to being sleepy. There was a good deal of tickling and giggling that seemed to last for hours. Had he not been so tired, Frank would have liked to join in.

Maisie was the first to see David and Amy walking up the path the following afternoon.

'*He's* coming,' she announced, turning wide-eyed from the kitchen window. 'Dave is!'

'Yes, we knew he was coming over today,' Lizzie said briskly. 'You can talk to him in the parlour, Frank, I'll get Maisie to take your tea through there.'

But Frank had no intention of talking to David in a place where Lizzie could so easily eavesdrop. 'No, I'll see him outside,' he said, going out to the porch to meet the visitors and to avoid further discussion with Lizzie.

Amy went on inside, and Frank led David away from the house. He was quite certain they were being watched from the kitchen; he chose to disappoint their audience by making sure they were shielded from view by one of the sheds before he halted.

He could not fault the shortness of David's hair. It had left the boy looking younger than ever, staring at Frank with large, anxious eyes. 'Well?' Frank demanded. 'What have you got to say for yourself?'

He saw David frowning in concentration, clearly going through words in his head. Frank suspected he had been practising this speech with his mother.

'I want to ask your permission,' David said carefully, 'to marry Beth.' He paused, waiting for a response; when none came, he ploughed on. 'I know I haven't got as much money as you, and my place isn't very flash. But I want to look after Beth, and I think I can. I'll try my hardest to.' When there was still no reply, he added, 'And there's the baby. It'd be better if we were married when the baby comes.'

David had clearly exhausted his arguments. He stood and waited for Frank to speak.

'I only want what's best for her,' Frank said at last. 'I want her to be happy. That's why I've been trying to figure out what's the right thing to do. It seems to me there isn't a right thing any more, not with what you've done. So I've got to pick the best choice of what's left to me.' He paused, putting his thoughts in some kind of order. 'Beth thinks she wants to marry you. Maybe that's the best choice. I don't know. But what with the baby and all, it doesn't seem like I've got a lot of options.' He shook his head in defeat. 'I'll let you have a go at making her happy. It's beyond me.'

David took hold of Frank's hand and pumped it vigorously. 'Thank you, Uncle Frank! I will, I'll really look after her.'

Frank let his hand be shaken briefly, then retrieved it and pointed a warning finger at David. 'I'll tell you this right from the start, boy—if you ever raise a hand to Beth, I'll fetch her straight back home, husband or no husband. And you'll never get near her again.'

David looked completely bewildered. Frank saw realisation gradually dawn. 'You think I'd hit Beth? I'd never do that! I'd never want to hurt her.' His expression grew wounded. 'It's because of Pa, isn't it? Pa used to knock Ma around, so you think I'd do the same to Beth.'

'I didn't say that,' Frank said, fully aware it was exactly what he had been thinking. 'I just want my daughter properly looked after. I'd say the same to anyone who came asking for her.'

David looked away. 'I bet you didn't say that to Richard,' he said in a low voice.

Frank found himself unable to answer. They walked back to the house in an uncomfortable silence.

Beth had joined Lizzie, Maisie and Amy in the kitchen when Frank walked in followed by David. Her eyes went straight to David's, clearly trying to guess what had happened from what she read there, but it was Frank who spoke first.

'Well, I've said yes.'

He was promptly rewarded when Beth rushed at him. She wrapped her arms around his waist and buried her face against his chest. 'Thank you, Pa.' She raised her face to show eyes bright with happiness and unshed tears. Lizzie beamed at him, and Amy smiled her gratitude as she slipped her arm through David's. For a brief few moments, Frank basked in the warmth of their approval.

'We'd better get on with sorting out this wedding, then,' said Lizzie. 'We'll have to see how soon we can have it.' She glanced at David, and at the sight of his serious expression her smile slipped. 'Cheer up, Dave!' she said, stabbing at his arm with her finger to punctuate her remark. 'Anyone would think we were planning your funeral, not your wedding!'

'Sorry,' David muttered.

'How about you two go out on the verandah for a bit while we decide what needs doing?' Lizzie said. 'Now you're properly engaged and all, you'll want to see more of each other.'

Beth and David went readily enough, leaving Amy and Lizzie to talk of licences and banns and such matters, while Frank sat and listened. They had only been gone a few minutes when the back door opened and Rosie and Kate erupted into the room, eager to talk about their day at school and demanding cuddles from anyone who looked likely to sit still for a few minutes.

Lizzie let them prattle away while they had their milk and biscuits, then she shooed them from the room. 'Get changed out of your school clothes, then you've got jobs to do. There's the parlour to dust—and you've got piano practice, Rosie. Aunt Lily's coming down tomorrow.'

Rosie pulled a face. 'Where's Beth?' she asked, obviously trying to put off both work and piano practice.

'Out on the verandah with Dave. They're having a talk. And don't you go—Rosie!' Lizzie called after the retreating child.

'I just want to say hello to Dave,' Rosie called back.

Frank was not surprised when Beth and David came back into the kitchen a few moments later; Rosie's noisy presence must have quickly put a stop to any tender moments. David still looked serious, and was as reluctant to meet Frank's gaze as Frank was his.

But Beth looked straight at her father. The fear and unhappiness he had become used to seeing in her face had gone, replaced by stern reproach. It was clear that David had reported Frank's words to her, with their implied slur against David's character, and equally clear Beth did not approve of what her father had said. Frank had never seen Beth look so much like her mother.

It was no use for Lizzie and Amy to attempt to carry on a serious conversation with Rosie and Kate running out to the kitchen whenever they could think of an excuse. Amy rose to leave soon after David had come back into the room. There was an awkward moment when David seemed about to offer to shake hands with Frank, then pulled back.

Amy kissed Beth goodbye, and Beth turned to David. She paused for a moment, then stood on tiptoe, pulled his face down to hers and kissed him on the lips.

'Beth!' Lizzie said, visibly shocked. 'You don't go doing that in front of everyone! You can just keep that sort of thing for when you're in private.'

'I just wanted to say goodbye to my fiancé,' Beth said, unabashed, though David was blushing and Amy was trying in vain to hide a smile.

Rosie and Kate, who had managed to be in the kitchen in time to witness the kiss, were staring wide-eyed at Beth when the door closed behind Amy and David. 'Well, you two, we've got a bit of news,' Lizzie told the little girls. 'We're going to have a wedding. Beth and Dave are getting married, and you can be bridesmaids again.'

'Can I have a new dress?' Rosie asked promptly.

'No, you can't,' said Lizzie. 'We'll use the ones from Maudie's wedding, and we'll cut Beth's down for you. Kate can have your old one, and Maisie can wear the same dress she did last time.'

If they were going to start on about dresses, Frank thought, it was time to make himself scarce. He remembered all too well the months leading up to Maudie's wedding, when the house had seemed full of pink satin and tempers had been strained. He glanced over at Lizzie, and saw her eyes light up as a thought struck her.

'You can wear my old wedding dress,' she told Beth.

Frank recalled Maudie's response to the same suggestion. Before Beth had a chance to answer, he spoke.

'She can have a new dress for it—she can have all the same stuff Maudie had. I won't have anyone saying I did more for Maudie than I will for Beth.'

'Frank, that's all very well,' said Lizzie. 'But we won't have as much time as we had for Maudie's. We can't be sending away to Auckland and all that.'

'It's all right, Ma,' Beth said. 'I'd rather wear your dress than have a new one. It's like you're saying you're happy that I'm going to marry Dave.'

'Of course I'm happy about it. There's no reason I wouldn't be.' Lizzie and Beth both turned to Frank and gave him a look that spoke volumes.

14

My darling Sarah, Amy wrote. *At last I have some proper news I can tell you. There's to be a wedding! Dave and Beth are getting married. It's all been quite a surprise to everyone, but with the two of them spending so much time together while I was staying with you, they got to thinking they'd like to be married. That's why Davie wrote wanting me to come home, because there was so much to be done in a hurry. They wanted to get married straight away once it was decided.*

It's only going to be a very small wedding, because they're neither of them ones for a big fuss. Just family and special friends, so of course you're invited. I'll understand if you can't come, I know you've a lot on with your business and everything. But I thought I'd write as soon as it was settled, because I knew you'd want to know about everything that's happened.

As much of what had happened as Amy felt able to put in a letter, at any rate. She tucked the invitation, written in Lizzie's most careful handwriting, into the envelope with her letter, ready to be sent off when she next went into town.

Sarah's reply came the following week, and included a note addressed to David. David opened it with a certain amount of trepidation when Amy passed it to him.

'I suppose she's telling me off.'

'I shouldn't think so,' Amy said, smiling at his expression. 'What does she say?' she prompted when she had given him a few moments to read the note.

' "Dear Dave," ' he read aloud, ' "Marriage seems a rather extreme step to have taken in order to get Amy away from me." See? I told you she'd tell me off.'

'She's just teasing, Davie.'

'Maybe,' David said, clearly unconvinced. He looked back at the letter. ' "But I wish you every happiness, and congratulate you on your excellent choice of bride. I'm sorry that I won't be able to attend your wedding." '

Another piece of paper was tucked into Sarah's note; Amy watched as David unfolded it. He stared at it in puzzlement, then his eyes widened. 'She's sent me some money. Ma, she's sent me fifty pounds!'

'Fifty pounds!' Amy echoed. 'That's nice, isn't it? That'll be a real help to you.'

David held the cheque out in front of him, looking as if he were afraid it might bite at his fingers. 'I don't know if I can take this. I mean, I don't really know her that well, and it's a heck of a lot of money. It doesn't seem right to take it off her.'

Amy studied his anxious face. David, she knew, could have little idea of the life Sarah led in Auckland, or the funds she had at her disposal. 'I think you should. I think Sarah would be quite hurt if you sent it back.'

'But fifty pounds? I wouldn't want her to go short from giving it to me.'

'I know it's a lot to you and me, but it's different for Sarah. Honestly it is, Davie. If you'd seen her house and everything you'd know.'

'Why's she sent me that much? It's not as if she's family or anything.'

How much simpler it would have been if she could tell him the truth. And how much more complicated. 'Sarah's a good friend, and she's been very good to me. She wants to do something nice for you—she likes you really, you know.' She placed a hand on David's arm. 'You'd be able to buy some nice things for Beth with the money.'

'I suppose I would,' David said thoughtfully, and Amy could see that the matter was settled.

Susannah had not been enthusiastic when Thomas had first suggested they get a house cow. It was only after he had assured her that he would take entire responsibility for looking after the animal that she had reluctantly agreed. Frank had given him a Jersey who was past her most productive years, a steady old matron who had adapted to her new home with every appearance of contentment. Thomas had fenced off part of their long backyard, and had built Blossom a byre.

The twice-daily milkings were the happiest part of Thomas's day. For a brief few minutes he would crouch on a stool in the shelter of the byre, leaning his head against Blossom's warm flank; his nostrils full of the scent of cow, his hands working at the task he had been familiar with almost since he could walk, hearing the swish of milk into the bucket and Blossom chewing her cud. If he closed his eyes, he could imagine himself back on the farm; could almost believe that he might open them to see his father smiling over at him.

And then if it were morning he would go inside and put on a suit, and a shirt with a stiff, uncomfortable collar, and prepare himself for another day spent within the brick walls of the bank; or if it were evening, he would go in for his dinner, and hope to find his mother in one of her easier moods.

September had brought mild days, but a chill came with the evenings. Thomas was relieved to enter the kitchen and feel the warmth of the stove. When his mother had dished up their meal and taken her seat, Thomas noticed an open envelope beside her plate, a sheet of pink notepaper jutting from it.

'Who's that from?' he asked idly.

'Your Aunt Constance. She says our mother's ill. Constance doesn't expect her to recover.' She said it without any great show of concern, but Thomas knew she was sometimes inclined to pretend an indifference she did not feel. On another occasion, she might appear far more agitated than she actually was. Reading his mother's moods was never a simple matter, for all the care he took over it.

'Are you going up to see her?' Thomas asked.

'Of course not. How could I possibly leave you?'

'I'll be all right if you have to—I could have my meals at the hotel.'

'No, it's simply not to be thought of—not when I've no idea how long I might have to stay there. My place is here, looking after you.'

It was clear to Thomas that, for whatever reason, his mother had no desire to go to Auckland and see her family. He did not mind being used as her excuse. 'Well, if you need to go up later—you know, if she does pass away—I can take my holiday and go up with you, if it's not for too long.'

She gave him a smile of genuine warmth. 'Thank you, Thomas. I'd be far easier in my mind if you were to come with me.' She frowned as a thought struck her. 'Though if it's before the wedding, we can't possibly go. It would be rude of me not to attend Beth's wedding, especially with your being best man for David.'

'I suppose not.' Thomas smiled pensively. 'Funny to think of Dave getting married. I keep thinking he's still a little kid.'

'Well, he *is* very young to be married,' said Susannah. Neither of them said aloud what Thomas was sure they were both thinking: David was five years younger than Thomas. 'Though he does have his own farm, which puts a different complexion on things.' Her lips compressed for a moment. 'Of course, *you* should have had your own farm, too, or at least a fair share of it, if your father had done the right—'

'Don't start that, Mother,' Thomas interrupted. 'Pa did the best he could. He did right by us all.' Not allowing any criticism of his father was the one thing Thomas was prepared to be firm with his mother over, and she had learned to respect his feelings on the matter.

'I'm only thinking of you, I'm sure. Though I must say I'm glad to have got you and George away from that place. Of course George had to go and find himself an even dirtier job than being a farmer, working with all that nasty cargo the way he does.'

'George is doing all right.' Thomas was unsure if their mother had any inkling of George's living arrangements, which had yet to involve marriage, but even without that detail George's situation was another subject that could become tedious. He changed it. 'I didn't really think of Dave asking me to be his best man. Nice that he did, though.'

'And who else should he ask?' Susannah said, gazing proudly at him. 'You're almost his closest relation. I'm so pleased you're to be part of it—it should be a most pleasant occasion. I've ordered a new dress specially.' She looked away, and spoke in a carefully casual tone. 'They're both very young, but people on farms seem to marry at that sort of age. There's no need for someone in your position to rush into things.'

'I'm not rushing into anything,' said Thomas. There was not much risk of his doing so. It would mean finding a girl who not only wanted to marry him, but was also willing to share a household with his mother. If such a girl existed, he had yet to meet her.

Using the bridesmaids' dresses from Maudie's wedding had seemed a good way to save time, but altering two of them to fit Rosie and Kate had turned out to be more difficult than expected. Lizzie announced that Rosie had grown suddenly. She made it sound as if Rosie had done it on purpose; Rosie took it as a personal insult, and hard words had been said. Maudie suspected that her mother had cut more off Beth's old dress than she should have when cutting it down, and was reluctant to admit her mistake. However it had happened, the dress altered for Rosie had dangerously narrow seams, and she had been sternly warned not to grow any more before the wedding. Kate paid the price by having to wear a dress that had been so cautiously altered as to be baggy on her; the five-year-old might not have noticed, but Rosie had helpfully pointed out the dress's shortcomings.

So tempers were frayed as the female members of the household crammed into the kitchen, pink satin dresses draped across every available surface. Maudie watched the proceedings, wavering between amused tolerance and aloof superiority. Really, the very idea of trying to organise a wedding in a few weeks! She remembered with satisfaction the months that had gone into preparing for her own day of triumph. Of course that had been completely different. *Hers* had been a proper wedding.

She flicked a crumb from Lucy's pretty dress, newly arrived in a package ordered from Auckland. 'Lucy's talking ever so well. She's very forward for her age.'

'Maisie, see if you can do something about the hem on Kate's dress,' said Lizzie. 'It's sagging down in the middle. Yes, Lucy's coming on all right,' she added absently. 'Up a bit more, Maisie.'

'She's saying whole words one after another,' Maudie said more loudly. 'Show Grandma, Lucy. Say, "I want a bikkie".'

Lucy obliged with a burst of sound that to Maudie was clear proof. 'See?' she said triumphantly. 'A whole sentence, just like that.'

'All kids do that,' said Lizzie. 'You were just the same at her age. I probably thought it was talking, too. I know it seems a marvel to you, but it's just noises. Pass me those pins, Beth.'

'It's not just noises! It's proper talking. Richard agrees with me.'

'Richard can't be bothered arguing over it.' Lizzie paused in her work to hand Lucy a biscuit and plant a kiss on the top of her head. 'She's a good little thing, and she'll talk soon enough. Now, just keep her out of the way so we can get on with this stuff. You know we haven't got time to waste with a lot of nonsense.'

Maudie drew herself up stiffly. 'Well, I'm sure I don't know why everyone's making such a fuss about this wedding. It's not as if things are as they should be.'

Rosie, always alert for signs of strife, looked up at once. 'What's she mean, Ma?'

'Never you mind what she means,' said Lizzie. 'Little girls should mind their own business. And so should some big girls,' she added with a dark look at Maudie. 'That hem's good enough, Maisie—no one'll be taking much notice of Kate, anyway. Rosie, get your old clothes on and you and Kate can go and tell your father to come up for afternoon tea.'

She watched as the little girls slipped out of the pink dresses, pulled on their everyday ones and went outside. 'Beth, you can… now, where did she go?'

'She went up the passage,' Maisie said, casting an accusing look at Maudie. 'She's probably gone off to have a cry.'

Lizzie glared at Maudie. 'Oh, thank you very much. We've just got her to stop bawling all the time, and now you set her off.'

'What's she bawling for?' Maudie asked in surprise. 'She's getting married!'

'Yes, now that I've finally talked your father round. The poor girl's been that miserable worrying if she'd be allowed or not, she's been making herself ill with it.'

'She was crying till she was sick some nights,' Maisie put in.

'And now you come in all high and mighty, with your "things aren't as they should be",' said Lizzie.

'Well, they're not,' Maudie said, struggling to maintain her sense of moral superiority. 'Richard and I didn't—'

'Richard and you weren't out of my sight long enough to get up to any mischief,' Lizzie cut in. 'And don't you go telling me you wouldn't have, given the chance,' she said before Maudie could express her outrage. 'If I'd kept a proper eye on Beth like I did on you, this wouldn't have happened either. But it did happen, and we're trying to make the best we can of it. She's not going to have a flash wedding like we gave you, what with us having to do everything in such a rush. And there won't be any nonsense with engagement rings or honeymoons, either. Dave can't afford that sort of thing. But it's still the girl's wedding, and she doesn't need you trying to spoil it for her.'

'I didn't know she'd been miserable about it,' Maudie said.

'Should I go and see if she's all right?' Maisie asked.

'No, leave her in peace for a bit,' said Lizzie. 'Take her a cup of tea when it's ready, she can have it in there.'

Maudie sat quietly, mulling over what her mother had said. The idea that she might have been responsible for marring Beth's pleasure in so wonderful an event as her own wedding, even the small and plain one this was to be, was too heavy a burden of guilt to bear.

When the rest of the family had come in, she placed Lucy on Frank's lap, took Beth's cup from Maisie and went through to her old room.

Beth was sitting on the edge of the bed she had once shared with Maudie, their mother's old veil on her lap and a needle and thread in one hand. She looked up when the door opened; on seeing who it was, she bent lower over the veil and appeared to be giving all her attention to the rent she was mending. But Maudie had seen the telltale red blotches on her face.

Maudie placed the cup and saucer on the dressing table and sat down beside her. 'Ma's veil's a bit ratty,' she said, fingering the net gingerly. 'You're going to have an awful job trying to mend all those ripped bits.'

'It doesn't matter. No one's going to worry what I look like.'

'Of course it matters!' Maudie hesitated for a moment, then said, 'Would you like to borrow my veil? You'd look really nice in it.'

Beth looked up, startled. 'I didn't think you'd want me wearing anything of yours.'

'Why wouldn't I?' Maudie took Beth's hand in hers and squeezed it. 'Sorry.' After a moment she felt a matching movement of Beth's hand that told her she was forgiven. 'It's good your baby and Lucy will be so close together, isn't it?'

'I hadn't thought of that,' Beth said. 'I suppose I haven't really thought much about the baby. Just about… you know. All the fuss and everything.'

'You'll have more time to think about it once the wedding's over. I hope you have a girl, too. Girls are best.'

The day of the wedding dawned grey, with a heavy, lowering sky that threatened rain.

'We'll have to squeeze everyone into the parlour if it pours,' Lizzie said, peering anxiously through the bedroom window. 'I want to put the food out on the verandah.'

Frank grunted. The weather was the least of his worries on this day when he had to allow Beth to go to David.

The leaden sky kept up its threat all morning, without ever delivering more than a few spots of rain. Lizzie had decided to risk the weather, and as the guests arrived they were shown to a mixed assortment of chairs in front of the verandah. Beth and the other girls had disappeared to their room some time before, with Lizzie dividing her time between supervising their preparations and keeping the boys busy and away from the food.

Maudie had had Richard bring her out the previous evening, and had somehow squeezed herself and Lucy into the girls' room for the night. She and her mother, united in the cause of making Beth's wedding a success, were getting on remarkably well.

Only a small number of guests had been invited. Beth had made it clear she had no desire for a large wedding, and given how short a time there was to organise the affair, Lizzie had agreed readily enough.

Amy and David arrived some time before the guests. Amy set to helping Lizzie, while David and Frank found themselves forced into an uneasy association. It seemed a long time to Frank before he was called into the house and David was told to take his place on the verandah, Thomas at his side.

Beth emerged from her room. She and Frank stood silent, staring at each other. It was the first time he had ever seen Beth with her hair up, and certainly the first time she had worn such an elaborate gown. Her small figure was almost lost in the pale pink satin, all gathers and ruffles. She and Lizzie had discarded the bustle as hopelessly old-fashioned, which made the dress even longer for her than it already was. She looked far too young to be wearing such a gown, but Frank thought she looked beautiful. To see her in Lizzie's wedding dress made his heart leap, until he recalled whom she was to marry. It should not have been like this, not for his little Beth.

'Are you two going to stand there all day?' said Lizzie. 'I need to get out there ahead of you.'

Beth took the simple bunch of flowers, picked from the garden that morning, that Maudie was holding for her. Lucy clung to her mother's skirts, looking like a tiny image of the bridesmaids in the little pink dress Maudie had made for her out of Kate's old one. 'I'm ready, Ma,' Beth said, and Lizzie walked off, casting a glance at Frank as she did. Frank held out his arm for Beth to slip hers through.

It was the first time she had touched him since the day a few weeks before when he had given his consent to her marriage. He had had a brief, grateful embrace from her that day, but when she and David had returned from their conversation on the verandah Beth had turned a disapproving glare on her father, and she had been distant ever since. She clearly believed he had been unfair in thinking David might behave in any way like his father. Frank fervently hoped she was right.

'You look really good, love,' he said, squeezing her hand.

'Thank you.' The pretty brooch that had been a gift from Amy and Sarah was pinned to the front of Beth's dress; she gave it a brief touch, as if for luck. Frank had hoped to raise a smile from her, though he could not produce one himself; instead she sent him a piercing look, in which he recognised a plea. If the plea was for him to be happy about her marriage, he found himself unable to grant it.

Maisie and the little girls clustered behind them. Maudie drew the veil over Beth's face before stepping quickly off in her mother's wake, Lucy on one hip. Frank led Beth out to the verandah.

David's eyes lit up when he saw her, and a small answering smile warmed Beth's face briefly. But they both looked serious as they faced the minister. Frank thought he felt Beth's hand tremble when he was asked "Who giveth this Woman to be married to this Man?"; almost, he thought, as if she feared he might refuse to do so. He felt Lizzie's eyes boring into the back of his head, and realised that he had hesitated for a moment. 'I do,' he said quietly, sensing Beth's relief as the words were uttered. He relinquished her hand and took his seat beside Lizzie for the remainder of the short service.

'I pronounce that they be man and wife together,' the minister said. David and Beth turned to face their guests, and Frank heard a murmur of approval that he felt no urge to join in.

'I hope to God I've done the right thing,' he muttered under his breath.

'Of course you have,' said Lizzie, as sharp-eared as if he had been one of her children. 'Now shut up about it before anyone else hears you.'

After the ceremony there were photographs to be taken. Old Mr Hatfield, who had served as Ruatane's photographer for many years, had become too tottery to haul his heavy equipment about, and had sold it to an energetic young man who had recently moved into the district. Young Mr Hart rushed about cheerfully, attempting to coax a matching enthusiasm from his subjects.

'Come along, there's no need to look so solemn!' he said. 'I'm sure you can all manage a smile for the camera on such a happy occasion.'

Frank knew he must look as sombre as he felt. He saw Lizzie and Amy smiling brightly, while Rosie was clearly revelling in the attention, and seemed to be cajoling Mr Hart into taking more photographs of her than were strictly necessary, but Beth and David stayed resolutely solemn. Frank might have thought Beth was already regretting her marriage, had he not seen her slip her hand into David's whenever she thought no one was looking at them.

'Ugh! Whatever is that animal doing?' Frank heard Susannah say. She gave a small squeal and moved away from the wedding party, but Beth laughed aloud.

'Look what Pip's got!'

Frank followed her gaze and saw the little black kitten walking towards Beth, stiff-legged and tail quivering with pride, a mouse clamped firmly in its jaws. It dropped the thoroughly dead mouse at her feet and looked up, clearly expecting praise.

Beth thrust her bouquet at Maisie and scooped up the kitten. 'What a clever boy.' She kissed the kitten on the top of its head. 'He's given us a wedding present, Davie!'

David fussed over the kitten with her, the two of them smiling and talking quietly. Beth looked happy and at ease for the first time all day. She persuaded Mr Hart to take a photograph of herself and David with the kitten, then insisted on taking the kitten up to the verandah and placing it on her lap when they were called for the meal.

The wedding was small, but some formalities could not be avoided. Frank made a brief speech, thanking the guests for coming and wishing the bride and groom every happiness. When David rose to make his own speech, Frank saw his hands shaking slightly as he gripped the edge of the table. Frank recalled how terrifying he had once found it to speak in front of a group of people, even one such as this, where everyone was known to him. Despite himself, he felt a tiny trace of sympathy for David.

David thanked everyone for their good wishes, then looked over at Frank. 'And thanks, Uncle Frank, for letting me marry Beth,' he finished in a rush. He sat down in evident relief, to a ripple of laughter from the guests.

After lunch Arthur and Edie remained sitting enthroned in the two most comfortable chairs, and Lily spent much of the time in the parlour playing the piano, but the other guests milled about, chatting to each other and to the wedding party.

'They grow up fast, eh?'

Frank turned to find Bill at his elbow. 'Yes, they do. Too fast.'

'Must be hard giving one of your girls away. I'm not looking forward to it with Emma.'

'It's harder some times than others,' Frank said in a low voice. Bill cast a quizzical look at him, but Frank did not elaborate. He suspected Lizzie had entrusted Lily with the knowledge of Beth's pregnancy, and it seemed likely enough that Lily would have told her husband, but this marriage was not something he wanted to discuss, even with Bill. He mumbled an excuse and moved away.

Lizzie saw him standing by himself, and brought a mug of beer over to him. Frank glanced around at the guests; his mood darkened when he saw David clutching a full mug.

'He's getting through that drink pretty fast,' he muttered to Lizzie. 'I saw him downing one a couple of minutes ago.'

'Well, it's not going to do him much harm drinking lemonade, is it? And we've got plenty of it.'

'Lemonade?' Frank echoed. 'You sure it's not beer?'

'Of course it's not. Dave doesn't drink.'

'Doesn't he?' said Frank, startled. 'I didn't know that.'

'You would if you took any notice of things. No, he promised his ma years and years ago that he'd never drink, and he's kept to it, even when he was away working at that mine place. He saw how his father got when he had too much, and Dave didn't want to turn out the same.'

'Humph,' Frank said, unable to find anything to counter this unexpected piece of information. 'Well, I suppose that's something.'

'He's not his father, you know.'

'I never said he was.'

Lizzie pursed her lips at him, but let the subject drop. 'They'll be wanting to get away soon. Make sure you catch Dave first and tell him you'll do his milking for him tomorrow morning.'

'I don't know about that,' Frank said, aware that he was embarking on an argument he was likely to lose. 'I don't know if it suits me to. We'll be milking till lunchtime if we have to do his as well.'

'It won't be that late, don't talk rot. Anyway, that wouldn't hurt you, just this once. You don't begrudge the boy a lie-in, do you? He'll have to milk this afternoon, you know.'

'That's his look-out. It's a silly time of year to get married.'

'Well, he didn't have a lot of choice, did he?'

'Yes, he did,' Frank said grimly. 'I don't see why I should do his milking. It's not as if he deserves it, the way he's carried on.'

He belatedly noticed how close to him Amy was passing, just as Lizzie gave him a sharp dig in the ribs. Amy's serene countenance showed no sign that she had heard, but Frank felt an uncomfortable stab of guilt to go with the after-effects of Lizzie's jab. 'Oh, all right, then, I'll do it for him.'

David looked at him warily when he approached. 'No need to worry about your milking in the morning,' Frank said.

'No, there isn't. Uncle John said they'd do it for me.'

'Oh,' Frank was taken aback. 'Well, that's all right then. You're sorted out.'

David sought Beth's eyes, then looked back at Frank. 'We thought we might get going about now.'

'Did you?' Frank said, unable to think of anything more useful to say.

He found Lizzie at his elbow. 'Are you two off? You'd better give me a kiss then, Dave, now you're my son-in-law.'

David obliged readily enough, and Beth embraced her mother and Amy. Tears welled in her eyes as the emotion of the day threatened to overwhelm her. 'Come on, don't be silly,' Lizzie said, but she gave Beth another hug, produced one of the extra handkerchiefs she always had about her person, and wiped the tears away quite gently. 'You'll be all right,' she said, tucking the handkerchief up Beth's sleeve.

Beth turned to her father, hesitated, then allowed herself to be enfolded in his arms. He thought he felt a suppressed sob, and held her more tightly, but after a few moments Beth pulled away.

Aware of Lizzie's eyes on him, he shook hands with David. 'You look after her,' Frank said, his voice made rough by the tightening in his throat.

'I will, Uncle Frank.'

The gig was brought around by Joe, with Mickey and Danny coming along behind leading three cows. Along with her kitten, a small bundle of clothes and an old pharmacopoeia that Richard had given Frank, but which had immediately been taken over by Beth as inspiration for her various animal remedies, Beth was leaving home taking with her the cows that Frank insisted were hers: Jewel, the once-sickly calf she had reared into a fine creature, and Jewel's two heifer offspring. The cows wore halters, and were tethered to the gig on long leashes. It would mean a slow walk to David's farm, but the distance was short.

David helped Beth into the gig. He climbed in after her, and they set off.

Amy waved as the gig pulled away, the young couple's attempt at leaving quietly thwarted by the hoots and yells of Beth's younger brothers. She was glad to see things settled for David, but mingled with her happiness was an awareness that her house would be a very different place from now on.

A voice interrupted her thoughts. 'Your dress is quite lovely, Amy,' Susannah, said, admiring the black satin gown. 'Really, you look very nice indeed.'

'Thank you,' Amy said, startled by a compliment from such an unexpected source.

'You surely didn't get that made in Ruatane?'

'No, it's from Auckland. Sarah's dressmaker made it for me.' There seemed no need to tell Susannah just how many other dresses had been ordered at the same time.

'Really?' Amy was quite sure Susannah was wondering how Amy could have afforded such a gown, and perhaps speculating on whether Sarah had paid for it. 'You were very fortunate to be able to stay with Miss Millish.'

'Yes, I was. Sarah's been very kind to me.'

There was a brief, awkward silence, which was broken by Susannah. 'I think it's very nice that your son should be marrying Lizzie's daughter, with the two of you always being such friends,' she said, her manner stiff, but her sentiments genuine as far as Amy could tell. 'You must be pleased to have him marrying so well. And... and I'm glad things are easier for you these days,' she finished in something of a rush.

And I'm glad for Tom's sake that you're in such a good mood, was the thought that came to Amy, but she contented herself with a simple, 'Thank you. It's good of you to say so.'

Susannah inclined her head and moved away, and Amy looked around at the remains of the meal. There were no servants here to pick up after her, even if she was wearing one of her Auckland gowns. She gathered up some empty plates and carried them to the kitchen.

It would be strange for her to spend the night in Lizzie's house, and to share a bed in the girls' room. And it would be a good deal stranger for her to share her own house with Beth.

It was indeed strange, and not something Amy found as easy to accept as she had hoped. She did love Beth, and loved her all the more for how

183

much she clearly cared for David, but Amy could not watch her own special place in David's life evaporate without feeling a pang of loss. Beth came first with him now.

It had to be so, Amy knew; it should be so, even if it never had been between Charlie and her. She had no right to feel resentment.

But it was not easy to consider things sensibly; especially when she had not had a good night's sleep since Beth's arrival. The noise those two made! Beth was such a quietly-spoken girl most of the time that Amy would not have expected to hear her through the wall. And had the bed really creaked so loudly during the years she had shared it with Charlie? She could not remember; but speculating on reasons it might be so much noisier under David than under his father led to thoughts Amy was not comfortable thinking about her own son. It was even worse when the bed head started banging against the wall. The rhythmic thump-thump-thump could not be ignored, even when Amy resorted to putting her head under the covers. When the noise stopped for a time, she lay awake waiting, knowing it would soon start again. David and Beth had sent off for a new bed with some of their wedding present money from Sarah; Amy could only hope that it would be a quieter one.

In the daytime David often looked more asleep than awake. Beth was almost as bad, but Amy found that concerned her less.

A few weeks after the wedding, she watched as David yawned hugely, rose from the breakfast table and made his way somewhat unsteadily towards the door. He almost missed his footing on the steps, she noted anxiously. A sensible voice inside her head told her that David was quite capable of looking after himself; she ignored it.

'Dave's looking very tired.'

Beth smothered a yawn with her hand. 'Yes, he is,' she said, not quite managing to hide a small, contented smile.

At the sight of that smile, Amy felt her own mouth tighten. 'Dave works hard, you know,' she said, more sharply than she had intended. 'It's all very well, this being just married, but he needs to have a proper night's sleep sometimes.'

Her words sounded prim in her own ears; she was not surprised when Beth looked hurt.

'I think he's all right. He's not complaining, anyway.'

'Well, no, he wouldn't,' Amy said, increasingly uncomfortable. 'It's up to you to look after him. And you should be careful, you know. You need to think about the baby.'

Beth looked startled. 'Could it hurt the baby?'

'I don't know for sure. I'm just saying you need to be careful, that's all.' Amy felt a pang of guilt at Beth's anxious expression; she remembered David's weary face, and resisted the urge to take back her words.

Beth was quiet as the two of them worked in the kitchen. It was barely half an hour before morning tea time when she said, 'I thought I might go and see Ma this morning. Is that all right?'

'Of course it is, Beth,' Amy said, still feeling somewhat guilty. 'You don't need to ask me whether you can go out or not.' She felt even more guilty over her secret delight at the thought of having David to herself over morning tea.

When she judged he must be on his way to the house she set the table for the two of them, and had the tea things and a plate of scones ready by the time he came inside.

'Where's Beth?' were his first words on entering the room.

'She's gone to see Aunt Lizzie. It's just the two of us.' Amy saw disappointment flit across his face, and had to fight down a rush of resentment. 'Just like it used to be, Davie,' she said, trying to make her voice light.

'I suppose it is.'

David turned his full attention on the fresh scones until the plate was empty. Afterwards he talked readily enough to his mother about his morning's work, but Amy noticed how often his gaze flicked across the table, unconsciously seeking the absent Beth. Whenever he realised once again that she was not there, that disappointed look would return.

The house was less bright without Beth, Amy had to admit, if only for the effect her absence had on David. He was lingering longer than usual, no doubt hoping Beth would come back before he had to go outside again. Beth usually went out on the farm with him after morning tea; she and Amy agreed there was not enough work for two women in so small a household as theirs, while Beth delighted in helping David with the animals.

David went off at last, and Amy cleared away their tea things. It occurred to her that this time after morning tea, when she had the house to herself, was the dullest part of her day. Beth, for all her quiet ways, was good company. Amy had grown used to having her about the place; a willing helper and a cheerful companion. Beth, she realised, had become part of them.

For this cause shall a man leave his father and mother, and shall be joined unto his wife; and they two shall be one flesh. The words from the marriage service came to her. David and Beth had certainly become one flesh, but it was more than that: they were like two halves of the same person. It was

185

hard for Amy to imagine that she was needed here. Perhaps, she reflected, it was time David's mother thought about leaving him.

Sarah had the habit of ending every letter by asking when Amy was coming back to her. In the last letter Amy had received, the familiar question was missing; in fact Amy had had the impression Sarah was preoccupied with a problem of some sort. But there was no sense worrying about that; Sarah was sure be more than a match for whatever (or perhaps whoever) was causing her difficulty. It was here on the farm that it was up to Amy to make things right. Sarah would soon enough be pressing her to come to Auckland again. And Amy rather thought she should accept the invitation.

Beth found her mother in the kitchen, holding Benjy's hands as the little boy took tentative steps. Maisie was putting a tray of biscuits into the range. Beth kissed them all, took a seat at the table, then quietly asked her mother if they could talk in private.

Lizzie picked Benjy up and whisked Beth off to the bedroom. 'Something about the baby, is it?' she asked as she plumped herself down on the bed. 'Everything all right?'

Beth took a chair near the window. 'I think so. I just wondered…' Now that it came to the point, she found her question was not easy to ask. 'Ma, can it hurt the baby if you… you know. If you do it a lot.'

'Eh? What are you on about, girl?'

Beth looked away, feeling her colour rise. '*You* know. With your husband.'

'Oh,' Lizzie said, sounding startled. Beth darted a glance at her mother; she looked thoughtful. 'It can't do,' Lizzie announced. 'You lot all turned out healthy. You'll find it can't be done when you get to be a real size, but that's a fair way off yet. You might as well enjoy yourselves for now.'

Relief flooded through Beth. 'Thanks, Ma.'

'You can ask your Aunt Amy things about the baby, you know. She hasn't had as many babies as me, but she can tell you what you need to know.'

Beth looked away again. 'I don't want to ask her things.'

'Why not?' Lizzie asked sharply. 'Aren't you getting on with her?'

'I thought I was. But now she thinks I'm not looking after Davie properly, and I am. She said I—'

'Now, don't you go carrying tales,' Lizzie interrupted. 'I don't want to hear a word of it. You just be a good girl for your Aunt Amy. She hasn't had things easy, you know.'

'I know she hasn't,' Beth said, resigned to losing the argument before it had begun.

Her mother was silent for several moments. 'You know she hasn't, do you?' she said at last. 'I'm not so sure about that. What's Dave told you about his ma and pa?'

'A little bit. He hasn't said much, but I know Uncle Charlie used to hit Aunt Amy sometimes. That's why P—' She stopped herself just in time. Her father's insinuation that David might be capable of hitting Beth was a detail she had chosen not to share with her mother. Annoyed as she still was with him over what he had said to David, she was not quite annoyed enough to get him into that amount of trouble. 'I know he doesn't like talking about it, though.'

'No, and he's quite right not to. The man was his father, after all. That's all very well, but I think perhaps it's time I told you a thing or two.'

Benjy wriggled on her lap. Lizzie opened her bodice and put him to her breast.

'He did used to hit her,' she said when the baby was suckling contentedly. 'Right from when they were first married. I'd see bruises on her, for all she'd try and cover them up.'

'Bruises?' Beth echoed. 'I thought—'

'You thought it was just the odd slap,' her mother finished for her. 'Lots of men think it's all right to treat their wives like that—not your father, I might add—and the law says they can do it. I don't think many of them are as bad as your Uncle Charlie was, though. You were only about Benjy's age when he did the worst of it, so Dave must have only been three or so. He mightn't even remember it.'

'I think he might,' Beth murmured. Some of David's vaguer remarks, quickly stifled, were now making more sense to her.

'She'd never talk about how he was carrying on. It was only that I popped in to see her not long after it happened.' Her mother fell silent again for a time. 'Her face. It was that cut and swollen you wouldn't have known it was her. He'd taken his fists to her as if he was fighting another man. Not just her face, either—she could hardly stand up, let alone walk. It's my belief he kicked...' She left the sentence unfinished. 'I think he jolly near killed her that time.'

'I didn't know,' Beth whispered.

'No, of course you didn't. It's not something to gossip about—and don't you go telling anyone else this stuff, either. Not Maudie or anyone. I'm only telling you because you need to understand a few things.'

'I won't tell anyone, Ma.'

'She told me he never laid a hand on her after that, but he still used to talk nasty to her all the time. And he'd have kept her locked up in the house if he could—she had to ask him every time she so much as wanted to go next door, and as often as not he'd say no, just to be contrary. That's the sort of thing she had to put up with all those years. I don't know how she stayed as bright as she did. She had her boys of course, but... well, I don't want to speak ill of Mal, but he was a trial to her, getting into bad company and all. And then she had the upset of him going off and dying like that, and your Uncle Charlie getting worse than ever. The only one she had for company was Dave. Do you understand what I'm saying, girl?'

'I know Aunt Amy's very fond of Dave—he is of her, too.'

'He was the one that kept her going, it seemed to me. When he went off to Waihi, I was worried she might go funny in the head. But we got him back in the end. He's been a good son to her, and you can't expect her to dance a jig about having to share him with someone else, even when it's you. I expect the two of you go off to bed early?'

'A bit early,' Beth admitted.

'And she's left sitting up on her own, when she's been used to having Dave for company. And when the three of you are together, he wants to talk to you as often as not—probably more than he does to his ma. Now, I'm not saying you're doing anything wrong,' Lizzie said; Beth realised her sense of guilt must be showing on her face. 'It's natural the two of you want to spend all the time together you can. I'm just saying you need to think about what it's like for your Aunt Amy.'

'What should I do, Ma?' Beth asked, still reeling from her mother's revelations. 'I want us all to get on and everything.'

'Just be patient. Things'll sort themselves out soon enough, especially once the baby arrives. She'll be that pleased—and you and Dave will settle down more, too, when you've got a baby to think about.'

Benjy had lost interest in feeding; Lizzie buttoned her bodice and held him against her shoulder. 'You'll be all right. Your Aunt Amy's very fond of you, she always has been.'

'I'm fond of her, too,' said Beth. 'I really am.'

Beth rode back to David's farm, so lost in her thoughts that the horse found its own way with little guidance. She entered the kitchen determined to say something to make up for any hurt she might have caused her aunt, but before she could utter a word Amy had crossed the room and placed a kiss on her cheek.

'I'm glad you're back,' Amy said. 'It's been too quiet without you.'

188

'Has it?' Beth said, mildly stunned at the warmth of her reception. She was still struggling to find the right words when Amy spoke again.

'Beth, I'm sure everything'll be all right with the baby. You wouldn't do anything that'd hurt it. And I think you're making a good job of looking after Dave.' She reached out and touched Beth's arm. 'I hope you know I'm very happy about you and Dave being married.'

Beth flung her arms around Amy's waist and felt herself enfolded in a hug. 'Thank you, Aunt Amy. And I do want to look after Davie—and the baby—and I like living here with you.'

Amy kissed her again, then extricated herself. 'I can finish getting lunch on. I think you should go and find Dave—he missed you at morning tea.' She smiled at Beth. 'He's a lot happier when you're here.'

15

A week after the wedding, Susannah had a cable from her sister to tell her their mother was considered to be in her last hours. Thomas could not detect any signs of grief as she calmly made arrangements for the two of them to travel to Auckland; not even when a further cable the morning before they were to sail told her that her mother had died. 'We'll be there in time for the funeral,' she said, as if that were the only thing to be concerned about.

Thomas had not seen George for some weeks; though his brother had, of course, been invited to the wedding, he had not felt it necessary to interrupt his sailing schedule in order to attend. Thomas knew that George would not be particularly interested in their grandmother's death, but he left a message for him at Ruatane's wharf in case his brother should call in while they were out of town and wonder where they were.

They arrived in Auckland the evening before the funeral was to take place, and were driven to his Uncle Henry's. To Thomas, the house seemed huge. The drawing room (as he was promptly informed it was called when he mistakenly referred to it as "the parlour") was sombre, its mantelpiece draped in black crepe while the house was in mourning. A constant stream of visitors seemed to call during the day to express their condolences. Many of them said they remembered Thomas from the previous time his mother had taken him to Auckland, nine years before when his grandfather had died; one or two ancient-looking women even claimed to remember seeing him on an earlier trip, one Thomas had only vague memories of, though he did recall that Amy had been with them on that journey. Thomas was not used to meeting so many unfamiliar people at once, and when at last he was able to go to bed he soon fell into an exhausted sleep.

At the funeral, his main concern was his mother. Although she continued to appear calm, Thomas wondered if the occasion might prove too much for her. But she remained serene and composed. Her only display of emotion was her surprise and evident pleasure when George arrived at the church while they were waiting to go in.

'I got Tom's note, and we were bringing the boat up anyway, so I thought I'd see if I could get here in time,' George said cheerfully. He looked more smartly turned out than Thomas had seen him in years, wearing a suit that appeared freshly pressed.

He and Thomas escorted their mother into the church, and sat either side of her during the service. On such a solemn occasion Susannah would not allow herself anything more than the hint of a smile, but Thomas was sure she was delighted at having the presence of both her sons. He suspected she was equally delighted that George took himself off soon after the funeral, staying just long enough for Susannah to display the two of them, but not long enough for any of the other mourners to start asking awkward questions about George's somewhat irregular private life.

Henry Kendall considered himself a fortunate man. He was successful in his profession; he had a wife who made his house a comfortable place to live, was a good hostess, and was for the most part sensible; and he had five fine children. It was hardly Constance's fault that her brother had so little to recommend him. Henry tolerated Jimmy's presence when obliged to, but he took no pleasure in it.

A family gathering at his house on an evening soon after the funeral of his mother-in-law was an occasion for the exercise of such tolerance. Of Henry's children, only Laura was present. His sons had returned to Wellington, where they both had positions in the public service, the day after the funeral, and his older daughters were at home with their own families. But Susannah and Thomas were still staying with the Kendalls, and Jimmy and Charlotte had been invited to dinner.

Jimmy seemed in no hurry to return to his own home after the meal, and Henry was treated to the sight of Jimmy helping himself to the best port. There was little chance of Henry's drawing Thomas into the men's conversation with Jimmy there. Jimmy's main topic of discourse was one that he appeared to find endlessly interesting: himself. After a modest amount of port he was merely boring; given long enough in the vicinity of the decanter, Henry knew he was quite capable of becoming offensive. It was a relief to be able to use the excuse of the ladies waiting in the drawing room to persuade Jimmy to bid the port a reluctant farewell.

Henry saw Susannah's face light up at the sight of Thomas when the men entered the room,. She indicated the space she had been saving for him, and Thomas took a seat on the sofa at her side.

Constance was looking more her naturally lively self this evening than she had in some time, Henry noted with pleasure. She and her mother had been close, and old Mrs Taylor had lived with the Kendalls for the last few years. Her mother's long illness had been a strain on Constance. Henry had engaged a nurse as soon as it became apparent that his mother-in-law needed a level of care he considered too much to ask of Constance, but she had still spent much of each day with her mother, and had watched her decline with mounting distress. Mrs Taylor had ceased to show any awareness of those around her some weeks before she finally slipped away. Henry was sure that mingled with Constance's genuine grief at her mother's passing was a sense of a burden having been lifted from her.

Laura was at the piano, playing a rather wistful piece that Henry thought might have been by Schumann. She looked up from her music and smiled at her father, then returned her full attention to her playing.

Laura had been a great support to Constance during this time, Henry knew. She had insisted on sharing the duty of sitting at her grandmother's bedside, so that her mother should not feel obliged to spend all her free moments there. Laura would read to the old lady, or occasionally sing one of her grandmother's favourite songs.

If anything could have given comfort to the dying woman, Henry thought, it would have been Laura's presence. Mrs Taylor had always doted on Henry's children, particularly his daughters. Henry's father-in-law had left the family home to his widow, causing Jimmy much indignation (and thus leading Henry to remember his late father-in-law with a good deal more affection than he might otherwise have); she had sold the house when she moved in with Constance and Henry, and over the years since had spent most of the proceeds on gifts for her grandchildren. Mrs Taylor's last major purchase before the onset of her illness had been the beautiful piano that now held pride of place in the drawing room, as she had considered their old one not a fit match for Laura's talent.

Laura finished the piece and came to sit between her father and Thomas. She spoke quietly with her cousin for a time; Henry had noticed that Thomas spoke more easily to Laura than he did to his older relations.

After a few minutes Constance caught Laura's eye and indicated the mantel clock. Laura nodded, and rose from her chair. She kissed her parents, and said goodnight to their guests with careful politeness and varying degrees of warmth; Henry fancied that Jimmy was not a favourite with her. Thomas actually stood to see her to the door, increasing Henry's already favourable opinion of him.

Henry had been impressed by how sensible a young man Thomas was. It took a little effort to draw him out of what Henry realised was shyness, but he found that, making allowances for Thomas' limited education, he was an interesting conversationalist and an attentive listener. He was also clearly a thoughtful son, constantly consulting his mother's wishes and checking on her comfort.

Henry had not seen Susannah since her father's death, nine years before. He found her greatly changed, and very much for the better. Gone was the stiffness that had always made him somewhat uncomfortable around her; gone was the slight air of self-pity; and best of all, gone was her pathetic attachment to Jimmy.

On her previous visit, Henry had observed her attempts to gain any sort of attention from Jimmy, and her distress at being studiously ignored. Susannah had not made herself conspicuous over the matter; her self-control was too rigid for that; but Henry prided himself on being a keen observer of people, and on noticing details others would not. He was quite sure that even if Jimmy had noticed Susannah's distress, he would not have been particularly concerned by it. As far as Henry could tell, Jimmy Taylor went through life blissfully untroubled by pangs of conscience over any pain he might have caused anyone else.

But this was a new, confident Susannah, who showed polite interest when her brother spoke, but who otherwise ignored him, much as Henry did. She seemed quite indifferent to his comings and goings, paying far more attention to Thomas, and to Henry's own family.

Her self-confidence had another effect, one that pleased Henry greatly. One of the few matters in which he considered his wife less than sensible was the delight she had always taken in needling Susannah. It was clear to Henry that Constance had been far more fortunate in life than had Susannah, not least in having married him; it seemed to him that that should have inspired her to be kind to her sister, rather than to rub the poor woman's nose in her deficiencies.

Things had become particularly unpleasant on Susannah's previous visit, when Charlotte had perceived her as a useful target for whatever her own frustrations were, and had taken what seemed to Henry a malicious pleasure in subtle but pointed attacks. Constance, who had what Henry had noted as an unerring instinct for backing the winning side, had joined forces with Charlotte in goading Susannah, to the point where Henry had been forced to scold his wife in private, and insist that she moderate her conduct.

There was no need for him to consider such a step now. While Charlotte was still making an occasional attempt at unsettling Susannah, Constance had observed Susannah's new poise much as Henry had, and she appeared to have changed her allegiance accordingly. Henry was relieved at the resulting harmony, especially as Susannah and Thomas were guests in his house.

Henry had noticed Thomas stifling yawns even before the men left the dining room. Thomas stayed in the drawing room just long enough to be sure his mother was comfortable before he made his excuses and went off to bed, only a few minutes after Laura had gone.

'Goodness, what early hours you must keep in the country, Susannah,' Charlotte remarked as Thomas left the room. 'But I imagine there's very little society of any sort to oblige you to go out.' She bestowed a condescending smile. 'It must be wonderful to have such a simple life, and not be bothered with constant invitations.'

'Actually, Charlotte, there's a good deal of pleasant society,' Susannah said calmly. 'But I do most of my visiting in the daytime. In the evenings I'm happy enough with Thomas for company.'

If Charlotte's lip had curled just a fraction more, Henry reflected, her smile would be more accurately called a sneer. 'Oh, yes, I'm sure he's excellent company for you, though perhaps his conversation is just a little limited?'

'I must say I've been taking a great deal of pleasure in Thomas's company these last few days,' Henry put in before Susannah had a chance to respond. 'He's a fine young man, Susannah. You must be very proud.'

Susannah turned a warm smile on him. 'Thank you, Henry. Yes, I'm very proud indeed of Thomas. In fact I'm proud of both my sons. Of course I'm only too ready to hear my sons being praised,' she said, turning her attention back to Charlotte. Her smile remained, though its warmth had gone. 'I believe I'm not unusual in that regard. I'm afraid, Charlotte, that you must excuse a mother's partiality.'

'You're quite right, Susannah,' Constance chimed in. 'I know I can be positively foolish about my children at times—I always think they're so clever and talented. We just can't help it, can we?' She beamed at Susannah in matronly pride.

Henry glanced from this show of sisterly unity over to Charlotte, in time to see her condescending expression slip for a moment, to be briefly replaced by a wounded look. He could find it in his heart to feel a degree of sympathy, both for her childlessness and for having married Jimmy.

He searched for a useful change of subject, and soon latched on one. 'Susannah, did Constance tell you that we met an acquaintance of yours earlier in the year? Well, I should say a family member—I believe she's your stepdaughter. Mrs Stewart, was it?'

'Oh, yes, I remember,' said Constance. 'We met her when we were out on Mr Dewar's boat. She was very smartly turned out, I recall—in quite the latest fashion. And with the *prettiest* hat.'

'How interesting,' Susannah said in a tone that implied otherwise. 'The evenings do seem to be getting warmer, don't they?'

Henry was surprised by her evident reluctance to discuss their mutual acquaintance, but he knew that stepmothers and stepdaughters did not always have the smoothest of relationships; this seemed to be the case with Susannah.

Constance seemed oblivious to Susannah's discomfort. 'And she was staying with Sarah Millish! Miss Millish hardly ever has anyone to stay, she must have been very taken with Mrs Stewart.'

This seemed a line of discourse that gave Susannah more pleasure. 'Oh, dear Miss Millish. We all became such good friends when she was staying in Ruatane.'

'Did you really?' Constance said, clearly taken aback. 'How odd. I sent invitations several times to have her bring Mrs Stewart here to dine, but she always made some excuse or other. However did you come to meet her?'

'We attended the same soirées.'

Charlotte gave a little laugh. 'You have soirées down there? How droll that must be—are they held in barns?'

'No,' Susannah said coolly. 'They are held in houses. Thomas and I are always invited to the best of them. Jack's niece married rather well, and she often holds soirées.'

Jimmy snorted, catching Henry's attention. 'You mean Lizzie? But she married Frank!' Jimmy seemed to be taking more notice of this talk of visits and soirées than Henry would have expected. 'You remember him, Charlotte, we met him on Queen Street one day. Straight from the farm—I almost expected to see the mud still on his boots.'

'Not really,' Charlotte said idly. 'I find it hard to keep track of all these country cousins of yours.'

'Well, Frank's not the most memorable of chaps,' said Jimmy. 'A decent enough fellow in his own way, I suppose, but hardly what I'd call marrying well.'

'I beg to differ,' Susannah said, unperturbed. 'Frank's done very well for himself. Among other things, he's chairman of the dairy co-operative.'

'Oh, really?' said Henry, finding himself well-disposed to this Frank fellow if for no other reason than Jimmy's professed disdain. 'Then he must be a person of some consequence in the area. Those co-operatives are important affairs these days.'

'And these farmhouse soirées,' said Charlotte, her condescending smile restored, 'what do they have as far as music goes? Does everyone sing along and stamp their feet to rousing tunes?'

'We're rather fortunate there,' said Susannah, still imperturbably calm. We have a very fine pianist who studied under some of the best teachers in Auckland. In fact it's Lily who provided our introduction to Miss Millish, as they're cousins.' She cast a glance around the room, checking that she had everyone's attention. 'And Lily is married to one of Jack's nephews.'

Had Susannah been a man, she might have made a good courtroom lawyer, Henry thought to himself as he admired her performance. She had certainly gained the ascendancy with that piece of information.

She had also irritated Constance. 'Well,' Constance sniffed, 'I'm sure I've no idea why Miss Millish should give herself airs and graces. What makes her so grand, when you think about it?'

'You're speaking of a young lady who is one of our most valued clients, my dear,' Henry reminded her.

'Oh, I know all that,' Constance said impatiently. 'But really, with her background? With no one knowing what sort of people she came from? She certainly has no business looking down on anyone.'

'Whatever do you mean?' Susannah asked, clearly startled. 'Surely the Millishes are one of the best families in Auckland?'

'Yes, Mr and Mrs Millish were,' said Constance. 'But Miss Sarah came from nowhere.' She observed Susannah's puzzlement, and her eyes lit up with the delight of having a revelation to impart. 'But don't you know, Susannah? They adopted Miss Sarah. Surely you knew that?'

'I had no idea.' Susannah's brow furrowed in thought. 'She's younger than Thomas, I think, so that must have happened after I left Auckland.'

'Miss Millish came of age last year,' Henry said. 'I recall a good deal of to-ing and fro-ing in the office when she was taking control of her own affairs.'

'Then she was born the year after George,' said Susannah, still looking thoughtful.

'But surely she was adopted from within the family, or least from among their acquaintance,' Charlotte said, frowning. 'They wouldn't have taken a child they knew nothing about—not people like that, who moved in the best society.'

'Oh, but that's just what they did,' Constance insisted. 'Henry knows all about it.'

'Well, I do recall it somewhat,' Henry allowed. 'Though I wasn't directly involved—I've never had the honour of handling the Millish affairs myself. But I remember discussions in the office when it was in process. They only had the one child—a son—and Mrs Millish dearly wanted a daughter. Dewar put them in contact with a lady who arranged such things, and that's how they came to find little Sarah.'

He smiled at the memory. 'It was supposedly for his wife's sake that Fred Millish went to so much trouble, but he was as besotted with Sarah as she was—probably more so. Especially after their boy died. I remember he used to bring her into the office occasionally, right from when she was quite a small girl. Such a bright little thing, she was. She had a way about her, even then—she'd look straight at you, with those huge blue eyes of hers, and somehow you felt you needed to make a good account of yourself.'

'But a child they knew nothing of,' Charlotte said, her distaste clear from her expression. 'That would be like taking in one of those grubby urchins one sometimes sees playing in the gutters. It's likely enough the mother was a woman of ill repute. Think of bringing such a child into one's house! It might be diseased. Or it might be inclined to wickedness—with a mother like that, it might carry bad blood.'

To Henry's annoyance, Constance was nodding in prim agreement. 'I must say I never quite approved of the idea myself,' she said.

'Fortunately for the child in question,' Henry said, making no attempt to keep the sharpness out of his voice, 'the Millishes didn't think in that way. Fortunately for them as well—Sarah brought them both a great deal of joy.' He gave Constance a reproving glance, and was pleased to see a look of chagrin flit across her face. 'And in fact—not that it's any of our business—they did know a little about the mother. She was a very young girl, from some tiny place out in the countryside. I can't find it in my heart to think ill of such a poor, misused creature. As for the father…' Henry grimaced. 'I believe we can make a reasonable assessment of his character by the fact that the girl was left to fend for herself in such a state. I have no desire for any further knowledge of such a man as that.'

The room was briefly silent. Constance looked somewhat abashed, and Charlotte's expression of distaste had slipped a little. And Susannah… Henry looked at Susannah in surprise. She had not said a word for some time, but she was gripping the arms of her chair so tightly that he could see her knuckles whitening.

She became aware that she was being observed. She placed her hands in her lap and looked across the room, as if the far wall had suddenly become of interest to her.

Prudishness, Henry decided. The mention of women of ill repute must have offended her sensibilities. Though it was surely not prudishness leading Jimmy to stare so intently at Susannah, who was resolutely ignoring his attention.

Constance remarked on the likelihood of fine weather the next day;

Susannah made an equally inconsequential response, and the strained moment passed. After a few minutes of such idle conversation around the room, Susannah rose from her chair.

'I think I shall retire for the night. I find myself rather tired this evening. Good night, everyone.'

She left the room too quickly for Charlotte to have the opportunity to make any further remarks about country hours.

Henry stood politely to see her out of the room, then strolled over to the mantelpiece, where he had left his cup of tea. When he looked back, he saw Jimmy slipping out of the room in Susannah's wake.

Jimmy was certainly taking a good deal more notice of his sister than was his habit. Henry contrived to cross the room without making it obvious he was following Jimmy; fortunately Constance and Charlotte were sharing some piece of interesting gossip. He paused in the doorway, from where he had a good view of the base of the staircase.

Susannah had one hand on the stair rail, and was standing on the lowest step with her face on a level with Jimmy's. They were conversing rapidly, but in low voices, so that Henry could not make out what they were saying. Susannah was clearly becoming more agitated by the moment. Her voice rose enough for Henry to catch the words, 'Of course I didn't know! And I don't wish to speak of it. Leave me alone.'

She made to turn away and mount the stairs, but Jimmy took hold of her arm. When she attempted to wrest it free, he took a firmer hold and brought his face closer to hers.

Henry took a few steps forward, deliberately making enough noise to be heard. 'Is everything all right, Susannah?' he asked.

Susannah gracefully removed her arm from Jimmy's grasp. 'Of course. I was just saying good night to James.' She nodded to both men, and glided off up the stairs.

Henry turned a quizzical look on Jimmy, who met it with his usual bluff smile. 'It's about time I took Charlotte home, I suppose,' said Jimmy. 'Any chance of a nightcap first, Henry? I noticed your brandy decanter's looking comfortably full.'

'Of course,' Henry said resignedly. He glanced up the stairs, but Susannah was already out of sight. It seemed unlikely that whatever was going on between those two needed his further involvement; Henry resolved to try and forget it.

16

'There's a gentleman at the door asking to see you, Miss Sarah,' said Nellie. 'He sent in his card.' She passed Sarah a small silver tray.

Sarah took the card from it. 'Mr Taylor,' she murmured. 'Well, well.'

For a moment, she considered having Nellie send the man packing. Had Amy still been with her, she would certainly have done so. He had called several times before, asking for Amy; on each visit Sarah had instructed the maid to tell him Mrs Stewart was out, until the last such occasion when Mr Taylor had been informed, quite truthfully, that she had returned to Ruatane.

There had been no further visits since then until today, and this time it was Sarah herself he was asking to see. He would be sure to call again; and again. Sarah had generally found it better to deal with unpleasant tasks promptly.

'Send him through to my study in a few minutes, Nellie,' she said. 'There'll be no need to bring refreshments, he won't be staying long.'

Her study was the obvious choice for Sarah when it came to receiving this unwelcome guest. She always felt at her strongest here, where the very furniture held memories of her father. With his massive desk placed between her and the world, she felt ready to take on a far more formidable opponent than she expected Mr Taylor to be. The photographs of her father were placed so that he appeared to be watching her as she sat at his desk, lending his silent support. Sarah's eye fell on the picture of herself with Amy; she took it up and carefully placed it in a drawer. She would not allow that man to leer at it.

She sat behind the desk and ran through the possible reasons Taylor might have for inviting himself to her house. A purely business meeting seemed unlikely. And he knew that Amy was no longer in Auckland. So the most likely explanation was something Sarah had known to be a possibility ever since Amy had reported her meeting with the man: he had discovered his connection to herself.

He entered the room wearing a smile Sarah was sure he considered charming. 'My dear Miss Millish,' he said, leaning forward and waiting for Sarah to extend her hand. But she left both hands resting lightly on top of the desk.

'Mr Taylor,' she said coolly, nodding towards the chair she had placed before it. She had made sure it was the least comfortable the room held. 'To what do I owe this unexpected visit?' She had no intention of referring to it as a pleasure; still less as an honour.

He kept his awkward leaning posture for a moment, then accepted that she was not going to proffer her hand. He took the indicated seat and perched on its front edge, still smiling brightly.

'I imagine that what I'm about to tell you will come as quite a surprise—a pleasant one, I hope.'

'I rather doubt that,' Sarah murmured. That smile of his was becoming more and more irritating.

'I hardly know how to begin.'

'Then let me begin for you. Let us waste no more of each other's time, Mr Taylor. I'm quite aware of who you are in relation to me. When Mrs Stewart was staying with me and had that rather unfortunate encounter with you, she told me all that I needed to know.'

'Oh, that makes it so much easier.' He gazed at Sarah with what she took for a proprietorial air. 'My dear girl. You talk of wasting time—the years we've wasted through not knowing each other! To think of our living in the same city and not knowing we were father and daughter!'

Sarah felt herself stiffen. He had no right to the name of father; her father was the man who had sat at this desk. She gripped the arms of the chair that had been his, and stared coolly at the man who dared try to usurp his title.

'Let there be no more wasted time. My dear Sarah—I may call you that?' His expression made it clear that he felt he already knew the answer.

'No, you may not,' Sarah said sharply. 'Mr Taylor, an accident of blood links us. Nothing more than that. I have no desire for a closer acquaintance with you, and I suggest you put such an idea out of your mind.' She pulled the bell cord to summon a maid.

His smile barely wavered. 'I'm prepared to be patient, my dear. I realise how strange this must seem to you—I'm still getting used to the idea myself of having such a lovely daughter.'

' "Strange" is not precisely the word I would have chosen.' Sarah looked up when she heard Nellie enter the room. 'Nellie will show you out, Mr Taylor. Good day to you.' She lowered her gaze to examine some papers on her desk, glad of the excuse to remove that maddening smile from her view.

'I'll call on you again soon,' he said as he rose from the chair.

'I suggest that in future you request an appointment first,' she said, not looking up from the papers. 'I have a good deal to occupy my time.' She waited until she heard the front door closed behind him before she pushed the papers aside. That, Sarah hoped, would be the last time she would find herself allowing Mr Taylor into her home.

*

Jimmy Taylor left the Millish house feeling thoroughly pleased with himself. Meeting Amy again the previous month had reminded him of that delightful summer long ago; it had also revived his almost extinguished hope of having an heir in spite of Charlotte's failure to provide him with one. But not in his wildest fancies had he dreamed of acquiring a daughter like Sarah Millish.

She was close to perfect. Quite apart from being a young woman any man would be proud to have fathered, she presented opportunities for making his life a good deal more agreeable than it currently was. He foresaw an end to the aggravation of having constantly to ask Charlotte for more money, and the resulting humiliation of being interrogated by his own wife as to where the money was going. It was, of course, completely inappropriate for Charlotte to question him in such a way, but Charlotte sometimes showed herself sadly lacking in proper womanly qualities.

Jimmy blamed his father-in-law for that. Not only had the man put the house he had bought them into Charlotte's name; he had also given her sole control of a substantial bank account, regularly augmented by the generous allowance he paid her. No wonder she was inclined to fancy herself as knowing how to manage money.

The same character flaw was likely to exist in his daughter, unfortunately. Not that it was the girl's fault. But cautious enquiries among his acquaintance had told him that Sarah had complete control of her financial interests, with no man's guiding hand. It was a ridiculous state of affairs, and one that Jimmy intended to rectify.

He would have to tread carefully. Sarah was used to having her own way (another flaw she shared with Charlotte), and it would take her some time to trust him. But it was worth being patient when the prize was so valuable.

He would leave it a few days before visiting again; that would give Sarah time to think things over, and perhaps to wonder if he would return. A small gift next time would do no harm. He needed to gain her affection, and get her to see that he had her best interests at heart. The girl was probably anxious over all her responsibilities, despite her outward show of confidence.

Once he had gained her trust, it would simply be a matter of getting the appropriate legal documents drawn up, giving him overall responsibility for her affairs, and getting Sarah to sign them. That was the good side of Sarah's having complete control over her holdings: all he needed was her signature. There was no one else whom he needed to convince that Sarah's own father was the proper person to watch over her interests.

He had always wanted a son, of course, but in these circumstances a daughter was infinitely preferable. A son would take more convincing that he needed the guidance of a mature man, but women were naturally more malleable, and less capable of understanding complicated matters of finance.

Jimmy stopped in his tracks as a dreadful thought struck him: what if Sarah were to be married? It would be disastrous. And she could be a target for any number of fortune-hunters with selfish motives. That made things rather more difficult. He would have to move more quickly than he had planned, but not so quickly as to risk her taking fright and fancying that his intentions were other than benevolent. In any event, things must be properly settled between them before Sarah married.

It was somewhat odd, though certainly fortunate, that she had not already married. Not only was she a substantial heiress; she resembled her mother enough to be a pretty girl. She could do with being more womanly, of course. It was a pity she hadn't inherited something of Amy's amiable nature, though that made the whole business more of a stimulating challenge.

He lost himself briefly in pleasant recollections of Amy's warm and obliging ways. There had never been any other woman quite like her. If only circumstances had not made it impossible for him to marry her. If only he could have found someone with Amy's nature and Charlotte's material advantages. Jimmy rather thought he might have managed to be faithful to such a woman.

He pulled out his watch and checked the time. Almost four o'clock; it was hardly worth going back to the office now. A few drinks and an early dinner at his club, perhaps. Then a game or two of cards; his luck at the table had not been the best lately, but it must be due to change. Fortune was certainly smiling upon him with the discovery of his daughter.

There would be no need to hurry home after that. There was a certain establishment where they knew his particular tastes. Damnably expensive, but he could afford to treat himself. He could afford a good many things now.

Jimmy sat in his office chair, staring absently at the far wall as he mulled over his plans. It was almost three weeks since his conversation with Sarah. He had attempted to call on her several times since then, but on each occasion had been told she was otherwise engaged. No doubt she was a busy girl, but he suspected it was more a case of her not yet being ready to meet him again. There was probably an element of shyness, which was quite becoming in a girl. He briefly considered penning a letter to her, but rejected the idea almost at once. It was best not to put anything in writing just yet.

A soft knock at the door broke into his thoughts. Jimmy looked over to see his young clerk, Osborne, standing in the doorway.

'What is it, Osborne?'

'Mr Hobbs is here again. He's quite insistent, sir,' Osborne said quickly, before Jimmy could tell him to send the man packing.

Jimmy sighed. 'All right, then, send him in.' He leaned back in his chair and assumed the expression of a man bestowing his valuable attention on one scarcely worthy of the honour.

Mr Hobbs owned a brass foundry; a small concern, with a handful of workers. Jimmy had done him something of a favour by putting an order for the fittings in a row of worker's cottages into his hands. The order had been large enough, coupled with Jimmy's suggestion that more business would be likely to come his way, for Hobbs to sell him the fittings at rather a good price, and Jimmy had to admit that his staff had told him the foundry's workmanship was excellent. But the man had become tiresome since, constantly nagging about his payment. Surely he knew that a business the size of Jimmy's could not be expected to pay every little invoice straight away? And naturally Jimmy needed to see that the more important suppliers were paid first. Men like Hobbs simply had to wait their turn.

Mr Hobbs slipped into the room, clutching his hat in his hands. He was a small, balding man in a worn-looking suit. He looked in awe around Jimmy's well-furnished office as he approached the desk.

'Ah, Hobbs,' Jimmy said expansively. 'Sit down, won't you? Now, what can I do for you?'

Mr Hobbs perched on the edge of the indicated chair. 'It's about the money, sir. The account's got quite overdue now.'

'Has it indeed? Dear, dear—I shall have to speak to my clerks about that.' The invoices concerned were in a well-stuffed folder somewhere in his desk, along with others liberally ornamented with "Overdue" or various synonyms.

'It's two hundred and thirty pounds. That's a lot of money for a man such as myself.' Mr Hobbs looked around the wood-panelled office again. 'I've wages to pay, you see, and a family to feed. I'm sorry to be a bother about it,' he added, lowering his gaze.

'Yes, well, I'm in a similar position myself, you know,' said Jimmy. 'The men's wages have to be paid, even if it means going short myself. And cash is just a little tight at the moment—business is brisk enough,' he added quickly, 'but much of my cash is tied up in some promising new developments. You know what it's like, Hobbs, you and I are both men of business. Sometimes one has to be patient with these things.'

Mr Hobbs turned his hat around in his lap. 'Not wanting to be rude, sir, but I've been patient over this for six months now. Patience won't put food on the table, or pay the wages. And now I've got rent due on the factory, and all manner of things I need money for. I need that bill paid, and that's the truth of it.' Having been roused enough to make such a bold speech, he seemed to shrink in on himself.

Jimmy took out his wallet and opened it. 'Now, I'll tell you what— here's five pounds out of my own pocket, just as a gesture of good faith.' He handed the note across his desk. After a moment's hesitation, Mr Hobbs took it, and studied it rather uncertainly.

'And there's no need for you to worry yourself about the rest of it,' Jimmy said. 'I'm going to take you into my confidence, Hobbs. I can see you're an honest fellow, so I'm going to trust you with this. You know of Sarah Millish, I suppose?'

'Miss Millish? Of course, sir.'

'Well—remember, this is in confidence—Miss Millish and I are on the point of coming to a business arrangement that will be highly advantageous to us both. Once that happens, any current difficulties regarding cash will become irrelevant.'

He watched Mr Hobbs puzzling it out. 'So you have dealings with Miss Millish?'

'Yes, I do. It's early days yet, but it's all looking very promising. And, I might add, once things start going forward I'm likely to be able to put a good deal more business your way.' Jimmy saw from Mr Hobbs' eyes that the man had taken the bait. He reeled him in carefully. 'Access to the Millish business, eh, Hobbs. That's worth a bit of patience, isn't it?'

'I suppose so. I can't wait for the whole amount, Mr Taylor.'

'No one's asking you to,' Jimmy said breezily. 'I've given you something on account, and if you come back in a week or two, I'll tell the clerk to have a little something more ready. The Millish business, Hobbs. Just think of that.'

He stood up and strode around to the front of his desk, extending his hand. Mr Hobbs hesitated before shaking the proffered hand. 'Well, I'm sure you have things you need to be doing, Hobbs, so I won't keep you any longer. We'll be speaking again before too long, I've no doubt. Just remember,' he added, giving Mr Hobbs the grin of a fellow conspirator, 'keep the Millish business under your hat for now.'

'I will, Mr Taylor. Thank you very much, sir.'

Mr Hobbs allowed himself to be shepherded out of the door, and Jimmy resumed his comfortable chair. It was time, he reflected, to try another visit to Sarah.

Sarah's letters continued to give Amy the sense that she was preoccupied with an irritating matter. But even if she had been pressing Amy to visit her again, Amy would have felt herself unable to leave the farm. For she had begun to suspect that Beth was unwell.

After having a barely perceptible bump for months, Beth seemed to have swollen almost overnight, so that her pregnancy looked more advanced than its five months. She moved clumsily, and seemed short of breath much of the time. Amy thought the baby must be lying awkwardly, though she was careful to say nothing to Beth that might alarm her. She told herself she was probably worrying needlessly. Beth had always been a healthy girl; there was surely no reason to think she was in any real danger.

Lizzie seemed unconcerned, though Amy suspected Beth made an effort to appear more cheerful when her parents came to visit, as Amy did herself. It helped cover the awkward silences when David and Frank were in the same room. And Lizzie had not been a frequent visitor of late; Benjy had been somewhat feverish during a recent bout of teething, making Lizzie reluctant to take him out of the house since.

But it wrung Amy's heart to see Beth grimace in pain if she moved incautiously. She would only allow Beth to help with the lightest of the household tasks, ones she could do while seated. Beth made little protest; she seemed to have barely enough energy to drag herself around the house.

Her moods swung between lethargy and irritability, both of them uncharacteristic, and with lethargy increasingly gaining the ascendancy. More and more often Beth chose to stay indoors rather than go outside with David. Amy could see that David was becoming anxious, and she did her best not to make him more so. But Beth loved to be out on the farm with him, and to see her unable to rouse the strength worried Amy more than anything else.

Beth rose ponderously from the table and carried a bowl of shelled peas to where Amy stood at the bench. As she turned to go back, she stumbled and almost fell. Amy hurried to her, and helped her back to her chair. She stood with an arm around Beth's shoulders until she saw her relax a little.

'Was it the baby moving?' Amy asked.

Beth shook her head. 'No, it just went all blurry for a bit, and I felt sort of dizzy. I had that yesterday as well.' She rubbed at her belly and grimaced. 'It does hurt here, though, like it's digging into me. Is it going to be like this the whole time?'

Amy hesitated before answering. 'I don't really know, Beth,' she said, choosing her words with care. 'It's different every time. I had a lot more bother with Mal than with Dave.' And the worst time of all with Alexander, but she was careful not to mention that pregnancy, with its sad ending.

She studied Beth's face, puffy and swollen as it was, and with threatened tears. 'It might get easier nearer your time, as the baby shifts. But I think you need to start resting more. How about you go and have a lie-down?'

Without giving Beth the chance to argue, Amy coaxed her upright and led her through to the bedroom. 'I think you should start having a lie-down every afternoon. Is that when things hurt most?'

'They hurt all the time,' Beth said in a small voice.

And it was only December. The hottest months of summer were still to come, with Beth getting larger and more uncomfortable every day. 'Well, perhaps it won't be as bad if you keep the weight off your feet more,' Amy said, trying to sound more cheerful than she felt. 'See if you can sleep for a bit. That always helps.' She kissed Beth's cheek and went out, closing the door behind her.

That Friday, Lizzie sent Danny to David's with a message, inviting them over for Sunday lunch if Beth felt up to an outing. When they failed to appear on the Sunday, Lizzie showed a lack of concern that only increased Frank's annoyance.

'Beth probably just felt like stopping in,' said Lizzie. 'She's getting big now, she's not going to feel like going out much.'

'She might have been too scared to ask him,' Frank said darkly.

'Oh, don't talk rot. Who could be scared of Dave? Benjy's over his teething for now, you can take me over there on Wednesday or Thursday and see her for yourself.'

Frank remained unconvinced. The following Tuesday he was loading his empty cream cans back onto the spring cart when he saw David bringing his own cart up to the factory. Frank marched over, and accosted the boy as David swung down from the front of the cart.

'You were meant to bring Beth over for lunch on Sunday,' he said without preamble. 'Why didn't you turn up?'

'Sorry, Uncle Frank. Beth didn't feel well, so we ended up staying home.'

An image of Beth, bruised and frightened, rose in Frank's imagination. 'Didn't feel well? What's wrong with her?' he asked sharply.

He could see that David had caught his implication. David opened his mouth as if to snap back an answer, then turned away before speaking. 'She just said she was too tired, and she had a headache. She's not the best today, either. I'll bring her over as soon as she feels up to it.'

'You just see that you do, or I'll have something to say about it.'

Frank fully intended to follow through on his warning, but he was not given the chance. Later that very morning, the back door opened and Beth walked in, closely followed by an anxious-looking David.

'Beth!' Lizzie said. 'I didn't expect you on an ironing day.'

'I've come to be inspected,' Beth announced, with a meaning look at her father.

'Sit down,' David urged. He dragged a chair back from the table and took Beth's arm to help her to it, but she shook his hand off.

'Don't fuss. I've told you, I'm sick of being fussed over.'

Frank saw dark rings under Beth's eyes that spoke of broken nights, and a tightness around her mouth quite foreign to its familiar sweet expression. His guilty awareness that he was the reason she had come out today did not improve his mood. He found a target near at hand.

'You didn't need to bring her,' he told David. 'You could have let her come on her own.'

David met his eyes, then looked away. 'Beth's not used to driving the gig. And I don't think she should be riding just now.'

'You're quite right, Dave,' Lizzie said, darting a frown at Frank. 'You don't look the best, girl. How are you keeping?'

'I'm all right,' Beth snapped. Her eyes widened at the realisation of how she had spoken to her mother. She looked warily at Lizzie. 'I'm just sick of people fussing over me. And I can't seem to get comfortable.'

David fetched a low stool from near the bench and put it in front of her chair. 'You might be better with your feet up.' He carefully placed Beth's feet on the stool. 'Her legs get sore,' he said to Lizzie over his shoulder before turning his attention back to Beth. 'Is that all right? Or would you rather have them up on a chair?'

'They're all right like this. Stop flapping around me like an old chook.'

Lizzie passed Benjy over to Frank. 'There's still tea in the pot. I'll get a couple more cups.'

'Would you rather have a drink of water?' David asked. 'How's your head? Do you want a damp cloth for it? She's been getting bad headaches,' he added to Lizzie.

'I have not!' Beth protested. 'Just the odd little one. Don't you go talking about me like that.'

Lizzie was studying Beth thoughtfully. She poured them all a cup of tea, and talked about inconsequential matters while it was being drunk.

Beth finished hers quickly, then lowered her feet to the floor and rose ponderously upright, leaning on the edge of the table for support. 'Right, you've seen me. Dave, take me home.'

'I think you'd better have a rest first,' said Lizzie. 'How about you stay on for a bit and have a lie-down? Your father can run you back later.'

'That's a good idea,' David said. 'I'll give you a hand up the passage. Aunt Lizzie's right, you could do with a lie-down.' He reached out a hand towards her, but Beth batted it away.

'I don't want to,' she said, her voice rising in irritation. 'Take me home, Dave.'

Undeterred, David put his hand on her arm. 'I really think you should stay here for a bit. You might feel better if you have a rest.'

'Stop nagging at me!' Beth cried shrilly. She swung her hand at his face.

David flinched, but made no move to avoid the slap aimed at him. Beth jerked back her hand just before it connected, then reached out again and stroked his face. 'I'm all right, Davie,' she said softly. 'You mustn't keep fussing.'

David took her hand and planted a quick kiss on the palm. 'Sorry,' he murmured. 'I'm just trying to look after you.'

Frank looked away, feeling awkward at having witnessed such a private moment. He caught Lizzie's eye, and could see she felt much the same. He also saw a certain smug satisfaction.

David and Beth left soon afterwards. Frank and Lizzie watched as David lifted Beth carefully into the gig and then drove away at a walk.

Lizzie coaxed Benjy to wave at the departing gig. 'Well,' she said, looking over at Frank, 'I don't know about you, but I wouldn't call that *scared*. Not her, anyway. I thought he looked a bit worried she might give him a clout. But if you think—'

'All right, don't go on about it,' Frank interrupted. 'I'd better get on and see what those boys are up to.' As he walked away, he could feel Lizzie's eyes following him. He did not need to see her face to know its expression.

She was right, of course. Try as he might, in the face of the tender scene he had witnessed Frank could not maintain the notion that David

208

was anything but kind and thoughtful to Beth. It was hard to see anything of Charlie in the boy who had quietly waited to see whether he would be slapped or caressed.

That afternoon Frank did his best to assume a casual air when he remarked to Lizzie, 'I thought I might pop up and see Bill this afternoon.' It was true enough; he did intend to pay a quick call on Bill. It was convenient that that meant passing David's farm.

'Don't be late back for afternoon tea,' said Lizzie. 'And while you're talking to Dave, tell him I said Beth had better stay home while she's not the best. I'll get you to take me over to see her later in the week.'

'I didn't say…' Frank began, but there was no use denying what they both knew was the main reason for his outing.

He soon found David, checking his potato paddock. David looked at him warily, clearly expecting a confrontation of some sort.

'You don't need to cart Beth down to see us again, not when she's not feeling the best,' Frank said. 'I can see you're looking after her.' It seemed to him that he owed David more than this. 'Look, I'm sorry I've been giving you a hard time, Dave.'

He had expected suspicion, and at best a gradual return into David's confidence. What he had not expected was the relief that flooded David's face, and the way he immediately thrust out his hand to shake Frank's.

'Thanks, Uncle Frank.'

Frank let his own hand be engulfed in David's, and patted the boy's shoulder with his free hand. David's ready forgiveness shamed him far more than resentment would have done.

'Well, you might have a daughter yourself one day. Then you'll know how worried you get about them.'

'A daughter.' David smiled at the notion. 'I'd like that.' His face fell. 'I'd like this business to be over, too.'

'Beth doesn't look too good, does she?'

David shook his head. 'No. I don't know what it's meant to be like for a girl, but I think Ma's a bit worried about her, too. She's that tired—she hasn't been sleeping well, that makes it worse. And everything seems to hurt her. I just wish I could do something to help.'

Frank studied David's anxious expression, remembering all too well his own feelings during Lizzie's illness. 'It can be hard on them sometimes. She might have a bit of what her ma had with Benjy. Something to do with her blood. Richard had a fancy name for it—he seemed to know a lot about it.'

'Do you think I should get Richard to take a look at her?'

Frank gave him a rueful smile. 'Good luck to you getting her to let him. Your Aunt Lizzie wouldn't have had a bar of it.'

'I might give it a go,' David said thoughtfully.

'Richard's come to see you,' David announced a few days later, standing to one side to let Richard into the kitchen.

Amy saw David and Beth exchange a look. He wore a set expression; Beth's suggested that she would have more to say on the subject when they were alone.

'I'm sorry you've come out specially,' Beth said, turning her attention on her brother-in-law. 'I told Dave I didn't need to see you.'

'That's quite all right, Beth,' Richard said. 'I was coming out this way anyway, so I thought I'd call in and see how you were keeping. Dave did happen to mention the other day that you were feeling a little under the weather.'

'Oh, did he just?' Beth shot a rapid glance at David.

'You'll have a cup of tea with us, won't you Richard?' Amy said, forestalling whatever Beth might have said next. 'We can have it in the parlour. Then you can have a talk with Beth afterwards.' She slipped her hand over Beth's. 'I think it'd be a good idea for you to talk to Richard. Tell him about your headaches—he can probably give you something for them.'

Beth looked down at the floor. 'I'm not going to take any clothes off.'

Richard almost succeeded in hiding a smile. 'I'm sure that won't be necessary.'

Beth and David were both silent while the four of them had their tea, with Amy and Richard managing to keep up a semblance of conversation. When they had finished, Amy put their tea things on a tray and rose to leave the room.

'I'd just like to ask you one or two things,' Richard told Beth. 'Would you be happier if Dave stayed while we talk?'

'No, thank you,' Beth said loftily, but Amy saw how nervous she was.

'Would you like me to stay?' she asked. Beth nodded, sending her a look of gratitude. Amy passed the tray to David, who took the hint and left the room.

Amy sat as far away as the tiny parlour permitted, trying to give the impression that she was devoting all her attention to a baby gown she was hemming.

Richard spoke quietly, but Amy could not help overhearing everything that was said. She heard him draw out of Beth admissions that she was unable to sleep properly at night, her head hurt much of the time, and she was having occasional dizzy spells.

'Thank you, Beth,' Richard said when he had asked all his questions. 'From what you've told me, I believe you have a blood disorder that sometimes occurs during pregnancy.'

'Is there something wrong with the baby? Is it something I did wrong?'

'Not at all,' Richard assured her. 'It strikes without apparent cause—there's certainly nothing to blame yourself for. It's an unpleasant condition, but there are measures we can take to help you through the worst of it. I'll give you a mild sleeping draught, and something for the headaches.'

'But will the baby be all right?'

'As long as you take the proper precautions, there's every reason to think so. May I call David in, please? I'd like to discuss this with you both.'

'All right.'

Richard returned a moment later with David, who had clearly gone no further than the kitchen. 'I can give Beth some medicines to help with the discomfort,' Richard said, 'but the most useful thing I can prescribe is bed rest.'

'I'm doing that now,' said Beth. 'Aunt Amy gets me to have a lie-down every afternoon.'

'I'm afraid that's not quite what I meant. What's required is total bed rest. From now until your baby's born.'

Beth's mouth opened in astonishment. 'Stay in bed from now till April? I can't do that!'

'Yes, you can,' said David. 'If it's what you need to do so you'll be all right.' He turned to Richard. 'She'll do it.'

Beth shot him a reproachful look. 'But what will I *do* all that time?'

'We'll keep you company,' said Amy. 'You can do some sewing if you feel up to it. And you can read my books if you like.'

'I'll have time to read them all if I'm stuck in bed for four months,' Beth muttered. 'Even the dictionary.'

Richard smiled at her. 'I can see you'll be well looked after.' He glanced into the bag at his side. 'Before I go, I'll just listen to your chest if I may? Just in case there's any congestion.'

Beth nodded, and Richard pulled out his stethoscope. David was holding Beth's hand and talking quietly to her, but Amy had a clear view of Richard's face as he placed the stethoscope against Beth's chest. She saw his smile disappear abruptly. He listened, frowning, then moved the instrument and listened again.

He removed the stethoscope and put it away in his bag, then sat for a few moments as if gathering his thoughts.

'I've a favour to ask you, Beth,' he said at last.

Beth looked up, startled. 'A favour? What do you mean?'

'Will you allow me to attend the birth of your baby?'

Beth's eyes widened. She clutched at David's hand. 'No,' she said, shaking her head. 'No, I couldn't do that.'

'It's your decision, of course,' said Richard. 'And perhaps Dave's, also,' he added, earning himself an indignant glare from Beth. 'But I hope you'll consider it further. I've observed an irregularity in your heartbeat.'

'What's wrong with her?' David asked.

'Oh, I'm sure it's nothing serious—or at least it wouldn't be, if there weren't Beth's condition to consider. I doubt very much if it's ever caused a problem up till now. But childbirth puts a severe strain on the body—particularly if it becomes drawn out.' Richard held Beth's gaze. 'I don't want you subjected to a long labour.'

'What does that mean?' Beth asked in a small voice.

Richard sighed. 'I'm so sorry, I should have thought… Amy, perhaps you could explain some of this to Beth later?'

'Of course,' said Amy. She would have to find a way to tell Beth as much as she needed to know without frightening her unduly.

'For now, let me just say that sometimes the process of childbirth takes longer than I think your heart should be made to cope with,' Richard said. 'If that were to happen, there are certain measures I can take to hurry matters along. But they're measures that require a doctor— it's not something a midwife could do for you.'

Amy gave a sharp intake of breath. 'Do you mean forceps?' She immediately regretted having spoken. But when she risked a glance at Beth, the girl looked puzzled rather than frightened.

'What's forceps?' Beth asked.

'Simply a tool for making childbirth easier,' Richard said smoothly. 'Don't worry yourself over the details. Beth, I know you'd rather be attended by a woman, but please think this over. You've plenty of time yet.'

'We'll have a talk about it,' David said, still holding Beth's hand. 'We'll do what's best for Beth.' David would talk Beth into it, Amy was sure, though it might take him some time.

Richard rose to go, and Amy showed him out to the kitchen, leaving David and Beth to talk in private. She stood at the back door and watched Richard walking down the path, but when he was halfway to the garden gate she hurried out after him.

'Richard, do you really think you might have to use forceps on Beth?'

He turned to face her. 'I do think it's likely, yes. If her labour shows signs of being protracted, which is probable enough with a first baby, then I'll intervene.'

'But…' Amy closed her eyes for a moment, and heard again in memory the harsh voice of Sister Prescott with her dire threats. 'But won't that be awful for Beth? And does it mean the baby will die?'

Richard looked startled. 'No, nothing of the sort! What makes you say that?'

'It was… I heard it once, a long time ago. A nurse told me. She said it was awful. She said it meant ripping the woman with things like butchers use, and pulling the baby out in bits. I'd hate that to happen to Beth.'

She saw Richard's face cloud with anger, but when he spoke his voice was controlled. 'I can assure you, Amy, that I have no intention of harming Beth or her child. Quite the reverse, in fact.'

'I'm sorry, I didn't mean—' Amy began, but Richard waved her apology aside.

'I'm afraid midwives tend not to approve of doctors who have the impertinence to attend births, and some of them are not above embroidering the truth to support their case. The nurse who said those things to you was one such. It's natural that you should be concerned, having been told such nonsense.'

'She wasn't a very nice nurse,' Amy said cautiously.

Richard smiled. 'I can quite believe it. Forceps, when used by a competent practitioner—and I believe myself to be one—can be a life-saving tool. It's true that it's likely to mean a degree of discomfort after the birth somewhat more severe than the usual, and a longer time of healing for Beth. But it's a good deal better than the alternative in a case like this. If Beth were to endure a long or specially difficult labour, I'd be seriously concerned for her safety. I think it's important that I attend her. I do urge you to use what influence you can to persuade her.'

'But you think she'll be all right if you're there to help?' Amy asked.

Richard hesitated longer than she would have liked. 'I'll do my best. Beth's always been a healthy girl up till now, and that's in her favour. But hearts are a difficult matter, especially when it comes to childbirth. Particularly if she has a big baby.' He did not say aloud what Amy was sure they were both thinking: given David's size, that seemed all too likely.

17

'Excuse me, Miss Sarah, there's a man here says he wants to see you.'

Sarah looked up from her desk to see Nellie in the doorway. 'Is it Mr Taylor?' Over recent weeks, Taylor had taken to calling every few days. Her consistent refusal to have him admitted to the house had not yet had the desired effect.

'No, Miss—he says his name's Hobbs. He's not a smartly turned out sort of man at all. He come to the back door, as he should. Mrs Jenson's been trying to get some sense out of him, but her and I can't make head nor tail of what he's on about.'

'I don't believe I know anyone of that name. But I'd better see him. Bring him through, please, Nellie.'

Nellie bobbed a curtsey. She disappeared, and was soon back with a frightened-looking little man trailing behind her.

'Here's Mr Hobbs, Miss Sarah,' she announced.

'Mr Hobbs, do come in,' said Sarah. 'Please, sit down.' She indicated the chair in front of her desk.

For a moment, she thought the man might be about to take to his heels. But she saw him gather his courage and step into the room, then walk over and sit down. Nellie curtseyed again and left.

'It's very good of you to see me, Miss,' Mr Hobbs said, his voice so low that Sarah could scarcely hear him.

'Not at all. What is it you wanted to see me about, Mr Hobbs?'

It was some time before she could get anything intelligible out of the man. He would mumble a few words, then trail off and look at the floor. Sarah began to wonder if he was a simpleton, and if she should call Nellie back and have him escorted from the house. Then amongst his mumblings she caught the name "Taylor".

'What was that?' she said sharply. 'Do you have some connection with Mr Taylor? Did he perhaps send you?'

'Oh, no, Miss. No, I expect Mr Taylor might be a bit put out about me coming here. He told me to say nothing about it, see—about you and him having dealings. But it's the money, Miss. To tell you God's truth, I don't know where else to turn.'

Sarah could see that in his face. The man looked desperate; in fact he looked on the verge of tears. 'Then you'd better tell me the whole story,' she said, making her voice as soothing as she could. She was not happy about that reference to "dealings", but she did not want the man to take fright. 'Take your time.'

She saw Mr Hobbs take a deep breath to calm himself. 'It was such a big order, you see,' he began. 'All the fittings for a whole row of houses.'

'Fittings?' Sarah prompted.

'All the brass—taps, and door knobs, and lighting bits, and all. I've a foundry,' he added belatedly. 'Just a small one, but we do good work, though I says it as shouldn't.'

'There's no reason you shouldn't take pride in work well done, Mr Hobbs. Pray, continue. So Mr Taylor gave you a large order?'

'Yes, he did, Miss. That was last year. I'd never had such an order—I thought we'd be properly set up after that. Mr Taylor told me there'd be a lot more work coming my way if we gave satisfaction. I wouldn't be making much money on it, because I had to give him a good price. But it was an opportunity, see?'

An opportunity for Taylor to take advantage of an honest man, Sarah thought to herself. 'Yes, I see how it was. Go on, Mr Hobbs.'

'So I put the whole factory onto it. I turned down a few other orders, and I took on more men. I had to pay for the materials, and that took a bit of doing to get the money together. We all worked extra shifts for weeks—I had to work on the Sabbath more than a time or two, me and my oldest boy both. But we did it, Miss. We had the whole lot ready on time for Mr Taylor. No corners cut, either. All top notch.'

Sarah saw the man's quiet pride in his workmanship, and respected him all the more for it. 'Well done,' she said.

Mr Hobbs slumped in his chair. 'And that's when the trouble started. They took delivery, and I sent my account at the end of the month. But I didn't get no money, Miss. I gave them a while, I didn't go bothering them as soon as it was a bit late. Then I started sending reminders, nice and polite, like.'

'And they were ignored?'

'Yes, Miss. Not so much as a word. After a bit I started going to see Mr Taylor, just to see if I could get to the bottom of things. He'd tell me it'd be the next week, then the next. I'd go and see him again, and he'd tell me the same.'

'It sounds as if this has been going on for a good while, Mr Hobbs.'

'Nearly eight months now. I saw him again six weeks ago—it was the first time I'd got in to see him for months, they'd been telling me he was away every time I went. I told him I had to have that money. That's when he told me…' Mr Hobbs looked nervously at Sarah. 'He said he had dealings with you. He said you and him was coming to an arrangement. So if I was patient a bit longer, I'd get the whole lot that's owed me, and there'd be more work to come. He gave me five pounds there in his office, and he said I could have a bit more in a week or two.

But I haven't seen him since. Every time I go there they tell me he's out, or in an important meeting or suchlike. And they can none of them do anything about the money without his say so.'

With an effort, Sarah kept her voice mild. 'What's the total sum involved?'

'Two hundred and thirty pounds—less the five pounds he gave me. I'm at my wit's end over it. I'm behind with my rent on the factory, and they're saying they'll get the law on me for that. I'll be turned out of the place. I'll lose the whole lot. I've a wife and children, and I don't know what's to become of us all. I'm sorry, Miss, I don't mean to cause you no bother. I just thought with you and Mr Taylor having dealings, you could maybe see your way clear to speak to him, and ask him to pay a bit more of what's owing?'

The naked plea in the man's face was almost too much for Sarah's composure. Two hundred and thirty pounds. It was a small enough sum for her; she had spent close to a third of that amount on Amy's gowns. But for this man it could mean ruination. And Taylor had used her name to deceive the man into trusting him.

'I'm afraid you've been misinformed by Mr Taylor. I have no business dealings with him whatsoever. But please don't distress yourself further over this, Mr Hobbs,' she added quickly, seeing the man's rising panic. 'I believe I may have a solution to your present difficulties.'

She waited a few moments till she was sure Mr Hobbs had calmed himself sufficiently to take in her words. 'I presume you have details of these transactions in writing?' she asked. 'The original order, and copies of your invoices and other correspondence?'

'Yes, Miss. My younger boy helps me with the accounts and all that. He's very neat and particular,' he added, a trace of pride discernible through his anxiousness.

'Excellent. Now, let me explain what I want you to do. I'm going to give you a letter to take to my business managers—they're the people that look after paying out money for me. I'll write out their address for you. I want you to gather up all your papers regarding Mr Taylor, and take them along with you when you go and see them. All right?' She waited for Mr Hobbs to nod his understanding.

'When you call and see them, they'll want to talk to you, then they'll give you some papers to sign. One will be an account of your dealings with Mr Taylor, noting particularly the way he used my name to make you think he intended to pay you.'

'I don't want any trouble,' Mr Hobbs said uncertainly.

'I can assure you there will be no trouble. Not for you, at any rate.

There'll be another paper for you to sign. It will state that you've signed over Mr Taylor's debt, so the money is now owed to me rather than to you. Once that's signed, my people will give you the full amount you're owed. Plus a little extra for the time you've been kept waiting. Does that sound satisfactory?'

Mr Hobbs was staring at her, his mouth open. 'It sounds bloomin' wonderful, Miss. I don't know how I can thank you.'

'There's no need. But I strongly advise that you have no further dealings with Mr Taylor.'

'I don't need to be told that! Begging your pardon, Miss,' he added hastily.

'No, I'm sure you don't.' Sarah studied the lines worry had etched into his face, and she wondered when he had last eaten a meal in peace. 'This letter will take me several minutes to write, Mr Hobbs. Would you like to wait in the kitchen in the meantime?'

'Yes, Miss. As long as I wouldn't be in anyone's way.'

'Not in the least.' She rang the bell, and Nellie soon appeared. 'Nellie, please take Mr Hobbs through to the kitchen while I finish what I'm doing here. Ask Mrs Jenson to give him some refreshments.'

Mr Hobbs rose from his chair. 'Begging your pardon, Miss, but... why? I can't thank you enough, and Mrs Hobbs is going to be beside herself. But why are you doing this for me?'

Sarah regarded him thoughtfully. 'Because my father brought me up to respect honest tradesmen, and to see that they're paid their due. It's not within my power to do that for every tradesman in Auckland, but your particular case has become my responsibility. I'm only too pleased to be able to put right something of the wrong that's been done here.'

'Bless you, Miss,' Mr Hobbs said fervently.

Sarah nodded her farewell, then began writing the letter for Mr Hobbs to take away.

After finishing that, she wrote a short note for the gardener's boy to deliver. When that note reached its recipient, she would have a less than pleasant task. She would have to allow Mr Taylor to enter her house one last time.

Sarah watched Mr Taylor enter her study and stride across the room. His self-satisfied smile was, if possible, even broader than on his previous visit. Until she saw that smile again, Sarah had thought its power to irritate must have been exaggerated in her memory.

'Sarah, my dear!' he exclaimed. 'You've been an elusive creature lately. I almost began to think you were avoiding me, until I got your note.'

The man was actually wagging his finger at her. Sarah stared at the gesture in horrified fascination, briefly lost for words. He dragged a chair in front of her desk and sat down, stretching his long legs out in front of him.

'Well, let's not speak of that,' he said, as if bestowing a favour. 'I'm here now, and we don't want to waste any of our time together.' He put his hands behind his head and leaned back, still gazing on her with a proprietorial air.

He was clearly waiting for her to speak. Sarah let the silence hang between them until she thought it must be obvious even to this man. Then she spoke, biting off each word.

'I did not invite you to be seated.'

He let out a snort of laughter. 'Oh, come now, my dear. There's no need for you and I to stand on ceremony.'

'On the contrary, there is every need for just that. I wish to have the appropriate forms observed.'

She held his gaze, and at last had the satisfaction of seeing that loathsome smile fade. 'I'm afraid I must say you're being rather a silly girl,' he said, drawing himself up to a standing position. 'Now, are you satisfied? May I sit in your presence?'

Sarah ignored the sarcastic edge to his voice. 'No, you may not. I would prefer to conduct this meeting with you standing.'

It was a good deal more satisfying to observe his obvious discomfort. His eyes were now at a higher level than hers, but her desk was deep enough to give him no opportunity of looming over her. It required only a slight tilting of her head to keep him fixed with a hard stare.

'Mr Taylor, it's come to my attention that you have been claiming a relationship with me, and using my name to gain certain business advantages. I will not tolerate this.'

He looked startled, then annoyed. 'May I ask where you've heard such tales?'

'That's of no concern.' Sarah knew that correspondence relating to the transfer of Mr Hobbs' account had been sent to Taylor's office; it did not surprise her that he apparently remained ignorant of the matter. He probably considered such mundane matters as the payment of invoices to be beneath his notice. 'What's pertinent is that such behaviour is to cease at once. Do I make myself understood?'

The smile had returned. 'But my dear girl, we *do* have a relationship! You can hardly deny that, given what we are to each other.'

'I most certainly can, and will, deny any meaningful connection with you. Mr Taylor, I strongly advise you not to attempt any deception of this sort again. If you do, the consequences will be most unpleasant.'

She saw his smile harden. 'And have you thought about the possible consequences of any falling-out between us, Sarah? Would you be quite happy with the details of your background becoming public knowledge?'

'Why ever should that concern me? I'm fortunate enough to bear an honourable name that I attempt to be worthy of. And I believe that if my "background", as you put it, became a subject for gossip, I would be considered an innocent party in the matter. Unlike yourself.'

His expression hardened further. 'Perhaps you need to consider how others might be affected, my dear. Your experience of the world has been rather narrow till now, but I can assure you that in such matters society tends to judge a woman far more harshly than a man. Think how this whole business might affect Amy.'

Sarah felt herself give a start, and to her annoyance she saw that he had noted it.

'I imagine you might want to have her come and stay with you again on some future occasion?' he went on smoothly. 'Amy might find herself somewhat uncomfortable in Auckland if her past became general knowledge. Especially if some of the more interesting details of her behaviour were noised abroad. I won't sully your innocence with such things, but I rather think it would attract a good deal of salacious talk.'

Sarah had thought she was angry with the man before. Now, as she heard him threaten Amy, she felt as if she had never in her life till this moment known what anger was. She could feel her cheeks burning; the fact that she was sure he would take it for embarrassment rather than the fury it was angered her all the more. She made herself wait until her voice was under control before she spoke; she would not allow him to hear any tremble in it.

'Mr Taylor, I could ruin you, financially and socially. If you ever misappropriate my name again—and if you ever attempt to harm Mrs Stewart, in even the slightest way—I will have not the least hesitation in doing just that. Please do not imagine that I am anything but serious in this.'

She rang the bell for the maid. 'And now I'll ask you to leave my house. I don't expect that we will meet again, other than by chance.'

She could see little outward sign that her warning had subdued his confidence. 'But I expect we will, my dear,' he said, before the maid arrived to usher him out and leave Sarah in blessed solitude.

It was to be a quiet Christmas at David's farm. Late in the morning Frank brought Lizzie over for a short visit, leaving all the children except

Benjy at home, but for the rest of the day Amy, David and Beth had the house to themselves.

With Richard's permission, David had helped Beth out to the parlour to lie on the couch, and Amy brought their Christmas dinner through from the kitchen. Beth had little appetite for the meal; 'I don't think there's room for anything else in here,' she said, resting her hand on the mound of her belly. She had brightened a little when her parents arrived, but soon lapsed into the subdued state now common with her. Not long after lunch, she asked to be helped back into bed.

At Frank's house it was noisy and lively. As well as his own children, Arthur's household joined them for the occasion. After lunch they overflowed the parlour and spilled out onto the verandah. The children were forbidden to go further than the garden gate, dressed as they were in their Sunday best.

Lizzie gathered most of her guests into the parlour for the musical part of the afternoon, though Frank noticed that his older sons, along with their male cousins, contrived to stay out on the verandah where they could largely ignore the music.

Rosie played first. Reluctant as he was to acknowledge any flaws in his children, Frank had to accept that Rosie showed no special gift for music. "Energetic" was the kindest word anyone managed to find for her effort. Even Benjy seemed unimpressed, wriggling in Lizzie's lap and beginning to grizzle by the time Rosie finished the thankfully short piece.

Lily's daughter Emma was a good deal better. She played two pieces, which were met with lively applause, then helped Rosie and Kate pass round plates of biscuits. Benjy had settled down again during Emma's playing, and now sat contentedly gnawing at a biscuit.

'Emma's good on the piano,' Frank said to Lily, who was sitting beside him. 'She takes after you.'

Lily smiled. 'Thank you, Frank, that's very kind of you. I think she does have something of a gift, and she's very good about practising whenever she gets the chance. Those were simple pieces, though—I really can't spend enough time teaching Emma to be able to take her much further.'

'Bring her as often as you like. You know you're welcome to come and use the piano any time.'

'Oh, you've always made that clear. And I'm very grateful to you and Lizzie. But...' She cast a quick glance at Arthur and Edie; Maudie was currently keeping them busy fussing over Lucy. 'I can't leave Father and Mother alone, you see,' Lily said in a low voice. 'Mother gets so forgetful now, I'm afraid she'll burn herself or leave something on the range. And before Emma finished up at school, Father had a fall one day when I happened to be outside and he tried carrying the tea things. Bill's very good, he insists on watching them himself at least once a week so that Emma and I can come here together, but the rest of the time either she or I need to be at home with them. I don't mind,' she said, seeing Frank's expression. 'They've been so good to me over the years, I don't begrudge them the attention.'

It seemed a shame, Frank thought, that his piano should sit idle most of the week, while Lily had to make do with snatched opportunities to play.

Kate appeared at Lily's side, and tugged at her skirt. She was a quietly-spoken child, easily hidden in Rosie's shadow. 'Can I play my song, Aunt Lily?'

'When you've learned one, dear,' Lily said, smiling at the five-year-old. 'I'm going to start teaching you next year.'

'But I know one already,' Kate insisted. 'I learned it by myself.'

'Did you really?' Lily said, gently amused. 'Well, we'd better hear it—if Papa says that's all right,' she added, looking at Frank.

'It's the first I've heard about you playing the piano, Kate,' said Frank. 'Let's hear you, then.'

Kate clambered onto the piano stool, which was rather too high for her. She screwed up her face in concentration, then slowly but quite recognisably picked out the tune of "Twinkle, Twinkle, Little Star" with her right hand.

Benjy had escaped from Lizzie's lap and made his way over to Frank, using various pieces of furniture and the occasional human leg for support along the way. He balanced himself against Frank's chair while Kate played, listening with interest. Frank gathered the little boy onto his own lap, and Benjy nestled in comfortably.

When Kate finished, there was a good-humoured burst of clapping. Benjy clapped his own chubby little hands and sang the last few notes, raising a laugh from his audience.

'Did you learn that all by yourself, Kate?' Lily asked.

Kate nodded solemnly. 'I learned it in my head. Then I tried and tried and tried it till it was right.'

'Why, Lizzie,' Lily said, still amused, 'I do believe your two little ones are the most musical of them all. Kate's obviously got an ear for music, and Benjy appreciates it as well. Perhaps I'd better start teaching them both!'

Benjy recognised his name, and knew he was being talked of. He giggled delightedly, and sang a few more notes.

'I never thought about getting any of the boys to learn piano,' Lizzie said thoughtfully. 'I don't think the rest of them would've been any good at it. I expect Benjy would be, though.'

'Well, let's wait till he's a bit older—perhaps when he starts school,' Lily said, her tone suggesting that she was taking the idea seriously, though Frank caught the twinkle in her eye.

With the children having performed, Lily at last allowed herself to take a seat at the piano. She started with a few familiar Christmas songs, playing them from memory, then arranged some sheet music on the stand. Frank was seated close enough to have a clear view of her face, and he could see from her expression that this was a piece she had been looking forward to playing.

Lily had barely finished setting out the music when Bill came to her side.

'I think we're going to have to take Pa home,' he said, keeping his voice low so that there was no risk of Arthur's hearing him. 'His leg's playing up.'

Frank looked around and saw Emma hovering near Arthur, attempting to adjust the cushions on his footstool. Arthur was insisting there was no need for anyone to be fussing over him, but his expression made it clear that he was in some discomfort.

Lily at once began tidying away her music. 'Of course. I'll be ready in just a moment.'

'Sorry, love,' said Bill. 'You didn't get the chance to play any of your fancy stuff.'

'Oh, I could do with practising that one a little more before it's fit for public performance,' Lily said, determinedly bright. 'Don't worry, Bill. It's high time we left, anyway—Mother and Father will be getting sleepy before long, they often have a doze around now.' She closed the lid of the piano and allowed her hand to rest on it for a moment; Bill's eyes followed the gesture.

Lily sent Emma out to find her brothers and tell them to bring the buggy around. Arthur deigned to allow Bill to help him out of his chair and pass him his walking stick, and Frank's family saw the Leiths out to the gate.

'Tell Beth we were sorry not to be able to see her today,' Lily said as Bill helped her up into the buggy. 'I thought we might call in on her, but we'd better get straight home. How's she keeping?' she asked, too quietly for the children to hear.

'She has her ups and downs,' said Lizzie. 'She wouldn't be up to seeing you all at once, anyway.'

'Poor dear,' said Lily. 'She'll be so glad when it's all over.'

'We all will be,' Lizzie said; Frank agreed whole-heartedly.

At Jimmy's club, the food was excellent and the company for the most part congenial. He often found it preferable to his own home as a place to pass the evening, though it had to be admitted it was not an inexpensive choice. But Charlotte had been indulging in one of her weepy moods lately, when she took to fretting over how far she was from her father and brothers back in Melbourne. There was a time when such moods had usually included laments over her childlessness, but that seemed to have ceased over the last few months, for some reason.

He studied the brandy glass in his hand, and idly considered what he might do with the rest of the evening. Luck had not been with him at the card tables earlier; nothing he considered serious, but perhaps it would be better not to seek expensive female entertainment tonight.

The deep armchairs were comfortable, and the brandy had given him a pleasant feeling of languor. Perhaps he would spend another hour or two here, then go home. With luck, Charlotte would have gone to bed by then, and he would not have to hear her complaints.

'Ah, Taylor, there you are,' came a hearty voice. Jimmy looked up to see the portly figure of the club's manager, Mr Ballard, standing over him. 'Can we have a word in my office, if you have a moment?'

Jimmy swallowed the last mouthful of brandy and hauled himself upright. The room gave a disconcerting tilt as he did so; he reached out and grabbed at the back of the armchair, hoping Ballard had not noticed. There had been a particularly fine claret served with dinner that evening; he had perhaps had a little more of it than was his wont, especially as he had enjoyed one or two glasses of port at the card tables afterwards. He found himself having to watch his footing as he followed in Mr Ballard's wake, and briefly considered whether it might not have been wiser to have stopped at one brandy once he had settled in to the lounge.

Still, there was no use worrying about that now. He followed Ballard into a small but well-furnished room, and hoped the man would not be too tedious over whatever it was he wanted to ramble on about.

Mr Ballard closed the door behind them, sat at a desk and indicated the chair nearest it. 'I've just been going over the accounts.' A large book lay open on the desk; he patted it with one pudgy hand. 'You seem to have overlooked settling up for a while, Taylor. I know these things can slip one's mind,' he said, smiling benevolently. 'But when they start to mount up, it's best to put matters back in order.'

'Oh, certainly,' Jimmy said, making an effort not to show his irritation. The man had dragged him from a comfortable chair for this nonsense. 'Yes, I'll look into it when I get home. Must have mislaid the account, eh?'

'You must have mislaid a few of them, old man. These are dating back some time now. Accounts from the bar, and the dining room—and your membership fee is well past due, I see.'

'Really? I can't imagine how that got missed. Yes, I'll look into that tonight.'

'That's the way. Wouldn't want to think you weren't going to pay, would we? We wouldn't want to eject you, ha ha!'

The man was becoming impertinent. Really, as a member of the club Jimmy was more or less his employer. He had no business taking that tone.

'I should think not,' Jimmy said sharply. 'Not with my connections.'

Rather than appearing chastened, Ballard looked amused. 'Connections? My dear fellow, with the greatest respect, I wouldn't call them anything out of the ordinary.'

'No? You wouldn't call Sarah Millish out of the ordinary?' Jimmy snapped, his own words taking him by surprise. He had not quite intended to mention Sarah by name. He had been treading carefully since their last rather heated meeting the previous month. He had made no further attempt to call on her, aware that it might take some time for her to settle down after having got herself in such a state.

The girl certainly had a nasty temper on her. The way she had spoken to him! Her own father! It was almost beyond bearing. Why the devil couldn't she have inherited more of Amy's nature? It was a damned shame that Amy hadn't stayed in Auckland longer, and not only for the possibilities it might have offered Jimmy. It had been on the tip of his tongue to tell Sarah she really should have Amy to stay again, and soon: she could do with her mother's influence.

Well, the words were out now, and he had the satisfaction of seeing that they had taken Ballard aback.

'Miss Millish? May I ask what your connection is with her?'

'Shall we say… both business and personal,' Jimmy said, affecting a lofty tone.

To his annoyance, Ballard looked sceptical. 'Personal, eh? I won't ask you to be indiscreet, then. I'd have thought she was a little young for you, Taylor.'

'I'm certainly not referring to anything improper!' Jimmy said, outraged at the suggestion.

'I'm pleased to hear it,' said Ballard, though in rather too salacious a tone to appease Jimmy. 'So what did you mean by a business connection, then? Hmm?'

'I mean that such trifling matters as the odd bill I've run up here will soon be of no consequence,' Jimmy said, stung once again by Ballard's superior manner. 'I have expectations of gaining access to considerable resources. Resources I'm perfectly entitled to, but there are matters of some delicacy involved.'

'Are you implying that Miss Millish owes you money?' Mr Ballard asked, regarding Jimmy with rather more respect.

Jimmy considered his words. 'Yes, she most certainly does,' he said after a moment. 'A substantial amount.' After all, he reflected, there could hardly be a greater debt than owing her very existence to him.

'Well, that does put a different complexion on things. And when are you expecting payment of this debt?'

'Oh, quite soon now,' Jimmy said airily.

'Is there a particular date it's due?' Mr Ballard probed. 'I'd like to see your account with us settled before too much longer, and if it's waiting on this matter…' He turned a quizzical expression on Jimmy.

'Well, it's all somewhat delicate,' Jimmy said, trying not to sound as if he was floundering for the right words. 'So it may take a little longer yet. It's not quite… it's not exactly in writing, as such. You might say it's more a matter of honour.'

Mr Ballard frowned. 'Just a verbal agreement, then? Hmm, that can be a ticklish business. One ends up relying on the other party's being honorable—which I'm sure Miss Millish is,' he added hastily. 'If things have got a little awkward, Taylor, I'd be more than happy to act as a go-between. I flatter myself that I have certain skills when it comes to handling negotiations.'

'No, no, there'll be no need for that. No, just leave it in my hands. Miss Millish and I are on the verge of getting everything sorted out. Goodness, is that the time?' he said, pretending concern as he glanced at the clock in one corner. 'I need to be off home, we're expecting guests this evening. Good night to you, Ballard.'

He rose and left the office, and soon after went out into the street to hail a cab. There was no chance of a peaceful evening at the club with Ballard hovering about making a nuisance of himself, so he might as well go home. It was unfortunate that the guests he had referred to were entirely fictitious; he would have to make do with Charlotte's company.

Sarah was working in her study when Alice informed her that a

225

gentleman was in the hall. Sarah studied the card the maid had brought in, puzzled as to what the man might want. She knew that her father had belonged to this club, though his visits to it had been rare. But she had no association with it herself, and was not likely to, given that it excluded women.

'You'd better show him in, Alice.'

Alice soon ushered in a rather red-faced man with a large moustache. He was breathing heavily; Sarah suspected that the walk uphill had been more vigorous exercise than he was used to.

She extended her hand to be shaken by a somewhat clammy one. 'Ah, Miss Millish. Delighted,' Mr Ballard said, beaming at her. 'I knew your late father, of course—sadly missed—but I've never had the pleasure of calling on you till now.'

'And to what to I owe the honour of this visit?' Sarah asked, withdrawing her hand as soon as she politely could.

'Oh, the honour is all mine, I assure you. But I decided to call just to see if I could be of use in certain matters. I realise it must be very difficult for a young lady in your position to keep on top of things.'

'I'm afraid I don't follow you, Mr Ballard,' Sarah said, quite aware that she was being patronised, but mystified as to what the man might be referring. 'I have no connection at all with the Empire Club, as I'm sure you know.'

'Ah, yes, we're deprived of such delightful company as yours. But I'm aware that you're acquainted with one or two of our more fortunate members—in a business sense, that is,' he added hastily. 'And I learned recently of a certain involvement with one particular member that seems to have become somewhat confused. In such cases it can be useful for a third party to become involved. That's why I'm here to offer my assistance.' He sat back in his chair and smiled benignly.

Sarah thought rapidly, unpicking Ballard's words to find the sense that she was sure must be hidden there. The man was somewhat pompous, but he was unlikely to be a fool. Awareness dawned, and with it an anger that she kept tightly under control.

'Could I ask the name of the person to whom you're referring?'

'Certainly, Miss Millish. I'm speaking of Mr Taylor.' He nodded knowingly. 'And if for whatever reason you'd prefer not to speak directly to him over this matter, I'm more than willing to act as agent for both parties.'

'I find myself at something of a disadvantage, Mr Ballard. I don't know the nature of the "matter" to which you refer. I must ask you to be more precise.'

'Ah, dear lady, I realise this is all rather delicate. And I certainly don't wish to probe into your personal affairs.'

'Oh, please have no compunction on that score,' Sarah said, aware that her voice had become sharp. 'I'd like to have the details of whatever is going on here.'

'Well,' Mr Ballard said, studying her somewhat apprehensively, 'I understand from Mr Taylor that a sum of money is owed him. I gather there isn't a formal contract as such, but there was an understanding that funds would be forthcoming. That's certainly how Taylor seems to have seen it, and... well, to be frank, Miss Millish, he appears to have found himself a little short of ready money as a result. I get the impression that he's understandably somewhat reluctant to broach the subject with you, so I thought I'd help matters along if I could, just to save any awkwardness on either side.'

To save himself from the embarrassment of having allowed a debt to be run up by an untrustworthy party would be a more accurate statement, Sarah suspected. But that was Mr Ballard's problem, not hers. This was no struggling tradesman who had been unlucky enough to fall into Mr Taylor's path, and trusting enough to believe him.

'Unfortunately, Mr Ballard, you are under a misapprehension,' she said crisply. 'Any debt owed by me to Mr Taylor exists only in his own imagination. There is no contract, verbal or otherwise. No agreement, no handshake, and certainly no obligation on my part. Mr Taylor has simply taken it upon himself to claim an association with me to further his own interests. I'm sorry to say it's not the first time he's done such a thing, though I believe it will be the last.' She fixed Mr Ballard with a hard gaze. 'I value my good name, and I won't allow it to be abused in this way—not by anyone.'

She had the satisfaction of seeing his composure slip. 'I assure you, Miss Millish—' he began, but Sarah pressed on as if he had not spoken.

'If Mr Taylor has incurred a debt with you, I advise you to take whatever measures are at your disposal to retrieve it, so long as such measures don't involve insulting other parties by implying less than honourable dealings. And I would advise you to take care against repeating slander.'

'Slander?' he echoed nervously. 'My dear Miss Millish, I had no—'

'Pray don't trouble yourself further. May I assume that you've spoken of this to no one other than Mr Taylor?'

'Oh, quite. I can assure you I've been discreet.'

'In that case I'm willing to let the matter rest, regarding your part in it.' She had frightened him enough, Sarah decided. 'In fact I thank you for bringing Mr Taylor's behaviour to my attention.'

Mr Ballard beamed in evident relief. 'Only too glad to have cleared things up. Please feel free to call on me at any time if I can ever be of assistance.'

That, Sarah reflected, would be difficult, given that she would not be permitted on the premises. But she nodded graciously and allowed Mr Ballard to take his leave.

Knowing what she did of Taylor's character, there was no reason to be startled by Mr Ballard's revelation. Nor, now that she had had time to absorb the facts, would she allow herself to waste energy on anger. Taylor was simply a problem to be solved, and she meant to solve it once and for all. Fortunately, she had taken certain steps against such an eventuality. That would make matters more straightforward now.

There were two letters to be written. The first was a short note to Mr Henry Kendall, directing him to call on her at his earliest convenience. The note suggested that his earliest convenience should be considered to be at or about ten o'clock the following morning.

The other letter took more thought. Sarah considered it for some time before writing a carefully-worded invitation. For this, she used her personal notepaper rather than the businesslike stationery she had used for Mr Kendall's message.

With both notes sealed, and despatched with the gardener's boy, Sarah sat back in her chair to consider the finer details of what she was about to put into effect.

18

Sarah spent much of the following two days in meetings with Mr Kendall. She satisfied herself that he understood what was required, then left the details in his hands. So she was alone in her study on the morning Charlotte Taylor came to call.

It would not be a pleasant occasion, Sarah knew. But she felt she owed Mrs Taylor this meeting. The blame for her husband's actions was not hers.

Sarah had Charlotte brought into her study, but rather than shelter behind her desk she sat at a small table to one side of the room. It was a spot where Amy had often sat, reading or stitching, and Sarah felt herself heartened by the memory. She invited Charlotte to take the chair beside hers, and had the maid bring tea and dainty biscuits.

Charlotte was a picture of understated elegance in her tailored costume of dark green wool, a cream silk blouse frothy with lace visible under the jacket. She wore a matching hat, her blonde hair making a striking effect against the dark green.

They exchanged pointless remarks about the weather as they drank their tea. Sarah was aware that Charlotte was darting glances around the room; she suspected her visitor would not be particularly impressed. The room was comfortable, and the furniture of high quality, but it was functional rather than luxurious.

She saw Charlotte's eyes fall on Sarah's photograph of herself with Amy. 'That's the person who was staying with you, isn't it?' Charlotte said when she realised she was being observed. 'Mrs Stewart, was it?'

'Yes,' said Sarah. 'She's returned to the countryside for the moment. I must say I miss her.' She took a quick glance at the photograph to strengthen herself for what must come next. 'You're probably wondering why I asked you to call, Mrs Taylor.'

'I'll confess that's so. We're not well acquainted, though we do move in similar circles.'

'I'm afraid it's not for a particularly pleasant reason.' Sarah saw the look of surprise in the other woman's eyes. She had rehearsed the words many times; that did not seem to be making the process easier. 'It's regarding your husband.'

Charlotte's expression tightened. 'Then it's my husband you should speak with.'

'Unfortunately, this concerns you as well. Your husband has behaved in a manner that—'

'Miss Millish,' Charlotte interrupted, 'I did not come here to listen to distasteful remarks. If you've been incautious enough to place your reputation in jeopardy, I hardly see that burdening me with the unpleasant details is the appropriate course of action.'

Charlotte had kept her voice well schooled, but her convulsive grip on the arm of her chair betrayed agitation. Sarah stared at her in confusion for a moment before she took her meaning.

'Oh! Oh no, Mrs Taylor, you misunderstand me. I meant nothing of that sort. My dealings with Mr Taylor have been... there has been no...' She stopped, furious at herself for the blush she could feel, and for her inability to find the right words. She was floundering in unfamiliar waters. 'I'm sorry for having given such an impression,' she went on more collectedly. 'It's more a matter of business—though there's a personal element as well.'

Charlotte was studying her warily, but her hands had relaxed. 'I still fail to see how it concerns me.'

Sarah glanced at Amy's picture again before returning her attention to Charlotte. 'I'm not sure if you're aware, Mrs Taylor, that I was not born a Millish. I was adopted into this family as an infant.'

Charlotte looked puzzled at the apparent change of subject, but she nodded. 'Yes, I'd heard that.'

'Well, some time ago I was fortunate enough to find my mother—my other mother, I should say. I've the great fortune to have had two.' She smiled, but Charlotte's expression remained distant. 'When we met after the concert last year, I referred to Mrs Stewart as my very dear friend. And she most certainly is. But she's even more to me than that. She is my mother.'

'Oh,' said Charlotte. 'I see.'

Sarah took a deep breath before plunging on. 'But it was more recently that I discovered who my...' Again, she found herself briefly lost for words. "Father" was not a word she was willing to use for Mr Taylor. 'Who the man involved was.' She saw a dawning awareness in Charlotte's eyes. 'It was Mr Taylor.'

She waited for Charlotte's response, with no idea what form it might take. Would the woman angrily deny it? Would she storm out? Might she dissolve into tears?

Charlotte Taylor did none of those things. She sat as if carved in stone. She seemed to be staring into some invisible distance, so absorbed in her thoughts that Sarah did not feel able to interrupt them.

Silence filled the room like a heavy, muffling blanket. Sarah waited until the absence of sound became unbearable. 'This happened before you and Mr Taylor were married,' she said cautiously. 'It was before he went to Australia. I believe I'm the reason he went there, actually.' Charlotte's gaze was on her now, and Sarah saw a deep resentment there.

'I gather your husband has never spoken of this to you?' A barely perceptible twist in Charlotte's mouth was the nearest approach she made to an answer. Sarah ploughed on. 'Believe me, Mrs Taylor, I would rather not have been obliged to bring this to your attention. I realise it must be somewhat painful.'

For a moment Charlotte's guard slipped, and a wounded creature looked out through her eyes. "Painful", Sarah realised, might be an inadequate word. But Charlotte's mask of composure was restored so quickly that Sarah almost doubted what she had seen.

'Mr Taylor learned of our... connection even more recently than I did,' she went on. 'I don't know how he came to discover it—it certainly wasn't from Mrs Stewart. If having been responsible for the existence of a child had slipped his mind, perhaps seeing her again that evening after the concert reminded him. The very fact that she was staying with me probably contributed.

'However it was that he discovered it, frankly I wish we had both remained in ignorance on the subject. When he came to see me—yes, he called on me,' she said, seeing Charlotte's expression. 'I made it plain to him I had no desire for any closer contact. I hoped that would be an end to the matter. Unfortunately, he chose to take advantage of the situation.'

Sarah was feeling increasingly uncomfortable at the one-sided nature of this conversation, but Charlotte showed no sign of wishing to speak. Sarah might almost have thought her bored with the whole affair, had it not been for the intensity of her gaze.

'Mr Taylor used our supposed relationship to gain certain financial benefits. To be frank, he took actions that I regard as fraudulent. After the first such incident came to my notice, I warned him there would be serious consequences if he did not desist. I'm afraid that my warning appears to have gone unheeded—in the most recent event he's descended into slandering me—and I now find myself obliged to take action.'

There was no point in going on without some sign that the woman was following her. Sarah waited, and Charlotte spoke at last.

'Does she want him back?'

'What?' Sarah said, thrown off balance by the unexpected response. 'I'm sorry, I don't—'

'Her.' Charlotte flicked a hand in the direction of Amy's photograph.

'Does she want him back? Is that why she came to Auckland?'

Sarah fought down the sharp retort that was her instinctive response to the implied slur on Amy's character. She could only guess at how distressing this must be for Charlotte. 'No, Mrs Taylor, she does not.' She debated within herself how much she should reveal, then came to a decision. Charlotte Taylor had the right to know everything in her husband's behaviour that was behind Sarah's course of action.

'When Mrs Stewart found herself face to face with Mr Taylor that evening after the concert,' Sarah said, 'he persuaded her to meet him the next day.' Charlotte said nothing, but Sarah saw her eyes widen slightly. 'I realise it was unwise of her to agree, but she was taken by surprise. She took care to meet him in a public place, but even so...' She found she could not meet Charlotte's eyes. 'Forgive me, Mrs Taylor, I know this is distasteful. He made certain suggestions to Mrs Stewart. He seems to have thought that she might want to... to re-establish their former relations.'

When Sarah made herself look, Charlotte again resembled a figure carved from marble. It was almost frightening to observe such rigid self-control grafted over what must be an inner turmoil. 'Mrs Stewart was deeply distressed by the incident,' Sarah said, unable to keep a tremble out of her voice. It was not easy to speak of such things. 'In fact, I suspect she's reluctant to return to Auckland for fear of another such encounter. No, Mrs Taylor, I believe few things would make Mrs Stewart happier than to know she would never have to see Mr Taylor again.'

'Then perhaps she and I have something in common.' Charlotte's voice was brittle. 'Though I suppose that rather goes without saying.' She closed her eyes for a moment, then turned an apparently composed face on Sarah. 'You spoke of taking action, Miss Millish. What is it you propose to do?'

It was a relief to move on from such uncomfortable matters. 'I propose to ruin your husband, Mrs Taylor.'

Charlotte did not seem shocked by the announcement. She gave a nod of understanding.

'I very much regret the unpleasantness this will cause you,' Sarah said, 'but I'm afraid it's necessary. I hope that you can take steps to avoid the wreckage for yourself.'

'Perhaps,' Charlotte murmured.

'I will not permit Mr Taylor to continue in his present situation. I consider that by his actions he's sacrificed a certain measure of freedom. Exactly what happens to him next depends to some extent on you.'

Charlotte raised her eyebrows a fraction. 'Indeed? In what way?'

'I don't wish to pry into your affairs, but with the imminent change in your husband's circumstances, I wonder if you'll wish to continue living in Auckland.'

'And if I don't?'

'Then—forgive my frankness—if you decide to return to Australia, I imagine the choice is yours as to whether or not Mr Taylor accompanies you.'

'Yes, it is,' said Charlotte.

'If he does not—'

'If he does not, Miss Millish,' Charlotte interrupted, 'his situation will no longer be any concern of mine.'

It was something of a relief to have Charlotte Taylor match Sarah's own frankness. 'No, I suppose it won't. And if that turns out to be the case, I'll deal with his situation myself.'

She knew that Charlotte would have no more desire for a further meeting than she did herself. 'Perhaps you'd be so good as to let Mr Kendall know when you've made your decision. Forgive me, Mrs Taylor, but I require that it be made promptly.'

'That won't be a problem.' Charlotte rose to leave. 'I suppose I ought to thank you.'

'There's no need.'

'No, I rather think there isn't.' She studied Sarah, and gave a small nod. 'There's quite a strong likeness. I'm almost surprised I've never noticed it before.'

Sarah smiled, and brushed her fingers across the frame of Amy's photograph. 'Not as much as I might wish.'

Charlotte's eyes narrowed. 'I didn't mean a likeness to *her*.'

Jimmy strolled home from his office in the late afternoon. He would rather have gone to the club first, but things might be awkward there. A letter had arrived recently with the club's address on the back; he had thrown it into a drawer, but he suspected it contained further demands for the payment of his account. And given that he had outstanding debts to some of his fellow card players there, it would be as well to avoid the place for the moment.

He was going to have to do something about those debts. Being obliged to stay away from the club was a serious inconvenience. There was clearly nothing to be hoped for from Sarah for the time being; he wished he had not been so careless as to let slip her name to Ballard that evening. The more he considered the matter, the more he realised he was going to have to ingratiate himself with Charlotte. It was not a prospect he relished.

As if that weren't annoying enough, Henry had been sending him increasingly pressing messages, insisting that Jimmy needed to come into his office for some sort of meeting. No doubt it was to lecture him on the state of his finances. Henry could be priggish at times.

He let himself in his front door to find the house barely recognisable. Boxes were piled up in the entrance hall, along with vast quantities of cotton dust covers, and the maids were dragging a heavy-looking trunk down the stairs. There was barely room to move between the staircase and the wall. Jimmy stood still in shock for a moment, then followed the sound of Charlotte's voice through to the drawing room.

She was standing in the middle of the room, talking to the housekeeper, Mrs Rushton. When she saw Jimmy, she abruptly dismissed Mrs Rushton, who left the room with barely a glance in Jimmy's direction.

'Charlotte, what in the world is going on?' Jimmy asked as soon as they were alone.

She closed the door before turning to face him. 'I'm going home,' she said simply.

If Jimmy had not been so aware of his need to get into Charlotte's good graces, he might have snapped at her. Instead he managed a semblance of a smile as he spoke. 'A holiday's a fine idea—I know you've been rather down lately—but you might have given me fair warning! We'll need to make some arrangements before you leave.' Given the amount of baggage she seemed to be amassing, she must be planning a long holiday; in any case, it would hardly be worth her while going to Melbourne for anything less than several months. He would need to be sure he had access to the necessary funds before he could allow her to be away for so long.

'It's not a holiday. I'm doing what I should have done years ago. I'm going home for good.' She fixed him with a steady gaze while Jimmy struggled to find words.

'Wh-what are you talking about?' he managed at last. 'You can't mean it! What's brought this on?'

She took a few steps towards him. 'I had a very enlightening conversation this morning. With your *daughter.*'

A band seemed to be wrapped around his chest, squeezing it painfully. 'You spoke to Sarah?' Her lips compressed as she heard the name; he saw them whiten. 'Oh, God, I'm sorry you had to find out like that. I was going to tell you myself.'

'Oh, really? And yet you've felt no need in the twenty years we've been married to tell me that you had a child.'

'There was no point in upsetting you, when I had no idea what had even become of it. I'd put all that behind me by the time I met you. I know it was a foolish thing to have let happen, but I wasn't much more than a boy! It meant nothing, Charlotte.'

'It meant nothing to you that you had a child? Is that why it slipped your mind?' Her eyes were dry, but he saw that the skin around them was red and swollen, as if she had done a good deal of crying that day.

Jimmy scrambled for words that might rescue him from the peril he knew he faced. 'I didn't want to hurt you. Especially when you were so upset about not being able to have a child of your own.' That had been a mistake, he realised the moment he had said it. Her mouth trembled briefly, then set into a thin line. 'It was before I even met you! Surely you know that from the moment we met there's never been anyone for me but you?' For a moment, swayed by his own eloquence, he almost believed what he said.

'Don't take me for a fool, Jimmy. All those nights you haven't come home till the early hours? I know perfectly well you haven't always been at the club. And when we've been out to the theatre or to concerts, I've seen the looks you've exchanged with some of the women who hover about such places.' He sputtered an ineffectual attempt at denial, but Charlotte ignored it. 'I know such things happen. As long as you were prepared to be discreet, I was prepared to act as if I hadn't noticed.'

'And you were quite right,' Jimmy said, reeling from the revelation that Charlotte had been aware of activities he had thought himself so cautious about. 'Why upset yourself over something that didn't matter? Oh, I'll admit that I've slipped up once or twice, especially when you weren't well. Remember all those times you were ill?'

Her expression showed that she knew what he was referring to. There had been a long period when she had gone from one quack to the next, lured into trying ever more bizarre remedies by the false hope they offered. Some of them had caused violent purging that had confined Charlotte to the house for days on end, and left her weak and wretched.

'I wasn't going to force myself on you when you were in that state,' he said, pleased at the thought of how considerate he had always been. 'But that sort of thing's not easy on a man, you know. Especially a man with such an attractive wife as you.'

He thought that might have coaxed a smile from her, but Charlotte's cool blue eyes seemed to be looking past him. 'And still you speak as if you think I'm a fool. As if I'm meant to believe those were the only times you went to such women. As if it was for my sake! I don't suppose you even remember the last of those supposed doctors I tried?'

Jimmy searched unsuccessfully for the memory. 'There were so many of them.'

'That one was particularly memorable. I had to submit to…' He saw her shudder slightly. 'I don't think he even washed his hands first,' she murmured. 'Then he sold me a horrid, smelly paste I was meant to use. He said it would warm my inner workings. I used it that very night, and I almost thought I'd die of the pain.'

'I think I do remember that.' It had been a particularly frustrating occasion, Jimmy recalled.

'It was so bad that I had to go to the doctor—the real doctor, I mean. At least he had clean fingernails. Of course I had to tell him about the man I'd been to. The paste I'd used had burned the skin so badly that I had blisters. He scolded me as if I was a naughty child, and told me I should be content with my lot.'

Her eyes met his, and her gaze bored through him. 'When I told you what the doctor had said—about being burned and blistered—do you remember what you said to me?'

'I… no,' Jimmy admitted, wondering whatever all this had to do with Charlotte's threat to leave him.

'I was in agony. I'd been injured and humiliated, and now the doctor had told me I should give up even hoping. I remember I came home and started telling you—I wanted to talk about everything the doctor had said. I wanted you to… I was foolish enough to think you might be…'

She turned away. 'I got as far as telling you about the blisters, and you said, "Well, a lot of good *that's* going to do us." After what I'd been through, you could say such a thing to me.'

'I don't even remember… Charlotte, I didn't mean…' Jimmy said helplessly.

'Yes, you did. You said it to hurt me, and it succeeded. But it was my fault. I was foolish enough back then to care about what you thought of me.' Charlotte had been holding herself very still; now she moved over to the mantelpiece and studied the ornaments on it, then turned back to face him. 'I kept thinking if only I could have a child, that would make everything all right. I was sure I'd be happy then, with a child of my own. And you'd turn into the man I thought I'd married. That's why I tried all those horrible things. I'd have tried almost anything.' She had lapsed back into stillness, her gaze once again distant.

'Charlotte, you know I've only ever cared about your happiness.'

'You've only ever cared for your own comfort.' Charlotte's voice dripped with scorn. 'And I knew you were paying other women to provide it. Discreetly,' she added bitterly. 'But I don't call it discreet when you want to bring your little farm girl to Auckland and take up with her again.'

Jimmy realised that his mouth had fallen open in shock. Not for a moment had he thought Sarah might know that particular piece of information; still less that she might have shared it with Charlotte. 'Did Sarah tell you that? Charlotte, you mustn't believe her!'

'But I do believe her.'

'You'd believe that vindictive little bitch over your own husband?'

'I believe she told me the truth. I've become an expert at detecting lies over the years I've lived with you. You've given me practice enough.'

'You know that's not true! You've let her upset you—not that I blame you, having to listen that sort of talk. Charlotte, I'm sorry. I know I should have told you about her. But when I found out so suddenly just who she was, I thought I'd try and get to know her myself a little first, and see if she was worthy of being introduced to you. She's shown herself to be nothing of the sort, and I want nothing further to do with her.'

Charlotte raised her eyebrows. 'I'd rather received the impression it was she who wanted nothing to do with you. And that you were the one trying to take advantage of the connection.'

'I was trying to show an interest in the girl! See the thanks she's given me for it? Trying to make trouble between you and I.' He took a few steps towards her. 'Don't let her succeed. Don't let her ruin things for us.' He grasped at what seemed an increasingly flimsy lifeline. 'You know, I think you're quite right. We need to get away from Auckland and all its petty gossip.' And its troublesome creditors, he added to himself. 'I'll come to Melbourne with you. Hang the business, they can just manage without me for a while. We'll get away from all this nonsense, and it'll be like it was when we were first married.' He reached out a hand towards her face. 'You'd like that, wouldn't you, Lottie?'

He had not used his pet name for her in years; at the sound of it, she recoiled as if she had been struck. 'I'd like you to get out of my sight,' she said in a low voice. 'I'd like never to hear another of your lies.'

'Charlotte, you've let her poison you against me!'

'No, I haven't. You did that all by yourself. It's been a long, slow poisoning, but I've decided to draw the venom.'

'But…' Appealing to her affections was clearly not working; he tried another tack. 'You speak of being indiscreet—it'd be a scandal if you were to leave me. Aren't you worried about what people would say?'

237

'So I should stay for appearances' sake? That's just what I've been doing for years.' She took a few aimless steps around the room, one hand trailing along the back of a sofa. 'The trouble with appearances is that they're such shallow things. You scratch the surface and you find what's underneath. And it might be something ugly—something that needs covering up. So that things appear to be as they should.' She turned to face him. 'Father didn't want me to marry you, you know.'

'No, he made that clear enough to me at the time.'

'He thought I was marrying beneath myself. But I coaxed and wheedled, and he let me have my own way. I remember exactly what he said to me. "It appears he's the only man who can make you happy, my dear. And that's all I want." *Appears*, do you see? Do you see how deceptive appearances can be? I don't remember the last time I was happy.'

All the sharpness had drained out of her voice. Jimmy had never seen her looking so wistful. There was a fragility about her that roused something as close to tenderness as he had ever felt towards her. 'Charlotte, what do you want me to do?' he asked desperately. 'I'll do anything you want.'

Charlotte picked up a notebook and pencil that lay on the nearest sofa, and walked past him to stand closer to the window. 'Get out of my light, Jimmy.'

She began writing in the notebook. 'I'm making an inventory of the furnishings before I have the house closed up. If there's anything I want to keep, I'll have it sent over to me later. Though I doubt if there is.' She gave the room a brief glance. 'There're one or two things here from your old house, or gifts from your parents. That clock, for one.' She indicated a fine clock on the mantel. 'I'll leave all those for you. Let Henry know where you want them sent.'

She walked around the room, writing rapidly. 'I'm going to move into a hotel until I can get a passage home, and I'll appoint an agent to sell the house as soon as I've moved out. I spoke to Henry today, and told him I'd be leaving Auckland almost at once. I didn't feel the need to share the details of your connection with Miss Millish, I'll leave that up to you. Henry recommended I engage a lawyer of my own before I leave, as it's awkward for him to have both of us as clients. My lawyer and Henry can deal with any questions you might have.'

She spoke of it as a thing settled beyond any need of discussion. 'And where am I supposed to live?' Jimmy snapped.

'That's no longer my concern. It's not as if you could have stayed on here, anyway, even if I'd allow you to.'

"Allow" him! Jimmy felt his temper rising, but he managed to bite back the words that came to his lips.

'I gather from Henry that there are several options for you,' Charlotte went on coolly. 'You mightn't find any of them particularly palatable, but again, that's not my problem.'

'What on earth do you mean, "options"?'

'You'll need to discuss that with Henry. I don't wish to speak of it further. I don't wish to *think* about any of it. Perhaps Henry can give you some advice on where you should stay tonight, because you're not going to spend another night under my roof.'

'Charlotte, don't be ridiculous. You can't throw me out of the house!'

'I believe I'm doing just that.'

'You can hardly remove me bodily.'

'No,' she agreed. 'But I've had your bed stripped and your clothes packed away. I've told the servants they're to take instructions from no one but me. Are you going to find the bed linen and make the bed up yourself?' She held his gaze, staring back with a composure he found infuriating.

Jimmy looked away. 'You're clearly too upset to talk sensibly. I think it might be a good idea for me to stay away tonight.'

'I've had the maid pack you a suitcase with the things you're likely to need in the next few days. You can send for it when you know where you're staying tonight. I'll leave instructions to have the rest of your belongings sent on later once it's settled where you're to live.'

'All right, I'll go and see Henry and see if I can get any sense out of him. We'll speak again tomorrow.'

'I doubt that.' She turned her back on him. 'Goodbye, Jimmy.'

19

Henry was clearing his desk with a view to going home for the day when Jimmy was announced.

'Oh, you've decided to turn up at last, have you?' Henry said, not bothering to keep the irritation out of his voice. 'I've been sending you messages for days.'

'Henry, can you make any sense of what's going on? Charlotte's being ridiculous—she's threatening to leave me—and she's talking some nonsense about where I can and can't live. She seems to think you know all about it.' Jimmy flopped into a chair in front of Henry's desk.

Where to begin? Henry thought to himself. 'Have you taken leave of your senses, Jimmy? What possessed you to think you could get away with claiming a connection with Sarah Millish?'

Jimmy had the cheek to look affronted. 'What's that to do with you?'

'Unfortunately, I happen to be your lawyer—not to mention your brother-in-law. At the moment I'm not particularly happy about either of those facts. But if you choose to indulge in criminal activity—'

'Criminal!' Jimmy snorted.

'The last time I checked, fraud and slander were both crimes. And that's what your actions amount to. Miss Millish has documentary evidence and witnesses willing to testify against you, and she's quite prepared to press charges unless you—'

'Oh, this is absurd. The silly little bitch has taken it into her head to cause trouble for me, and now she's even got you taking her seriously.'

'If anyone's being absurd, Jimmy, it's you. And I'll thank you to show proper respect for the lady in question. Rather than calling her names, you should be grateful that Miss Millish is showing such forbearance. I certainly am.'

'Forbearance! Is that what you call threatening to charge me over this nonsense?'

'I do indeed. Rather than go ahead and press charges, she's indicated an alternative solution that she'd find acceptable.' Henry felt a profound gratitude towards Sarah Millish; it had been all he could do not to fawn over her when she had suggested that charges were not inevitable. 'Have you any idea how embarrassing it would be for me to have a convicted criminal as a brother-in-law? Particularly one who'd attempted to take advantage of a valued client. But she said she'd rather avoid scandal if she could, and that's why she specifically asked me to deal with it. I don't usually look after her affairs, you know. I can only assume she meant avoiding scandal for myself, as the case hardly reflects badly on her.'

Jimmy gave him calculating look. 'I wouldn't be so sure about that. But what's all this talk about these supposed options I have?'

Henry wondered briefly what was behind Jimmy's odd remark, but decided to ignore it in favour of the matter at hand. 'You had three, but I suspect that one of them has already slipped from your grasp. All three involve removing you from the possibility of doing more of the sort of harm that's brought you to this pass.'

Jimmy rolled his eyes. 'Must you lecture me, Henry?'

'Yes, I believe I must, since you show no sign of taking this seriously. Miss Millish said that if she could be assured you were about to settle permanently in Australia, she'd take matters no further. I don't know if that's because she doesn't much care for Australians, or if she thought Charlotte and her family would keep you on a tight rein.' Jimmy scowled at him. 'That would have been the best outcome for you, but Charlotte made it rather clear to me when she called earlier today that she had no intention of taking you with her, and I gather you failed to win her over this evening.' A deeper scowl was the only response.

'So you'll be staying in New Zealand, but with the requirement that Miss Sarah be assured of your incapacity to do further damage. That means leaving Auckland—'

'Oh, that's out of the question,' Jimmy interrupted. 'All my business contacts are here.'

'That hardly matters, considering that very shortly you will no longer have a business.' Henry sat back and waited for his comment to sink in.

'Eh? What the devil are you talking about?'

'Miss Millish informed me that she spoke to you after the first of these unfortunate incidents. She told you that the consequences of any further lapses on your part would include being ruined financially. It was not an idle threat, Jimmy. She took steps to ensure she'd have the ability to follow through if necessary. She holds various debts against the company, either directly or through some of her financial interests, and they're substantial enough to bring down the business if called in. Which is exactly what she's in the process of doing.'

'She can't do that!' Jimmy protested. 'I won't allow it! Surely we can put a stop to it?' He looked outraged rather than concerned; Henry could see that Jimmy had not yet comprehended just how grave a situation he had created for himself.

'No, we can't. And that's your doing—you've allowed the business to get into such a state that it's vulnerable to such action. Without Charlotte's assistance to prop it up, it would probably collapse even without Miss Millish's intervention. Although she's hastening the process somewhat.'

'That's not true! I'll admit we've had trying times lately, the market hasn't been the best, but—'

'Don't waste your breath, Jimmy. I've a fair idea of the state of your books. If we manage the process carefully, what assets the business has should clear the bulk of its debts. And speaking of debts, we'll need to see what we can do about your personal liabilities. I'm going to need a comprehensive list of your creditors. I realise it might be rather long. How much do you have in the bank?'

'Ah... not a large amount,' Jimmy said, looking away as he spoke.

That meant somewhere from a zero balance downwards, Henry was sure. 'Any other assets? Apart from the business, that is, which we must assume to be worthless.'

'Not really,' Jimmy admitted. 'There's... well, some of the furniture belongs to me. Things from the old house.'

'Hmm, you've one or two nice pieces. I'll see we use a reputable dealer so you'll get a fair price.' If Constance had a sentimental attachment to any of the items from her childhood home, Henry thought, he might well buy them off Jimmy himself. 'I doubt if that'll cover your debts, given your style of life, but I'll do my best to persuade your creditors to accept so many shillings in the pound. I don't particularly want a bankrupt for a brother-in-law, either.'

'Bankrupt! But... look here, Henry, I'm not going to put up with this. I don't see why I shouldn't defend myself in court. Let a judge and jury hear this nonsense of hers—surely there's a fair chance it'd be thrown out?'

'It's not easy to predict the outcome of any particular case with certainty. But I'd give you an extremely low chance of success. Miss Millish has convincing evidence, and quite frankly she'd cut a more impressive figure in court. A young woman alone in the world, trying to defend herself against an unscrupulous businessman, et cetera, et cetera. You'd be battling against their natural sympathies before you even stepped into the courtroom.'

'I'm inclined to chance it. I don't see how it could make things much worse. Even if I lost and got some sort of fine—'

'A fine! Jimmy, have you still not got it into your head how serious this is? We're not talking about a fine—you'd be thrown in jail, man!' Henry took a grim pleasure in seeing Jimmy's composure slip. 'Yes, jail,' he repeated. 'With hard labour, I'd imagine. Do you know what that means? I expect you've seen men working at the harbour reclamation—pick and shovel work, breaking rocks and hauling them about in

242

barrows. How long do you think you'd last at that sort of work?' Henry was aware that he was painting the worst case scenario, but he felt no compunction in doing so.

Jimmy looked badly shaken. 'The little bitch would do that to me? What sort of unnatural creature is she?'

'Unnatural?' Henry echoed, startled. 'Whatever do you mean by that?'

Jimmy paused for a moment as if deciding whether or not to speak, then his mouth curled into a grimace. 'What else do you call it when a girl plots something like this against her own father?'

Henry did not often find himself lost for words, but this was one such occasion. 'You... you're Sarah Millish's father?' he said at last. 'I knew she was adopted, of course, but... you?'

'Yes, though you'd hardly know it from the way she's carrying on,' Jimmy said bitterly.

Henry gave his head a small shake in an attempt to clear his thoughts. 'And may I ask who the unfortunate mother is?'

'You met her when she was staying with the girl. Amy—Mrs Stewart, she is now.'

Henry frowned, struggling to recall the name. 'Mrs Stewart? You mean that sweet little creature from Ruatane, or whatever it's called?' The woman was surely a good deal younger than he was; she had looked far too young to be the mother of the self-possessed Sarah Millish. 'How old was she, for heaven's sake?'

'Fifteen.'

Fifteen. Laura's age. Henry's memory of the small figure from the yacht, tiny alongside Sarah, merged with Laura's face to give him all too clear a picture of a frightened girl betrayed and abandoned. When old Mr Millish had spoken of the young girl who had been Sarah's mother, Henry had known that the man involved must be a scoundrel. But he had never suspected it might be a member of his own family.

'I wasn't very old myself, you know,' Jimmy said when he saw Henry's expression. 'It was that summer I went and stayed with Jack and Susannah. I was only twenty.'

The mention of Susannah brought to mind further implications. 'Good God, Jimmy, she's your sister's stepdaughter! She's more or less your niece!'

'Not by blood—we're not related at all.'

'You're morally her uncle—if the concept of morality means anything to you. And I'm sure you were more than willing to take advantage of the relationship. No doubt it allowed you unsupervised access to her.' He studied Jimmy, all sullen resentment and wounded dignity. 'Why didn't you marry the girl?'

'Oh, don't be ridiculous.'

'And exactly what is ridiculous about marrying a girl you'd got with child?'

'She had nothing, Henry! I could see that her father wasn't in a position to help me get established. And Father would have made an awful fuss about it, with me getting her with child, and her being Susannah's stepdaughter and all that. It would have held me back dreadfully—I'd already had the idea of trying my hand in Melbourne, but getting myself set up there with a wife and child in tow, especially if Father had decided to be difficult about it all... well, it just wouldn't have done.'

He glanced at Henry, who was making no attempt to hide his disgust. 'It wasn't an easy decision, I'll have you know. I was very fond of Amy. I wish I *could* have married her—in fact I've sometimes wished I had, in spite of all the bother it would have caused me. I expect I'd have been a good deal happier than Charlotte's made me. And I wouldn't have allowed Sarah to turn out the way she has, if she'd been under my authority,' he added grimly. 'But it just wouldn't have been sensible, not with my position at the time. I'd have been doing Amy no favours, either, dragging her up here for Mother to look down her nose at.'

Henry did not waste his breath attempting to make Jimmy see the feebleness of his arguments. 'I certainly hope that Stewart fellow she married treated her well.'

Jimmy gave him a quick, suspicious glance, then looked away. 'I wouldn't know,' he said with an unconvincing air of casualness. It was enough for Henry to see that Jimmy did indeed know something of the matter. He did not press the point, knowing that there was little chance he would be told the truth.

He dragged his thoughts back to the present. 'I find I must return to my original question—what made you suddenly decide to try and profit from your connection with Miss Sarah, after all these years?'

'I had no idea she was my child. It was at your house that I found out, as it happens. When Susannah was staying with you, and you started talking about Sarah—about her being adopted, and her mother being a girl from the country. I put two and two together, especially when I saw that Susannah knew more than she was letting on. And I knew Amy had been staying with Sarah earlier in the year—I saw her one evening after a concert, and I managed to get her to meet me the next day.'

'You met Mrs Stewart? Why ever did you distress the poor creature by doing that?' Henry was rapidly replaying events in his head; no wonder, he realised, Mrs Stewart had become so suddenly shy on the yacht when they had discovered their connection.

Again he saw Jimmy's gaze shift away from his. 'That's none of your business. A fat lot of good it did, anyway—every time I tried to visit her after that, I'd get some maid telling me she was out, or indisposed, or some other story. Sarah must have poisoned her against me.'

'I expect you did that without any assistance,' Henry remarked.

'Oh, don't go thinking I forced her. She was a willing participant, I can assure you. Positively eager, in fact, once I'd introduced her to the pleasure of the whole business. Such an affectionate little thing she was,' he said, smiling as he gazed into an invisible distance. 'It really was a dreadful waste that I couldn't marry her.'

'You had a choice in the matter, unlike the poor girl in question. I daresay she believed marriage was a possibility when she allowed you to ruin her.'

'Spare me the sermons. I've no appetite for them.' Jimmy's brow furrowed in thought. 'I've a good mind to try it,' he murmured. 'That might give the little bitch something to think about.'

'What idiocy are you plotting, Jimmy?'

'I may just have a way to make Miss Sarah,' Jimmy gave the title a scornful edge, 'sit up and take notice. She might decide to think again about this whole business of pressing charges.' He leaned forward eagerly. 'Henry, if Sarah persists in this idea of a court case, how would it be if we were to threaten to call Amy as a witness?'

'What in the world has Mrs Stewart to do with the matter?'

'If we could find some way to get Amy involved in the case, it might be enough to frighten Sarah out of taking it any further. And if she did decide to go ahead anyway, for all she claims to be so fond of Amy, surely that would only help my case? It would all come out in court— about Sarah being my daughter, I mean. The chaps on the jury would think a girl owed her father something. They'd hardly find me guilty of some crime just for wanting her to show me a little proper respect. And I wouldn't allow her to get away with painting me so very black regarding Amy, either. If it's a matter of defending my reputation, I don't see why I shouldn't let slip a few details about Amy's behaviour. That would show Sarah what comes of defying me. If they heard—'

'Enough!' Henry thundered. He rarely shouted, but he had a strong voice, and the room rang with it. Jimmy's head jerked back, and he stared at Henry in shock.

'I won't listen to another word of such talk,' Henry went on in a lower voice. 'And I won't attempt to appeal to your better nature, as I'd clearly be wasting my breath, so I'll confine myself to pointing out the likely consequences of such actions. I said earlier I'd give you a low chance of success if it came to a trial. If you chose to divulge your link with Sarah Millish, and even more so if you chose to drag Mrs Stewart before the court, you'd change the outcome in only one way—you would make it even more certain that you'd be found guilty. And you'd impel the judge towards choosing the harshest sentence available.'

Jimmy was frowning in confusion. 'Why should that be the case?'

'Because a good half of the men on the jury are likely to have daughters of their own, and we've all spent our share of time worrying about some scoundrel getting his hands on our girls. They'd see their own daughters' faces when they looked at little Mrs Stewart cowering in the witness box, with filth being spouted against her. And when they looked at Miss Sarah, they'd see the child you abandoned when you'd ruined her mother—the child you wanted nothing to do with until you saw that she could be of some use to you. I wouldn't be surprised if they asked whether hanging was an option in this case. It's not,' he added, seeing the question on Jimmy's lips. 'Some people might say that's unfortunate.'

Jimmy was silent for several moments. 'I suppose I'll have to take your word for all that.'

'Since there's no way of allowing you to bring the well-deserved wrath of the court down on yourself without causing harm to innocent parties, then yes, I'd urge you to proceed no further. In which case, let us get on with making new living arrangements for you.'

'Because the dear girl says I must leave Auckland.' Jimmy scowled. 'I must say I'm feeling no great affection for the place, with all the trouble I've had lately. I suppose I could try Wellington. Your boys seem to be doing well there, and I could probably get some sort of government job.'

Henry shook his head. 'No, Wellington won't do. That would be far too comfortable an option. Miss Sarah was quite adamant it had to be a small place, somewhere out of the way. One with no scope for you to do further harm, because there won't be much you *can* do there.' He was relieved that there was no need to risk any close contact between his sons and their uncle; Jimmy's was not an influence he would like to see them exposed to. 'I went over several possibilities with her, and we settled on one that was acceptable.' He patted a folder on his desk. 'You're to go and live in Russell.'

'Russell!' Jimmy looked stunned on hearing the name of the tiny seaside settlement. 'I can't go and live in Russell! Good Lord, I'm not sure I even know where it is.'

'You certainly can't continue to live in Auckland. Unless prison appeals, that is. And I'll see that you find your way to Russell, you need have no fear on that score. It's quite a distance north, but a boat goes there occasionally. I understand a good deal of fish is shipped out of Russell—I believe it's the only real activity in the area these days—so it's possible the boat may be somewhat odiferous, but that can't be helped.'

'And what am I supposed to do in a place like that?'

'Oh, Russell has several advantages as a place to dispose of you. There's a position vacant that Miss Sarah can use contacts she has in Customs to get you into. Nothing demanding—in fact it's the sort of job that might normally go to a retired civil servant from one of the lower rungs of the public service. You're to act as customs agent there, for the occasional boat that might require such offices. I understand there aren't a great number, so you'll have a good deal of free time to consider how matters came to such a pass. It's better than prison, Jimmy. Some might say a good deal better than you deserve. Your daughter is a merciful young woman.'

'My daughter is a spoiled little bitch.'

'There's even a house that goes with the position. Well, when I say a house... I understand there's an office with a room behind it as living quarters. That should do you nicely. The remuneration is, of course, very small. But then I don't suppose you'll find much to spend it on in Russell.'

'I... I won't put up with it. What sort of place is that for a man such as myself?'

'A quiet one. You'll need to accustom yourself to a rather retired style of life from now on. But I imagine there are some pleasant walks, and perhaps you could take up fishing.'

'Fishing! I hardly think so.'

'Gardening then, if you prefer. It's good exercise.' Henry put the last few files still on his desk away. 'You must excuse me, Jimmy, Constance will be thinking about serving dinner soon. I'll need you to call in again tomorrow to finalise the arrangements.'

'Ah, Henry... I don't quite know where I'm staying tonight. I thought it might be best if I left Charlotte alone to calm down, and, well...'

'Oh yes, I'd forgotten Charlotte planned to evict you. Can't you stay at the club?'

'I'd sooner not go to the club just at the moment.'

Henry studied his expression. 'I take it that means I can expect to see the club on your list of creditors?' There was no response beyond a quick grimace. Henry sighed. 'Oh, I suppose you can come and—'

He stopped abruptly. 'No, I'm afraid you can't come home with me. In fact I don't believe I want you in my house again. I have Laura to think of.'

Jimmy looked puzzled, then indignant. 'What are you suggesting? Good Lord, Laura's my niece!'

'Yes, exactly.' Henry opened a drawer of his desk and withdrew a card. 'Here's the address of a boarding house we sometimes recommend to clients who find themselves in sudden difficulties. The terms are most reasonable. I believe it's very clean, though of course rather basic.'

'A boarding house!' Jimmy said in disgust. 'One of those places with a hatchet-faced landlady, and everything smelling of cabbage?'

'I haven't met the lady in question, so I can't comment on her physiognomy. And perhaps you could request a vegetable other than cabbage, though it's wholesome enough. If it doesn't match up to your standards, you can always find yourself a hotel.'

'Well, that might not be possible just at the moment,' Jimmy said, avoiding his eyes.

'No, and I'm certainly not paying for you to stay in one. If the boarding house is beyond your means, I don't mind helping out. I can hardly have you sleeping on a bench in the park—you'd only get picked up as a vagrant.' He took ten shillings from his pocketbook and passed it to Jimmy. 'Don't book in for too long, we need to get matters settled soon. I don't want to try Miss Sarah's patience.'

'Russell,' Jimmy muttered. 'I don't know about that. I'll go and see Charlotte again tomorrow,' he said, brightening visibly. 'She was upset today—that's understandable, after the way Sarah spoke to her. She'll calm down overnight. I'm not sure you'll need to take this Russell nonsense any further, Henry—I expect I'll be leaving for Melbourne soon.'

Henry raised his eyebrows at Jimmy's seemingly boundless capacity for self-deception, but made no answer. He strongly suspected that Jimmy would find the door of Charlotte's house closed against him, with no response beyond being told that the mistress was "out", but he would let Jimmy discover that for himself.

He watched as Jimmy left the office. Organising the details of his exile to Russell was demanding a fair degree of time and trouble, but Henry considered it thoroughly worthwhile if it meant he would soon never have to see Jimmy again.

20

Late in January, Amy had a letter from Sarah that was as cheerful as she could have wished. Sarah wrote of tennis parties and of croquet on the lawn; of sailing on the harbour, and afternoon tea with friends. She mentioned in passing many of the people Amy had met while at Sarah's. Mr Kendall, she said, had been particularly helpful recently. After her long silence on the subject, Sarah renewed her invitation for Amy to come to Auckland again, preferably to settle there this time, and pressed her to name a date. There would be concerts and plays, she reminded Amy. A new bookstore had opened, and Sarah was looking forward to taking Amy there.

Do say you'll come, and soon, Sarah wrote. *Surely you need have no qualms about leaving David now that he has a wife to look after him?*

Towards the end of the letter Sarah added, as if it were a matter of no great consequence,

You may be interested to hear that Mrs Leith's brother, Mr Taylor, has left Auckland. He has chosen to settle in a secluded area, quite some distance north of here. I've heard it surmised that his health has obliged him to seek a retired life. It's understood that Mrs Taylor has returned to Melbourne, and is paying an extended visit to her family. Neither of them is expected to return to Auckland.

Amy laid down the letter and pondered what might be behind Sarah's words. Jimmy had looked well enough just a few months before, and she could not believe he would willingly choose isolation. However it had come about, Auckland seemed a more inviting place with the knowledge that it no longer held Jimmy.

Inviting, but for the moment quite unattainable. In the privacy of her room, Amy took up pen and paper and began her reply.

Of course I'd love to come and see you again, my darling, she wrote. *And I will as soon as I can. But I don't know when that's likely to be.* She paused, and chose her words with care. *Beth's rather poorly, you see, and I don't feel able to leave her just now. Once she's well again I can think about going away. But that won't be for a while, I'm afraid. Not for a few months.*

Amy's hand hovered over the page as she debated how much she should say. Her reference to Beth's being "poorly" would probably mean little to Sarah. Should she tell her about the baby? Which was worse: to risk overstepping the bounds of propriety by telling an unmarried woman that Beth was with child, or to have Sarah think that perhaps Amy was making excuses to stay away from her?

The answer was obvious. *There's to be a baby, you see. We're all very excited about it, but things aren't going quite as well as they could. Beth needs me here just now. Once it's all over and I know she's able to manage on her own, then I can think about coming back to you. I promise I will, my darling, just as soon as I can.*

She set the letter aside to give the ink time to dry, and left the room. She did not like to leave Beth by herself for too long, to make herself more frightened than ever by dwelling on what was to come.

With March almost over, Amy knew that Beth could go into labour at any time. She watched her closely for any sign of it. A day came when Beth was clearly even more restless and uncomfortable than usual. Amy went to bed that night fully expecting to be woken before many hours had passed.

A sharp rap on her door roused her from a fitful slumber. It was pitch dark; Amy guessed that it was probably some time past midnight. 'Ma?' she heard David call, the anxiousness in his voice clear even through the muffling of the wood. 'Beth thinks it's started.'

Amy was out of bed and had her dressing gown pulled on over her nightdress in moments. She followed David through the cottage to where Beth was sitting up against the pillows, her eyes wide and frightened in the light of the candle at her side.

'What should I do, Ma?' David asked. 'Shall I go and get Richard? It's pretty dark out there, but I'll go as fast as I can. Or should I do something here first? What can I do?'

When Amy managed to silence him for long enough to allow Beth to speak, she found that what had sent David running through the house in his nightshirt was Beth's report of a single, sharp pain.

'No, Dave, there's no need to go out in the middle of the night,' Amy said. 'It's much too soon—nothing's going to happen for a long while yet.'

'But how will we know when he should go?' Beth asked.

'You'll start getting pains closer together.' There was no need to tell her that they would also be a good deal stronger. 'Don't worry, Beth, I'll know when it's time.' She studied Beth's expression. It was important, she knew, to keep her as calm as possible. 'Would you like me to stay in here with you?'

'Yes, please,' Beth said in a small voice.

'But what can I *do*?' David persisted.

'The best thing you could do is try and get back to sleep,' Amy said. 'We'll need you to run all the messages in the morning.'

David insisted that he would not be able to sleep, but he lay down on top of the covers and rolled over to face Beth. Amy lit a lamp and turned it down as low as it would go, blew out the candle, and settled into a chair close to Beth's side.

'Aunt Amy?' Beth said a few minutes later.

'Mmm? Have you had another pain?'

'No, just that aching in my back I've had since this morning. I'm sorry I'm such a nuisance, making you sit there all night.'

'Of course you're not a nuisance! I don't mind—I often used to sit here of an evening, getting your Uncle Charlie off to sleep when he was having trouble settling.'

David's breathing soon told them both that despite his protestations he had nodded off. Beth's contractions seemed mild so far; they were frequent enough to prevent her from sleeping, but when they came she made no noise beyond a faint whimper. There was little risk that Amy might fall asleep, sitting upright in a none-too-comfortable chair. She and Beth spoke in whispers, careful not to disturb David, though he showed no sign of waking.

In the grey light of dawn Amy stood up, and was abruptly made aware of how stiff she was. She went around to the other side of the bed and placed a hand on the dark mound that was David. 'Time to get up, Davie.'

He sat up at once. 'Should I go and get Richard now?'

'No, not just yet. You can do your milking first, but don't take too long over it. Run next door and ask Uncle John to take your milk to the factory—I don't want you too far away from the house.'

Amy went to her own room to get dressed, leaving David to get himself ready for the day. He took some convincing that the birth was not imminent before Amy managed to shoo him out of the house. She made Beth as comfortable as she could before she set to work in the kitchen, popping into the bedroom every few minutes in between getting breakfast underway.

When David had come back from milking and gulped down a hasty breakfast, Amy judged it was time to let him go into town; more because his increasing agitation was likely to upset Beth than from any imminent need for Richard.

'There's no need to gallop,' she told him as he pulled on his boots. 'We don't want you to end up in a ditch. And let Aunt Lizzie know what's going on—you can leave that until you're on your way back,' she added, seeing the protest on his lips. 'I know you want to get on.'

She persuaded Beth to have a slice or two of bread, along with a glass of water, knowing it was best not to offer her heavier food. The contractions were stronger now, making Beth cry out with the worst of them.

'I'm sorry for making such a fuss,' Beth said after a particularly bad one.

'No, don't say that—you make as much noise as you want to. I'm sure I did when I was having the children.'

'Will it get really bad later?'

Amy set aside the old sheet she was ripping up to add to her pile of clean rags, and brushed a strand of hair away from Beth's forehead. 'Not so very bad, no. Richard will give you something to make you go to sleep before the worst of it.'

Beth seemed to shrink against the pillows. 'I wish I didn't have to have Richard,' she murmured. Amy suspected she was almost as fearful of that as of the birth itself. 'No, I know I have to,' she said before Amy could speak. 'It's no use being silly about it.'

David returned rather sooner than Amy would have thought possible without some hard riding, and with the news that Richard was on the way.

'He said he'd bring the nurse,' David added.

Hiring a nurse had been Amy's idea. Richard had supported her, as aware as she was that it would be easier on Beth if she did not have to be handled by Richard until she was unconscious. Finding a nurse willing to work under Richard's supervision had proved difficult, but at last someone had mentioned Mrs Dalton. She was a widow who had moved to Ruatane the previous year, to keep house for her bachelor brother. She had been a nurse at a London hospital, and was used to working with doctors. Amy had found her a stolid, taciturn woman, but she seemed clean and capable.

Beth brightened visibly at the mention of Mrs Dalton.

'Perhaps he'll get the nurse to do everything, and he'll just tell her what to do,' she said, looking hopeful. 'Do you think so, Aunt Amy?'

Amy hesitated. The nurse, she knew, would not be able to use forceps. 'I'm sure he'll get her to do as much of it as he can,' she said carefully.

Frank and Lizzie arrived a few minutes later, and David was unceremoniously ejected from the bedroom by Lizzie. 'We don't need you getting under foot,' she said, taking his arm and leading him to the door. 'Go and talk to your Uncle Frank. You can help him bring some stuff in from the buggy.' She closed the door firmly behind him.

'I brought a bit of food over,' she told Amy. 'I thought you wouldn't have had time to get much done today. Just some biscuits, and a few loaves of bread, and a bit of cold meat. Oh, and a couple of pies. Now, is everything going all right?' she asked Beth. 'Of course it is, you've got your Aunt Amy looking after you. I'll just see if there's anything that needs doing.'

She bustled about the room with Benjy clutched to one hip, checking the clean cloths and basins Amy had ready, and finding everything to her satisfaction. Then she plumped herself down on the bed and studied Beth's face. 'You haven't been getting in a state, I hope? You know you're not supposed to get upset, with you turning out to have that thing wrong with your heart, though I'm sure I don't know how you came to have such a thing without me knowing about it.'

'No, I haven't got upset,' Beth said, looking guilty.

Amy patted her hand. 'She's being very brave about it all.'

'That's a good girl,' Lizzie said. 'I'll just pop out to the kitchen and tell Frank and Dave where to put the stuff I brought.'

She was back some time later, this time without Benjy, whom she had entrusted to Frank. 'Your father's looking after Dave. He'll stop him working himself up into a state.'

'Can't Davie stay in here with me?' Beth asked, but Lizzie shook her head.

'It's no place for a man in here. Well, except we've got to have Richard. That's different, though, he's a doctor. He can make himself useful.'

When Richard arrived, ushering Mrs Dalton into the room ahead of him, Amy saw Beth's mouth tremble. She took Beth's hand and squeezed it, and felt the ghost of an answering squeeze.

Richard smiled encouragingly at Beth, but as he looked around the small room his smile faltered. 'I'm afraid there won't be room for all of us.'

'Of course. I'm sorry, I'll get out of the way,' Amy said. She released Beth's hand and made to stand up, but to her surprise Lizzie waved her back to her seat.

'No, you stop where you are,' said Lizzie. 'You don't take up much room. I can do cups of tea and stuff while we're waiting for something to happen.'

'Are you sure you don't want to stay with Beth?' Amy asked, reluctant to usurp Lizzie's place with her daughter.

'You'll be all right with your Aunt Amy, won't you?' Lizzie said to Beth. 'I won't be far away, anyway. It's better you stay here than me, Amy, you've got more of a quiet way about you—you'll keep her settled better than I would.'

'I did have some difficulty persuading Maudie to stay home,' Richard told Beth. 'She wanted to come, but I managed to convince her there'd be plenty of people to look after you. She sends her love, and I'll bring her out to see you in a day or two.'

The room seemed a good deal less crowded when Lizzie had gone. Richard sat on the bed and spoke quietly to Beth. Amy could see that he was studying Beth carefully as he asked her questions about how she was feeling. He listened to her heart, though it was impossible to tell from his manner how satisfied he was with what he heard.

While he spoke, Mrs Dalton set about checking the progress of Beth's labour, carefully arranging the sheet to keep what she was doing invisible to the other occupants of the room. She seemed to have a gentle touch; although Beth tensed and turned her face away so as not to look at Richard, Amy could see no sign that the nurse was hurting her.

'It feels as if the baby's lying properly, Doctor,' Mrs Dalton announced. 'She's only two fingers dilated, though.'

'We've quite a wait ahead of us,' Richard said to Beth. 'The most important thing is for you to stay as calm as you can. Try not to push when you feel a contraction, just let it pass over you.'

Amy watched as Beth made herself look at Richard. 'Will you give me something to make it stop hurting?' Beth asked.

'Yes, I will. I don't want you to suffer unduly. But do you think you can manage without it for now?'

'I... I think so. It's going to get worse, isn't it?'

'The contractions will get stronger, yes. As soon as you feel it's too much for you, I'll give you chloroform.'

'Couldn't you do it now, Richard?' Amy asked quietly. 'Do we have to wait till it gets bad?'

Richard hesitated before answering. 'I'd like to wait until things are further along if I possibly can. Chloroform is not without its risks, you see—and unfortunately, those risks are particularly significant when there's any problem with the patient's heart. It should be safe if I can use it for a very brief period—ideally, just for the actual delivery itself. I'm afraid that's some way off yet.'

'So should I try and do without having it at all?' Beth asked, a quaver in her voice.

Richard shook his head. 'No, we've moved beyond such barbarism in the treatment of women. I certainly wouldn't attempt a forceps delivery without giving you chloroform first. And if the pain gets too much for you in the meantime, I'll give it to you earlier.'

Beth spoke so quietly that Amy saw Richard incline his head to be able to hear her, but the quaver had gone from her voice. 'I'll wait till you say it's time. I can manage.'

254

*

The day dragged on. Beth was clearly in increasing pain, but she continued to insist that it was bearable. Things were moving slowly, according to the nurse. From time to time Lizzie brought in cups of tea, and spoke reassuringly to Beth. Once or twice she spelled Amy at the bedside, giving Amy the chance to stretch her stiff legs. Rather later than they would usually have eaten, Amy cobbled together a makeshift lunch from the food Lizzie had brought and some soup left over from the day before. People came in and out of the kitchen to snatch a hasty meal.

For the first time Amy could ever recall, David needed to be persuaded to eat. She had to take him by the hand and tug him before he would leave the parlour and come to the kitchen table. Once there, he jumped at every real or imagined noise from the direction of the bedroom, taking far more notice of that than of the food Amy put in front of him.

'You have to eat, Davie,' she said. 'You won't do Beth any good like that. You need to keep your strength up, so you can help me look after her when it's all over.'

That was enough to make him gulp down what was on his plate and hurry back to the parlour. When Amy came through on her way to the bedroom, he was perched uncomfortably on the edge of his chair, staring intently at the bedroom door. Frank, who was jiggling a somewhat fractious Benjy on his lap, seemed to be doing his best to engage David in conversation, but it was a one-sided affair. Amy hurried past them with only the briefest of glances. Right now it was Beth who needed her.

Lizzie emerged from the bedroom moments after Amy had entered it. 'I heard Benjy grizzling, give him here,' she said, sinking onto the couch and opening her arms for the little boy.

Benjy snuggled up against her when Frank placed him on her lap, but he soon began wriggling again, trying unsuccessfully to escape her firm hold.

'I'll give him a feed in a bit, see if that settles him down. I don't know if I'll be able to get him to have a sleep in a strange place, though. Dave, stop that!' Lizzie said sharply.

David, who had let out a yelp of alarm as Beth cried out, turned a bewildered face to Lizzie. 'Stop what?'

'Getting in such a state. If you keep that up, Beth'll hear you, and next thing she'll be worrying about you getting upset. She's got enough on her plate without that.'

'Sorry,' David said, his face a picture of guilt. 'I didn't mean to bother her.'

Lizzie heaved herself to her feet, Benjy in one arm. 'I'm taking Benjy out to the verandah. Frank, do something with this boy,' she said, waving her free hand in David's direction.

Frank studied David, who looked as tense as a coil of wire. 'How about we go outside for a bit?' he suggested. 'I could do with some fresh air.'

David glanced at him, then returned his attention to the bedroom door. 'I'd sooner stay close, in case they want me for something.'

'I shouldn't think they will, Dave. There's that many people running around after Beth, they don't need you and me just now.'

David showed no sign of having heard him. When Beth next cried out, he leapt to his feet and took a few steps towards the bedroom, then stopped and stood in the middle of the parlour, head down and looking utterly dejected.

Frank rose from his chair and moved towards the kitchen. 'Come on, Dave, let's take a look around the place,' he said, looking back over his shoulder. 'You can show me what you're thinking you might get done over the winter. You were talking about doing a bit of work on your cowshed, weren't you?'

David reluctantly followed him outside. Frank allowed David to choose their direction, which meant an aimless wander along the nearest fence line.

'It's hard, this waiting,' said Frank. 'Harder for her than for you, though.'

David turned a stricken face to him. 'I didn't know it was like this. The way it's hurting her! Beth's not one for making a fuss, it must be really bad. And she didn't want to have Richard, I said she had to.'

'You couldn't have made her if she'd put her foot down—she's got enough of her ma in her for that. It's good you've got Richard here, anyway, he'll see that she's all right.'

'I hope so,' David said in a low voice.

'This thing with her heart—it's not that bad, is it? I mean, she's always been that healthy, she can't have much wrong with her.' Frank had had a vague account from Lizzie, who had herself relied on what Beth had told her, and had not seemed unduly concerned. Now, faced with David's distress, an answering fear was gnawing at Frank. 'It's something to do with her missing a beat every now and again, isn't it? That doesn't sound so bad.'

'I don't know. Richard said it's a strain on her heart, having a baby. And that's my fault.' He met Frank's eyes, clearly expecting to be berated.

Frank shook his head. 'There's no sense talking about anyone's fault. Beth would've had a baby sooner or later, however it had turned out. It's a good thing you got Richard to look at her, or we wouldn't have known there was anything wrong. It's thanks to you we've got him onto it.' Lizzie had not been able to tell him just what it was Richard was expected to do, but everyone involved seemed agreed that it was something useful.

The afternoon was wearing on, and Frank noticed the cows bunching up near a gate. 'Must be about time to think about milking.' Perhaps, he hoped, the familiar task would steady David somewhat; especially if he had some company. 'How about I give you a hand? Joe'll be all right getting the other boys on with it at my place, I told him he might have to do without me this afternoon.' He saw David look uncertainly back towards the house. 'They'll know where to find you if there's any need, Dave.'

When they reached the gate, Frank saw the three Jerseys at the front of the herd, dwarfed by the Shorthorns. 'Beth's cows don't let the Shorthorns boss them around, eh?'

For the first time that day, he saw the ghost of a smile on David's face. 'No, they're always at the front of the line. They're cleverer than the others, they want to get milked and back in the paddock as quick as they can. The littlest one isn't even in milk yet, but she likes hanging around with the other two.'

'I hope you get a couple of heifers out of them come calving time. You'll want to build your herd up a bit now you and Beth have started having kids.'

That did not raise the spark of interest Frank had hoped for. 'I just wish this could all be over, and I knew she was all right,' David murmured.

Beth lay limp against the pillows. The front of her nightdress was drenched with sweat, and her hair was plastered to her scalp. She no longer seemed to have the strength to do more than moan when the pains took her. The months she had spent confined to bed had left her weak, and this labour was exhausting her. Amy patted at Beth's face and neck with a cloth wrung out in cool water, and wished she could do something more to ease the girl's suffering.

Richard checked Beth's heartbeat from time to time, and did what he could to reassure her that she was doing well. Things were moving along, the nurse said, but they seemed to be moving with agonizing slowness.

With the milking done and the cows moved to a fresh paddock, Frank could think of no further pretext to keep David out of the house. They were again sitting in the parlour, David picking distractedly at a worn patch on the arm of his chair, when Lizzie emerged from the bedroom.

'It doesn't sound as though anything's happening soon,' she said. 'I think you'd better take me home, Frank.'

'You don't mind leaving her?' Frank asked.

'I told her I'd be back in the morning, and she said she'd be all right without me till then. She's got Amy looking after her.' Frank knew that Lizzie considered Amy second only to herself in competence when it came to household matters. 'And there's Richard for if he's needed, and that nurse seems to know her business well enough. No, they can manage without me. I'd as soon not leave Maisie to get the dinner on by herself, let alone try and make them all behave at the table. You know what those boys are like, there'll be a riot if I'm not there to keep an eye on them. And Rosie'll play up for her and say she won't go to bed, and Kate copies what she does, so they'll have Maisie tearing her hair out.'

Frank did not like to leave David by himself, but he had no argument to counter Lizzie's. 'We're off home then, Dave,' he said, rising to leave. David nodded, but Frank was not sure if the boy was aware of what he had said. He glanced over his shoulder as he held the kitchen door open for Lizzie. David was slumped in his chair, still staring at the door into the bedroom.

The sun was getting low in the sky, and Amy began to worry about how she was to feed the four people in the house who might have some interest in eating.

'I'd better see about getting dinner on,' she said. 'Beth, will you be all right without me for a while?'

To her dismay, she saw Beth's eyes brimming with tears. 'No,' she whispered.

Beth clearly did not want to be left alone with Richard, and with the nurse who was almost a stranger to her. Amy could understand her fear, but it left Amy in an awkward position. 'I have to feed everyone, Beth. I'll be as quick as I can.'

Beth clutched at her hand. 'Please, Aunt Amy. Please stay here.'

Mrs Dalton got to her feet. 'I'll put a bit of food on, if you like. I've nothing useful to do in here till things get further along.'

Amy was only too glad to take up the nurse's offer. 'There's some cold meat left that Mrs Kelly brought over. And Dave can show you where the potatoes and carrots are.'

Mrs Dalton looked amused when she returned to say that she had food on the table. 'Your son insisted on peeling the potatoes himself,' she told Amy. 'You've trained him well.'

'No, that was Beth,' Amy said, patting Beth's hand. 'Dave never used to do anything in the kitchen till she started getting him to help.' She saw a faint smile flit over Beth's face.

'Well, she's made a good job of it,' said Mrs Dalton. 'He wanted to dish up a plate for her, but I told him she's got more on her mind than eating dinner.'

Richard went out to the kitchen at Mrs Dalton's invitation, but Amy assured the nurse that she was not particularly hungry. Mrs Dalton looked sceptical, and was back a few minutes later with a plate for her.

It did not seem right to sit at Beth's elbow and eat while the poor girl lay exhausted and in pain. Amy got up and walked around the room, stretching her cramped legs as she picked at the food on her plate. She saw Beth following her with her eyes, too weary to speak but watching her intently. Amy ate a few mouthfuls, then put the plate down on the chest of drawers and returned to her seat.

'Don't worry, Beth. I won't leave you on your own.'

The younger children were in bed, and peace reigned in Frank's parlour. But he found himself unable to settle. He pictured David sitting alone in his own parlour, no doubt working himself up into worse terrors as the hours wore on. Frank remembered those long, fear-filled hours all too well.

'I think I might go back over to Dave's for a while,' he told Lizzie. 'It's hard on him, waiting by himself.'

'That's a kind thought. He could do with the company—he's as bad as you for worrying when there's no need. Don't go staying there all night, though.'

'I won't.' Frank rose from his chair and placed a kiss on Lizzie's cheek before heading for the door. 'Don't sit up waiting, Lizzie. I might be a while.'

Frank found David in the kitchen, drying the last of the dishes from dinner.

'Still waiting, are you?' Frank asked.

David grimaced. 'How much longer do you think it'll take? That nurse wouldn't tell me.'

'I don't know, Dave. It's different every time.' Frank had a vague memory that Lily had been in labour for days with her first child; he chose not to share this with David. 'You've been keeping yourself busy—that's a good idea.'

'I thought it'd take my mind off worrying about her. It hasn't,' David said bleakly. He draped the dish towel over the back of a chair and went through to the parlour, Frank following in his wake. They sat down, and David resumed his vigil, staring at the bedroom door.

The nurse looked up from checking Beth's progress and gave Richard a nod. 'Nearly there, Doctor. She's fully dilated now.'

'Good.' Richard smiled encouragement at Beth. 'You've been wonderfully brave, Beth. I think it's time I gave you something for the pain.'

Amy had expected him to produce a wad of cloth to be soaked in chloroform, just as her old midwife had used. But instead Richard withdrew a small box from his medical bag. He opened the box to reveal two bottles, and an oddly-shaped device with a beak-like protrusion on one side. He put some liquid from each bottle into the device.

'I'll place this over your face, and all you need do is breathe deeply.'

Beth flinched as Richard brought the mask closer. Her expression might have suggested a bird of prey was menacing her. 'What does it do?' she asked, her voice trembling.

'It's chloroform,' said Richard. 'It'll allow you to be unconscious while the baby's delivered. There's no need for you to suffer through that.'

Beth closed her eyes for a moment, then opened them to turn a pleading gaze on Richard. 'Couldn't I see Davie first? Please? Just for a minute—before I have to go unconscious. Just in case,' she added in a whisper.

'Beth, I don't think—' Amy began, but Richard held up a hand to stop her.

'Do you know, I think perhaps you might,' he said. 'Amy, would you mind bringing David in? Just for a moment or two—he can say goodnight to Beth before she goes to sleep.'

Amy stared at Richard, more frightened than she had been all day. For Richard to allow this, she was sure, must mean he was afraid Beth would not survive the birth.

But speaking such things aloud was unthinkable. She waited for the nurse to arrange a sheet over Beth's lower parts, then hurried out to the parlour, noting vaguely that Frank had come back, and beckoned David. 'You can come in and see Beth before she goes to sleep,' she said. 'Just for a minute.'

David did not need to be told twice. He was through the door and crouching at the bedside almost before Amy had finished speaking.

'Are you all right?' he asked Beth.

From some unexpected reserve of strength, Beth managed to produce a smile for him. 'Yes,' she said, in the face of all evidence to the contrary.

'David, I'm afraid I can only allow you to stay for a moment,' Richard said from the other side of the bed. 'Beth's being very brave, but the sooner I can put her under chloroform the sooner she'll be out of pain.'

David leaned forward and gently kissed Beth. 'I'll see you later, then.' He went out, looking over his shoulder as he closed the door behind him.

Beth gave a great shudder, and the smile she had conjured for David's comfort turned to a grimace of pain. As Richard brought the chloroform mask close to her face she snatched at it and breathed in deeply.

'That's better, isn't it?' Amy said, seeing the lines of pain begin to ease from Beth's face. 'Now you'll go to sleep for a while, and when you wake up it'll all be over and you'll have a lovely little baby.' As she watched Beth slip into unconsciousness, she prayed fervently that it might be true.

'That was good you were allowed to see her,' Frank said to David. 'They never let me with your Aunt Lizzie.'

David flopped back into his chair. 'She looked that worn out and in pain. I don't know how she's putting up with it.'

'She's strong, like her ma. It's a hard thing, but she'll come through. You'll see.' Frank wished he could have put more conviction into his words.

'What if… what if she doesn't?' David said, the last few words coming out in a rush. 'I don't know what I'll do if Beth—'

'Don't talk like that, Dave,' Frank interrupted. 'That won't do anyone any good.'

David fell silent. 'I can't hear her any more,' he said after a few moments.

'They've put her under. That's good—you don't have to worry about it hurting her now.'

'No,' said David. 'But at least when I could hear her I knew…'

He left the words unspoken, but Frank could finish the sentence easily enough in his head: while David could hear Beth crying out, at least he knew she was still alive.

Richard took off his jacket, rolled up his shirt sleeves and washed his hands. Mrs Dalton stood aside for him to take her place at the foot of the bed.

'Amy, I need you to watch Beth carefully,' he said. 'Check her breathing—if there's any sign that she's struggling for breath, or any hint she might vomit, tell me at once.'

Amy moved her chair even closer to the bed so that she could hear the rhythm of Beth's breathing. When she felt able to risk taking her eyes from Beth for a moment, she darted a glance at Richard. She saw something metal in his hands, and knew it must be forceps. A shudder ran through her, even as her head told her that Richard had Beth's welfare in mind.

'The head's engaged,' she heard him say to the nurse. 'It's early to use forceps, but this is the stage that would put her heart in the most serious danger if I were to let nature take its course.'

Amy could see little past the mound of Beth's belly, but she thought Richard had removed something else from his bag.

'I'll need to cut, to make room to insert the forceps,' he said.

'So much?' the nurse murmured. 'She'll be a long time healing, poor child.'

Amy wiped away a trail of saliva forming under Beth's mouth, and dabbed at the girl's damp forehead. She did her best to ignore what was going on at Richard's end of the bed, though she could not avoid catching an occasional glimpse of a bloodied cloth being dropped into a basin.

She did not dare distract Richard by speaking to him, to ask if things were happening as they should. It all seemed to be taking a long time, and she thought she could hear Richard grunting with effort.

'This baby isn't eager to enter the world,' he muttered. 'Nurse? Would you mind?' Out of the corner of her eye, Amy saw the nurse leaning over to mop Richard's forehead.

Amy fought down the nausea she felt at what was happening to Beth; at the thought of metal tools scraping their way inside her, grasping at her unborn child to drag it into the world. She concentrated on her task of watching Beth, bending low over her face and occasionally stroking an unresponsive cheek.

Beth's breathing seemed steady, though from time to time her mouth twisted, as if she were dimly aware of what was being done to her. Amy fretted over whether Beth might wake up before this horrible business was over. Even worse was the fear that she might not wake at all.

'I think we're almost… just a little more… yes.' Amy heard Richard heave a breath of relief. She looked down the bed to see him holding a bloodied creature in his hands. Richard seemed barely interested in the baby; as soon as he had ensured it was breathing, he passed it to the nurse and turned his attention back to Beth.

Amy was vaguely aware that the nurse had taken the baby to the other side of the room to wash it and wrap it warmly; her concentration, like Richard's, was all on Beth. Beth was making small noises, almost like sobs. Amy wondered if she should tell Richard, but she did not want to interrupt what he was doing. The nurse was back at his side helping him; more bloodstained cloths appeared, and then something that made a wet, slapping noise as it was dropped into a basin. Amy guessed that it was the afterbirth. Now Richard seemed to be doing something that took finer movements; when she saw the nurse passing him a pair of scissors, Amy realised he had been stitching Beth where she had been cut.

Richard stood up, wiped his hands on a towel, and approached the head of the bed, leaving the nurse to finish cleaning Beth. He listened to Beth's chest, felt her forehead, then looked across her to where Amy sat watching him. His mouth eased into a weary smile. 'I think she's safe.'

'Thank heaven,' Amy murmured.

'And now let's have a look at this little girl,' Richard said more brightly. 'Yes, it's a girl—you've a granddaughter, Amy. Come and see her.'

He carefully lifted the baby and placed her in Amy's outstretched arms. 'She's a fine size. It's a good thing she wasn't any bigger, things were difficult enough as it was. Don't worry about those marks,' he said, indicating the red lines on either side of the baby's head. 'They're from the forceps—they'll fade in a day or two.'

Amy gazed at the little creature in her arms. Vivid blue eyes were studying the world with an expression that suggested it had yet to prove itself satisfactory. The baby's head was crowned with a blazing mop of hair.

'She's got red hair!' Amy said in delight and astonishment. 'Fancy her getting Charlie's red hair!' She planted a careful kiss on top of the baby's head. 'Can I take her out to show Dave? Only if Beth's not going to wake up for a bit, though—I should be here when she does.'

'Beth won't wake for some time yet,' said Richard. 'Yes, by all means go and see the new father, and set his mind at rest. Don't let him in here, though—better that he waits until we've been able to make Beth more comfortable.'

Amy carried the precious bundle out to the parlour, where David and Frank sat in the small circle of light cast by the lamp. David erupted from his chair at the sight of her, and took a step forward.

'She's going to be all right, Davie,' Amy said, anxious that he should not have to worry a moment longer. 'Beth's safe. And look!' She stepped into the lamplight and lifted the baby to show an awed David. 'You've got a daughter!'

21

Beth opened her eyes to find a sea of faces looming over her, and a warm weight pressed just below her chest. Pain nagged at the edge of her awareness, but she was too weary to give it any attention.

The faces resolved into David's, Aunt Amy's, and her father's; Richard and the nurse seemed to be there, too, but the lamplight was too dim for her to be sure.

She looked down to see what it was that nestled against her, small and soft and warm. Huge blue eyes looked into hers, from a little face crowned with red hair.

'See what a lovely baby you have?' That was her Aunt Amy's voice. 'You've got a little girl, Beth. You've got a daughter.'

Beth stared into those unfocussed eyes as she slowly unravelled the meaning of her aunt's words. It was all over. She was alive, and the most beautiful baby there had ever been lay in her arms. Her very own baby.

Hot tears welled up in her eyes and spilled unchecked down her cheeks. Her chest heaved with sobs till she was gasping for breath. The sobs hurt; everything hurt. But it didn't matter. Nothing mattered except her baby.

Aunt Amy was shooing the others out of the room, even Richard. She put an arm around Beth's shoulders and held her, making little wordless soothing noises until the sobs eased.

Beth felt herself being lifted forward slightly, just enough for her aunt to place another pillow behind her shoulders. A handkerchief appeared in front of her, and her eyes and face were gently wiped. It was a relief to be rid of the blurring of tears, because it meant she could see her baby properly. Aunt Amy was saying something about red marks—don't worry about the marks on her face, they'll fade. As if a few silly little marks mattered. As if they could stop her baby from being beautiful.

Her nightdress felt cool and crisp against her skin. She seemed to have had a fresh one put on her while she had been asleep. The buttons down the bodice were being opened, and her aunt was nudging at Beth's arms—no, she mustn't take the baby away, Beth wanted to tell her, but before she could make her mouth form the words, she realised that Aunt Amy was just moving Beth's arms to lift the baby a little higher.

'There won't be anything there yet, but this'll help the milk come in,' her aunt said. She brought the tiny, questing mouth close to one of Beth's breasts.

The baby nuzzled at her, licking at her nipple. It felt funny and strange and lovely. How clever her baby was, to know just what to do straight away. Beth looked up at her aunt, wanting to say this aloud, but she could not seem to get the words out.

Aunt Amy smiled at her and nodded. 'I know,' she said.

Beth looked back down at her baby. She was going to stay awake and watch her for whatever was left of the night. She felt as if she never wanted to close her eyes again, for fear of missing a moment's opportunity to study this wondrous being.

But her eyelids were drooping, refusing to obey her, and she felt her arms slackening their grasp. Aunt Amy was helping, holding the baby in place with her own arm under Beth's.

'You can go to sleep, Beth,' Aunt Amy murmured close to her ear. 'Baby will still be here when you wake up. It's all right.'

And it was all right. Everything was all right now. The baby had let go of Beth's nipple, but she was still pressed close against her, warm and soft and immeasurably comforting. Beth let her eyes close.

She would have to stay in bed for one more month, Richard told her. They all seemed to think she might make a fuss about it, but it hurt so much to do anything, even to be washed and have a fresh nightdress put on her, that it was easy to agree to whatever meant she could move as little as possible.

Amy looked after both Beth and the baby during the daytime, but if David was in the house when the baby needed to be fed, he assigned himself the task of carrying her to Beth. He would sit on the bed and watch her feeding, and when she had finished he would take his turn at cuddling her before putting her back in the cradle. After the first few days, when Beth had got used to the idea of letting anyone but herself hold her baby, she found she enjoyed watching them together, the baby tiny in David's big hands. It was almost as nice as cuddling her herself. As moving became less painful, she would sometimes nestle against David while they held the baby between them. That, Beth thought, was the best thing of all.

At night, Beth found that no matter how deeply she had felt herself to be sleeping, the moment the baby stirred she was wide awake. The same did not apply to David, who in spite of his good intentions would, if left alone, have slept until the little whimpers turned to full-blown wailing, but Beth soon discovered that a sharp jab of her elbow in David's side solved that problem.

When the baby was just over a week old, and Beth was finding herself less inclined to fall asleep without warning, she had David call Amy in one afternoon so that they could ask her opinion.

266

'We can't think of a name,' Beth told her. 'Well, not one that someone in the family hasn't already got. It has to be something nice. Not too fancy, though, or people will make fun of it.'

Rather to Beth's surprise, her aunt had a suggestion at once.

'What about Margaret?' she asked.

'That's quite nice,' said Beth. 'What made you think of that one? Is it from one of your books.'

Amy shook her head. 'No, it was the name of your Uncle Charlie's mother. She died when he was just a little boy. When Alexander was on the way, I told Uncle Charlie I'd name the baby after his mother if it was a girl. But of course I had another boy, and then after Alexander… well, there weren't any more babies to name.'

'Margaret,' Beth said thoughtfully. 'It's a bit long, though, and I wouldn't want people to call her Maggie. I don't like that much. Not Meg, either—we had a dog called that once.'

'Well,' said Amy, 'one of the books I read at Sarah's had a girl called Meg in it. She had a baby girl, and they called her Margaret after her mother, but the family called her Daisy. I think it's a sort of play on words—there are those little daisies called marguerites.'

'Daisy.' Beth tried the word out in her mouth. 'She looks like a little flower, don't you think? With her pretty face, and her hair so bright around it.'

'Of course she does,' said Amy.

'What do you think, Davie?' Beth asked.

'I don't know about that looking like a flower business,' David admitted. 'But Margaret sounds all right, especially if we can call her Daisy for short.'

'All right, that's decided,' said Beth. 'She's to be Margaret Amy.' She had the satisfaction of seeing her aunt's eyes light up with pleasure.

As the month wore on, and Beth found herself gradually less likely to be met by a stab of pain every time she moved, she began to look forward to being allowed out of bed. It would mean she could start looking after Daisy herself, instead of having to watch as her aunt tended the baby. Aunt Amy's friend Sarah had sent the most beautiful layette from Auckland; her aunt had spread out the tiny dresses and other garments on the bed for Beth to admire, but had suggested they wait until Beth was up and about before using the layette. Beth longed to put those pretty things on her baby with her own hands.

She also longed to go outside again. She had spent the entire summer trapped indoors, and now autumn was half over. The thought of being out in the fresh air, feeling the sunshine on her upturned face, and going about with David as he checked the cows, was enticing. Her Jerseys would be calving in a few months; Beth wanted to see for herself how they were faring.

Once she had allowed herself to look forward to such freedom, she became more and more frustrated at how long she still had to wait. The days seemed be dragging at an absurdly slow pace.

'I'm feeling really well,' she insisted to Richard whenever he called. A few lingering pains in places she preferred not to talk about with Richard did not seem reason enough to be trapped in the house. 'Couldn't I get up now?'

But every time she asked, Richard would say, 'I think we'll wait the full month. It's not much longer now,' and David and Amy would both say she had better do what Richard said. It did not seem fair to have them all siding against her, even when she secretly admitted to herself that they might be right.

At last came the day when Daisy was a month old. Richard listened to Beth's chest, asked her some questions about how she was feeling, then nodded his head. 'Yes, I think you can get up tomorrow,' he announced. Beth cast a look of triumph at David. 'I do want you to take things gently, though,' Richard went on before Beth had had the chance to voice her delight. 'You've been confined to bed for a long time now, you'll find you tire easily at first. Don't try to do too much.'

'She won't,' David answered for her. 'I'll keep an eye on her. I want you to get back to your old self again, Beth, not wear yourself out.'

Richard gave David what struck Beth as an odd sort of smile; it seemed almost sad. 'Dave, could I have a word with you before I leave?' he asked.

'All right,' said David. 'I'll walk you out to your gig, then.'

Beth heard the gig rattling away a few minutes later, but it was some time after that before David came back into the bedroom. The look on his face made her catch her breath. He closed the door behind him, sat on the edge of the bed, and told her what Richard had said.

Frank was checking the fences in a paddock near the road when he saw Richard approaching.

'You've been to see Beth, have you?' he asked. 'She's looking good now—Daisy's coming on well, too.'

'Yes, they're both doing well,' Richard said, though he sounded unconvinced by his own words.

'You want to come up to the house for a cup of tea? Lizzie'll have the kettle on.'

'No, thank you, I'd better be on my way. Please make my excuses to Lizzie. Frank, how old is Dave?'

'Eh?' Frank said, startled by the unexpected question. 'He's a year younger than Maudie, I think.'

'Nineteen, then. It's a heavy responsibility for a boy of nineteen.'

'Having a wife and kid already, you mean? Well, yes, it is. But Beth's a sensible girl, she's a real help to him.'

'Yes, of course she is, but I rather think there are matters that he feels are his responsibility alone. If you can spare the time, I think it would be a good idea for you to pay him a visit in the next day or so. He could do with a father's advice just now, and I don't think anyone could be better fitted than you to give it.'

'I might pop over tomorrow, then. What's up with him?' Frank frowned, taking in Richard's grave expression. 'There's something you're not letting on about, isn't there? Something to do with Beth.'

'There are things I can't speak of, Frank. I have to respect the privacy of those involved—yes, even when it's family,' he said, seeing the protest on Frank's lips. 'But Beth's quite well at the moment—in fact I've just told her that she can get up and about tomorrow—and Daisy's a picture of health. Beyond that, I'd rather leave it up to Dave to decide just what he wants to discuss with you.'

There was clearly no point in trying to press Richard for more. Frank took comfort from Richard's assurances that Beth and Daisy were both well, and resolved to visit David the very next morning.

Frank found David in one of the sheds, sanding down a flat piece of timber. Four long, thin lengths of wood were leaning against a bench.

'What are you up to there, Dave?' Frank asked.

There was a weary set to David's mouth and eyes; not at all surprising in the father of a small baby, but signs of strain that had not been there a few days before.

'I'm making a sort of table thing. It's so Beth'll be able to dress Daisy and change her without having to bend down. She's not meant to bend over in case it hurts her.'

Frank studied David's carpentry, impressed. 'Eight kids, and I never thought of anything like that. That's a good idea.'

'I want to look after her,' David said, as if to himself.

'Of course you do.' Frank seated himself on a sturdy-looking stack of wood to watch David at work. 'I was talking to Richard yesterday,' he said, careful to sound casual. 'He was on his way back from here.'

David looked up from his task. 'So you know what he told me.'

'No, I don't. Richard won't let on about things to do with doctoring, even when it's family. And you don't have to tell me, either. But if you want to talk, I'm listening.' He leaned back against the wall of the shed and waited.

David seemed to be giving all his attention to a roughness in the wood, rubbing vigorously at it. The sandpaper slowed to a halt, and he turned to face Frank, a haunted look in his eyes.

'Richard said having the baby's just about sure to have made Beth's heart weaker,' he began in a low voice. 'He said she'll be all right as long as...' He trailed off, then the words came out in a rush. 'He said she mustn't ever have another baby. He said if she does, it might kill her. I asked him, and he said women can keep having babies till they're over forty. Beth's only seventeen now. That's thirty years! Thirty years for me to mess things up. And it'd be my fault. If I mess up, I'll have killed Beth.'

Frank stared at him, shaken. He wished Richard did not take his duty of respecting confidences quite so seriously, so that Frank might have been prepared for this revelation.

This was his Beth whose life might be at risk. A small part of Frank wanted to encourage David to think that it would be his fault if she ever conceived again; to make him even more fearful of the very idea. But one look at David's eyes told him that the boy had no need of anyone else to make him feel the burden; he was being more than hard enough on himself.

'That's a hard thing for you to hear, Dave. I don't know what to tell you. I wish I did.'

David dropped his gaze. 'Thought you might want to take her back home once you found out.'

'I suppose I do, in a way. She's my daughter, and I'll never stop wanting to look after her. But that wouldn't be right.' Frank gave a rueful smile. 'Even if I could talk her into it, and we both know I'd have no show of that. Beth wants to be here with you, and I know you want to take good care of her.'

'But what if I don't take care of her?' David said, raising his eyes to show that same haunted look. 'What if I kill her?'

'Don't go saying things like "kill". It's no good talking like that.' Frank racked his brains for a response that would not be completely inadequate. 'You know, your Aunt Lizzie was really crook years ago, when Joe was a baby. I don't know if you'd remember—no, you were just a baby yourself, now I come to think about it. Your ma had Joey up here for a long while, she was feeding the two of you at the same time.

'Your Aunt Lizzie had this thing wrong with her insides—she was really bad with it. I thought I was going to lose her. It was the worst time of my life.' The memory still had the power to make his chest tighten. He had to wait a moment to recover himself before he could go on.

'Well, she came right in the end—and that's as much thanks to your ma as anyone else. But I was still worried about her, she'd been that crook. So I decided she'd better not have another baby for a good long time, give her the chance to get her strength back properly.' He snorted at his own misplaced confidence. 'We had another baby before the year was out. So I've no business getting all high and mighty with anyone else. But you know what, Dave? That was how we came to have Beth. I know this sounds a bit dopey, but it's as if… well, it's as if it was meant to be. It turned out all right, because we were meant to have Beth.'

David had listened politely, but Frank could see that his story had not made much of an impression. 'I know it's not the same thing, Dave, and… well, I don't know what I'm trying to say,' he admitted. 'But all you can do is your best. That's all anyone can ask of you. I trust you to do that—I think you might make a better job of it than I did, come to that.'

David made a movement somewhere between a shrug and a shake of his head, but said nothing.

It was all the encouragement Frank could find to offer, and he knew it was not enough. He let the subject rest, and thought of one that might raise David's spirits.

'You know, I've been thinking lately, I never did get around to giving you and Beth a wedding present.'

David roused himself enough to respond. 'But you paid for the wedding. You don't need to give us a present as well.'

'There was precious little needed paying for, just a bit of food. I didn't even get to buy Beth a new dress. No, I've thought of what I want to give you. How about we build you a new house?'

He had David's attention now. 'A… a new house?' he echoed. 'You mean it?'

'Well, I remember throwing off at you over the state of this one when you asked for Beth. So I thought I should do something about it. We won't be able to make a start for a few weeks, not till we dry the cows off, but with you and me and the boys all on it, it shouldn't take too long. What do you say?'

'That'd be really good. I'd like to have it a bit nicer for Beth. I can put in some money,' David added quickly. 'Sarah—that's Ma's friend in

271

Auckland—she sent some money for a wedding present, and we've only spent a bit of it so far. We bought a new bed out of it.' He looked away, but not before Frank caught the hint of a blush.

'No, I won't take a penny of your money—it wouldn't be much of a present if I let you pay for it. You can spend it on some more furniture when the house is ready. I'll tell you one thing I'll put towards it, though,' Frank said as a thought struck him. 'There's some money I've had sitting around for a while, because I've never been easy in my mind over it. I lent your ma a bit when Mal wanted to go away to the war—he needed it for his gear and all that. I told her there was no rush to pay it back, and of course when we got the bad news I didn't want to let her pay it back at all.' Belatedly, it occurred to Frank that reminding David of his brother's death was not likely to raise his spirits, but it was too late to stop now.

'But she wouldn't take no for an answer, she kept turning up once a quarter with her money. I found out she was putting all the money your grandpa left her towards it—I managed to put a stop to that, anyway. I told her I'd only take ten shillings a time, and she kept at it till she'd given me back the lot. And I've had it sitting in a drawer ever since. I couldn't give it back to her, and I couldn't spend it on myself. You'll be doing me a favour if you let me put Mal's money towards a new house for you and Beth.'

'I never thought of getting a new house,' David said, sounding a little dazed at the notion. 'Thanks, Uncle Frank.'

'Well, it's not going to be a mansion. Two bedrooms should do you to start with, so you've got one for your ma as well. I can give you a hand putting another one on when…' *When you have more kids* he had been on the point of saying; he caught himself in time to change it to, 'when Daisy gets big enough to need a room of her own,' but wished he had not raised the subject of bedrooms.

David's shoulders slumped. 'Maybe we should build one on for me,' he muttered.

'Dave, don't…' Frank began, but he could think of nothing useful to say.

22

When Frank shared the news with Lizzie, she was as shocked as he had been. She considered the fact that Beth would not have any more children as a greater tragedy than it had struck Frank, but she agreed with him that the responsibility of ensuring Beth did not conceive again was a heavy burden on David.

But there was nothing either of them could do, beyond expressing sympathy and concern. And there were more mundane matters on Frank's mind.

'How did it go?' Lizzie asked when he came home from a visit to town the week after his conversation with David.

'Pretty good. We shook hands on it.'

He waited until dinner time to tell the whole family.

'I've got a bit of news,' he announced. 'I've bought another farm.'

All the children (except Benjy, who sat on Lizzie's lap laughing and babbling away to himself) looked at him in surprise.

'Are we moving, then?' asked Danny.

'Of course we're not,' said Lizzie. 'I'd go distracted if I had to move all you lot.'

'No, it's as well as this one,' Frank said. 'I've bought Mr Carr's place. He's been trying to make a go of it, but it's got too much for him now he's getting on. He's buying a little place in town for him and Mrs Carr and Martha.'

'So we've got two farms now,' Rosie said, looking awed. 'I'm going to tell everyone at school.'

'Don't you go getting big-headed over it,' said Lizzie. 'Anyway, it'll be all over town by tomorrow, you won't need to tell anyone.'

'So why do you want another farm, Pa?' asked Mickey.

'Well, because of you boys, really. This one won't be big enough when you all get married and have families of your own.'

'As if anyone would want to marry those boys,' Rosie said, but her brothers ignored her.

'Mr Carr's farm's not a bad place, but it's been let go lately,' Frank went on. 'We'll have to do a fair bit of work on it over the winter. I won't be taking ownership till June, though, so we've got time to make a start on the new house for Dave and Beth before then.'

'You know, Pa, some people think winter's the time to have a bit of a rest,' Joe remarked with a smile.

'Not your pa,' Lizzie said. 'You won't catch him lazing around, any time of the year.'

'I just hope we get some fine weather,' said Frank. 'There's a lot to do. Now, the four of us will work on the new farm once it's all signed and sealed—Joe and me'll get you two started,' he said to Mickey and Danny. 'The fences aren't bad—a couple of them'll need fixing up before we put stock in there, that's all. The cowshed's only fit for firewood, but we won't need to do anything about that for a while. We'll use some of the paddocks as a runoff, and then there's a good flat part that'll be just right for spuds. We'll have to get the thistles out of it first, that's the only thing.'

'That sounds a lot of work,' Danny said, pulling a face.

'It'll keep us busy. Once it's all cleared and ploughed, you can get the spuds planted—no sense trying maize, not after last year.' The disastrous summer frosts of the previous year had destroyed maize crops throughout the Bay of Plenty, and Frank was thankful that he had devoted only a small area to the tender plant. 'Still, spuds are fetching a good price, what with so many places having the blight, so I'll get you to put a good lot in. Then it'll be up to you two to look after things till harvest time. It'll be your place one day, yours and Mickey's.'

Mickey's face brightened. 'So can we stay there while we're working on it? Maybe stay a few nights a week, anyway, so we don't have to ride there every day,' he added quickly, as if afraid he had asked for too great a liberty.

'You two, stay there on your own? Ha!' said Lizzie. 'I suppose you'd cook your own meals, would you? The only question would be whether you'd starve to death or poison yourselves first.'

Mickey started to scowl, caught his mother's eye and thought better of it. 'I thought maybe we could go into town and have a feed at the hotel some nights,' he mumbled. 'Or just go to the hotel, anyway,' he added in an even lower voice.

'Yes!' Danny said, catching his brother's enthusiasm. 'It's much closer to town than we are here, it wouldn't take long to ride in.'

'You boys are too young for that sort of thing,' said Frank. 'Hanging around hotels at your age can get you into all sorts of trouble.' He hoped that what made the notion of visiting the hotel appeal to the boys was the thought of drinking beer with men, rather than the female company on offer at a price. Mickey was not yet fifteen, and Danny on the point of turning thirteen; surely they were both too young to be thinking of such things? Frank certainly had no intention of encouraging it. 'And your ma's right, you're too young to stay at the new place on your own. No, I'm going to rent out the house and its bit of garden, probably with a horse paddock, too. That'll help with paying the bank. I don't want the house standing empty, either, not with—'

He saw the quick, warning movement of Lizzie's hand, and stopped in time. It was being rumoured around the town that Liam Feenan had been released from jail. He had been in prison for the last six years, after breaking into Reverend Simons' house and beating him so badly that the old man's life had for some time hung in the balance, but now Liam was said to be making his way back to Ruatane in the company of other men as unsavoury as himself.

Lizzie had reported that Maisie, when told of these rumours, had said little, but had clearly been upset. There was no sense troubling her further by referring to her cousin by name when there might be nothing to the story. 'An empty house that close to town, we might have kids breaking into it or something,' Frank said instead.

Mickey still looked mutinous. 'I dunno why we can't go into town on our own. Arfie's only the same age as me, and Grandpa gave him some money and said he could.'

'Yes, and Uncle Bill took it off him and said he couldn't,' Danny added.

Mickey elbowed his younger brother sharply. 'I wasn't going to tell them that bit,' he said, glowering.

Frank hid a smile. 'As a matter of fact, I already heard about that from Uncle Bill. Hard to keep secrets around here, Mickey.'

'And you can stop talking back to your father, if you want to see any pudding,' Lizzie added. Mickey subsided into aggrieved silence.

The rumours were true: Liam Feenan was back in Ruatane. At the dairy factory, Frank heard it from men who had seen him around the town.

'He's got a couple of other fellows with him,' Frank reported to Lizzie. 'That brother of his—Des, is it? And some bloke he was in prison with—he's a bit simple, they reckon, but he does what Liam tells him.'

'And they've gone back to their old place?' Lizzie asked.

'So they were saying down at the factory. Apparently the rest of the Feenans have pretty well cleared out over the last few years. Liam and Des's ma's still there, as far as anyone knows. Maisie's father, too, from what I hear. No one seems to have seen much of them for a while.'

'I don't suppose Liam and those other fellows will stay around Ruatane for long,' said Lizzie. 'Not with everyone knowing who they are—they wouldn't get away with any of their nonsense now. With a bit of luck, we'll none of us even see them before they take themselves off.'

*

Lizzie's optimism proved unfounded. Only a few days later, Frank was in a paddock near the road when a rider approached on a rangy, unkempt horse. He slid from his mount, leaving it to pick at the grass along the roadside, sauntered over to Frank and leaned on the top rail of the fence.

'A fine place you have here, Kelly,' he said in a pretence at affability.

Liam Feenan's time in jail had left him more heavily muscled, and certainly more liberally scarred, than when Frank had last seen him loitering on the streets of Ruatane. His clothes were ill-fitting, as if they might have belonged to someone else, and extremely dirty, but what struck Frank most was Liam's air of menace. It was as much a part of the man as his matted hair; heavy brows; and hard, dark eyes.

'What can I do for you?' Frank asked curtly.

Liam grinned at him, displaying an array of blackened teeth with several gaps. 'I've come to see my little cousin Maisie. I heard you've got her living with you. Very nice, I'm sure.'

'I don't think she's keen on seeing you. What do you want with her?'

'Well, I've been talking with my Uncle Kieran about you having Maisie here. We think it might be time she came home. Her dad's not too well, and my old mam's not the best, either. We could do with the help.'

Frank shook his head. 'No, this is Maisie's home now. I'm sorry for your troubles, but you'll have to sort it out yourself. You're not taking Maisie.' He put no real credence in Liam's assertions of illness in the family, but there was no point in openly accusing him of lying.

Liam looked him up and down. 'I don't know as it's up to you to decide where our Maisie lives,' he said, an edge of malice in his voice. 'It's up to her family.'

'It's up to Maisie. And she's said she wants to live here with us. I sorted that out with her pa a couple of years back.'

'Oh, yes, I heard about you buying her off Uncle Kieran. I've been talking about that with him, and I think you got too good a bargain. Ten pounds wasn't enough to buy her—you've just been renting her for the last couple of years.' His lips curled into an ugly leer. 'Rent's due again, Kelly. Either that, or time to give her back.'

Frank returned Liam's hard stare. 'Get out,' he said, surprised at how controlled his voice sounded. 'I'm not letting you near Maisie. You can tell her father that from me.'

Somewhat to his surprise, Liam turned to go. 'I'll be off home now,'

276

he said over his shoulder. 'You'll be hearing from me again. Be sure and give my love to Maisie,' he added before mounting the horse and setting off down the track.

Frank watched till Liam was out of sight, then walked up to the house. He found Maisie in the kitchen with Lizzie, the two of them doing a batch of baking while Benjy was having a nap.

'I saw that cousin of your just now, Maisie,' he said. 'Liam, I mean.'

Maisie let the tray of scones she was carrying fall heavily to the table. She stared at Frank with frightened eyes, but said nothing.

'What'd he want?' Lizzie asked.

'Never mind what he wanted. I sent him packing. But...' he looked at Maisie in concern. Her hands gripped the back of a chair; he saw them trembling. He wondered what memories were dredged up for her by the knowledge that Liam had been so close to the house. Frank hesitated, deliberating over how wise it was to frighten her further, then decided it was better that she be properly warned.

'He probably won't come around again. But just in case he does... you'd better not go too far from the house by yourself, Maisie. All right?'

Maisie was still trembling. She seemed to be staring into the distance rather than focussing on Frank.

Lizzie went to her and slipped an arm around her. 'Come on now, you're all right.' She guided Maisie to a chair, sat down beside her, and looked at Frank over the top of Maisie's head, frowning in concern.

Maisie gripped Lizzie's hand, took a deep breath, and spoke for the first time since Frank had entered the room. 'What about the girls?' she said in a low voice.

'What do you mean, Maisie?' Lizzie asked.

'Rosie and Kate.' She gave Frank a fierce glare. 'I don't want them going to the school and back on their own. You or one of the boys'll have to take them.'

'I don't think...' Frank stopped himself when he saw distress mounting in her eyes. He was sure that Liam and his cronies had no interest in anyone in the house except Maisie, but it seemed a small enough thing to agree to. 'All right, that's a good idea. We'll get Danny or Mickey to go with them, just till things settle down.'

'Those two'll be happy enough to get out of doing their work,' said Lizzie.

In fact she was wrong, somewhat to Frank's surprise. Mickey and Danny both grumbled over the task of escorting their little sisters, feeling it beneath their dignity, and only grudgingly agreed to take it in turns. Maisie suspected they might conveniently "forget" to pick the girls up after school, so every afternoon she would track them down and dispatch one of them, ignoring their complaints.

Frank was sure Rosie and Kate were in no danger, but Maisie's safety preyed on his mind. If Liam Feenan posed a threat to her, Frank wanted to know just what protection might be available beyond what he himself could offer. The next time he was town, he called in to Sergeant Riley's house to speak to the policeman.

'You know Liam Feenan's back in town?' Frank asked after they had exchanged perfunctory greetings.

Sergeant Riley scowled at the name. 'Him and his brother, and some other fellow who's probably as bad. Yes, I know. He been giving you any bother?'

'Maybe. He came poking around after Maisie—she's his cousin. You know she lives with us?'

'Yes, I heard that. You're a brave man, Kelly, taking in a Feenan brat.'

'Maisie's a good girl, and she's like one of our own now. Well, Liam started talking a lot of rot about wanting to take her back home with him. Says her father wants her back. I don't know if Liam'd be fool enough to try it, or if he was just throwing his weight around. We're keeping an eye on Maisie, there's probably nothing to worry about. But I just wanted to let you know, in case he does try something.'

Sergeant Riley looked at him blankly. 'If the girl's father wants her to come home, that's none of my business. None of yours, either.'

'Eh?' Frank said, startled. 'But Maisie doesn't want to go back there! She wants to stay with us.'

'That's as may be, but the girl's father's got the right to say where she lives. You can't go taking other men's children and saying you'll hang on to them, Kelly. And you can't have young girls deciding for themselves where they'll live. That's how those other Feenan girls ended up in the whorehouse.'

Sergeant Riley's response was so unexpected that Frank was briefly lost for words. 'But... but Maisie's not a little kid,' he managed at last. 'She's come of age.'

Riley looked at him skeptically. 'Maisie Feenan of age? That little runt? You sure about that?'

'I know she's small, but she's a couple of years older than my girl Maudie, and Maudie's twenty. So Maisie must be twenty-two.'

The sergeant continued to look unconvinced. 'I don't suppose you've got a birth certificate to prove it?'

'No,' Frank admitted.

'That's if her father ever bothered to register her, which I doubt. No, the girl's underage, and she's none of my concern. Now, I've things to attend to, Kelly, so if you've nothing else on your mind?'

Frank took the hint and left, a good deal more troubled than when he had arrived.

Maisie had become a careful clock-watcher ever since Liam's visit. 'It's about time for one of those boys to go and get the little ones,' she said to Lizzie one afternoon.

Lizzie glanced up from Benjy, who was claiming her full attention as she fed him. 'Mmm? Yes, I suppose it is. Don't fret, Maisie, they won't be too far away.'

'I don't know, they might have wandered off somewhere. They'll be larking about, with the mister not here to keep an eye on them.'

'It's about time *he* got home, come to that,' Lizzie remarked. 'He always ends up spending longer than he says he will when he goes to see the factory manager. He took Joey with him today, though, and I'd have thought Joey would start moaning if he thought he was going to miss his afternoon tea.'

'Well, I'm going out to find those boys if they're not here in ten minutes,' said Maisie.

Mickey and Danny had not appeared when the ten minutes were up, and Maisie set out in search of them.

She could not see the boys from the house, nor from the paddocks nearest it. Her fruitless search took longer than she had intended; she glanced at the lowering sun, anxiously aware that the afternoon was wearing on. She looked back at the house and briefly considered asking Lizzie's opinion on what she should do. Her mouth set in a firm line. If she did not ask permission to go on her own, she would not have the bother of arguing with her when Lizzie said no.

Maisie looked around apprehensively when she reached the end of the farm track and turned onto the road, but there was no one in sight. She set off briskly towards the school, and was nearly there when she met the girls trotting towards her on the fat little pony they shared.

'Those boys didn't turn up,' Rosie said indignantly. She had been enjoying the distinction of an escort to and from school; all the more so since she was aware how reluctant her brothers were to provide it. 'They're meant to be there when we get out!'

'I know,' said Maisie. 'I'll give them a piece of my mind, don't you worry about that.'

She rested a hand on the bridle as they walked back towards the farm, Rosie and Kate prattling away about their day while Maisie darted quick glances around her. There were patches of scrub on the far side of the road, and once or twice she thought she saw movement behind them. Probably just her nerves, she told herself.

They reached the entrance to Frank's farm, and Maisie allowed herself to relax. She looked up at the chattering little girls and smiled at the sight. Until they abruptly fell silent, and their eyes widened in alarm.

'Who's that—' Rosie began, then she let out a shriek.

Maisie turned and saw a man running towards her. She had not seen him for six years, but she knew him at once: her cousin Liam.

For a moment she was frozen to the spot. Then she let go of the bridle, slapped the pony on the rump and shouted at the girls, 'Go home! Go on! *Hurry!*'

A slap was not enough to startle Lumpy into rapid movement. The pony gave a snort, took a few steps forward, then halted as Rosie hauled on the reins. Both little girls were screaming now.

Liam reached Maisie, and by way of greeting he backhanded her across the mouth, knocking her head to one side. 'Well, if it isn't my little cousin Maisie,' he said, grinning at her. He snatched at her arm. 'I've missed you something awful, girlie. Your old dad's fretting, too. Time you came home.'

His fingers were digging into her arm like pincers, and she could taste blood in her mouth. He was dragging her towards a tall patch of scrub. She now saw the horse tied to a branch. Maisie pulled back, trying to ignore the pain in her arm, and twisted around to face the little girls. '*Run,*' she sobbed. 'Get *out* of here.'

Liam's grip tightened. 'That's right,' he called to the screaming girls. 'You run home and tell your old man that Liam's taken Maisie home. He knows what to do to get her back. You be sure and tell him that.'

He snatched a length of rope from behind his saddle and tied Maisie's hands with it, tightening the knot till she felt the rope rasping at her wrists. He flung her face-down across the horse's back just in front of the saddle, then mounted. When Maisie tried to move, he dug his elbow into her back until she cried out. 'Just behave yourself, Maisie, and it'll all be a lot easier. Get out of here, you little brats,' he called to Rosie and Kate.

By twisting her head, Maisie could just see the pony. Rather than running away, Rosie was kicking vigorously, trying to come nearer. Maisie felt the horse move awkwardly; out of the corner of her eye she saw that Liam had hold of a rough branch. He rode at the little girls, raised the branch, and whacked the pony with it.

Lumpy snorted, reared, and set off for home at a gallop. Maisie saw

Kate fall to the ground, and Rosie haul with all her strength on the reins, trying to stop the pony. Liam turned his own horse and kicked it into motion. The sudden lurch knocked the wind out of Maisie, and robbed her of one last chance to call out to Rosie and Kate.

23

Frank returned home to find the house in an uproar. Rosie and Kate, who had subsided into occasional sniffles, broke into loud weeping at the sight of their father.

'Maisie's gone,' they sobbed in unison.

'Liam Feenan's taken her,' Lizzie told Frank. 'He did it right in front of Rosie and Kate.'

'He grabbed her, and he *hit* her,' wailed Rosie, who had never before seen a girl hit by a man. 'I tried to chase him, but Lumpy was too slow.'

'And he hit Lumpy,' Kate put in. 'And I fell off.' She displayed her grazed knees.

'And then Lumpy tried to jump over the drain, and *I* fell off,' said Rosie. 'Then Lumpy went lame, and we had to walk home, and Kate could only go really slow.'

'Danny saw them coming up the track,' Lizzie said. 'He piggybacked Kate the rest of the way.'

'Danny and Mickey were meant to come and get us,' Rosie said, glaring at her brothers. 'Maisie wasn't even meant to come.'

One look at the boys' ashen faces told Frank there was no need for him to admonish them. They were clearly aware of their guilt. 'How long's she been gone?' he asked Lizzie.

'Nearly two hours now.' Her face was drawn with worry.

'You're going to get her back, aren't you, Papa?' Kate asked, her lower lip quivering.

'That man said to tell you he's taken her home with him, and you know what to do to get her back,' said Rosie. 'You're going to, aren't you?' She gazed trustingly at him.

'Frank, you're not to go there on your own,' Lizzie said in a low voice. 'We don't know how many fellows Liam's got with him.'

'I'll go with you,' Joe put in eagerly.

'And me,' said Mickey.

'Me too,' Danny added. 'Please, Pa.'

The younger boys looked at him with pleading in their eyes, but Frank shook his head. 'No, you two had better stay here. You can look after your ma and the girls. Joe, you can come with me.' He saw Lizzie's expression. 'I'm not going on my own, Lizzie. I'm not that dopey. I'll go and see Bill and the others, see if they'll come with me. Dave'll probably want to, as well. I know Bob Forster's fed up with Feenans thieving from his place, I might as well ask him, too.'

'Frank…' Lizzie said, as if about to protest, then gave a small shake of her head. 'No, I know you've got to go there. Just be careful, all right?'

'I'll do my best.' He kissed her uptilted face, and went outside with Joe.

Frank sent Joe on ahead to Arthur's, while he called in to David's farm. He was pleased to see Richard's gig by the garden fence. Richard had called in to check on Daisy's progress, and Frank found both his sons-in-law in the house.

He quickly explained what was going on, and David announced he would join him before Frank had the chance to ask. 'I'll go and tell Uncle John and Uncle Harry, too,' said David. 'The more the better, eh?'

Richard had said nothing in front of Beth and Amy, but he followed Frank outside, where they watched David jump over the nearest fence on his way next door. 'Frank, do you think this is wise?' Richard asked.

'Eh?' Frank said. 'What do you mean? I'm going to get Maisie back.'

'And what gives you the right to demand that she's returned to you? If her father—'

'Her father?' Frank broke in. 'Her father was happy enough to sell her to me for ten pounds. He didn't care what happened to her then.'

'He... I beg your pardon?' Richard frowned. 'Whatever do you mean?'

'Back when we decided to have Maisie live with us instead of going back and forth to the Feenans. Just after you and Maudie got married. I used to pay Maisie for helping Lizzie, and her pa took every penny off her. She was under age then, and I knew he wouldn't let her come unless I made it worth his while. I think he thought I'd try and beat him down over the price, but I wasn't going to haggle over Maisie. I just gave him what he asked for. And now he wants more. Or at least that bastard Liam does. And if I was fool enough to pay it, he'd do the same thing again in a month or two.'

'You *bought* Maisie?' Richard said in astonishment. 'Frank, you can't trade in human flesh! And I hardly think whatever bargain you struck would stand up in a court of law.'

'Law's no help with this,' Frank said bitterly. 'I asked Sergeant Riley about it, and he said Maisie's pa can take her back if he wants. The law might do something about it if I could prove she's of age, but we haven't got her birth certificate. So it's up to me to fetch her back with us, where she belongs.'

'So you're going to march up to this Feenan chap with a crowd of men and try to scare him into handing over Maisie?'

'That's about it, yes. Are you coming or not?'

Richard was looking at Frank as if he were a stranger. 'When I told people back in England that I was coming out to the colony, many of them warned me the country was full of savages, white as well as brown. They said this was a lawless place. I laughed it off, and told them New Zealand was as civilised as England. But I've never been as close to agreeing with them as I am at this moment. And you of all people! Frank, what makes us better than savages is something called the rule of law. If one abandons that, one abandons—'

'That's a lot of fine words,' Frank interrupted. 'And if I had some time to waste I'd stand here and listen to a few more speeches from you. But I'd like to get there before they start raping Maisie.' He saw the shock on Richard's face. 'Yes, I said rape. That's what she was scared of, and that's what they're likely to do. Your rule of law business might be interested after Maisie's family's finished with her, but I'm not going to wait for that. I'm fetching her home.' He turned on his heel and walked quickly over to mount his horse.

Frank looked around at the dozen men assembled on the beach, close to where a rough track led off to the Feenan farm. Bill had brought Alf and Ernie, John and Harry had come, and Matt Aitken and Bob Forster had both readily agreed to help. Matt and Bob had each brought their oldest sons; the Leith men had managed to forbid their own much younger sons from joining the party.

'All right, no sense hanging around here,' said Frank. 'Stay in a bunch, we want them to see us all at once. I'll—'

He stopped speaking when he heard the rattle of wheels. He looked over his shoulder, and was startled to see Richard's gig approaching.

'I didn't expect you to turn up,' he said when Richard had drawn closer. 'You coming with us?'

'If that's all right with you?'

Frank shrugged. 'I suppose so. Come on, you fellows, let's go.'

As the group moved off, Frank dropped back until his horse was beside the gig. 'What happened to that stuff about the rule of law?'

'I'm not saying I approve,' said Richard. 'But I thought there might be some broken heads that need patching up after you've finished here.'

Frank grunted, and guided his horse back to the front of the group.

They dismounted where the track degenerated into a narrow, rutted path edged with gorse bushes, tethered their horses to what passed for a fence, and approached the house on foot.

When they were close to the rough building, they halted, and Frank called out.

'Liam Feenan? You there?'

It was not Liam who emerged onto the verandah, but his younger brother, Des. He took one look at the assembled men and swore loudly, then called over his shoulder.

'Liam! There's half the bloody town out here!' When there was no response, he disappeared back into the house, calling Liam's name as he went.

Liam emerged, clutching a bottle. He stared at the assembled men, but his gaze soon settled on Frank.

'What the hell do you think you're doing, Kelly? What you got all this lot for? This business is between you and me.'

'Where's Maisie?' said Frank.

'What's it worth to you? I hope you brought some dough.'

Frank shook his head. 'You're not getting a penny. I want to see her.'

'Well, you can just come back tomorrow. I might let you see her then, if you ask nicely. And if you make it worth my while. Go on, get out of here. I've got plans for tonight.' He glanced towards the house, smirking.

'We're not going until I've seen Maisie. I want to see if she's all right.'

'Oh, she's happy as a pig in mud, now she's back home with us. She gave me a big kiss just now.'

It was all Frank could do to stop himself from leaping onto the verandah and taking Liam by the throat. But that would not help Maisie, still in the house with at least two other men who had probably been drinking all afternoon. 'I want to see her for myself. Bring her out here.'

Liam took a gulp from the bottle and wiped his hand across his mouth. 'I'll see if she's decent for visitors,' he said as he went back inside.

Frank heard a door open somewhere within the house. There was a thin, high-pitched wailing that turned his stomach, but the wailing was cut short by the slamming of a door, and a moment later Liam reappeared. With one hand he had hold of Maisie's wrist, which he had shoved high against her back. His other arm was across her throat as he half-led, half dragged her onto the verandah.

Her eyes widened when she saw Frank and the other men, but she did not make a sound, even when Liam lessened the pressure on her throat. Her dress was smeared with dirt; one of the sleeves had been ripped off, and Frank could see the marks where fingers had dug into her thin arm. There was a cut on her lip, and a bruise was forming on one cheek.

'All right, you've seen her,' said Liam. 'Come back tomorrow and you can have her. Just make sure you bring your rent, or I might get a little bit annoyed with Maisie.'

Frank looked into Maisie's terrified eyes, then turned his gaze on

Liam. 'I'm taking her home with me now. Let her go.'

Liam forced Maisie's arm higher up her back. Frank saw her face twist in pain, but still she did not utter a word.

Frank stepped forward. 'I said let her go.'

Liam lowered his arm from Maisie's throat, and Frank felt the men around him relax slightly. But Liam's hand snaked down to his belt, and came up with an ugly-looking knife. 'Don't take another step, Kelly.'

Frank did not pause for thought. It was crystal clear to him what he must do. He took another step forward, then another.

'Frank!' he heard Richard hiss. He was vaguely aware of Bill holding Joe back on one side, and John restraining David on the other. He ignored them all, walked forward, and climbed onto the verandah.

Liam stared wild-eyed at him. He waved the knife in Frank's direction, then held it to Maisie's throat. Frank was so close now he could hear the tiny whimper she gave. 'You want me to kill the little bitch? Eh?'

'Put it down, Liam,' Frank said quietly.

Liam waved the knife again. 'I'll slice the pair of you, Kelly—you and your little whore both.'

Frank shook his head. 'No, you won't do that. There's a dozen witnesses here. You use that knife and you'll swing for it. Is it worth getting hung for?'

He held Liam's gaze for what felt like an age. Something close to madness was there, but with a spark of cunning at its clouded core. Frank concentrated on that spark, willing Liam to see what was to his own best advantage.

Liam's hand dropped. He bared his teeth like a snarling dog, gave Maisie's arm one more savage wrench, and shoved her at Frank. 'Ah, you want the little bitch that much, you might as well have her.'

Frank got an arm around Maisie's waist just in time to stop her collapsing to the floor. He helped her down the steps and the few paces across to where the other men were converging on them. He kept his arm firmly around her; beneath his hand he felt her quick, light breaths like the fluttering of a tiny bird.

Maisie took a great gulp of air. She seemed about to speak, when once again Frank heard a wailing from the house. Maisie's eyes followed the sound, then caught Frank's.

'That's Aunt Bridie. She's really bad.' She clutched at Frank's sleeve. 'Can you help her?'

Frank looked at the plea in her eyes, and resigned himself to making the attempt. 'What's wrong with your ma?' he called to the figure still standing on the verandah. 'Does she need the doctor?'

Liam gripped his knife more firmly and spat on the floor. 'You want my old mam as well? You can have her, then. She's no bloody use here.'

He went inside, and returned carrying what looked like a bundle of dirty rags. 'Go on, then,' Liam snarled. 'Help yourself.' He dropped his burden onto the verandah, went back into the house and slammed the door behind him.

Frank was still supporting Maisie, but some of the other men quickly gathered up the bundle that he now saw held a feebly moving body. Bridie was gently lowered to the ground, and Richard crouched beside her.

'I can't do anything for her here,' Richard said after a quick examination. 'I need to get her into town. Would one of you mind fetching my bag? I'll have to anæsthetize before I try moving her.'

Bobby Forster went running towards the gig. While he waited for his bag, Richard came up to Frank. 'Maisie,' he said quietly, 'I need you to tell me if there's anything I should do for you right now. No broken bones?' He ran his hands quickly down her arms; she flinched at the touch, but Richard seemed satisfied. 'What about wounds? Is there any bleeding? Anything that needs to be bandaged straight away?'

Maisie shook her head. Richard held her gaze for a moment, then turned to Frank. 'All right. It'll be easier on Maisie if Lizzie sees to whatever else needs doing. I'll come out and see her tomorrow. Now, get her home, Frank. That's what she needs most.'

When they got to where the horses were tethered, Frank hoisted Maisie in front of the saddle. 'It won't be too comfortable, sorry. We won't go faster than a walk, though—I don't want to shake you around any more than I have to.' It would have been easier to have Maisie ride behind the saddle, but he wanted to be sure of holding on to her if she should faint.

The other men had mounted, ready to set off. Frank heard Bill sending Alf and Ernie on ahead, and he roused himself to speak to Joe. 'Don't wait for me. You get home and tell your ma we're on our way— she'll be worried sick. You too, Dave—no need to have Beth worrying. Thanks, you fellows,' he called to the others. Most of his companions headed off at a trot, and were soon out of sight.

Bill remained at his side. He said nothing, but Frank was aware of his presence and grateful for it. The horse plodded along patiently, needing no guidance. For the first minute or two Maisie gripped the mane where Frank had placed her hands, but she soon slumped against him. Her arms slid around his waist under his open jacket, and she leaned her head on his chest. It was an awkward pose, with the pommel of the saddle between them, but Maisie seemed content with it.

Anxious that she should stay conscious, he spoke quietly to her as they made their slow way along the beach. She roused herself to ask if Rosie and Kate were safe; once reassured, she listened to him in silence. Frank talked on and on, aware that much of it was nonsense. He pointed out the waves breaking on the shore, and the stars gradually appearing in the darkening sky. All the while Maisie clung to him, sometimes looking around as he pointed out some object, but much of the time staring up into his face.

The journey was becoming dreamlike. Beneath the drone of his own voice, Frank could hear the soft thud of the horse's hooves on the sand, replaced by a harder sound when they left the beach and started up the valley road.

They reached the track to Frank's farm. Bill said goodnight and went on his way. For the few minutes it took to approach the house, they rode in silence.

As they drew close, the whole family ran out to meet them. Frank disengaged Maisie's arms from around his waist so that he could dismount, then caught her as she slid to the ground. He gathered her up in his arms and carried her inside, leaving the boys to take care of his horse.

Directed by Lizzie, he took Maisie through to the girls' room and placed her gently on the bed. Lizzie ordered everyone from the room. Frank went back out to the kitchen, vaguely aware of Rosie clamouring to be told all that had happened. He reached up to one of the highest shelves and took down a bottle Lizzie kept there for medicinal purposes. Frank could not remember what it contained; a glance at the label told him it was brandy. He took a glass from the bench, sat down at the table with bottle and glass, and poured himself a generous measure.

He took a gulp. A line of heat traced its way down to his belly. Frank stared at the glass in front of him, but instead of the brown liquid he saw a long knife with a notched edge. He saw again the madness in Liam Feenan's eyes. He felt himself begin to shudder. With an effort, he held the glass steady long enough to take another gulp.

Rosie tugged at his sleeve, but Frank waved her away. He drained the glass, put it down heavily, and closed his eyes for a moment. Then he opened them, and looked around the warm, comfortable kitchen.

Joe and the younger boys were sitting along one side of the table, looking at their father in some awe. Rosie seemed to have wandered out of the room; Kate had probably trailed after her. With all that was going on, Lizzie had somehow contrived to prepare a meal, and the pleasant aroma of whatever was keeping warm on the range filled the room. Frank became aware that he had stopped shuddering.

There was an indignant squeal from the direction of the passage; Frank recognised Rosie's voice raised in complaint. 'That's what you get for listening at keyholes,' Lizzie said, shooing the little girls into the kitchen in front of her. 'Frank, come up here, I want to talk to you.'

Frank got up and followed her into the passage. Lizzie closed the door behind them, giving Rosie a warning glance as she did so, then led Frank far enough away from the kitchen to thwart any listeners.

'How is she?' Frank asked.

'Bruised from head to foot, and those fellows put their hands where they had no business going, but nothing's been done that won't heal. It's a good thing you got there smartly.'

Frank slumped in relief. 'The way that bugger talked, I wasn't sure what he might've done already.'

'It seems he thought you'd turn up tomorrow morning, cap in hand and with a pocket full of money. So him and those other fellows were in no hurry. From what she's said, that Liam fellow told her what they were going to do with her, then they shut her in a room with her aunt—in the dark, if you please—they'd boarded the window up—while they sat around drinking. They thought they had all night to play with her.'

The words that came to Frank were not ones he wanted to use in front of Lizzie. He shook his head, and swallowed down the bitter taste in his mouth. 'Well, we've got her back, and that's what counts.'

'I'm going to give her a good, strong dose of laudanum to make sure she sleeps, but she wants to see you first. Just for a minute, mind.'

They went into the girls' bedroom. Maisie was propped up against the pillows, dressed in a crisp, white nightdress. Her face shone with cleanness, marred only by a bruise on one cheek. She saw Frank, and lifted her arms like a child wanting to be picked up.

Frank sat on the edge of the bed and leaned over so she could wrap her arms around his neck. She pushed her face close to his. Her breath tickled his ear as she murmured, 'Thanks.'

She released her hold and lay back against the pillows, smiling up at Frank. 'I wasn't going to let anyone take off with one of my girls,' he told her.

'So, are you happy now?' Lizzie said, approaching the bed with a small glass. 'Come on, my girl, a good dose of laudanum for you.'

Maisie gave Frank a conspiratorial grin. 'I told the missus I wouldn't take it till she fetched you.'

Frank watched as she obediently took the medicine. 'You know,

Maisie, it's about time you stopped that "Mr" and "Mrs" business.'

Maisie looked startled. 'What should I call you, then?'

'Uncle Frank and Aunt Lizzie, if you like. Or maybe…' He glanced across the bed at Lizzie. She met his eyes, smiled, and nodded her agreement. 'Maybe you should just call us Ma and Pa.'

Lizzie insisted that Maisie stay in bed all the next morning. At lunch time she allowed her to get up and join the family in the kitchen, but made Maisie sit quietly rather than helping. There was little chance of her tiring herself; Mickey and Danny vied with each other to pass her whatever she might need, to see that her glass was kept topped up, and to wrap a shawl around her shoulders when Lizzie asked if she was cold.

'Make the most of it,' Lizzie remarked when their fussing had gone on long enough for Maisie to complain. 'It won't last.' She fixed the boys with a hard look. Frank had given both boys a stern talking-to that morning about doing as they were told in future, especially when it involved looking after one of their sisters. He knew their contrition was genuine; like Lizzie, he also knew that it would not last long.

Richard called in during the afternoon. Maisie declared that she did not need to be "poked at"; when she was backed up by Lizzie's assurance that all was well, Richard gave in graciously.

'I'm sure you know best, Lizzie,' he said, demonstrating just why he got on so well with his mother-in-law. 'Maisie, your aunt was asking after you, so I'll be able to tell her how well you are. She's in the infirmary at the convent, and the nuns are taking good care of her.'

'Is she going to be all right?' Maisie asked.

Richard shook his head. 'I'm afraid she's not. She has a growth, and it's quite advanced. But I'll do what I can to see that she doesn't suffer unduly.'

Frank could see that the news did not come as a shock to Maisie. 'Can I go and see her?'

'As soon as Lizzie says you're well enough for outings. I'll be calling in to see her every afternoon, so I'll tell her to expect you. It'll give her something to look forward to.' He looked over Maisie's head at Lizzie. 'Don't leave it too long, Lizzie.'

Frank walked with Richard out to his gig. 'So Bridie's pretty bad, eh?'

Richard grimaced. 'I thought I was inured to such things, but seeing that wretched creature has given me a new understanding of the tenacity of life. How a person can cling on in such a state… Her womb is rotten with cancer, Frank. It's half eaten away. When I examined her, I found maggots there.' He shook his head. 'It's the closest I've come to vomiting at the sight of a human body since I was a medical student.

'I took a gamble that the nuns would take her in. It's good of them, especially since I gather she hasn't exactly been notable for her attendance at Mass. They're excellent nurses, and they'll see that she dies clean, and as comfortable as possible. That's the best that can be done for her.'

Frank nodded. 'I'll bring Maisie in as soon as I can. Bridie was the only one at that place who ever took any notice of her.'

'Frank...' Richard hesitated a moment. 'To be quite honest, I'm not sure what I think about what happened last night. The idea of taking the law into your own hands like that—it seems like mob rule.' He smiled ruefully. 'But certainties have a way of evaporating in the face of a frightened child. Whatever the law might say, it's clear to me that Maisie belongs with you and Lizzie. And I'm glad you have her back, however you went about it.'

Maisie persuaded Lizzie into allowing a visit to Bridie on an afternoon a few days later. The cut on Maisie's lip was already healing, and Lizzie helped her arrange her hair so that the bruise on her cheek would not be visible to a casual observer.

Frank took Maisie in the buggy. They made their way to the convent tucked behind Ruatane's Catholic church. A nun took them through to the convent's infirmary, where they found Richard in a corridor talking to an older nun.

'She's on heavy doses of opiates for the pain,' Richard said as he led them along the corridor. 'You may find she's rather sleepy. But she should know you, Maisie.'

He opened a door and ushered Maisie ahead of him. Frank followed Richard, and found himself in a small room with a metal-framed bed taking up most of it. The floor was bare wood, the walls were painted white, and a window looked out on a peaceful patch of garden.

Bridie was propped up against the pillows. What Frank could see of her looked a good deal cleaner than on the previous occasions he had met her, but the skin was stretched taut over the bones of her face. Her hands rested limply on the bedcovers, all knuckle and sinew. Her hair had been cut short; it stuck out around her head like a dark halo.

Maisie sat by the bed on the one chair the room held, while Frank and Richard stood against the wall opposite. Bridie seemed pleased, in a languid fashion, to see her. She listened while Maisie talked quietly, but her attention soon wandered. Her gaze drifted idly around the room until it fell on Frank. Her lips curved in the ghost of a smile.

'Come here, handsome,' she said, one hand moving slightly against the covers.

Richard blinked. 'Which of us do you mean, Miss Feenan?'

Bridie glanced at him for barely a moment. 'Ah, you're all right for those as fancy pretty boys, but this fellow's an old flame of mine. He gave me five pounds once, I'll have you know. He's the only man who ever did that.' Her hand moved again, in what seemed to be an attempt to pat the covers invitingly. 'Come on. I won't bite you. Well, not unless you want me to.'

There was surely no harm in humouring her. Frank crossed the room to stand beside the bed. 'That's better,' said Bridie. 'Now I can look at you properly. Who'd have thought I'd end up with the nuns, eh? Do you see who I've got here?' A slight tilt of her head directed Frank's attention to a small painting on the wall above her bed. It showed a young woman dressed as a nun, smiling mildly down as if on the bed's occupant. 'That's Saint Bridget. She's me name saint, see? The nuns put her up there to keep an eye on me.' Bridie smiled, and Frank saw a trace of the spark he had once noticed in her dark eyes. 'Ah, but she's an Irish lass, so she'll not be one for passing judgement on the likes of me. What about a kiss, then?'

'Eh?' Frank said, startled. 'I don't know about that!'

'Ah, go on. There's no harm in a kiss, is there? Don't worry, I won't be carrying tales to your missus. Come on.' She pursed her lips.

Frank looked across the bed at Maisie. Her expression was unreadable. He looked down at the plea in the eyes of the dying woman, and admitted defeat. He leaned over to give her a chaste peck on the cheek, but Bridie tilted her face just in time to ensure that the kiss landed on her lips. Her breath was like a cesspit; it was all Frank could do not to gag. As he straightened up, he saw her hands moving. He strongly suspected that, had she had the strength, she would have wrapped her arms around his neck.

'Not bad,' she said. 'That'll have to do me, then. I'm not likely to get another in here.'

A nun came in with a pile of clean bedding. 'And what are you up to, Bridie Feenan? Trying to lead respectable married men astray, are you? You're a shameless creature.'

Frank felt an irrational rush of guilt as he stepped quickly back from the bed, but when he met the nun's eyes he saw a twinkle there. 'You'd best be getting along,' the nun told him. 'I've things to do for this saucy piece. The girl can stay if she likes, though I'll be dosing Bridie up before I start on her.'

Richard went out into the corridor with Frank, leaving Maisie in the room. 'She looks pretty bad,' Frank said.

'Yes. The nuns have done fine work cleaning her up and making her comfortable, but she won't last long. I shouldn't think it'll be worth bringing Maisie again—another day or two and her aunt won't know her. I doubt if she has more than a week of life left in her, if that. She's livelier today than she's been since I brought her in.' He gave Frank a sidelong glance, and smiled. 'Though I must say you brightened her up rather more than Maisie did.'

'I can't say I grudge it, the poor beggar. Do you want to know what I gave her five pounds for?'

'Out of Christian charity, I expect. It's none of my business, Frank.'

'I don't mind telling you. It was when I gave Maisie's father the ten pounds. I slipped Bridie five pounds as well, just for taking a bit of notice of Maisie.'

'Well, you obviously made quite an impression on Bridie Feenan, one way or another,' Richard said, still smiling. 'You might like to tell Maisie her cousins and their crony have left town—I imagine she'll be relieved to hear it.'

'I'll say she will! They didn't hang around long, eh?'

'No, and I might have had just a little to do with that, as it happens. I took it upon myself to call on Sergeant Riley and tell him about an upstanding citizen being threatened with a knife in front of witnesses. I suggested rather strongly that it wasn't something authority could ignore. I've heard since that he paid Feenan a visit—I presume he took a few burly chaps with him—and gave the fellow to understand that if he didn't take himself away from Ruatane rather promptly, the consequences would be unpleasant. Feenan's not likely to return, either, knowing he'd be facing arrest if he did so.'

'Well, that's a bit of good news, all right,' said Frank. 'I didn't think he'd be fool enough to try anything like that again, but Maisie wouldn't have been easy in her mind, knowing he was still around.'

'No, I imagine not. I've found out somewhat more of what's going on in her old home—the nuns are rather a good source of news. Someone from the church has been out there to check on Maisie's father, and it's been decided to ship him off to an Old Men's Home. And it seems the family's many creditors are clamouring for payment, so the property will be auctioned and any proceeds put towards the debts. The house will be torched first—it seems generally agreed that would increase the value of the property rather than the reverse.'

'I wouldn't have the place if it was offered me for nothing,' said Frank.

Maisie came out a few minutes later, when Bridie had lapsed into unconsciousness. Richard went back to talk to Sister Bernadette, the nun tending Bridie, and Frank took Maisie out to the buggy. He waited to help her up into it, but she stood looking across the road. Frank followed her gaze, and saw two young women there, staring back. They were dressed decently enough, albeit somewhat gaudily, but the elaborate care with which he saw several women take a wide berth to pass them told Frank just what profession they followed.

'That's my sisters,' Maisie whispered. 'They must've heard about Aunt Bridie.'

Frank studied Maisie's face, trying to decide the right thing to do. 'Do you want to go and talk to them? You don't have to if you don't want to.'

'Yes,' Maisie said in a small voice, but she did not move. She clutched at Frank's sleeve.

Frank sighed. 'Do you want me to go with you?' Maisie nodded.

It was easy to imagine what the main topic of conversation would be in many Ruatane homes that evening, Frank reflected as he led Maisie across the road. "I saw Frank Kelly talking to a couple of the whores from the Royal Hotel—right there in the main street!" It was a good thing Lizzie was too wise to be bothered by such talk; though Frank rather hoped Arthur would not hear this particular piece of gossip.

Close up, the two looked much younger; almost like girls dressed up in their mother's clothes, Frank thought. Until he looked into their faces, and saw eyes that seemed far older than Lizzie's.

'This is Sally and this one's Norah,' Maisie said. 'This is Mr Kelly.' She looked down at the ground.

Sally was easily recognisable as Maisie's sister, though she was not quite as small. She had the same sharp features, and the same dark eyes. The wicked glitter in those eyes reminded Frank of the first time he had met Bridie. He managed with an effort not to show any sign of recognition at her name; Sally Feenan had a certain fame among the young men of Ruatane, and Frank had occasionally heard her mentioned during his visits to the dairy factory. He had noticed that the boys who spoke of her in the most awestruck tones were those who were clearly too young to have enjoyed her services, and he was quite sure the stories were exaggerated. But the fact remained that Sally had a reputation for entering into her work with enthusiasm.

Norah came closer to being pretty than did either of her sisters. Her hair was thicker and somewhat wavy, and her eyes were large and a dark blue. They were currently directed on Frank in such a baleful glare that for a moment he wondered if Norah had mistaken him for someone else. He saw bitter resentment there, mingled with defiance and just a hint of something else. She hid it well, but Frank remembered how Maisie had looked at him before she learned to trust him. He recognised the same fear deep in Norah's eyes.

Frank had never felt the least temptation to visit the whorehouse, but he could understand why an unmarried man might occasionally crave some willing female company. But it was beyond his comprehension how any man could take pleasure in buying the reluctant services of Norah Feenan. He slipped a protective arm around Maisie's shoulders, and blessed the day he had brought her into his house and away from the shadow of her sisters' fate.

'How's Aunt Bridie?' Sally asked without preamble.

'Bad,' said Maisie. 'She won't last long. She says it doesn't hurt any more, though.'

'Who'd you get this from?' Norah asked, fingering the bruise on Maisie's cheek and turning her glare back on Frank.

'Liam.' From the scowls on her sisters' faces, Frank was sure they believed her. 'He caught me and took me back to the old place. But he,' she pointed to Frank, 'came and got me off him.' Her eyes met Frank's for a moment; Frank could see that she was too shy to call him "Pa" in front of her sisters.

Sally Feenan gave Frank an openly appraising stare. 'This is the bloke you live with, eh?'

Frank felt Maisie stiffen under his arm. 'Maisie lives with me and Mrs Kelly,' he said. 'She's like one of our own daughters.'

Sally continued to look him up and down. 'Haven't seen you at the hotel—or upstairs where we work. You should come around one of these nights. I'd see you enjoyed yourself.'

'Thanks,' Frank said cautiously. 'But I like to stay home with my wife and kids of an evening.'

Sally gave a low laugh. 'Didn't know there was blokes like you. You done all right for yourself, Maisie.' She turned to Norah. 'What do you reckon?'

Norah looked at Frank and nodded slowly. 'Yes. You done all right.'

She threaded her arm through Sally's, and the two of them walked off down the street in the direction of the hotel, heads held defiantly high.

Frank had hoisted Maisie into the buggy, and was about to climb in himself, when Richard emerged from the convent gate and beckoned him over.

'I spoke to the Mother Superior a few days ago about Maisie's problem with proving her age,' Richard said. 'She said she'd see what she could do. I've just spoken with her again, and she gave me this for you.'

He handed over a sheet of paper, tightly rolled and tied with a thin ribbon. 'I think you'll find this has as much legal force as a birth certificate would. It's Maisie's baptismal certificate. She's most definitely of full age—and she has the right to say where she lives.'

24

Daisy was almost three months old, and in Amy's opinion an enchanting child. She was as good a baby as David had been, sleeping through much of the night and easy to coax to smiles and giggles when she was awake. Amy delighted in any opportunity she had to play with Daisy and hear that magical little laugh, or just to sit with the baby on her lap, seeing those clear blue eyes turned on her, still with a touch of wonder in them at the newness of the world.

Such opportunities were not common. Now that Beth had regained much of her former strength, she spent all the time she could out and about on the farm with David, but she had no intention of leaving Daisy behind. She fashioned a carrying sling out of an old sheet, and she would set off with the baby nestled cosily in it, but somehow if the three of them came back to the house together David would always have persuaded her to let him carry Daisy.

Lizzie did not approve of all this. 'You shouldn't cart her around like that all the time,' she told Beth when she heard what was going on. 'Babies need their sleep. You just get her settled down in her cradle before you go wandering off with Dave.' Beth listened politely, and with what appeared to be careful attention, then proceeded to ignore her mother's advice.

Only if Daisy happened to be asleep when Beth decided to go out with David would Amy find herself left in charge, and only if Daisy then happened to wake up before her mother returned did Amy have an excuse to take her out of the cradle and play with her. She knew she should leave Daisy to soothe herself for a few minutes rather than rushing in to pick her up, but somehow she always found she was by the cradle moments after hearing the first hint of a cry.

A good start had been made on the new house during May, but things had come to a standstill after that. There had been a spell of wet weather, and now Frank and his sons were busy on work that had to be done on Frank's new farm before spring. David had done a little on the house since then, but there were not many tasks that could be done by one person. He accepted the delays patiently enough, knowing Frank would come back to it as soon as he could spare the time.

Amy enjoyed seeing David's delight in his baby daughter. She was sure he would never be afraid of spoiling Daisy by showing her too much affection. If firmness was ever needed, Amy strongly suspected it would be up to Beth to provide it.

David and Beth had both changed since Daisy's birth; even more than might have been expected from such a momentous event in their lives. When Amy saw them together, she was struck by how careful they often were of each other. It was not awkwardness or distance; it was a tender attention to the other's comfort, so foreign to Amy's own experience that she watched it with something like awe.

Richard had visited several times recently. Amy had wondered if he was anxious about Beth's health, but when she cautiously asked if all was well, Beth assured her that Richard said both she and Daisy were in fine form. Perhaps, Amy thought, Richard felt a special interest in Daisy because of his own role in her delivery; especially since he was also her godfather. It was not hard to understand why anyone would want to spend time with Daisy.

One Monday afternoon Amy carried a pile of freshly laundered bed linen into David and Beth's bedroom, where Beth had just settled Daisy into her cradle after feeding her. Amy placed the sheets and pillowcases on the end of the bed. As she turned to leave the room, a strange looking object on the windowsill caught her eye.

'What's that?' she asked, moving a little closer to get a better look at the thing. It was round, an inch or two in diameter, and appeared to be made of rubber.

Beth glanced around. When she saw where Amy was looking, her eyes widened in alarm. She moved quickly to the windowsill, snatched up the rubber object, and shoved it into a small box that she picked up from a chair beside the bed. 'Nothing.' She sat down on the bed and stared at her lap. 'It's nothing.'

'I'm sorry, I didn't mean to be nosy,' Amy said, startled at the strength of Beth's reaction. She made to leave the room, but she had only taken a few steps when Beth spoke again.

'I'm not supposed to have any more babies.' Her eyes were still downcast, and she was fiddling distractedly with the box in her lap.

Amy sat on the bed beside her. 'Yes, I know. Your ma told me. I thought I'd wait and see if you wanted to tell me yourself.'

Beth raised her eyes to meet Amy's. 'I don't really mind about not having any more babies, not when I've got Daisy. I suppose it would've been nice for Davie to have a son, but he says he doesn't mind either, and he really loves Daisy, and I can help him on the farm, especially when Daisy gets a bit older—I can milk and things.' She paused for breath, then seemed in no hurry to continue.

Amy sat and waited patiently, careful not to press Beth into saying more than she wanted to.

'It's just... we have to make sure I don't have any more,' Beth said at last. 'And Davie said he'd try… But it's hard, Aunt Amy. It's hard to say we'll never… He was talking about going back to his old room out on the verandah, but I said that wouldn't be right… And it was getting like he was scared even to have a cuddle or anything…'

Beth shook her head. 'We were going to try our best. Then Richard came out to see us, and he said he'd been worrying ever since he'd had to tell Davie about not having any more babies. He said…' Beth paused, as if calling to mind the exact words used. 'He said he knew it was asking too much of us, and it would only be a matter of time before the inevitable happened. So he'd been writing to a doctor he knows in Auckland—do you know they have doctors up there that just do delivering babies and things to do with women's insides?' she said, wide-eyed at the notion. 'He told this doctor about me not being meant to have any more babies—he didn't say my name or anything, he just said I was a patient—and they wrote back and forth about what we might be able to do. Then the other doctor sent Richard this thing.'

She opened the box on her lap, and Amy peered in at the rubber object. 'Whatever is it?' Amy asked.

Beth looked away, her face reddening. 'It's to stop a baby from happening. I have to put it up inside me before we… you know. Then I have to leave it there for a while before I can take it out and wash it. I let it dry on the windowsill before I put it away.'

'What a good idea,' Amy said, staring at the nondescript piece of rubber that held such power. 'I've never heard of such a thing.'

'Richard said we can't rely on it, though,' Beth said, regret clear in her voice. 'Things like this help, but they don't work every time. So we still have to be careful. We should be all right with using this thing while I'm feeding Daisy, especially if we… if Davie… if we sort of stop before…' She trailed off, leaving Amy somewhat mystified, but reluctant to ask for more details.

'But we'll have to be a lot more careful once Daisy's weaned,' she went on. 'Once my bleeding gets back to normal, that's when I'll be really fruitful again. Even with using this thing we'll only be able to on the day or two just after my bleeding finishes every month. But that's good, isn't it?' she said, turning a pleading face to Amy. 'That's much better than saying we never can ever again.'

It seemed a very long time since the brief period of Amy's life when she had found pleasure in such matters. But she knew that for Beth and David it would mean rigid self-control.

'Yes, it's very good,' she said, squeezing Beth's hand. 'It's lucky we had Richard to get that for you.'

Beth closed the lid of the box. 'Don't tell anyone—especially about this thing. I know you wouldn't gossip, it's just that Richard asked us not to say anything about it. Lots of doctors think it's awful, you see, for women to have a way to stop having babies. I don't see that it's any of their business,' she said fiercely, and Amy nodded her agreement. 'But it's even in the law that you're not meant to send things like this through the post—they put that in the law last year, Richard said. It should be all right when it's doctors sending them, but I'd hate to get Richard in trouble when he's been so good about everything.'

'I won't say a word.' Amy wondered how she could find out Richard's favourite sort of baking, so she could make it specially when he was next expected.

It was now hard to believe that Beth's health had caused so much concern. She spent her days caring for Daisy, helping David on the farm, and helping Amy in the house, and seemed to have enough energy to make a fine job of it all. It was clear to Amy that Beth was ready to run the house on her own. That meant it was time to consider once again Sarah's proposal that Amy should come to live with her.

She chose a day when they were all in the kitchen lingering over their morning tea to raise the subject. Daisy was snuggled in David's lap, her eyes drooping as she drifted off into a well-fed sleep, one of David's fingers clutched in her little fist. Beth stroked Daisy's hair and shared a contented smile with David. Amy studied the tableau, feeling her resolve strengthen as she watched them together.

'I think I might go up to Auckland soon,' she announced.

Beth and David turned surprised faces to her. 'Again?' David said. 'But you were there for ages just last year.'

'Sarah wants me to come back, and I think it's a good idea.'

'How long do you think you'll stay this time, Aunt Amy?' Beth asked.

Amy paused for a moment to prepare herself for their reaction. 'Actually, I'm thinking of moving up there.'

They both frowned, puzzled, then looked startled.

'Move?' said David. 'What, leave the farm and go up there for good? You can't do that!'

'Wouldn't you miss Daisy?' Beth asked, wide-eyed at the notion that anyone could willingly deprive themselves of her baby's company.

'Of course I will. I'll miss all of you. But I'll come back for visits—I don't want Daisy forgetting me. And it's not as far as all that.' She would simply have to get used to making that wretched boat trip several times a year; she knew it was futile to hope she would ever become a better sailor.

Beth looked unconvinced, while David was clearly troubled. 'You can't, Ma. I can't let you do that.'

'That's not up to you to decide, Davie,' Amy said. 'It's for me to say what I'll do.'

Now he looked close to distraught. 'But why do you want to go away?'

'I think it'd be better for us all. Sarah's in that great big house of hers all by herself, and she wants me to come and live with her. And it'd be nice for you two to have the place to yourselves, instead of having me here all the time.'

'But we *like* having you here,' Beth said. 'I don't want you to go away because of me! It'll be like I've chased you away.' She seemed almost on the verge of tears.

'Of course you haven't chased me away. I just think it's time I went. And I wouldn't be able to if you weren't here to look after Dave for me.'

'No,' David said, shaking his head. 'You can't. You mustn't. You're meant to stay here. I don't want you going off just because of me and Beth. I don't want to kick you out.'

'You're not kicking me out. It's me who's decided I want to go.'

David's distress had communicated itself to Daisy, who stirred and began whimpering. Beth gathered the baby onto her own lap to soothe her; David barely seemed to notice.

'Pa thought I might, you know,' he said, speaking rapidly and showing no sign of having heard Amy. 'He even put it in his will.'

'That's just a thing they put in wills,' Amy said. 'Your father didn't mean anything by it.'

'No, he did mean it,' David insisted. 'He told me he was going to have the lawyer put it in—it was one of those days when he wasn't muddled. He said I was to look after you, and he said, "Don't you go thinking you can kick your ma out as soon as you get wed. She's as much right to live here as you have." I said of course I wouldn't kick you out, and he said he'd make sure I couldn't.'

'You never told me that,' Amy said, taken aback.

'It never needed saying before. It does now, if you think you have to go and live with strangers just because of us.'

'Sarah's not a stranger. She's… she's a good friend to me.'

'But she's not *family*,' David said. 'If you go up there, it means I've shoved you out to go and live with someone you just met last year. It's not right. I can't let you.'

Not family. The force of David's emotion and the shock of hearing those words robbed Amy of speech. She clasped her hands tightly in her lap until she felt them stop shaking. It was clear what she needed to do, but she doubted her own courage to do it.

'All right, let's not talk about it any more just now,' she said when she could trust her voice. 'I didn't mean to upset you.' She rose to take the dishes to the bench, and soon afterwards David went outside.

All through the rest of the day, the task ahead loomed over Amy. She was sure David and Beth were sincere in saying they wanted her to stay; she was equally sure they would be happier on their own. Going to live with Sarah was the right thing to do; her head and heart agreed on that. But she could not allow David to feel it was his fault. She could no longer allow him to think of Sarah as a stranger.

She waited till the evening, when Daisy was asleep in her cradle and the three of them were in the parlour, enjoying the warmth of the fire. Beth and David were talking about the calving that would soon begin, and about their plans for improving the herd, while Beth stitched at a small tear in one of David's shirts. Amy waited for a pause in their conversation, took a deep breath, and spoke.

'I need to tell you two something.'

She saw David stiffen, and Beth look at him in concern. 'Is this about you going away?' he asked. 'I thought we decided about that.'

'No, it's not. Well, in a way...' It was so hard to find the right words. They were both watching her, sitting side by side on the sofa, Beth's sewing lying forgotten on her lap. Beth had taken David's hand, a movement that seemed so natural Amy suspected she was not even aware she had done it.

The waiting silence hung between them, daring Amy to break it. Daring her to risk what must be done.

'Before I married your father,' she began, and saw David's tense expression change to a puzzled one. 'Before I even thought of such a thing... there was another man I thought I was going to marry.'

Now David looked astonished. 'Who was it?'

'No one you know. He wasn't from Ruatane. Please... I don't want you to ask me a lot of questions. This isn't easy for me to talk about.'

David opened his mouth as if to press her further, but at a nudge from Beth he closed it.

'He asked me to marry him, and I said yes. But I was only fifteen, and we thought your grandpa would say I was too young. So he—the man— said we'd better keep it a secret engagement for a while.' She saw David and Beth exchange a look, and was sure they were thinking of their own secret courtship. 'He was going to write and ask his father's permission, then ask Grandpa, but somehow the time kept drifting on.'

And now came the hardest part.

'Then one day...' She found she could not look at David. Instead she stared into the fire, watching the flames twisting and writhing as they devoured the dry wood. 'I told him I was going to have a baby.'

She thought she heard a sharp intake of breath from Beth's side of the couch, but there was not a sound from David. What would she see if she dared look at his face? Shock, certainly. But what else? Understanding? Concern? Or disgust and loathing?

She was not ready to meet what might be there. Not yet. Not till she had said all she had to. 'He said he'd go back to... to where he lived, and tell his father about it, then he'd come back and tell Pa. I was to keep it a secret till he came back. So he went, and I waited. I waited a long time. Then I found out he wasn't coming back. He didn't want to marry me. He didn't want me, and he didn't want the baby.'

Amy made herself turn to face David, and saw blank bewilderment in his eyes, as if her words had been in a foreign language.

She opened her mouth intending to ask, 'Do you think I'm awful now?' but what came out was the question that was eating at her heart. She had to know, even though she was terrified of what the answer might be. 'Do you still love me, Davie?'

He hesitated for what might have been a fraction of a second, but to Amy it felt an age. 'Of course he does!' Beth said fiercely. She prodded David's arm. 'Davie, tell Aunt Amy you do!'

'Ye-yes. Yes, I do. But...' He shook his head helplessly, unable to give voice to all the questions clamouring to be asked.

'What a horrible man,' Beth breathed. 'Just leaving you like that, with a baby coming! But what did you do, Aunt Amy? You must have been so frightened.'

'Yes, I was. I didn't know what to do. I was too scared to tell anyone—that was silly, of course, I knew they'd find out sooner or later. Your ma was the first person I told, Beth. It gave her an awful shock, but she was so good about it. She wanted to help me tell Pa, but I kept putting it off, and saying it had to be the right time. As if there could be a right time for something like that.' She fixed her eyes on Beth as she spoke, only risking an occasional glance at David. It was easier to face Beth's earnest look of sympathy than the bewildered expression David wore.

'Then Aunt Susannah noticed, and Pa...' The memory of the pain and confusion in her father's face robbed Amy of speech for several moments. 'He was so upset, and I knew it was my fault. It was... it was a bad time.'

She swallowed, and went on. 'I knew it upset Pa just looking at me after that.' Amy saw Beth nod her understanding. 'I couldn't talk to him about it, that would only have upset him more. I didn't have anyone to talk to—your ma wasn't allowed to come and see me once everyone found out.

'Then one day I was wandering around the farm, just trying to keep out of everyone's way so they wouldn't have to look at me. I wasn't thinking about where I was going, and I ended up near the boundary fence. Your father saw me, Davie, and he could tell there was a baby on the way. He must have thought... I don't know. We never really talked about that.

'Well, he came over a bit later to see Pa, and he asked if he could marry me.'

'And you said yes?' Beth asked.

'I didn't want to at first. I was frightened. I didn't really know him, I didn't know what he might... But Susannah said—I mean, I thought it over, and... I'd upset everyone so much with what I'd done, especially Pa. And Pa was so happy at the thought of me getting married—it was as if I could make it up to him, make up a bit for the bad things I'd done. So I decided I would. I said yes.'

She saw David's brow furrow. 'So Mal... was that Mal?' he asked, getting the words out with obvious difficulty.

Amy shook her head. 'No, Mal was your father's son. No, he said he wanted to marry me, but he didn't want the baby, not when it wasn't his. And I didn't know... you can't know what it'll feel like to have your own baby. Not till you see it there in your arms.'

'That's right,' Beth whispered.

'So the grownups talked about it among themselves, and I just went along with what they decided. Aunt Susannah organised it all. She took me up to Auckland, and I stayed there till the baby was born. I had a little girl. The prettiest little girl you've ever seen—as pretty as Daisy.'

Again she had to pause for some time before she could bring herself to go on. Beth was leaning forward, listening avidly, while David still looked dazed.

'I was allowed to keep her till she was nearly three weeks old. Then I woke up one day and she was gone. The nurses had taken her away while I was asleep, and she'd been sent off to be adopted. They told me she was going to have a new mother. A good mother, not a bad girl like me.'

Beth rose from the sofa and took a step towards the bedroom all in one movement, as if afraid Daisy might have been spirited away from under her nose. She turned and stared at Amy, her mouth an O of horror. 'They took your baby?' she breathed. 'How could you bear it, Aunt Amy?'

Amy spread out her hands in a gesture of helplessness. 'I don't know. It was like having my heart torn out. I felt as if I wanted to die. But I found out you don't die just from wanting to. You just carry on, because you have to.'

'But it wasn't *fair*.' Tears were streaming unchecked down Beth's face. She crossed the room and sank to the floor, resting her head on Amy's lap. Amy stroked her hair, then retrieved a clean handkerchief from her sleeve and dabbed at Beth's cheeks.

Beth raised her head, sniffed, and reached out a hand to David. 'Come here, Davie.' When he did not immediately respond, she took hold of his hand and tugged at it until he came and sat on the floor at her side.

Amy looked from one upturned face to the other, Beth's eyes still brimming with tears and David's expression unreadable. 'I came back home, and I got married. Mal was born the year after my little girl, then you came along, Davie. I tried to make the best of things—and there were good things, as well as the hard ones. Especially you—and Mal, of course,' she added belatedly. 'But not a day went by when I didn't think about her, and wonder what was happening to her, and if she was happy.'

'Of course you did,' Beth murmured. She placed her hand over Amy's and squeezed it.

'And then last year the most wonderful thing happened.' Amy felt her heart lift as she recalled that day. 'She found me again. She sat here in this very room—just where you two are sitting—and she told me she was my daughter. My little girl, come back to me after all those years.' She closed her eyes for a moment to savour the memory, then opened them to meet David's. 'It's Sarah, Davie. She's your sister.'

Beth had her hand up to her mouth, while David's was hanging open in astonishment. 'Sister?' he echoed. 'I've got a sister?'

'Yes, you have.'

It was done now. She had offered up her secret, and it was in David's hands how he chose to judge her. Amy felt a sudden weariness, and an overwhelming need to be alone. She freed her hand from Beth's grasp and stood up. 'I'm going to bed now.'

Beth rose, took hold of Amy's arm and walked with her to the door, so solicitous that Amy realised she meant to put her to bed. 'I'm all right, Beth. You stay here and talk to Dave.' She was sure they would be discussing what she had told them well into the night.

She hovered in the doorway, hoping to catch David's eye. He was staring down at the floor, but as she watched he lifted his gaze and met hers.

'That's why Pa used to talk how he did, isn't it?' he said slowly. 'Calling you names and all that.'

'He stopped doing that in the end. But yes, that's why. He knew before he asked to marry me what had happened, but... well, it was hard for him.'

David nodded. Amy stood and waited, wondering if he would speak again.

'He... he shouldn't have said those things,' David said at last. 'He shouldn't have talked to you like that. And... and I'm glad about Sarah and everything,' he finished in a rush.

Relief flooded through her. 'Thank you, Davie. That means a lot to me.'

25

It was now a settled thing that Amy would go to Auckland, but there seemed any number of reasons that she should be in no hurry to do so. Beth and David wanted her to be there when the first Jersey calves were born on the farm; something they were a good deal more excited about than she was.

'And you should stay for Davie's birthday,' Beth urged. 'Twenty's quite a big one.'

Amy drew the line when they suggested she wait until the new house was completed; at the current rate of progress, she was not convinced that would happen before the end of the year. But she let herself be persuaded to wait till after David's birthday. That was less than two months away; it would be easy enough to wait those few more weeks. In the meantime she and Sarah were exchanging letters more frequently than ever. Amy could tell that Sarah was looking forward to the imminent move with as keen anticipation as she herself was.

Amy was quietly relieved when David added his own urging to Beth's. In the first days after her revelation he had been a little subdued, and there was still sometimes an awkwardness in his manner towards her, but she could now allow herself to believe he still cared for her. She felt a weight had been lifted now that David knew her secret.

Her move to Auckland was never far from her mind. She was thinking about it one afternoon, enjoying the thought of seeing Sarah again and imagining the long talks they would have, catching up on the things that had happened to them both in the months they had been apart, and which had not made their way into letters. Beth was out on the farm with David, having taken Daisy with her, so Amy had the kitchen to herself. As well as scones and biscuits, she had made a small batch of the fudge that had always been a favourite treat for her boys.

She moved about the kitchen, clearing up after her baking, the room and the tasks so familiar that her mind was left free to wander. So caught up was she in her thoughts that the knock on the door took her by surprise. She had not heard the sound of hooves or wheels, and when family members visited they did not wait to have the door opened for them.

She peeped out the window, but there was no sign of a horse; her visitors must have arrived on foot. Wondering who it could possibly be, Amy opened the door…

…and clutched unsteadily at the doorpost for support. For Malcolm was dead and buried half a world away. How could he be standing there on the bottom step, scowling at her in the way she remembered so well? But not the sixteen-year-old Malcolm she had seen riding away on that fateful night; this was Malcolm as a little boy, before he had even started school.

For the first time, she became aware that a young woman was standing beside the red-headed child, holding his hand firmly as if afraid he might run off. 'What... who...' Amy began, then trailed off, unable to find words.

The young woman's face softened in evident relief. 'He's like him, isn't he?' she said eagerly. 'He's just like his dad.'

'His dad?' Amy echoed. She gave her head a small shake. 'You'd better come in,' she said, opening the door more widely.

'Come on, Eddie,' the woman coaxed. The child gave Amy a dubious look, then allowed himself to be led up the steps and into the kitchen. Just inside the door he came to a sudden stop. 'No,' he said, thrusting out his lower lip in a deeper scowl, and looking more like Malcolm than ever. 'I don't like it here.'

'Please, Eddie,' the woman pleaded. 'Be a good boy for Mama—you said you'd be good.'

With an effort, Amy took her eyes from the small boy to his mother. She looked to be in her mid-twenties, with brown hair and a broad face, wind-reddened after the long trek she must have had. The hand that was not clutching Eddie's carried a shapeless bundle tied with a length of rope. Her boots and the hem of her dress were caked in mud, her hair was escaping from its pins, and she looked close to exhaustion.

Eddie held his ground stubbornly. With a flash of inspiration, Amy darted to one of her cake tins and returned with a slab of fudge on a plate.

'I bet you like fudge, don't you, Eddie,' she said, holding out the plate so he could see what was on it. 'Come and sit at the table to eat it, then Mama can sit down and have a rest.'

He looked at her doubtfully, but the fudge won him over. He allowed his mother to lead him to the table, sat down, and took a large bite.

The young woman sank into a chair at his side, letting her bundle drop to the floor. 'It's a long way out here. And I had to carry Eddie on the last bit, he said his feet were hurting. He's been growing that fast, he probably needs new boots again.'

Amy took her own seat and stared at the two of them. 'Is this... is he really...' She hardly dared ask the question, for fear the answer might be "no".

'He's Mal's son,' the woman said, and Amy's heart leapt. 'Thank God he looks like him—they wouldn't let me put Mal's name on his birth certificate.'

'But how—I'm sorry, I don't even know your name,' said Amy.

'I'm Milly Dobson. I know you're Mal's ma, I used to see you in town sometimes when me and my ma lived here.'

'And you and Mal…' Amy looked at Eddie, but his attention was completely devoted to the fudge. 'I didn't… he never…' She shook her head helplessly.

'We went around together, right up to when Mal went off to the war. Me and Ma lived in Elliot Street, around behind the carpenter's yard. Mal and his mates used to hang around there at nights, drinking and stuff, and some of them'd race their horses and jump the fence, things like that. I'd go out there when Ma was asleep and watch them, and give them cheek if they saw me. Then I started hanging around with them.'

'I knew Mal sneaked into town some nights, but I never knew there were girls there,' Amy said, still finding it difficult to think straight.

'I was the only one,' Milly said, a mixture of defiance and pride in her voice. 'I went with a couple of the other blokes before Mal—Eddie's Mal's, though,' she added quickly.

'I can see that,' Amy said, careful to keep any disapproval out of her voice. This young woman was the mother of Malcolm's child; that covered a multitude of sins. 'It's written all over his face.'

Eddie finished off the fudge, slid from his chair and climbed onto his mother's lap, from where he watched Amy

'I couldn't put Mal down as his father, 'cause we weren't married, but I put it in his name. He's Edmund Malcolm—Edmund after a little brother I had, he died when he was only two or three. And Malcolm for his dad. They couldn't stop me giving him his dad's name.' Milly stroked Eddie's hair.

'They were a rough lot, most of those blokes,' she said, pulling a face. 'I didn't like them much. Especially that Liam Feenan—he tried to get me to go with him once, but I just wouldn't. Mal was the pick of them,' she said proudly.

It seemed to Amy a dubious honour to be considered the best among a group led by Liam Feenan, but she kept that thought to herself.

'Was Mal really eighteen?' Milly asked.

'Eighteen? No, he was only sixteen when he… when he passed away.'

'I thought as much. He told me he was eighteen—that's just because I was eighteen, I reckon. He didn't want to let on that he was younger than me.' Milly gave a conspiratorial grin. 'He told me he'd been with girls before, too, but I could tell he hadn't. I just about had to tell him where to put the thing the first time we did it.'

There was no denying it: Milly was not a girl Amy would have chosen to have in her house, let alone as someone who might have been her daughter-in-law.

'He was like a big kid, Mal was,' Milly said, smiling fondly. 'He wasn't like the other blokes. He was sort of wild, you know? Never scared of anything. When he was riding that horse of his he'd have a go at jumping anything—if he fell off he'd just laugh, and if he made it he'd be that excited. He put his whole self into things. He was the same between the sheets,' she added smugly. 'He never held back there, either.'

Amy winced. She searched for a polite way of suggesting to Milly that this was not an appropriate subject of conversation, but nothing came to mind that would not sound like condemnation. 'Mal was always very good with horses,' she said, her voice sounding prim in her own ears.

'That's my dad's name, Mal is,' Eddie put in. 'He could ride a big horse.'

'That's right, Eddie,' Amy said, settling gratefully on the distraction.

'He was the best rider in the whole world,' Eddie said.

Amy smiled. 'Well, I don't know about that. But yes, he was very good. He won a special race once, and there were much bigger boys than him in it.'

Eddie was staring avidly at her. It was clear that Milly had made his father a hero to him. When Amy glanced from Eddie to Milly, she saw the same eager expression in Milly's brown eyes that was lighting up Eddie's blue ones. Whatever Milly might lack in social graces, there was no doubting she had genuinely cared for Malcolm.

Amy heard voices outside the door, and it opened to admit David and Beth, with Daisy in David's arms. David and Beth seemed to have been in the middle of an animated conversation, but they fell silent at the unusual sight of strangers in the house. David nodded politely to Milly, turned to Eddie and blinked in surprise.

'Milly, this is my son Dave,' said Amy. 'And his wife, Beth, and Daisy's their little girl. This is Milly Dobson, you two. And this is Eddie.'

'He looks just like...' David turned a questioning face to Amy.

Amy nodded. 'Yes, Dave. Eddie's Mal's son.'

David sank into a chair, Daisy held in one arm. Beth gave a quick glance at them all, then crossed to the bench. 'I'll put the kettle on,' she said.

'So... so you're Mal's girl,' David said when he had recovered the use of his voice.

'You knew about this?' Amy asked, astonished.

'No, I didn't really... I mean, Mal said he had a girl, but I thought...'
He trailed off awkwardly.

Milly stiffened. 'He never paid me for it, if that's what you're getting at.'

'No! I didn't mean that! I just thought... well, I thought he might have been making it up.' David suddenly found it necessary to bend low over Daisy and fuss with the edge of her sleeve.

'So you thought he couldn't get a girl of his own?' Milly said. 'Just because he didn't have a pretty face as if he was a girl himself?'

'Of course I didn't! I just—'

'Dave was only fourteen when Mal went away,' Amy interposed before David could dig a bigger hole for himself. 'He wasn't thinking about girls at all. I didn't think Mal was, either. I'm glad he was,' she said, studying Eddie as he sat on his mother's lap and surveyed the room's occupants. 'But it's been five years, Milly—why didn't you come to us before?'

'I couldn't while Mal's old man was around. Not with the way him and Mal hated each other.'

'No, they didn't,' Amy said, remembering similar arguments with Malcolm himself. 'I know you'd have thought it at times, the way they used to fight, but they didn't hate each other.'

'Mal used to go on and on about his dad. I got fed up with it. In the end I asked him if he hated him so much why did he want to talk about him all the time?'

'Yes, exactly,' Amy murmured.

'But the old bloke would've kicked me down the road, and Eddie after me, if I'd turned up here.'

'Oh, he'd have wanted Eddie, all right.' Though it was doubtful, Amy privately agreed, that Charlie would have welcomed Milly's presence. 'Well, what's done is done.'

Beth brought the tea things to the table and took her own seat beside David. David seemed grateful for the distraction of teacups and plates of biscuits; it gave him an excuse not to talk to Milly.

The two children were not burdened with any sense of the situation's awkwardness. They studied each other with interest. Daisy beamed and gurgled and waved her arms at Eddie, while he regarded her solemnly. He looked at Daisy, then at the biscuit in his hand, pondered the matter for a few moments, and held the biscuit out towards the baby.

Beth intervened, taking the biscuit before it could make its way into Daisy's hand. 'Thank you, Eddie, but Daisy's too little for bikkies yet,' she said, smiling as she returned the biscuit, and getting a cautious answering smile.

David shifted awkwardly on his chair, moving Daisy to the other side of his lap. 'Do you want to have a look around the farm?' he asked Eddie.

Eddie looked dubious at the prospect, but before he had a chance to answer, Milly did it for him. 'He's not used to blokes,' she said, gripping Eddie more firmly. 'He wouldn't want to go off with you on his own.'

Whether intentionally or not, she made it sound like an accusation, and that was how David appeared to take it. 'Sorry,' he muttered, looking down at the floor. Amy was not surprised when soon afterwards, having gulped down his tea and passed Daisy across to Beth, he said that he needed to go back outside.

Beth seemed torn between indignation at any slight towards David and the need to show politeness to their guest. She gave Milly a hard look, then stood up with Daisy in her arms. 'I'll feed her in the bedroom, I think,' she announced.

Milly watched as David left the room. She turned back to Amy. 'I suppose that one got on all right with the old man.'

Amy smiled at the notion. 'He did at the end, when his father was old and sick, and just needed looking after—Davie was very good with him. But when he was a boy... well, not really. Mr Stewart always took more notice of Mal, anyway.'

Milly considered this, then nodded, apparently finding it easy to believe that Malcolm would be of more interest than his brother. 'Mal reckoned getting away from his old man'd be just about worth going off to the war. That wasn't really why he went, though.' She shot a challenging look at Amy. 'Do you know why?'

'He wanted an adventure,' Amy said quietly. She watched Eddie, who appeared to be doing his best to follow this conversation that included so many tantalising references to his father. She ached to reach out and draw him into her arms, but made herself tread carefully. She was still little more than a stranger to him, and there was no sense in frightening the child.

'Yes!' Milly said. 'He used to go on about getting out of Ruatane and seeing other places. He had pictures and things out of the paper—he'd bring them to show me. I thought he was just making it up about going away, you know what blokes are like for telling stories. But he kept on about it, then he told me he had the tickets and money and all.'

She stroked Eddie's hair and looked into an invisible distance as she spoke. 'He stayed at my place the night before he went. I think that was the night we got Eddie on the go.' She planted a quick kiss on his shock of hair. 'I left the window open for him, and he ended up staying right till it was daylight. We lay there and talked for hours and hours, about foreign countries and riding his horse across the plains, and seeing wild animals. He said he'd come back and get me when the fighting had finished, and take me to Africa to see it all for myself. Mal talked a lot of rot sometimes,' she added fondly, her eyes suspiciously bright. Amy felt tears pricking at her own eyes at this revelation of an unsuspected tender side to Malcolm.

'He gave me this just before he went away.' Milly stretched out her wrist to reveal a silver bangle. 'I saw them in the jeweller's window afterwards—they cost two shillings! He pinched this one for me,' she said proudly.

While Amy could not pretend to be impressed by Malcolm's effort, she hid her reaction. She would have to find some way of leaving the money anonymously in Mr Hatfield's shop.

'Then he went off, and a couple of months later I found out Eddie was on the way. Ma wasn't too pleased, but she said we'd just have to wait till Mal got back and hope he'd marry me. I don't know if he would have or not.'

'He would have if I'd had any say in it.' Though Amy knew her own influence would have had little sway over Charlie.

'I thought maybe I could write to him or something, but I didn't know where to write, and I didn't know who to ask about it. So I just waited, and hoped he'd come back soon. Then I found out he wasn't coming back at all.' Her head drooped, and Eddie raised a finger to touch the shining trail making its way down one cheek.

'I'm so sorry,' Amy murmured. 'I wish I'd known about you and Eddie.' She reached out and stroked Milly's arm, but felt it stiffen beneath her touch. Milly, it was clear, was not someone easily persuaded to let down her guard.

Milly wiped her sleeve over her eyes. 'Ma said we might as well move away after we heard about Mal. She said people would only be poking their noses in and gossiping. I wanted to stay and see that memorial thing once I heard about it, though—I put my foot down over waiting for that. I was showing by then, but I didn't go out much, and no one took any notice of me at the service. We went to Tauranga just a couple of weeks later, and that's where Eddie was born. And we've been there since.'

'I'm glad you've brought Eddie to see us at last. It's a long way to come with a little one.'

Milly sighed. 'Ma got sick last year. Then this year she got really bad, and she died a couple of months back.'

'I'm sorry to hear that,' said Amy.

'It was sort of a relief in the end. She was wanting to go. And she was never that fond of Eddie—she said she was past putting up with little kids at her age. But it's been hard to manage since.' Now they were getting to just what had finally prompted Milly to approach Malcolm's family, Amy realised. 'Ma had a bit put to one side, but it mostly went on doctors. And her and I used to both work before she got sick, cleaning people's houses and taking in washing and things. It's been hard getting enough work to pay the rent and everything with just me to do it, and I've got to try and keep an eye on Eddie, too. He gets into everything—you're a brat,' she said, without the least hint of censure. Eddie giggled with satisfaction.

'Do you need some help with managing?' Amy asked cautiously, wondering how best to avoid giving offence. 'I've got a little bit of my own, I'd be only too glad—'

'I don't want money!' Milly said indignantly. 'I didn't come here looking for charity.'

'Eddie's my grandson, Milly. It wouldn't be charity.'

Milly looked away, discomforted. 'Well, anyway, I didn't come asking for money. I've got myself a job,' she said, her eyes lighting up. 'A really good one. It's at a hotel down on the Strand in Tauranga—one of the flash places, with a dining room and all. I'll be helping in the kitchen, and they said if I do all right at that I'll be able to wait on tables in the dining room. They have fancy white cloths on the tables, and flowers in vases, and real silver knives and forks. I'd get to wear a black uniform with a white cap with real lace on it.'

'That sounds very nice.'

'And I can live in, so that's my room and board all covered. They've got a few rooms for the maids out the back. The only thing is, I can't have Eddie with me.'

'Ah,' said Amy. 'I see.'

'It'd just be for a while,' Milly said, a plea in her eyes. 'Just until I've got enough saved up. It won't be costing anything for my keep, I'll be able to save my whole pay, pretty well. Then I thought once I had enough put by, I could get a job just in the daytime, even though that wouldn't pay as much. Eddie'll start school at the end of the year, so I wouldn't have to leave him on his own all day. I thought maybe I could rent a nice little place with a bit of yard for Eddie to run around in. That'd cost a bit, but if I do extra shifts at the hotel I'll be making good money.'

It sounded a precarious plan to Amy. She could not believe that this hotel job would provide Milly with the sort of nest egg she seemed to be dreaming of, no matter how carefully she saved. Amy's conscience prodded at her, telling her she should offer Milly a home on the farm, but the voice of logic easily silenced it. Given David's and Milly's reactions to each other, neither of them would welcome the idea.

Eddie, however, was another matter. 'I'd love to have Eddie here. He can stay with us for as long as you need.'

She saw Milly's shoulders slump with relief, while Eddie frowned, clearly aware he was being discussed but unable to fathom the details. Amy leaned forward so her face was closer to his level. 'Eddie, you're going to stay with Granny for a little while,' she said. 'Just while Mama's busy with her new job. That'll be nice, won't it?'

Eddie looked dubious, while Milly gripped him more tightly. 'You'll like it with Granny,' Milly said, her voice unconvincingly bright. 'Lots of these fancy biscuits, eh? And lots of places for you to run around without getting in trouble. And Granny can tell you all about what your dad was like when he was a little boy.'

Eddie considered the notion. 'All right. Can I have another biscuit?'

Now that the matter was settled, all vigour seemed to have drained from Milly. Her head drooped, and she responded to Amy's offer of a second cup of tea with nothing more than a quick shake of her head. Amy studied her face, grey with weariness, in concern.

'You'll be staying the night with us, of course,' said Amy. 'And a bit longer, maybe?'

'Two nights, if that suits,' Milly said, rousing herself to speak with an obvious effort. 'I've got a passage booked for the day after tomorrow.'

'Why don't you have a lie-down till dinnertime? You must be worn out after that long walk.' Milly would also, Amy suspected, appreciate a little time away from prying eyes as she took in the fact that she would be leaving Eddie behind when she left Ruatane.

'I wouldn't mind,' Milly said. 'And Eddie usually has a sleep in the afternoon.'

Amy rose from her chair. 'I'll show you where you'll sleep. We've only got the one spare room, I hope you don't mind sharing with Eddie.'

Milly blinked in surprise. 'Of course not. I've always shared with him, right from when he was a baby.' She slid Eddie from her lap, stood and picked up her bundle, and followed Amy from the kitchen, leading Eddie by the hand. 'He'll have to get used to sleeping on his own,' she said in a low voice. 'It might be a bit hard for him.' And at least as hard for Milly, Amy thought to herself.

'Here you are,' Amy said as she ushered them into the small room that had been made by walling in the verandah of the cottage. 'This was Mal's and Dave's room.'

'You hear that, Eddie?' Milly said, brightening visibly. 'You're going to have your dad's old room.'

Amy left them looking around, a good deal more impressed than the cramped space warranted, while she collected clean bedding. On her way back through the parlour, the photograph on the mantel caught her eye. She placed it on top of the pile of sheets and pillowcases she was carrying.

'I thought you might like to have this in here,' she said, setting the photograph on top of the small chest of drawers. 'Mal must have been near enough to Eddie's age when this was taken.'

Milly had opened the bundle, and was pulling out the clothes it contained. She abandoned the task at once and snatched up the photograph. 'Look, Eddie, it's your dad,' she said, holding the picture out for Eddie's inspection. 'See, he looked just like you.'

'And here's the cup he won.' Amy picked up the small silver trophy. 'That was for being the best rider.'

Eddie seemed more impressed by the trophy than by the photograph. He held out his hands for it, then turned it round and round, examining it from all angles. He refused to let go while Milly was undressing him ready for bed, passing it from one hand to the other as she pulled a nightshirt over his head.

Amy made up the bed, then fetched a jug of water. When she came back into the room, Milly had taken off her dress and was standing in her petticoats and chemise, studying the photograph again. 'Just in case you want to have a wash,' Amy said, lifting the jug onto the chest of drawers.

Eddie was in the bed now, lying close to the wall, and to Amy's amusement he was still clutching the trophy. 'That's a lumpy thing to try and sleep with, Eddie! It might dig into you.'

'I don't care.' Eddie wrapped his arms more firmly around the cup.

'He's like that,' Milly said, taking her eyes off the photograph for a moment. 'When he gets an idea in his head, he's that set on it. I usually let him have his own way.'

Amy studied the little face on the pillow, his bright hair sticking out at unruly angles, and the sense of slipping back seventeen years left her lightheaded. She hesitated for a moment, then bent over Eddie and planted a soft kiss on his forehead. She stood up, expecting to be met with a scowl, but instead Eddie gave her a smile of such sweetness that it lit his whole face, and made Amy's heart leap.

'What a lovely boy,' she said, turning to Milly. 'Thank you for bringing him to me.'

Milly looked startled, then gave a cautious smile. It softened the pinched, anxious lines of her face, and made her look much younger. 'Mal never really talked about you. He went on about his old man, and he talked about his brother sometimes. He quite liked his brother,' she added grudgingly. 'I remember one time I asked him if he had a ma at all, with him never saying anything about you.'

Amy could not think how to respond, so she said nothing. Milly seemed to be working herself up to say more; at last she spoke again.

'He should have told me. Mal should've said what you were like. Then I wouldn't have been so worried about whether you'd want Eddie. I'd have known you would.'

Amy felt it was the greatest compliment Milly could have paid her. 'Thank you,' she said, then slipped from the room, leaving Milly to her rest.

26

Milly and David had not got off to a good start, and relations remained strained for the remainder of her stay. But on the morning after Milly and Eddie's arrival, David lifted Eddie onto the back of one of the farm's horses, led him around a paddock, and found he had become a hero.

Lizzie came to see them that same morning. David had told Frank of their unexpected visitors when they had met at the factory, and when Frank passed on the news to Lizzie she had lost no time in coming to confront what she was sure was a sly creature who intended to take advantage of Amy's soft heart by foisting an unwanted child, fathered by some man who had refused to take responsibility, upon her. Lizzie entered Amy's kitchen in a whirl of indignation, took one look at Eddie and stopped in her tracks.

'It's uncanny, that's what it is,' she said when she had recovered the power of speech. 'I've never seen a boy so much like his father.' She turned to Amy. 'You're going to have your work cut out.'

'What's that supposed to mean?' Milly said, indignant at the implied slight to Eddie.

Lizzie regarded her coolly. 'Mal was a handful. I expect this one will be, too.' It was a relief to Amy that Lizzie's visit was a brief one.

David and Beth had both calmly accepted the news that Eddie would be staying on, and made valiant attempts to hide their satisfaction that Milly would not be. David kept out of Milly's way as much as he could, but there was no avoiding the need for him to take her into town when it was time for her to leave. Amy decided to go in with them, though it made for a crush on the single seat of the gig, with three adults and one sturdy child.

Milly had wavered over whether or not she wanted Eddie to see her off, concerned that she might upset him; on the day of her departure she allowed Amy to persuade her to let him come along. Amy was sure Milly would regret depriving herself of that precious last hour with Eddie before she had to sail away.

Milly was keeping up a brave face, but when they got to the wharf and found that the boat would be sailing a little late because of a delay in loading the cargo Amy saw her composure slip. It was as if Milly had screwed up her courage to get through the exact number of minutes she had expected to have to wait on the wharf, saying goodbye to Eddie and coping with his questions; faced with another hour of this, her mouth drooped and her hands began to tremble.

Amy suggested they walk up and down the main street, while David took himself off to the general store. As they passed the photographer's studio a sudden inspiration struck her, and she darted into the shop to ask if the photographer was busy. She found the young man in question on the premises and with time on his hands.

Amy ushered Milly and Eddie into the studio, helped Milly to brush the dust of the road from her clothes and Eddie's, and to place her hat at a more respectable angle, then watched as they were photographed together, Eddie perched on his mother's lap.

Having their pictures taken used a large part of the time they had to wait for the boat to sail. 'I'll get him to make two copies of the nicest one,' Amy said to Milly as they walked back towards the wharf. 'I'll send you one as soon as it's ready, and Eddie can have the other one in his room.'

A sailor stood at the end of the gangplank, waiting for the last stragglers to come aboard.

'You're going back to the farm now,' Milly told Eddie. 'You're going to have a good time there, aren't you?'

'Yes,' Eddie agreed readily. 'Uncle Dave's going to teach me to ride a big horse. And Granny said she'd buy me some lollies.'

Milly managed a smile. 'Well, you'll be all right, then.' She glanced over her shoulder to where the sailor was rattling the gangplank meaningfully. 'I've got to go now.' She bent down and folded Eddie in her arms, determinedly dry-eyed but biting her lip so hard that when she stood up again Amy saw a drop of blood there.

Eddie clutched at her skirt, confusion on his face. It had all been explained to him: that his mother would be going away for a time, while he stayed behind on the farm, but it had meant nothing to him until this moment. His mother had been there every day of his life; the idea that the boat was about to take her away was too big for his head to hold.

'It won't be for long,' Milly told him, disengaging her skirt from his fist. 'I'll send for you as soon as I can. Now, you be a good boy for Granny.' She raised her eyes, now glittering with unshed tears, to Amy's. 'Will you write and let me know how he's getting on?'

'Of course I will,' Amy said. 'Every week.' She took Eddie's hand in hers and held it firmly as Milly made her way onto the boat.

Eddie watched the boat pull away, Milly standing on the deck and waving at them. His face was solemn, and he gripped Amy's hand tightly, as if afraid she, too, might slip away from him.

The boat rounded a bend in the river and disappeared from sight. Eddie stood and looked after it for a few more moments, then he let

Amy lead him away from the wharf and off to buy a large bag of sweets.

Eddie was uncharacteristically subdued for the rest of the day, though he ate his dinner with his usual enthusiasm. By the time he had had his second helping of pudding he was yawning hugely. Amy took him through to his little bedroom, got him into his nightshirt and tucked him in bed. Cautious enquiries as to whether he was used to saying prayers at night brought a determined 'yes!', followed by something that sounded like 'Now lay me sleep soul keep die wake soul take,' but said at such speed that she could not distinguish the individual words.

'We might try saying that a bit slower next time,' Amy suggested. She studied Eddie's face, his bright eyes on her, showing little sign of sleepiness now. 'Would you like a story?'

Eddie looked puzzled. 'What's that mean?'

'You don't know about stories?'

He shook his head.

Amy smiled. 'It's a long time since I had a little boy to tell stories to. Move over a bit so there's room for me.'

Eddie wriggled across the bed towards the wall, and Amy lay down next to him. She cast her mind back to when she had been Eddie's age, and her grandmother had told her stories from what had seemed a never-ending hoard of them. The details had blurred in her memory, so that some of the stories had become entangled with each other, but she did not think Eddie would mind.

'Once upon a time,' she began, 'there was a castle on a mountain...'

Telling the story took a long time, as Eddie had a stream of questions regarding such matters as castles and dragons. But there was no hurry. It was not like when Malcolm and David had been small children. Back then she could only steal a few minutes when putting them to bed, before Charlie would call her away.

Eddie fell asleep before she had finished, and Amy left the room without waking him. But later, when the whole household had gone to bed, she found herself wakeful, thinking of the little boy who had never before slept on his own.

She went quietly through the house, every inch of it so familiar that she had no need of a light, and crept into the verandah room. There was a moon that night, and a gap between the two scraps of sacking that covered the window let in enough light for her to see the small figure in the bed. Each of his cheeks bore a telltale trail, turned to silver by the moonlight.

'I'm not crying,' said a small voice.

Amy crossed to the bed and slipped under the covers. Eddie snuggled into her arms, his body warm and solid against her. She stroked his hair and kissed his forehead, whispering soothing words.

Eddie was soon asleep again. But Amy lay awake for a long time, holding her precious burden close and planning the letter she needed to write to Sarah, explaining why she would not be coming to Auckland.

A day spent running around the garden, climbing trees, being led around a paddock on horseback, and eating a good deal of food kept Eddie from brooding on his mother's absence, and when Amy put him to bed the following evening he assured her that he was a big boy, and not a bit frightened to sleep on his own. She checked on him during the night, found him peacefully asleep, and gave silent thanks for the resilience of children.

Amy had forgotten just how much energy a four-year-old boy had. Fortunately it tended to come in bursts, and after encouraging Eddie to run around wearing himself out she would be rewarded by times when he was content to sit quietly.

To her surprise and delight, Eddie appeared to enjoy her company. He was often happy to sit with her in the kitchen, most notably when she was baking. He took over the task of scraping out the mixing bowls, much to David's disappointment. He had an inexhaustible appetite for stories; not just the fairy tales Amy told him at bedtime, but stories of when his father had been a small boy, and Amy's own childhood memories of riding horses and swimming in the creek. He was even, she found, interested in her visit to Auckland the previous year, and fascinated by her account of seeing plays; 'stories acted out', as she explained them to him.

The first letter from Milly arrived a week after her departure. Her handwriting and spelling were both a good deal better than Amy had feared; Milly must have been far more regular in her school attendance than had Malcolm, and was capable of writing a perfectly legible message.

There was a determinedly cheerful tone to the letter. Milly's work was going well; everyone was very nice; and there was a promise that she would get a chance at serving in the dining room in another week or two.

The latter part of the letter was devoted to asking after Eddie, and its very last sentence was 'Give Eddie a big hug from me.'

'Come here,' Amy said, holding out her arms to Eddie, who was busying himself with a large glass of milk and a plate of biscuits. He came at once, clambering onto her lap and nestling against her. Eddie's ready affection was still strange and precious to Amy, difficult to reconcile with his startling likeness to his father. For the first few days she had hardly dared ask for these cuddles, as if she might break the spell that had produced this loving creature in Malcolm's image.

She squeezed him gently. 'There,' she said, relaxing her hold. 'That's from Mama. She said in her letter I was to give you a big hug.'

Eddie looked at the notepaper on the table in front of Amy. 'Where's it say hug?'

'Right here.' Amy took his hand in hers and guided it along the words. ' "Give Eddie a big hug from me",' she read. 'There's your name, see?' She placed his finger under it.

Eddie was fascinated by the idea that some scratchings on a piece of paper could convey such a thing as a hug and his very own name. He had Amy read them out to him several times, and afterwards he said them to himself under his breath. Amy watched him, amused by his intense concentration.

He lifted his bright eyes to meet her gaze. 'How do you know what it says?'

'That's what reading is. You learn letters, then you learn how they join together into words.'

'Can you show me how to do it?'

'How to read?' Amy said, startled. 'Would you like that?'

Eddie nodded.

Cool logic suggested she should tell him to wait a few months till he turned five years old and started school. Amy ignored it. 'That's a good idea, Eddie. I'll draw you some letters nice and big, and we'll start tomorrow. And I'm going to write back to Mama in a bit—I'll help you do your name at the bottom, so Mama can see what a clever boy you are. I think we'll use a pencil for that, though,' she added, envisaging the mess that would result from letting Eddie try a pen.

Eddie's first effort at writing his name, even with Amy guiding his hand, required the partiality of a grandmother (or, Amy hoped, the mother who would receive the letter) to be recognised, but she praised him for it, and was rewarded with a beaming smile.

With Eddie so keen to learn, it seemed a waste not to try and teach him while he was in her care. Amy was careful to keep such lessons short; it was too much to ask a four-year-old to spend more than a few minutes at a time working at learning his letters. She soon found that when Eddie became frustrated with a task, he could show flashes of temper that recalled his father's and grandfather's. Fortunately he was more easily calmed than either of them had been.

Beth, used as she was to younger brothers, had an easy friendship with Eddie from the start, but Amy could see David struggling over just how he should behave with him. Sometimes he romped with the little boy as if he were a child himself, clearly enjoying their play as much as Eddie did. At other times he felt the need to show some sort of authority, and would try to tell Eddie what to do, or scold him when he did not respond promptly to one of Amy's gentle requests. As Eddie ignored his instructions on any subject other than horses, on which he considered David an oracle, these attempts only made David uncomfortable while having no discernable effect on Eddie. Amy did not intervene; she was confident that David would, given time, realise he was wasting his energy on someone whose will was stronger than his own. Eddie, Amy could see, was a child better led by persuasion than command.

Milly wrote faithfully once a week; letters that tended to be short and unvarying. Her work was going well; she was saving her money (though Amy sensed that the amount was building up more slowly than Milly had expected); she hoped Eddie was being a good boy. She made much of Eddie's gradually improving attempts to write his name, and of the drawings Amy sometimes had him do for his mother. And she ended each letter with a hug for him, which Amy was only too happy to pass on.

It was clear that Eddie was going to be staying with them for some time, and after the first month Amy's fund of stories was running low. None of her own books seemed suitable for a small boy, so she wrote to Sarah, explaining the situation and enclosing a few shillings. A short time later a well-wrapped parcel arrived, and Amy opened it to find several small books with pictures of animals, dressed in human clothes, on the covers. A note from Sarah enclosed with the books explained that she had taken the advice of a bookseller, had been told these were quite new and very popular, and trusted that they would be suitable.

Eddie was entranced by the books, demanding to have them read to him night after night until Amy knew the simple stories by heart. When he asked if there were squirrels on the farm, she had to tell him the disappointing fact that there were none in the whole of New Zealand.

Eddie was not downcast for long; instead he turned his attention to the animals available to him. He searched the house for mouse holes, and prowled through the vegetable garden looking for rabbits, but there was no chance of finding such creatures in an entire state anywhere near the house; Pip, Beth's cat, was too good a hunter for that.

When Eddie tried talking to Pip, he suffered nothing worse than a dignified silence, but when he tried dressing the cat in one of Daisy's knitted jackets, Pip showed his disgust by leaving a trail of bleeding claw marks on the back of Eddie's hand before making his escape.

'Animals in stories aren't like real ones, Eddie,' Amy told him as she cleaned the blood from his hand. 'You can't dress them up. It's just pretend.' She dabbed away without comment the tears that had spilled onto Eddie's cheeks. He was not a child who often cried, and on the rare occasions when he did, he usually tried to hide it.

When Beth and David came in, Beth was clearly torn between amusement and sympathy, with amusement gaining the advantage once she had seen that Eddie's wounds were not serious. She fussed over his scratched hand, gave Pip some extra scraps to soothe his wounded pride, and repeated Amy's advice that real life cats would not submit to being dressed, whatever stories might say.

'Davie tried the same thing with Ginger when he was little,' Amy remarked. 'He put a baby's dress on him.'

This time Beth did not bother to hide her amusement. She demanded all the details, and laughed aloud as she heard the story.

David did not seem to find much humour in it. 'I don't remember that,' he said huffily.

'Well, you were only little,' said Amy. 'Littler than Eddie—I think you were only three.'

'Fancy trying to rock him in the cradle,' Beth said through a fresh burst of giggles. 'It's a wonder he didn't bite you.'

David scowled. 'Anyway, you shouldn't go opening people's drawers and helping yourself to stuff,' he said to Eddie.

'I didn't open no drawers,' Eddie said, unabashed. 'That jacket thing was just lying on the bed.'

'I was thinking about putting it in the ragbag,' Beth said. 'Maisie was trying to teach Rosie to knit, and it turned out with one arm longer than the other. I don't want to put a funny-looking thing like that on Daisy, especially with all the nice things Sarah sent her. Eddie's welcome to it.'

'Well... he shouldn't have done it,' said David. He gave Eddie a stern look, which was ignored.

Whenever the weather was fine enough, Amy made sure that Eddie spent much of the day outside. After having lived up till now in a series of rented rooms with no place more inviting than the street to play in, he delighted in running around the paddocks, climbing trees, and using the rope swing David made for him.

Once the paddocks were dry enough for a long walk, Amy took him to visit her old home. Her brothers and their households welcomed Eddie as part of the family, with their children cheerfully accepting the arrival of another cousin. They were all older than Eddie, and all at school, so could not be playmates for him, but he was a self-sufficient child, used to having only the company of adults.

And with the discovery of books and stories, he was showing every sign of a vivid imagination. When Amy was working outside and Eddie was playing nearby, she would often hear him talking away quietly to himself, though he seemed unaware that he was doing so. If she was close enough to make out the words, she usually found that Eddie was telling himself a story, something featuring himself and Daisy and, invariably, a horse.

Considering Daisy's limitations as a playmate, Eddie seemed to find her surprisingly good company. When they both happened to be in the house at the same time, he would often chatter away to her, and Amy almost had the impression that he garnered some meaning from Daisy's gurglings. He would sometimes sit beside her with one of his precious storybooks and "read" to her, as he insisted on calling it, though it was clear that he was telling the story from memory, with his own embellishments. Daisy showed every sign of delighting in the attention, whatever she made of the stories.

When the year's batch of calves were born, Beth showed Eddie how to teach them to drink from a bucket, and he appeared to enjoy the novelty. But he showed no interest at all in the adult cows. After milking resumed, David took him down to the cowshed one afternoon while Beth was busy with Daisy, but he sent Eddie back to the house before the task was over.

'He was playing up,' David said when he arrived back himself. 'I could see he'd be upsetting the cows if I kept him there much longer.'

'Cows are stupid,' Eddie grumbled.

'No, they're not!' Beth said, visibly shocked. 'They're clever, in their own way. Especially the Jerseys.'

'But they're no *use*. You can't play with them or get them to do anything.'

'They pay the bills and put food on the table,' David said, but this was too abstract a notion for the little boy. David shook his head as he studied Eddie's obstinate expression. 'I don't think we'll make a farmer out of you.'

He smiled as he said it, but Amy was suddenly reminded of Malcolm and his contempt for farm life. Had Eddie inherited her own desire for a wider world than the valley could offer, just as his father had?

While Eddie found cows boring, his fascination with horses grew with his experience of them. Only bad weather excused David from what Eddie considered his obligation to give a daily riding lesson. He was as fearless as Malcolm had been. If he took a tumble (though this had become rare), he would pick himself up and at once demand to be hoisted back onto the horse. He could already walk and trot the patient old horse that David was using for him to learn on; in spite of his pleas, Amy had forbidden any attempt at teaching him to jump.

'He's going to turn out a better rider than I am,' David said, watching Eddie urge the horse into a trot. 'Just like Mal was.'

David insisted that Eddie learn to tend the horses as well as ride them, and in this he had no problem getting Eddie to obey him. They made a comical sight as they groomed the horses together, the little boy standing on tiptoe to reach as high as he could before stepping back to let David finish the job. David showed him how to clean the tack, which he had to lift down from its hooks for him, and was endlessly patient with his clumsy attempts. Eddie would self-importantly stride along beside David when it came time to feed the horses, fondly imagining that he was carrying a useful share of the weight of a feed bag.

August came and went, with a small celebration to mark David's twentieth birthday. The weather grew finer, Frank spared some time from his own tasks to work on the new house with David, and Amy found that they had built in part of the verandah to make a third bedroom.

'You'll be using the other room, so we'll need it for Eddie,' David said when she asked him about the addition.

No more was said on the subject; it was clear that David and Beth felt that Eddie was not likely to return to his mother any time in the near future. And that Amy was no longer planning to move to Auckland.

Milly still wrote regularly, and her letters still had the same forced cheerfulness. Eddie might not be fretting for his mother, but she was certainly fretting for him.

September arrived. Eddie had been with them for almost three months. Amy had sensed from Milly's last few letters that something was on her mind beyond her usual preoccupation with her work and with Eddie's wellbeing. A line would be crossed out mid-sentence, followed by an abrupt change of subject to something as innocuous as the weather.

The month was half over when David came back from town one day bringing a letter from Milly somewhat longer than her recent ones.

Eddie had run out to help with the horse and cart, leaving Amy to open the letter while Beth put the kettle on. She read the first few lines, and gave a sharp intake of breath.

The noise caught Beth's attention. 'What is it, Aunt Amy?'

Amy stared at the words to see if she had somehow misunderstood them. But Milly's message was plain enough. She looked up from the letter to meet Beth's concerned gaze.

'Milly's got married.'

27

'Who to?' was Beth's first question.

'Someone she met at the hotel, I think she said. I'll read it all properly—don't say anything to Eddie,' Amy added, seeing that Beth was about to call David and Eddie in for their afternoon tea. 'I'll need to think out how to tell him.'

She tucked the letter away in her apron pocket, and left it there till she had the room to herself. Then she unfolded both sheets of paper and placed them on the table.

Milly, the letter informed Amy, had married a man called Sidney Carter. *He's very nice*, the letter said. *He's a fair bit older than me, but he's a good, steady bloke, and I think he'll be a good provider.* She had indeed met Mr Carter at the hotel, where he had been an occasional guest. *I've told him about Eddie, and he says I can have him with us, but to leave it for a bit till we're settled.* It seemed there was some discussion as to just where they might live; Milly's new husband had for the moment rented a room in Tauranga for the two of them, but it might suit him to set up house somewhere out of the town. *Don't tell Eddie just yet*, she said, much to Amy's relief. *Not till I know when I'll be able to send for him.*

Amy turned to the second sheet of paper. There were only a few lines on it. *It's not like being with Mal was*, Milly had written. *But you can't expect to have that twice in your life, eh?* She ended the letter with her usual hug for Eddie, but instead of signing it off with the familiar "Milly", she had carefully written "Amelia Carter". Amy put the letter away in her top drawer. It was not something to leave lying around for a casual observer; especially with its tender references to Malcolm.

Milly still wrote regularly, though much of the content of her letters had changed. She had left her job at the hotel shortly before her marriage, and was now occupied with keeping house for her husband. He had taken a house close to the mining town of Waihi, with a small yard in which Milly was trying to establish a garden. She sounded contented enough, though there were none of the affectionate remarks that might have been expected from a newlywed. While she continued to end every letter with a hug for Eddie, and it was clear that she missed him, she said she was not yet ready to send for him.

Eddie had his birthday in October. Now that he was five years old, the family had assumed Amy would send him to school, but she found herself reluctant to. Milly kept insisting she would be sending for Eddie 'in a bit', and there seemed little point in starting him at the valley school only to have to uproot him soon afterwards.

That was a good enough reason, but it was only part of Amy's decision to keep him at home. Eddie was enjoying his lessons with her, and she was thoroughly enjoying the opportunity to teach him.

She walked down to the school one afternoon to consult the teacher, and was told that while a child could be sent to school from the age of five, it was not compulsory to do so until the child turned seven. So she continued Eddie's lessons at home, and wondered how long it might be before he was taken from her.

It was Sarah's birthday in November. Before Eddie's arrival, Amy had expected to be settled in Auckland well before then, and to have been able to celebrate Sarah's birthday with her for the first time. Now she had no idea when she might be able to indulge in that pleasure. Much as she was enjoying Eddie's company, it did not stop her from longing for Sarah's.

A letter from Milly arrived not long after Sarah's birthday, containing news that came as no real surprise to Amy.

I'm expecting. I've got the morning sickness bad this time, but people say it doesn't last long. I didn't have it hardly at all with Eddie, I didn't know it took it out of you like this. Sid's being very good, fetching and carrying for me, and all. He's that pleased about the baby.

I hope you don't mind hanging on to Eddie a bit longer. I can't have him just yet, I've got to sort a few things out first.

Amy folded the letter back into its envelope. It was fortunate, she mused, that Eddie did not ask questions about his mother, now that they would have been so difficult to answer.

There was something troubling Amy about all this. Milly repeatedly said she would send for Eddie soon, and yet continued to delay doing so. She was in what sounded like the most settled home she had had since Eddie's birth, and was no longer having to try and earn money to support the two of them. There was no obvious reason for her to put off sending for him. Amy found herself having to fight against a nagging suspicion that now Milly was carrying a legitimate child she no longer wanted Malcolm's. The thought seemed ungenerous, and she would not allow herself to dwell on it.

There were other things to keep her busy. The new house was finally ready for the family to move into in early December. Frank brought his older boys, and Amy's brothers arrived with their sons, so there were many willing hands to help with moving. Amy's main task was to keep Eddie from getting underfoot badly enough to have a piece of furniture dropped on him, and to work with Beth providing morning tea for everyone. When their helpers had gone, she and Beth spent much of the afternoon and evening cleaning and dusting. She was worn out by the time she was finally able to go to bed, much later than usual, but seeing David and Beth's delight at their smart new house was more than worth the effort.

The size of Lizzie and Frank's family had meant that for several years now Arthur's household had gone to Frank's for Christmas dinner. But this year it was clear to everyone that making Arthur travel even so short a distance was not to be considered. The leg he had injured several years before not only made it difficult for him to walk more than a few steps, but also meant it was painful for him to keep it bent for any length of time. So buggy rides, even brief ones, were no longer possible.

None of this was discussed with Arthur himself, who would have felt the need to insist that he was perfectly capable of leaving the farm if he chose, and would have made himself and everyone around him wretched in the process of attempting to prove it. But when Christmas Day arrived, each of the households had its Christmas dinner at home. In the evening, Lizzie and Frank brought their family to Arthur's for a casual meal consisting mainly of leftovers.

After having been confined to the house the previous Christmas, Beth was eager to spend Daisy's first Christmas with her family. So the five of them went to Frank's then to Arthur's house that day, Amy driving the gig with Beth and Daisy, and an excited Eddie riding beside David on the oldest and slowest of the farm's horses, the first time he had been allowed to ride so far.

After their makeshift evening meal it was still light enough for the children to be sent outside to play, while the adults sat on the verandah. Eddie was absorbed into a group of the younger children, but when Rosie, who had decided to organise a complicated game of some sort, started trying to assert what she imagined to be her authority, Eddie wandered off on his own, exploring the unfamiliar garden. Amy kept an eye on him from the verandah, but he showed no inclination to go out of sight.

Eddie searched under a small grove of fruit trees, and came back to the verandah cradling something in his hands. He clambered up the steps and over to where Beth sat next to Amy, Daisy on her lap, and held out his hand to the baby. On it, Amy saw, was a small blue half eggshell, obviously dropped from a nest that spring.

Daisy's method of exploring the world consisted of putting everything that fell in her grasp into her mouth, and Amy was sure the experiment would do neither Daisy nor Eddie's treasure much good. She retrieved the eggshell before Beth, who was talking to her grandmother, had quite noticed what was happening.

'Keep it till Daisy's a bit older,' Amy told him. 'We'll put it in your room for now.' Eddie was gradually acquiring a collection of such things as dried leaves and berries, and pebbles of unusual shapes or colours. She wrapped the eggshell in her handkerchief and placed it carefully on the arm of her chair.

Instead of going back out into the garden, Eddie clambered onto her lap and snuggled into place. 'You're getting a bit sleepy, aren't you,' Amy said, seeing his eyelids drooping. 'I think we'll go home soon, or it'll be getting dark.'

'Do you want to hold Daisy for a bit before we go, Granny?' Beth asked Edie. She placed Daisy on Edie's lap, but kept her own arm around the baby, to stop Daisy wriggling from the unfamiliar perch.

Edie beamed. She seemed to know who Daisy was, though she called Eddie "Mal" whenever she spoke to him. The first few times she had done so, Arthur had tried to correct her, but as he struggled to remember Eddie's name himself he soon gave up the attempt.

Arthur looked on benignly at Daisy perched on Edie's lap. 'She's a bonny little thing. She's not a Leith, but there's a lot of Leith in her,' he announced.

Amy laughed. 'So there is, Uncle Arthur. Two Leith grannies, that must count for something.'

'I've two great-grandchildren now. Yes, Edie, I know you have as well,' Arthur added when he saw Edie about to speak. 'Jack would've had two, if he'd been spared,' he said, his expression growing heavier as he looked from Eddie to Daisy.

Amy held Eddie more tightly. 'He would've liked that.'

Eddie shrugged off his sleepiness and insisted on going with David to help get the horses ready to take them home. While they waited, Amy exchanged farewells with Lizzie. She noticed Frank and Bill off to one side, heads close together as they talked about what appeared to be a weighty matter.

'Frank and Bill look so serious!' Amy said, smiling at their expressions. 'They look as though they're plotting something.'

Lizzie looked around, checking that they were not being overheard. 'They are,' she confided. 'Don't let on to anyone, but…' She leaned closer to Amy and told her the secret.

Bill Leith was forty-two years old, but to his father that merely meant he was the oldest of "the boys", as Arthur referred to his sons. Now that his father rarely left the house, it fell on Bill's shoulders to see that the work of the farm went smoothly, as well as doing a large share of it himself. He conducted the day-to-day business of the farm, dealing with the factory and the general store. But his father held the chequebook, and held it firmly.

Arthur had never felt any need to pay his sons a wage. The farm fed and clothed them, and kept a roof over their heads. If he was moved to be generous he would occasionally give out a small amount of cash for the boy involved to treat himself, but any money beyond that had to be asked for. And Bill knew his father well enough to know what was worth asking for. The biggest purchase he had ever successfully requested his father to fund was Lily's wedding ring, but what he wanted now was a good deal more expensive.

It had started as more of a vague longing than a settled plan, but it had been in his mind for almost ten years now. Ever since the day he had first heard Lily play the piano.

She had stunned him with her playing, so unlike any music he had ever heard before. And then he had been startled by the sight of his calm, competent wife weeping, as she was buffeted by the abrupt rediscovery of what music meant to her. Lily was not a woman who readily wept.

He had asked Frank how much the piano had cost, and the answer had almost made him abandon the idea before it was even fully formed. Almost, but not quite. Perhaps he could not buy so smart an instrument as the one that graced Frank's parlour, but Lily deserved a piano of her own.

From that day, he had got into the habit of putting aside any money his father might give him for his own use. It accumulated, but painfully slowly. This was going to require more money than he had ever been able to call his own, and a good deal of patience.

He had let Frank into his confidence from early on, making the most of what Frank could tell him about the process of buying a piano. Though Frank could give him no advice on what to be careful of when it came to a used piano, as Bill had soon realised he would have to settle for. He had had to risk asking the one person who could give him a knowledgeable answer: Lily herself.

'Do pianos last a long time?' he had asked her one day with studied casualness, when he had just picked her up from Frank's house.

'If they're properly cared for, certainly. I've heard of antique pianos that are still in fine condition.' Lily had smiled, and placed a hand on his arm. 'Don't worry, dear, Frank's piano's not going to wear out in a hurry. Lizzie's very particular about not letting the children be rough with it—she doesn't let any of them touch it unless they're actually playing—and of course she keeps it beautifully clean. I'll be able to go on playing it for as long as I wish.'

She only had the chance to play it, of course, for brief periods each week, and most of even that small amount of time was in the course of teaching Lizzie's children. But it was a relief to be told by an expert that a piano did not have to be new to be worthy of Lily.

He had decided it had to be a Broadwood, the make of piano that Lily had owned until straitened circumstances had forced her to sell it after her mother's death, and the brand she had recommended to Frank. He could have bought a lesser one more cheaply, but since the whole project was as much dream as solid plan, he felt he might as well dream extravagantly. In any case, it seemed to him something like the difference between buying a broken-down nag of unknown origin, and a well-bred horse with quality lines.

When he had managed to put together a few pounds, he wrote to the firm Frank had used, asking about the possibility of buying a secondhand Broadwood from them. Writing letters was not something Bill was used to doing, but he found himself needing to become familiar with the task as his negotiations went on. It had to be done when Lily was out of the house but he himself was not busy on the farm, which was an extra difficulty.

He was told that used Broadwoods were only rarely offered, but with the estimate the firm supplied of the price he would probably have to pay for one, delay was hardly a problem. The company would put his details in their files, they said, and would inform him of any suitable instrument that might become available.

Once or twice in the intervening years he had heard again from the music shop, when they had acquired a Broadwood that was "almost as good as new". Almost as good, and almost as expensive. Bill had had to let such opportunities pass him by.

But a few months before Christmas, he received a letter from the firm that seemed, when he unravelled its meaning, to offer a ray of hope. The letter was full of words with which he had only a passing familiarity; words that he would in other circumstances have asked Lily to decipher for him. Instead, he read and re-read the letter several times, and when he felt he had made it out, he took it to show Frank.

'They say it's "fundamentally sound in the vital internal components relating to the quality of its tone," ' Bill read aloud carefully. ' "It has

333

sustained a degree of superficial damage to parts of the exterior, not including the keys, which are largely unmarked. Such damage is of a trifling nature, affecting only aesthetic details." I think they're saying its insides are all right, but the outside's a bit knocked about. What do you reckon?'

The words were as remote from Frank's vocabulary as from Bill's. But his brother-in-law agreed that seemed to be the gist of the letter. 'So you think you might send off for it?' Frank asked.

'Maybe,' said Bill. 'If they've still got it when I've put a bit more by.' *Quite a bit more*, he added to himself. The firm was asking seventeen pounds for the piano, including the cost of sending it to Ruatane, and when Bill had added up his savings he had found that they came to the disappointing total of twelve pounds, one shilling and fourpence.

Frank appeared to guess his thoughts. Bill sensed that he was on the point of offering to lend (or, even worse, *give*) him the money. He was grateful for the generous impulse, but even more grateful that Frank chose not to make an offer Bill's self-respect would have forced him to refuse.

Self-respect was all very well, but he needed to find a way to build up his savings that did not rely on his father's fitful, not to mention extremely modest, bursts of generosity. And then an idea came to him one day when he was ordering a new wheel for the spring cart.

'I hear there's a new bloke started up doing wheels and suchlike, out the other side of town,' he remarked to Mr Winskill. The wheelwright scowled at the reference to his rival, but made no reply beyond a grunt. 'He's doing a good price, I heard,' Bill added.

'A good price if you're not bothered about the quality,' Mr Winskill answered curtly. 'When do you want this wheel of yours by?'

Bill hesitated, as if considering a matter of some weight. 'I might leave it just now,' he said after a long pause. 'I was thinking of taking a look at the new bloke's place.'

Mr Winskill's scowl darkened. 'Don't come complaining to me when the wheel falls off your cart and you break your neck.'

'Well, it won't cost anything to look. And it might save me a few shillings.'

Bill made ready to ride off, deliberately being slow about it, and shooting covert glances at the wheelwright.

'I'll knock two shillings off, with you being a good customer,' Mr Winskill said abruptly.

'That's very good of you,' Bill said, careful not to let his triumph appear in his face. There would be no need to show his father the account before getting the money from him to pay the wheelwright; Arthur knew perfectly well what they were usually charged for wheels. He had an excellent memory for prices. The two shillings Bill had just saved could go straight into his secret hoard.

Over the following months those two shillings were joined by others, as Bill developed new skills at bargaining. Every purchase was subjected to scrutiny, to see whether or not he could save even a few pennies on it. He would allow the would-be seller to believe the purchase was all but settled, then begin to hem and haw, saying that perhaps he might leave it till the next quarter, or even hinting that he might find himself travelling to Auckland in the near future, where everyone knew things were cheaper. So adept did he become at these measures that he began to experience a certain coolness of manner towards himself. But he hardened himself against it, and remained steadfast.

He felt only the tiniest prickings of conscience over keeping the resulting savings for himself, rather than handing them over to his father. The fact that he found the whole business so unpleasant, going as it did against his easygoing nature, made him feel more justified in keeping the money. But most important of all was that this was for Lily. She deserved this.

Late in the year Bill received another letter from the piano shop. It surprised him, coming as it did unsolicited rather than in response to any approach from him. Once again, he had to find his way through the letter's unfamiliar language before he could understand its import, and when he had done so he was torn between hopefulness and unease. The used Broadwood was still available, but he sensed that the firm was not happy with its presence.

He recalled one or two rather grand shops he had seen when he had gone to Auckland with Frank; stores they had both found too intimidating to enter, knowing they would look out of place. Perhaps the owners of this piano shop, which prided itself on supplying only the finest instruments, were embarrassed by having on their premises a piano that had seen better days.

When Lily was safely occupied elsewhere in the house, Bill retrieved the tin box he kept in a drawer and counted his money. Even with his recent hard bargaining, it only came to fourteen pounds, two shillings and sixpence. Still almost three pounds short of the seventeen pounds that was being asked.

He dashed off a letter to the piano shop, assuring them that he was still interested but asking if any reduction in the price was possible. A reply came promptly. Its tone was polite but rather chilly. "After due consideration of the circumstances," he was told, the piano was now being offered to him for fifteen pounds ten shillings. No further reduction would be possible. If this reduced price did not meet with his approval, and if he did not find himself in a position to accept their offer in the near future, "an alternative method of disposal" would be sought.

Disposal! That sounded like getting rid of a dead cow. They couldn't be allowed to do that to Lily's piano!

It was time for desperate measures. Later that same day, Bill lingered on the verandah when they had had their afternoon tea and his father was settling in for what he called reading the paper, although to anyone else it might appear that he was taking a nap. Edie had wandered out to the kitchen to help Lily with getting dinner on; Bill knew Lily's heart always sank when Edie decided to help, and when he could spare the time he generally found ways of keeping his mother away from the kitchen at such moments. But just now it suited him to be alone with his father. Edie was inclined these days to forget within half an hour anything she had been told, but before forgetting it she was likely to repeat it to anyone within hearing.

Bill decided to take a direct approach. 'I want to get a piano for Lily,' he said when he was sure they would not be overheard.

'Eh?' said Arthur. 'Those things cost a lot of money, boy.'

'I know. I've been putting a bit aside for a while now. There's one I've got my eye on—secondhand, but a good brand. It's a good price, too. Frank put me on to this place. He knows a bit about buying pianos,' he pointed out before his father could bristle at not having been consulted first. 'His seems to be lasting all right.'

'That's true enough,' Arthur allowed. 'A piano,' he mused. 'I wouldn't mind hearing Lily play of an evening. I can't be bothered going down to Frank's all the time, I've too much to do here.'

Bill made a noise vaguely indicative of agreement. 'The thing is, I want to get on and buy it before someone else snaps it up. And I'm still a bit short.'

Arthur narrowed his eyes. 'How much?'

'One pound, seven shillings and sixpence.'

Now Arthur looked surprised. 'That's all? You've saved up all the rest?'

'Yes,' said Bill.

'You haven't done too badly, then,' Arthur said with grudging praise. 'I don't give you that much.'

Bill shrugged. 'I've been at it for a good while now. Years and years.'

He could have pressed his father; could have pointed out all the work

336

he did, and how rarely he asked for anything. And that would have guaranteed an indignant refusal. Instead, he schooled his face into meekness, and waited as patiently as he could, watching Arthur's thoughts play over his face.

'Lily's been a real help to your ma over the years,' Arthur said at last. 'You were lucky to get a good, steady woman like her.'

'I know I was.'

There was another pause; this one went on so long, and Arthur's eyelids drooped so much, that Bill began to fear his father had fallen asleep. At last Arthur shifted in his chair, reached for his pipe and started fiddling with it, then raised his eyes to Bill's.

'Go and fetch the chequebook,' he pronounced.

Bill sent off his order, along with the money, the very next day. Just before Christmas he received an acknowledgement, and an assurance that the piano would be sent early in the new year. On Christmas Day, when Frank's family were at Arthur's, Bill took the opportunity to tell Frank about the piano's imminent arrival, and to discuss with him what could be done to keep Lily away from the farm on the day it came.

'I want it to be a surprise,' said Bill. 'I don't want her to see it till it's all set up and ready for her.'

'Hmm, and there's a lot of fiddling about to get it put together and all, it'll take a while,' Frank said thoughtfully. 'You'll need to get the tuner out, too.'

'The tuner?' Bill echoed in sudden alarm. 'Couldn't I leave getting him out for a bit?'

Frank shook his head. 'No, you'll need him on the day. I remember when we got ours, he had to give it a good seeing-to before it sounded right. Sorry,' he added, seeing Bill's expression. 'I should have told you that before.'

Bill shrugged off his apology. 'Don't worry about it. I'll go and see him next time I'm in town.' He pushed the new complication to the back of his mind. 'So on the day it gets here, do you reckon you could keep Lily down at your place long enough for us to get it all sorted out? She's usually just there for a couple of hours when she goes down to teach the kids.'

'I'll ask Lizzie. She'll think of something.'

'Don't let on to anyone else, though—I want it to be a real surprise.'

Frank smiled at him. 'It'll be that, all right.'

'Jam!' had been Lizzie's suggestion. 'I'll tell Lily to come down for the day, and we can make jam together. She'll enjoy that.'

Lily had been less enthusiastic about the idea than Lizzie had predicted. 'Jam?' she said doubtfully. 'I'm not sure I can spare the time for that just now. Even if I could, it would suit me better to stay home and make it with Emma.'

'But Lizzie asked specially, and she's expecting you now,' said Bill. 'She said she'd get the kids to pick a lot more plums when I told her you'd come.'

Lily blinked in surprise. 'You told her I would? Without asking… well, that makes it awkward to refuse,' she said, the slightest trace of a frown drawing her brows together. That was as close as Lily would come to scolding him, even if they had not had an audience. 'I don't know, Bill, I really don't like to leave Emma on her own to look after Mother and Father all that time.'

She had lowered her voice, but Emma had sharp hearing. Emma had also been taken into Bill's confidence that very afternoon. She might be only twelve years old, but she was a sensible girl, and Bill knew she could be trusted with the secret, although he would not have said the same of her brothers.

'I'll be quite all right with Granny and Grandpa, Mother,' Emma said. 'And I can do a big load of baking while you're out, without us getting in each other's way.'

Lily smiled. 'You never get in my way, dear.' She gave in gracefully. 'In that case, it seems I'll be making jam with Lizzie tomorrow.'

'Good,' Bill said, careful not to show how relieved he was. 'I'm going into town tomorrow, I'll drop you off on my way.'

The next morning Bill set out with Lily, complete with buckets of plums from their own trees, several boxes of jam jars and a half-full bag of sugar, on their way to Lizzie's. It was all he could do to hide his anticipation; as it was, Lily noticed something of his mood.

'You seem very cheerful, dear,' she commented soon after they had left the farm.

'I'm looking forward to that jam,' he said for want of a better answer.

Lily laughed in her quiet way. 'I'd better make sure it's specially good jam, then.'

He dropped her off, then made his way into town to collect his piano.

The *Waiotahi* was already tied up at the wharf, with the cargo unloaded, by the time he got there with the large dray that Frank had arranged for him to borrow from the dairy factory. With the help of several of the wharf hands, as well as some of the boys who always

338

seemed to be hanging around the area, he soon had the large case holding the piano safely loaded, and was on his way home, the piano tuner riding alongside him.

He had told Emma she could let her brothers into the secret as soon as their mother was out of hearing. The two boys, as well as Bill's brothers Alf and Ernie, and Mr Reid the tuner, all joined in to help haul the piano into the house once it had been removed from its packaging, while Arthur stood by, leaning on his stick and giving instructions. The piano was pushed and pulled into the parlour, where Emma had been at work clearing a space for it and giving the area a thorough, though quite unnecessary, sweeping.

With the piano in place, for the first time Bill could take a proper look at it. His heart sank.

'My goodness, this instrument has had a hard life,' the tuner said, echoing Bill's thoughts. Where the wood of the piano could be seen through a layer of ancient grime, it was scuffed and scratched all over. Along one side, a strip of veneer had lifted from the wood beneath. The pedals and candle holders were so tarnished they were almost black. 'I hardly dare hope...' Mr Reid murmured as he opened his bag of tools.

The boys, and Bill's brothers, soon lost interest and wandered off, while Edie twittered away, largely ignored, and Arthur stared grimly at proceedings from his armchair. But Bill and Emma hovered near the tuner like anxious loved ones at a sickbed, hardly daring to breathe for fear of disturbing the healer at work.

After what seemed a long time to Bill, though it was in reality only a few minutes, the tuner looked up from his work and smiled. 'Well, the outside appearance is no reflection on the inside, I'm pleased to say. There's no sign of rot, and nothing important is warped or cracked. I'll need to replace a few of the felts, but that's trivial.' He patted the piano. 'Its heart is sound, and that's what matters.'

Bill exhaled a slow sigh of relief and sank into the nearest chair. He watched the tuner at work, vaguely aware that his father was making a few caustic remarks about the foolishness of buying a piano sight unseen.

'That should be quite satisfactory,' Mr Reid said. He played a few scales, then packed away his tools and stepped back from the piano. 'Now, who'd like to try it first?'

'That has to be you, love,' Bill told Emma.

She took a step towards the piano, then stopped and turned to face Bill. 'You don't want to wait for Mother to have first go?'

Bill shook his head. 'I'm not going to be easy in my mind till I've heard a tune out of it.'

He brought a chair through from the kitchen for her, making a mental note as he did so that he would have to see about getting a piano stool when he could next scrape together some money. Emma perched on the chair, frowned in concentration, and began a pretty little tune. Her playing was rather slow and deliberate, but the room rang with the strong, clear sound.

'Very nice,' said Mr Reid. 'The instrument has a fine tone, as I'd expect of a Broadwood. It obviously hasn't had the treatment it deserves, but I can see it's found a good home at last.'

'Yes, it has,' said Bill.

He saw Mr Reid to his horse. By the time he got back to the parlour, Emma had already taken to the piano with an armoury of dusters and polishing cloths. Arthur had removed himself from the scene of such womanly tasks, but Edie hovered about. Emma worked away vigorously, and Bill watched the operation in some awe.

She stood up from where she had been crouched over the pedals. 'That's the best I can do,' she said, studying her handiwork with a slight frown. 'I can't do anything about those really bad scratches.'

'You've done wonders,' Bill said. All trace of grime had disappeared, and generous amounts of polish had hidden the more minor scratches. The loose section of veneer, and the spots where it had been gouged through to the wood beneath, were still visible, and no one could miss the signs of the piano's rough treatment, but its woodwork and brass gleamed, right down to the pedals. He put his arm around Emma and squeezed. 'You'll get as good on the piano as your ma is, now there's one in the house.'

'No, I'll never play as well as Mother.' Emma had a thoughtful, considered way of speaking, weighing each word carefully before she uttered it, that Bill was quite sure she had not inherited from the Leith side of the family. 'But I think I might be quite good.'

Bill planted a kiss on the top of her head. 'I think so, too.'

Under Emma's direction, Bill pulled an armchair closer to hide the dangling veneer, which he told her he would make an attempt at gluing down when he had a moment; and she placed a cloth on top of the piano where an ancient water stain had defeated her polishing skills.

'Time to go and get your ma, I think,' Bill said. Emma's bright eyes reflected his own eager anticipation.

Lily was helping Lizzie and the girls wash up after their jam-making session, but Lizzie insisted that she leave as soon as Bill arrived. Lizzie exchanged a glance with Bill, who gave her a quick nod to indicate that all was well. Bill loaded the boxes of now-full jam jars, helped Lily onto the seat of the cart beside him, and set off, careful not to give away his eagerness by pushing the horse beyond a gentle trot.

'Well, I won't need to make jam again for a while,' Lily remarked. She sniffed delicately at one of her sleeves. 'Goodness, I smell of plums.'

'You could smell of a lot worse than that.'

Lily laughed. 'Yes, I suppose I could. I'm glad you came when you did, it was getting so warm in the kitchen—I was hoping I might manage a little time on the piano, but there really wasn't a chance.'

'That's a shame,' Bill said, turning aside to hide his smile.

When they pulled up to the house he called Arfie and Will over to take charge of the cart, warning them with his eyes to say nothing about the piano. He walked with Lily into the kitchen, where Emma had the room to herself.

Bill was still puzzling over how he could coax Lily into the parlour without giving away the surprise, when Emma took her mother's hand.

'I just want to show you something, Mother,' she said, her tone giving no indication of anything out of the ordinary. 'Come up here for a minute.' Emma's face was a picture of calm unconcern, although Bill knew she was almost as full of anticipation as he was himself. He watched her, impressed; he had had no idea that his daughter had such a gift for subterfuge.

Lily allowed Emma to lead her up the passage, Bill following in their wake. Just before they reached the parlour door, Emma let go of her mother's hand and stepped aside, allowing Bill to take her place. 'It's Pa who wants to show you, really,' she said.

Lily turned a quizzical face to Bill. 'Whatever's going on?' she asked, a slight smile playing on her lips.

The moment called for a touch of ceremony. Bill looped her arm through his, and ushered her into the room. Edie smiled benignly from her armchair, while Arthur was already regarding the piano with a proprietorial air.

They were halfway across the room before Lily saw the piano. She stood stock still, and Bill felt a tremor run through her. He tugged gently at her arm until she began walking again, still trembling. When the piano was close enough to touch, she reached out a quivering hand that hovered above the keyboard, then slowly lowered until it rested on the keys, so lightly that it made no sound.

The moment she touched the piano, her trembling stopped. She turned to Bill, eyes wide and mouth slightly open. 'Oh, Bill,' she breathed. 'Oh, Bill!'

The damage that had defeated Emma's best efforts at hiding it stared accusingly at Bill. 'I know it's a bit knocked about, but Emma had a go playing, and it sounds pretty good. Anyway, it's yours. You'd better try it out.'

'It's wonderful,' Lily said, her voice faint. She let Bill help her onto the chair, placed both hands over the keys and began to play.

Bill had difficulty distinguishing one piece of music from another, but he knew without being told that Lily had chosen to play a piece by Chopin. 'He lets my heart speak through my hands,' Lily had once told him when he asked her why Chopin was her favourite. That had been a more poetic answer than he had expected, but when he watched Lily bent over her piano, oblivious to the world, and heard the music coming from her, he felt that he was poised on the brink of understanding what she had meant. He sank into the nearest chair, moving carefully so as not to disturb Lily, and settled himself to watch and to listen. Emma perched on the arm of his chair and rested a hand on his shoulder, as engrossed in the scene as he was.

Lily looked up at last. Bill saw awareness of her surroundings seep into her face. Her eyes met his, and her mouth curved into a smile. 'Thank you,' she said, her voice scarcely above a whisper.

She gave herself a small shake, and stood up. 'Goodness, look at the time,' she exclaimed on checking the mantel clock. 'I must get on with my work.' She ran her fingers soundlessly over the keys, and looked over with evident relief at Edie, who had managed to nod off during the last piece of music, so would not trail out to the kitchen after her. Emma was fussing over her grandfather, moving his footstool to a better position and plumping up the cushion that had slipped to one side of his chair. She gave a quick nod to Lily to indicate that she would join her in a few moments.

The sight of Lily's face bright with happiness was so beguiling that Bill found himself reluctant to part from it just yet. He followed her out into the passage, caught her up and was about to speak when Lily flung her arms around his neck and pressed her mouth on his.

Bill wisely abandoned the notion of speech, and responded in kind. When he came up for air, Lily smiled at him, her eyes shining. She looked past him, and a flush spread over her face. Bill glanced over his shoulder just in time to see Emma disappearing back into the parlour, grinning broadly.

'Caught in mischief by our own child,' said Lily. 'I hope you realise that rather diminishes our authority.' Her blush was already fading; she was too brimful of delight for anything as trivial as embarrassment to take firm hold.

'So you like it?' Bill asked, knowing the answer but wanting to hear it anyway.

'I love it. I was past dreaming I'd ever have a piano of my own again. You even found a Broadwood!'

'I couldn't manage to get a new one for you, but it sounds all right, even if it doesn't look too flash. The tuner bloke said it'd probably been forgotten about, just left in a store room or something.'

'Do you know, I think I love it all the more for its having been neglected like that, and then rescued by you.' Lily laughed softly. 'It's a sort of fellow feeling, I suppose.'

Bill was not entirely sure what she meant, but he kissed her anyway, rather more sedately this time.

She disentangled herself with every sign of reluctance. 'I really do have work to do. But I'll play again this evening—I'm going to pull out every piece of music I own! You may come to regret this.'

Bill smiled back at her. 'I don't think so.'

He returned to the parlour. Emma was sitting with her hands folded in her lap, looking very prim and proper until he noticed the glint in her eye. 'I'll just go out and help Mother,' she said, almost managing to hide a smile as she rose and left the room.

Bill sat down where he had a good view of the piano, reviewing in his mind the picture Lily had made when seated before it. He had an odd sense that the piano was already missing Lily's presence. A fanciful notion, he knew; but a harmless one. Lily would soon be back there. It had almost been worth having to wait so long, when the fulfillment was so very satisfying.

Arthur stirred in his chair. 'You know, Lily's jolly good on that piano.' His tone suggested that Bill might not have realised this without the benefit of his father's wisdom.

'Yes, she is,' Bill agreed.

'It'll be good to have a bit of music in the house,' said Arthur. 'Yes, it's a good thing we got that piano. I don't know why we didn't do it years ago.'

It was clear to Bill that it would not be long before his father decided the whole business of getting a piano had been his own idea all along. That did not matter to him. What mattered was that Lily had her piano at last; and she knew perfectly well who had managed it.

In any case, it was fortunate that Arthur was beginning to take responsibility for the idea; that could only make him more obliging when it came to ongoing expenses. And at the moment, Bill had no idea how he was going to pay the account the piano tuner had left with him.

28

Just before Christmas a parcel had arrived, addressed to Amy and postmarked from Tauranga. It showed signs of having been hastily wrapped, with a sheet of brown paper crumpled around it and held together by a clumsily knotted length of string. Amy opened it to find a bundle of waxy-looking coloured sticks that seemed to be meant for drawing. The printed label around them said they were wax crayons, a thing Amy had never seen before. There was no letter with the crayons, only a scribbled note on a roughly torn piece of paper that said, 'Love from Milly.' Amy blinked in surprise when she saw the note; the crayons were clearly meant for Eddie, but Milly seemed to have been so flustered when sending them that she had forgotten to sign herself as "Mama".

Amy told herself there was nothing to be wondered at in a pregnant woman's vagueness; she recalled how hard she had found it when carrying her own children to concentrate on anything beyond the simplest tasks. She did her best not to dwell on how strange it seemed for a woman to forget that she was addressing her own child, and how much it seemed of a piece with Milly's odd behaviour ever since her marriage. She wrapped the crayons up again, more neatly this time, and put them aside until Christmas Day.

Milly's letters were no longer arriving every week. Amy wondered if Eddie had noticed the longer gaps between them, but she did not want to question him on the subject. It was not as if there was anything she could do about it.

She was relieved when a letter arrived in the middle of January, a somewhat belated response to her own note of thanks on Eddie's behalf.

I'm glad you got the parcel all right, Milly wrote. *I couldn't even remember afterwards if I'd written the address on it properly or not. I came over funny when I was in the Post Office. I had to sit down for a bit, and someone got me a glass of water.*

Sid had to go to Tauranga for his work that day, and he thought an outing might buck me up. I wasn't showing so as anyone would notice, I've swelled up a bit since. I don't think I'll go again. He left me to have a look around the shops, so I thought I'd get something for Eddie and get it sent off while I had the chance. I thought those crayon things would suit, with him being keen on drawing.

Sid took me out for lunch at a flash tearoom before we came back home. I didn't like to let on that I was feeling a bit crook. I've felt a bit funny ever since. I suppose it's the heat. I carried Eddie through the cooler weather, so it wasn't so bad. It seems a lot harder this time. And I've got a few months to go yet. Still, there's no use moaning about it.

Amy wrote a short reply that same afternoon, seated at the kitchen table from where she could keep Daisy and Eddie in her sight.

The children were sitting on the kitchen floor, Eddie with a magnificent book that Sarah had sent from Auckland as his Christmas present, and which had immediately become his most treasured possession, propped on his lap. It was a large volume, bound in rich brown leather with gold lettering, and filled with stories of dragons and castles and brave heroes, all beautifully illustrated. Eddie was recounting one of the stories to Daisy, in a mixture of actual reading and telling from memory.

Daisy's attention was divided between listening to Eddie and the apparently fascinating possibilities of her own feet, one of which she was currently engaged in putting into her mouth. She removed it, took hold of both feet and waved them vigorously, chortling as she did so. It was hard to believe she was the same child who had kept the adult members of the household awake much of the previous night, howling at the discomfort brought on by her current bout of teething. Daisy seemed quite untroubled by her broken night, her overly-bright cheeks the only sign today of the offending tooth.

'Do you want to come and do one of your nice drawings?' Amy asked when Eddie seemed to have come to the end of a story. She placed a sheet of notepaper on the table beside Eddie's crayons. 'I've got a letter to send off to Mama, and I'll put your drawing in with it.'

'All right.' Eddie got up and came over to the chair Amy pulled out for him.

'Don't leave your book on the floor, Daisy'll get into it,' Amy reminded him, not for the first time. She rose and picked the book up herself, and put it on the table out of Daisy's reach.

Daisy crawled on the floor while Eddie worked at his drawing and Amy put the vegetables on for their dinner. When they were almost ready, she set the table, carefully stepping around the baby.

Daisy pulled herself upright against Eddie's chair and tugged at his arm. Eddie held his drawing down to her level to show her.

'See, that's you, and that's Granny, and that's me on Patch's back,' Eddie said, pointing out each coloured blob in turn. 'It's for Milly.'

'For Mama, you mean,' Amy corrected him.

Eddie looked back at her, a hint of defiance in the set of his head. His new habit of referring to his mother by her name was proving hard to break. It had started when he saw the note she had enclosed with his crayons, signing herself as "Milly". Eddie could now read well enough to sound the word out for himself, and recognise it as the name he

346

sometimes heard Amy use to Beth or David when one of his mother's letters arrived.

He seemed to have taken Milly's failure to called herself "Mama" to heart. Ever since the arrival of her note he had been behaving a little oddly whenever she was mentioned. His odd behaviour did not, however, extend to the crayons Milly had sent, which were well-used and already noticeably shorter than they had been when new.

'It's for Milly,' Eddie repeated, still talking to Daisy. 'She was my mama. She went away.'

'She's still your mama, Eddie.' Amy thought she had caught the hint of a tremble in his voice. She wished she could take him in her arms and tell him that of course his mother would come back for him, but she could not when she was so unsure of it herself. She was not going to lie to Eddie.

She sighed, and chose a more down-to-earth distraction. 'I think Uncle Dave and Aunt Beth might be late again tonight. You can have your dinner now, and then have pudding when they're back.'

Eddie brightened visibly at the suggestion of dinner. Amy dished him up a plateful and placed it before him, then smiled at the sight of Daisy, who was still holding herself precariously upright against Eddie's chair, and was now looking up at his laden plate with a rather woebegone expression. Amy cut a chunk of bread from the loaf in front of her, swept Daisy onto her lap and gave her the bread to gnaw on.

Daisy was soon all smiles and crumbs. Amy popped her back on the floor so that she could finish getting their pudding ready to go in the range, while Eddie chose to take his plate and continue his dinner sitting on the floor with Daisy, talking away to her as if he was sure she understood every word. When he finished eating, he retrieved his book from the table and opened it to where he had left off.

David and Beth came in just as Amy was beginning to think she would have to dish their meals up and keep them warm by the range. They both looked tired and strained. One of Beth's Jersey cows had been ill, and Beth had been getting up several times a night to dose it with medicines of her own invention that she brewed on the range. The heifer was on the mend, but Beth was still keeping it in a shed close to the house so that she could check on it frequently. The run of broken nights had been capped by Daisy's efforts of the previous evening.

Amy waved aside a weary Beth's attempts to help dish up their meal. She made them both sit down, and was relieved to see them gradually look a little more like their usual selves under the influence of a good dinner. Neither of them made any move to pick up Daisy, who was still contentedly sitting beside Eddie, gnawing on an increasingly soggy crust.

Amy placed bowls of stewed fruit and custard on the table. 'I've filled your bowl a bit full, Eddie, so come and start it up here.'

Eddie came readily enough; a large helping of roast mutton, potatoes, peas and beans had not spoiled his appetite for pudding. He had just plunged his spoon into the bowl when Amy glanced down at Daisy, and saw that she was taking an unhealthy interest in Eddie's picture book.

'Eddie, you've left your book on the floor again. Pick it up—quickly, now—look, Daisy's going to chew it!'

Daisy had indeed managed to get a corner of the book's cover into her mouth. She closed her eyes, a look of contentment on her face, and sank her little teeth into the leather.

Eddie scrambled from his chair, crossed the few steps to Daisy, and snatched up his book. 'You leave my book alone!' he cried, his voice shrill. He clutched the book to his chest with one arm, and to Amy's shock he swung his other arm at Daisy, catching her a blow on the side of her head.

Time seemed to stop. Eddie stared down at Daisy, his eyes wide with the enormity of what he had done. It had been a clumsy blow, with no real force behind it, but everyone in the room was stunned into silence. Then Daisy opened her mouth and began howling her outrage, Beth moved to scoop her up into her arms, and at the same moment David erupted from his chair.

'Don't you touch her, you little bugger!' he roared. He grabbed the front of Eddie's shirt, lifted it till Eddie was on tiptoe, and shook him like a dog with a rat.

Amy had never seen such rage on David's face. She wanted to take hold of him and pull him away from Eddie, but as if she were in a bad dream she found herself unable to move, not even when she saw David raise his fist.

Eddie did not seem to take in the significance of the fist so near his head, but he was certainly aware of the anger suffusing the man who loomed over him. He hung limp in David's grip, staring back into the eyes glaring at him.

David abruptly let go of Eddie's shirt. Eddie staggered back a step or two, and swayed on his feet. Through it all, he had somehow managed to keep hold of his precious book. The rage had seeped out of David's face, to be replaced by something closer to horror. He turned away from Eddie and pounded both fists on the table, setting the dishes rattling.

'I don't know what to do,' he cried, his face contorted with distress. 'I don't know what to *do!*'

Amy recovered the power of movement at last. She took hold of Eddie's arm, left Beth to cope with her distraught husband and child, and dragged Eddie from the room. She hurried him though the house, not stopping until they were in his bedroom. She pushed Eddie onto the bed and stood over him.

'That was a wicked thing to do, Eddie! Hitting a little baby who can't stick up for herself!'

'But she was wrecking my book,' Eddie protested. 'Look!' He held it out to show Amy the damage, which consisted of the small marks of Daisy's front teeth and a generous smear of dribble, with a few crumbs of bread stuck to it.

'That doesn't mean you're allowed to hit her.' Amy knelt beside the bed and put a hand on each of his arms. 'Listen to me, Eddie. You're never to hit girls, and you're never to hit little kids smaller than you. That's just being a bully. You don't want to be a bully, do you?'

Eddie lowered his eyes. 'She was wrecking my book.'

'And that's because you left it on the floor again. She's a baby, Eddie. She doesn't know any better. You gave her an awful fright—and look how you upset Uncle Dave.'

Amy thought she saw a trace of contrition in Eddie's face. 'I didn't mean to hurt Daisy,' he said, so quietly that she barely caught the words. 'She just made me wild.'

'Well, you can't go around hitting people just because you get annoyed. I want you to think about what you did.' Amy unbuttoned his shirt as she spoke. 'You're going straight to bed with no pudding.'

'I don't care,' Eddie muttered, his face taking on the defiant expression that made him look so like his father. He reluctantly let her take the book out of his arms so that she could finish undoing his buttons.

Amy pulled the nightshirt over his head. 'And no stories tonight, either.' Eddie's face fell at that, but he said nothing. He climbed into bed; when Amy leant down and attempted to kiss him, he turned his face away.

She picked up his book from the chest of drawers where she had placed it. 'I'm going to put this book away until I'm sure you're sorry for what you did.'

Eddie sat up in bed, his mouth open in shock. 'That's not fair!'

'Hitting a little baby's not fair.' With an effort, Amy hardened her heart against his disconsolate expression. 'You can have it back when you've learned your lesson.'

Eddie's mouth trembled. 'Are you going to send me away?'

'Send you away?' Amy frowned in confusion. 'What do you mean, Eddie?'

'Milly said it. When her and me came here. She said if you didn't want me she didn't know what she'd do. She said she'd have to send me to a boys' home. She didn't want to, but she'd have to. And if I was bad you wouldn't want me. And hitting Daisy was a really bad thing.' The last words came out muffled as Eddie buried his face in the covers.

Amy placed the book back on the chest, crouched beside the bed and put her arms around the small figure. 'Of course I want you, Eddie. You're my little boy—mine and Mama's. I'm so very glad you came to live with me. And even if Mama…' She caught her breath, but it was too late to call back that "if". 'Even if Mama fetches you away, I'll still want you to come and have holidays with us. So will Aunt Beth and Uncle Dave.'

Eddie's expression suggested he was recalling how he had last seen David looking at him. Amy gave him a squeeze. 'Come on, let's do your prayers, then you can have a quiet little think about what you did, and why you'll never do it again. Then tomorrow you'll say sorry to everyone, and you'll all be friends again. Yes, even Uncle Dave.' She kissed his smooth cheek. 'You're a good boy, really.'

The kitchen was surprisingly peaceful when Amy entered the room. Daisy was nestled in the crook of David's arm, the traces of tears still visible on her lashes, but showing no other sign of her earlier distress. Amy bent to kiss the baby, and sat down.

'Is Daisy all right?' she asked Beth, who was in the process of pouring out cups of tea.

'Yes, she's just fine. She got a fright, but I don't think it really hurt her. There's not a mark on her.' Beth stroked Daisy's cheek, and Daisy gurgled contentedly. 'Boys can be a bit rough when they get worked up—I remember Danny gave Rosie a shove once and knocked her over, and she hit her head on a chair. She made a heck of a fuss, but it was no worse than what she'd get running around outside, or falling off the pony. Ma did Danny a lot more damage than he'd done Rosie. He was a lot older than Eddie is, though, he should've known better,' Beth added, with a quick glance at David. 'I know Eddie shouldn't have done it, but there was no harm, really.'

'No, he shouldn't have done it,' Amy said. 'I've sent him to bed with no pudding, and I've taken his book off him for now.' She turned to David. 'He's sorry for what he did. And he loves Daisy, you know he does. I'm sure he won't do anything like that again.'

350

Beth had done a fine job, with Daisy's assistance, of calming David down, but he still looked troubled. 'I don't know what to do with Eddie,' he said earnestly. 'I mean...' He lowered his eyes for a moment, then raised them to meet Amy's. 'I know you don't like me going on about Pa, but... I don't want to be like he was, thumping Mal and me so we were scared stiff of him.'

'You won't be,' Amy said. 'Your father couldn't help the way he was made, but you're not like that. I know you got a shock just now, but you stopped yourself before anything happened.'

'But I don't know what to do. What am I supposed to do when he plays up?'

'Don't do anything. It's not up to you—Eddie's my responsibility.'

'But... but he hasn't got a father,' David said, looking uncomfortable.

'That's right, Dave. Eddie doesn't have a father. That's just how things are. It's not your job to try and be one to him.'

David appeared more willing to be convinced than Amy had expected. It was clear that his attempts to act as a father to Eddie were prompted by duty, not by any wish for the role that should have been Malcolm's.

Next morning, Amy waited till David and Beth had come back from milking before she went to get Eddie up and dressed, leaving Beth to dish up their breakfast. She took him by the hand and led him into the kitchen, where David and Beth were now seated at the table.

'Eddie's got something to say.' Amy gave his hand an encouraging squeeze before letting it drop from her grasp.

Eddie went to stand in front of Daisy, who was on Beth's lap. 'Sorry, Daisy,' he said solemnly.

Daisy clearly bore no grudge. She gave a giggle, and reached out her arms towards Eddie. He took one little hand in his own, leaned forward and kissed her on the cheek. Daisy responded with a milky bubble, then startled the adults by quite distinctly saying 'adda'.

'That sounded like "Eddie",' said Beth. 'I think she's saying your name.'

Eddie appeared unsurprised by Daisy's feat, or by the fact that she had said his name before "Mama" or "Papa". 'I've been teaching her how to say it.' He remembered his task of the moment. 'I'm sorry I hit Daisy, Aunt Beth.'

Beth folded her free arm around him and drew him close. 'I know you didn't mean to. And you won't do it again, will you?' Eddie shook his head vigorously. 'That's a good boy.' She kissed him on the top of the head.

Eddie hesitated a moment, then marched across to where David sat. 'I'm sorry, Uncle Dave. I promise I won't ever hit Daisy again.' He thrust his hand out, and David carefully took it in his own much larger one to shake it.

David let go of his hand. Eddie continued to stand there, both of them looking awkward. 'Well, that's all sorted out, then,' David said. Another awkward silence followed, once again broken by David. 'Do you want to come down to the factory with me this morning?'

Eddie's face lit up. This was a rare treat; Amy considered him too young to be entirely safe at the factory, which she knew would be crowded with carts coming and going, heavy milk cans being unloaded, and men too engrossed in the task at hand and in talking to each other to take much notice of one small, lively boy. She had only allowed him to go with David once or twice before, and had worried the whole time they were gone. But this morning it seemed well worth the risk.

Eddie took his seat. He and David attacked their breakfasts with vigour, showing every sign of having put the awkwardness behind them. Amy met Beth's gaze and returned her smile. Peace reigned, and as long as David contented himself with being an overgrown big brother to Eddie, there seemed a fair chance that it would continue to do so.

Things quickly returned to normal on the farm. The morning after his outburst, Eddie picked Daisy a bunch of flowers that, as they were no use to chew on, she quickly pulled to bits and scattered over the floor. He then took to carrying her about, something that made Daisy crow in delight. She was a sturdy child, and Eddie did not look entirely steady under the burden, but he managed not to drop her. In any case, as Beth pointed out to Amy, it was not far for either of them to fall.

It was the end of January before Milly wrote again. She was full of apologies for her tardiness in replying, but when Amy had read the whole of her note she could not find it in herself to be at all irritated with Milly. There was a bleakness about the letter that seemed to Amy to go beyond the weariness that might be expected of a woman in the last half of her pregnancy.

I haven't got hardly anything done lately, Milly wrote. *I should be sewing and things for the baby, but I can't seem to settle to anything. I think this baby must be quite a size, the way it hurts every time I sit down or get up or just move. I had a dizzy spell the other day, then I was up half the night being sick. Sid's been that worried, he wanted to get the doctor to me. But I wouldn't let him—I didn't want some strange bloke poking around at me. I feel bad enough without that.*

It's funny I should be so bad with it this time. I kept as well as anything with Eddie even though I was worried about Mal and all, and this time when there's nothing to worry about I've been that crook I wish I

The last three words had been crossed out, and the sentence left unfinished. The letter gave the appearance of having been folded away for a time, then taken up again and continued.

It's such a long time since I saw Eddie. I bet he's grown. I hope you haven't had to buy him a load of clothes—I'll try and send you some money when I get the chance, but I can't just now. Fancy him turning out keen on reading and all. He must be pretty clever. Doesn't get that from me, eh?

Sorry for all this moaning. I haven't been sleeping much lately, that gets me down. I'll be all right when this business is over. Then I'll be able to get Eddie back. I feel like I won't be right again till I've got him. I'll manage it somehow.

Amy wrote back promptly, and with an assurance that there was no need for Milly to send money. Eddie was part of the family, she wrote, and Amy was more than happy to provide whatever might be needed. In fact, as she told Milly, with cousins of various ages scattered through the valley there had been little need to buy clothes for Eddie; he had simply become part of the round that passed clothes from one house to the next as they were grown out of.

Milly's remark that she would "manage it somehow" to get Eddie back puzzled Amy, but she put it down to the helpless feeling that went with Milly's obviously delicate health. She was clearly pining for Eddie, which was no doubt making her feel even worse. Amy was guiltily aware of her own earlier suspicions that Milly might not want him back. She was also aware of how painful she herself was going to find parting with Eddie when the time came.

There was no further word from Milly by late February, and this time Eddie left Amy in no doubt that he had noticed how rare his mother's letters had become. David was opening an envelope at the kitchen table one day, when Eddie came and stood at his elbow.

'Is that from Milly?' Eddie asked.

'Nope, it's just a bill from the store,' David told him.

Eddie said nothing, but he gave the table leg a kick as he walked back to his chair.

Amy slipped another biscuit onto his plate. 'Mama will write again before long, Eddie. She's probably just tired lately, with the hot weather.' He shrugged, but made no other response.

Beth arrived from the bedroom with Daisy in her arms. She and David set off to get the cows in for milking, taking Daisy with them. It was a time of day that Amy often devoted to Eddie's lessons, but today she decided that a change of routine was in order.

'It really is hot today, isn't it, Eddie? Would you like to go for a swim?' 'Yes!' Eddie said, his face brightening at once.

Amy gathered up towel and rug, and more biscuits for the appetite she was sure Eddie would have after the outing, and the two of them set out for the creek. She chose a spot close to the house, rather than the more secluded stretch of water David and Beth favoured when they went off for a swim together. Amy had been careful never to suggest that Eddie go with them.

The creek was shallow at this time of year, but Eddie only needed a pool deep enough for him to crouch down and splash away wildly. When he tired of that, he clambered around on the rocks of the creek bed, searching for interesting creatures that might have taken refuge in the mud between the stones. He claimed he could see an eel in one of the pools, but Amy declined his offer to try and catch it for her. She sat on the creek bank in the shade of an overhanging tree and watched Eddie darting from one spot to another as something caught his attention, occasionally plunging back into the water for a moment or two to cool off again.

When Amy judged he had been out in the sun for as long as was wise, she called him to her. He scrambled up the bank and let her enfold him in the towel.

'Look how long your legs are,' Amy remarked as she dried him off. Eddie was no longer the chubby toddler who had arrived at the farm eight months before. He seemed to have shot up several inches since the beginning of summer. Lily had recently sent over a bundle of clothes her younger son had outgrown; Will was four years older than Eddie, but Amy had only had to take up a small amount on the hems to make his trousers fit. 'You're going to be tall like your father was.' She wrapped the towel around him and sat him on her lap.

Eddie nestled against her, warm and soft. He had what seemed an insatiable appetite for hearing about his father; Amy only wished she might have had a larger fund of uplifting tales for him. 'Was my dad really tall?'

'Yes, even taller than Uncle Dave. I suppose Uncle Dave might have caught him up, though—he was only fourteen when your father went away, he's grown a lot since.'

Eddie shook his head. 'No,' he announced. 'My dad was the tallest out of everyone.'

Amy smiled at his certainty. 'Maybe he was, then. And maybe you'll be even taller than him one day. So I'd better do *this* while I'm still bigger than you.' She tickled him through the towel. Eddie squirmed and giggled till he hiccuped, and Amy held him close until he had calmed down enough to eat a biscuit without being in danger of choking.

'I remember bringing your father and Uncle Dave down here for a swim when they were little.'

Eddie looked up, bright-eyed. 'I bet he was a really good swimmer.'

Amy laughed softly. She had no wish to crush Eddie's determination to see his father as a master of all manly virtues. 'He might have been when he was older. I don't really know.'

'Did Milly used to come and swim here, too?' Eddie asked, startling her.

'No, the first time Mama ever came here was when she brought you.'

He looked at her solemnly, almost as if he knew what she was wondering: would that first visit turn out to be Milly's only one?

'We'd better go and see about dinner,' Amy said, seeking a distraction from the uncomfortable thought. 'Let's get you dressed.' She unwound the towel from Eddie and helped him into his clothes, then the two of them set off back to the house, hand in hand.

Amy took Eddie swimming most days after that, taking advantage of the warm weather that continued into March. He had ceased asking whether the mail contained anything from his mother, though Amy scanned every envelope that came, hoping to see Milly's handwriting.

She was relieved when another letter finally arrived, though the envelope was so clumsily addressed that she wondered if it had been written in near-darkness. She slipped it into the pocket of her apron while she and Beth put away the week's supplies, and waited till David had taken Eddie outside to help tend the horses before she went into her room and opened the letter.

It took only a glimpse of its contents to tell her that things were not right with Milly. A single sheet of notepaper was covered in an untidy scrawl, barely recognisable as Milly's handwriting. There were ink blots in several places, and in others what looked like the marks of tears. The letter itself was little more than a jumble of incoherent phrases that could only be made out with an effort. Amy recognised Eddie's name scattered through the letter, and she managed to decipher "wish I could see him" and "just about forgotten me by now". The last line of the letter, which had been written a little more clearly, was "I've messed everything up. I'm sorry."

Amy sat on the edge of her bed and, as calmly as she could, thought over what she should do. Milly was clearly in great distress, and quite possibly ill. There was only one way in which Amy could help her, though it would not be without complications.

She took her writing supplies out to the kitchen, sat at the table and wrote a brief letter to Milly.

I'm so sorry you're not feeling well, she began. *Would you like me to bring Eddie to see you? I'm sure that would brighten you up. Don't worry about having us to stay, I know you won't feel up to that. We'd just come for a day or two, and we could stay in a boarding house. I expect we could get a coach from Tauranga to Waihi, if that's the nearest town to you, and perhaps Mr Carter could pick us up from there, or if it's not too far we'll walk. Just say the word, and I'll see about booking a passage right away.*

She had David make a special trip into town the very next day to send off her letter, then settled herself to wait for a reply. Even as wretched and unwell as Milly seemed to be, Amy expected a prompt and eager response to the idea of seeing Eddie again.

But no answer came. Amy waited two weeks, then wrote again, repeating her offer and stressing how willing she was to bring Eddie to see his mother. She felt an urgency that she was unable to explain fully, even to herself, and at the same time she felt a sick helplessness. She had no proper address for Milly, just the name of the general store where mail was held for her. If it had been a matter of going on her own, Amy might have set out without hearing from Milly, and trusted to asking directions along the way. But she could not drag Eddie on such a journey, with no certainty of what might be at the end of it.

No letter ever came. But at the end of March, just after Daisy's first birthday, Amy was sitting at the table with Eddie one afternoon when she heard the sound of a horse's hooves coming up the track. Eddie got up at once, abandoning the arithmetic lesson Amy had been giving him, and ran to open the door.

'It's a man,' he announced. 'It's not one of the uncles.'

As every man in the valley was some sort of uncle to Eddie, this visitor must have come from further afield. Amy went to the doorway and looked over the top of Eddie's head, in time to see the rider dismounting his horse close to the garden gate. The man was a complete stranger to her.

She quickly took off her apron and hung it on a hook behind the door, then went out to greet the visitor, Eddie trotting along beside her.

The man stood outside the gate, holding the reins of his horse. He was tall and rather thin, with a slight stoop. He took off his hat as Amy approached, revealing thinning brown hair streaked with grey.

'Is Mrs Stewart at home?' he asked, his voice low.

'That's me. I'm Amy Stewart.' Belatedly she remembered that there were two Mrs Stewarts on the farm, but it was most unlikely that a stranger would be seeking Beth.

She saw the man's gaze flick to Eddie, then back to her. 'I'm Sid Carter,' he said, dipping his head uncertainly as if wondering whether she would recognise the name.

'Oh! You're Milly's—'

Amy suddenly found herself unable to speak. She reached out blindly to draw Eddie close as she stared at Sid Carter's sleeve, drawn in above his elbow by the black armband of mourning. Her eyes met his, and he nodded slowly.

29

With an effort, Amy recovered herself.

'Eddie, you fetch a bit of rope so you can tether Mr Carter's horse,' she told the little boy, who was staring at Sid Carter with frank curiosity. 'And then I want you to go and see Uncle Dave and Aunt Beth. Ask them... ask them what sort of jam they want with the scones later,' she said, flailing for an excuse, however feeble. 'There's no need to come straight back, you can stay with them for a bit. Tell Daisy about getting all your sums right.'

Eddie hesitated for a moment, still staring at Mr Carter, then appeared to decide that the visitor did not hold much promise of excitement. He slipped through the gate that Amy was now holding open, and set off at run.

Mr Carter tied the reins loosely to the fence and came through the gate, a leather satchel held under one arm.

'That's Milly's boy?' he asked, looking after the small figure.

'Yes, that's Eddie.' There was a pause, just long enough to be awkward, then Amy spoke again. 'Would you come in? I'm sure you could do with a cup of tea.'

Mr Carter followed her up the steps and into the kitchen. He took a seat at the table, placed the satchel on a chair beside him, then sat turning his hat between his hands.

Amy sent covert glances at him as she quickly tidied away the remains of Eddie's lesson and set out tea things. Milly had said her husband was some years older than she was, but this man, Amy judged, must be at least fifty, which would make him ten years older than Amy was herself. Perhaps it was the pall of grief hanging about him that bowed his shoulders so; for he was grieving, Amy had no doubt. He had soft brown eyes that struck her as kind, but full of pain.

She set the teapot down and sat opposite Mr Carter.

'When did Milly pass away?' she asked.

'Three weeks ago, it would be. The tenth of the month.'

Just a few days after the last letter she had ever sent. 'And how did it happen?' Amy prompted gently.

'It was when the child came. You knew she was with child?'

'Yes, she wrote and told me.'

'She hadn't been keeping well for some time. I was worried sick about her. But she wouldn't hear of letting a doctor see her. She kept saying it was nothing to worry about, it would be over soon enough. And I'd never had anything to do with a woman in that state before, so I thought perhaps I was worrying more than I needed to.'

Amy nodded in what she hoped was an encouraging way, anxious not to interrupt Mr Carter's flow.

'She was taken poorly one evening not long before it happened. She still had two months before the child was due, and she told me she didn't think it had started, but she was quite ill in the night. I nearly went for the nurse then, but it passed. She was... she was never quite right again after that. It was as if she knew what was to happen.'

He took a gulp of the hot tea that Amy had just placed before him, and stared into the distance. 'And then a week later her pains started. I didn't think she should be left on her own, but I had to fetch a nurse to her. There aren't any other houses close by, but some men were working on the road not too far away, and one of them said he knew where the nurse lived, and offered to go and tell her.

'I went back to Milly and got her to lie down. I think I made her a cup of tea. I didn't think the nurse would be long, I thought the best thing I could do was try and keep Milly calm till then.' He gave his head a small shake. 'She was calmer than I was, I think. Though I don't know if calm is the right word. It was as if she was beyond worrying. Worrying about herself, at any rate.

'It felt like hours we waited for the nurse—it *was* hours, come to that. Milly's pains eased for a time. It was happening so long before the baby was due that I thought perhaps it wasn't that at all, perhaps it was a false alarm, but Milly said no, this was childbirth. I argued the point—I remember I almost tried to make a joke of it, asking her how she could be so sure. That's when she told me. "Because I've been through it before, Sid," she said. "I've got a little boy." '

Amy frowned, trying to make sense of his words. 'But you knew that already. Milly had—' She stopped in mid-sentence, awareness flooding in.

Sid Carter had noted her reaction. 'You thought I knew about her boy. Yes, she told me she'd said that to you. We had a long talk while we waited for that nurse, in between the pains. She told me about her boy's father dying in the war, and how she'd had to leave the child with his grandmother when she started working at the hotel. And that you thought she'd told me about Eddie, and I'd said he could come and live with us once things were more settled.'

He gave a heavy sigh. 'Of course I would have let her have him with us—right from when we were first married—if I'd only known about him. I didn't like to think she hadn't felt able to tell me. But I couldn't scold her over it.

'She said she'd been scared to tell me before we got married—she thought I'd want nothing to do with her if I knew she'd had a child by another man. And then afterwards she was scared because she hadn't told me before. She'd been missing him all that time, poor girl. She started crying then, for all she was being so brave over the pains. She asked me to see that her boy would be all right. I told her we'd fetch him as soon as she was well again, but she was having none of it. Things weren't going right this time, she told me. She was too weak by then to argue over it, but she kept shaking her head when I told her she'd come through it. And she kept saying she had to know her boy would be all right. I promised her then. I promised I'd see that he was. That settled her a little, until the pains got bad again.'

'Poor Milly,' Amy murmured. Milly's deception seemed a small thing in the face of her suffering.

'I tried mopping her forehead and holding her hand, and giving her a bit of water, but there was nothing much I could do. I could see by the clock a couple of hours had gone since I'd sent off for the nurse, and I was starting to think I'd have to leave Milly and go out looking myself, but then the woman turned up.'

Amy expected to see some small sign of the relief Sid must have felt at the nurse's arrival, but instead his face hardened.

'I'd booked the nurse already. It was early, but I didn't want to leave anything to chance, and I'd been told she was the best in the district. But of course she wasn't expecting to have to attend Milly just then, and she was off with another patient, as I discovered later. The chap who'd gone to fetch her found she wasn't home, but someone on the street told him there was another nurse living not too far away, and he went there. That was the woman who turned up. I could see she was the worse for drink the moment she walked in.' Amy saw in his face that he had heard her sharp intake of breath.

'She wasn't even clean in her person. But I didn't have a choice by then,' he said, his mouth twisting with the effort of speech. 'I had to trust the woman knew her business. I made her wash her hands before I'd let her touch Milly, I had enough sense for that, at any rate. Not that it did much good.'

Amy did not dare interrupt him, even with a murmur of sympathy. He had clearly come to the darkest part of his tale.

'I had to… to help the woman. She wasn't steady enough on her feet to manage on her own. Just fetching and carrying, but I hadn't expected to be there during it. Though I'm glad of it, really. At least Milly had someone she knew with her.

'The child was definitely on the way, the woman said, for all it was so much before its time. But it wasn't sitting right. She'd have to turn it, she said.' He shuddered. 'I'd thought it was bad before, but the noises Milly made when that woman had her hands on her…'

He recovered himself and went on. 'I don't know how long it all lasted. I do know the fool of a woman took her time giving Milly anything for the pain. She asked if I had whisky in the house, but I'm not one for strong drink. She might've wanted it for herself, for all I know. She took little enough notice of the state Milly was in.

'It was past midnight when she said things were well enough along for her to put Milly out. She had some chipped old bottle with a few drops of something in the bottom—she put it on a dirty old rag and held it over Milly's face, but there wasn't enough to put her properly under. It dulled the pain, I think. She was groaning instead of screaming, anyway.

'The child…' His voice broke; he swallowed noisily. 'It was stillborn. I caught a glimpse before the woman wrapped it up in a towel. Such a tiny thing, but it seemed… broken, somehow. I think she'd damaged it trying to turn it in the womb. But I was told later a child born that early would never have lived.'

'No, it wouldn't,' Amy murmured in agreement. She fumbled for a handkerchief and dabbed at her eyes.

'The woman cleaned Milly up, then she took herself off. I put the baby beside Milly, and I sat there with them both. She came to herself after an hour or so, and she cried a little, but she didn't have strength to do much more than lie there, drifting in and out of sleep.'

He moved in his chair. Amy waited quietly for what she knew must be about to come.

'When it got light, I could see Milly had more colour in her face. I thought it was a good sign. But when I put my hand on her cheek I felt how hot it was. She'd taken a fever.

'I cooled her down as much as I could with wet cloths, then I ran off to the nearest house and asked them to send for the doctor. When I got back to Milly she was bad with the fever, tossing about and moaning. She was burning up worse than ever by the time the doctor arrived, and he said she was bleeding badly.

'He did what he could to make her more comfortable, and he had a woman come in to tend her and keep her clean. There was nothing else to be done. She died the next day. I had them bury the baby with her.'

'I'm so sorry,' Amy said.

Sid Carter looked up, startled, at the sound of her voice, as if he had forgotten where he was. 'She was calling out for her boy at the end.

361

"Eddie, Eddie," she kept saying. Calling for him and… I think your son's name must have been Mal.'

'Yes, it was,' Amy admitted. 'Milly would have been muddled in her head by then, she must have slipped back a few years.' Sid looked unconvinced. 'She talked about you a lot in her letters,' Amy said. 'She was always saying how good you were to her. You… you made her very happy.' She felt a little awkward making such a personal comment to a man she had just met, but she was rewarded by a tiny spark of life in Sid Carter's eyes.

'As she did me,' he said in a low voice. 'Perhaps not always the most truthful of girls, but a warm-hearted one.'

Amy let the silence rest between them for several moments before she spoke again.

'It was very kind of you to come all this way to let us know.'

He blinked at her. 'I had to. I promised Milly I'd see her boy was all right. I told her I'd look after him myself if need be.'

'No!' The word escaped from Amy before she had the chance to formulate a calmer response. 'I'm sorry, I didn't mean to… It's very good of you, Mr Carter, but there's no need for that. I want to keep Eddie with me.'

'You're quite sure? It's not every woman would welcome a child dropped on her like that.'

'He's come to feel like my own after having him all this time. I wouldn't want to part with him. And he's…' *He's all that's left of Mal.* Amy left the thought unsaid, rather than remind Sid Carter that Eddie was also all that was left of Milly.

'I'm glad of it,' Mr Carter said, his shoulders slumping. 'I'd have done my best by him, but I've no notion how to raise a child. And I'd have had to get someone to mind him during the day, and see that he ate properly, and whatever else boys need.' He hesitated, then asked diffidently, 'I can see the lad's healthy, but I wonder if I might speak to him before I leave? Just a few words. It would set my mind at rest, after promising Milly.'

'Of course,' Amy said. 'Would you like to stay the night? You've come a long way.'

'Thank you, but I couldn't put you out like that. No, I've a room at the hotel for the night, then I'll be on the boat tomorrow.'

'Well, stay until Eddie comes back, anyway. He'll probably come up wanting something to eat before too long. If he doesn't, I'll go and fetch him.'

Mr Carter nodded absently. He lifted the satchel onto his lap and opened it, removing a neatly-wrapped brown paper parcel tied with string. He slid the parcel across the table to Amy.

'Your letters are all in there. And the boy's drawings. Milly told me where she'd been keeping them. The last letter arrived after she'd passed away—I haven't opened it. You'll find his birth certificate in with them, too. And this,' he said, reaching into the satchel again. 'Milly used to wear this all the time. I thought her boy might like to have it.'

'Thank you. I'm sure he will.' Amy took the silver bangle from his outstretched hand, recognising it as the one Milly had proudly announced Malcolm had stolen for her. No need to tell Mr Carter that. She had slipped an envelope containing enough to cover the price of the bangle under Mr Hatfield's door one Sunday, so she could keep it for Eddie with a clear conscience.

Mr Carter removed something else from the satchel. He seemed about to pass it over, then hesitated, holding it between fingers that trembled. 'I've brought the photograph, too—the one of Milly and her boy. But I wondered if… I don't like to ask, but… I've no pictures of Milly.'

'Oh, you keep that one,' Amy urged. 'I got the photographer to do two just the same, one for Eddie and one for Milly. It was taken the day she left.'

'Thank you,' Mr Carter said with evident relief. He put the photograph away carefully. 'I've her wedding ring, too—I'll get a nice frame, and put the ring in with her picture.'

Amy poured out more tea. 'You met Milly at the hotel, didn't you?' she asked, wanting to turn the conversation along happier lines.

Sid Carter's face brightened. 'Yes, I did. I'm a bookkeeper, you see. I do the books for all sorts of little concerns that don't have enough business to employ a bookkeeper of their own. Mainly in and around Waihi, so I was living in a boarding house there. But I found I was spending a day most weeks in Tauranga, so I decided I could treat myself to staying the night there sometimes. It made a pleasant change— boarding house fare is rather monotonous.

'I noticed Milly straight away. The staff there are competent enough, but they're inclined to be a bit stiff and formal. Milly had a spark about her that set her apart. I remember the very first morning I saw her—the food's excellent at that hotel, but the portions aren't overly generous. Milly was serving my breakfast, and she gave me a bit of a grin and slipped me an extra knob of butter.' He smiled at the memory. 'It became something of a game between us after that. She'd look about as if there might be spies watching, then make a great show of sliding me the extra butter under cover of her hand.

'We'd talk away whenever she wasn't too busy with her work, and it got so as things seemed rather dull on the days I didn't see Milly. I soon started making sure I had enough work there to take me to Tauranga every week—in fact I found an excuse to stay two nights a week when I could. And then when I was walking about the town one day I saw a sign up for a concert, and… well, I hadn't been in the habit of putting myself forward like that, but I found myself asking Milly if she'd like to come to it with me. And she said yes.

'After that, I took her out every week, even if it was just for a walk along the Strand. She seemed to enjoy my company,' he said, a touch of wonder in his voice. 'And when I was responsible for her being dismissed, I thought I'd better do the right thing and get on and marry her at once.'

'Milly got the sack?' Amy said, startled. 'What, for giving you an extra knob of butter?'

Sid's eyes slid away from hers. On his face was an expression somewhere between embarrassment and shy pride. 'Actually, it was for being caught coming out of my room one morning,' he admitted. Amy suddenly felt the need to fuss about with the tea things.

'We got married straight away, as soon as all the forms were filled in. Just a simple exchange at the courthouse—Milly didn't want a fuss, though I wouldn't have grudged her a proper wedding. I bought her a new hat for the occasion,' he said pensively. 'One of the girls she'd been working with at the hotel came along to be a witness, and she ran back and got one of the boot boys when we realised we needed two of them. We didn't bother with photographs. I wished afterwards that we had.

'I rented a house for us, and Milly seemed happy getting it all set up the way she wanted. Then we found there was a baby on the way, and…' He picked up his spoon and began stirring his tea. 'I hadn't expected to marry,' he said, turning the spoon slowly round and round as if the task took great concentration. 'Not at my age. I was contented enough with how things were. Well, used to how they were, at any rate. But to come home every evening and find someone pleased to see me, and wanting to talk about all the little things that had happened in the day, and then with the baby… It was…' He trailed off and shook his head, and Amy quickly dashed her hand across her eyes to clear them.

Mr Carter looked up from stirring his tea. 'Would you mind writing from time to time to let me know how Milly's boy is getting on? Once a year would be enough.'

'I'd be glad to. And when Eddie's old enough, I'll get him to write himself sometimes.'

'Oh, I doubt if he'd be interested in writing to an old fellow like me.'

'Yes, he will. He'll want to when I tell him how good you were to Milly. But I think I'll leave that till he's old enough to understand.' Amy sighed. 'For now, it'll be enough for him to try and understand about Milly passing away.'

'I'll make sure you have an up-to-date address for me.'

'I've got the address—I used it to write to Milly.'

Sid shook his head. 'I won't keep the house on. There's no point, just for myself. When the rent's up on it, I'll go back into a boarding house.'

Back into the grey, plodding routine he must have had before Milly erupted into his life. Back to a world of dusty offices all day and a drab room to return to at night. Years stretching out ahead of him until those few months when he had been a husband and about to become a father would seem like a foolish daydream. Amy's heart ached for the man. But it ached more sharply for the little boy who had become an orphan.

'Shall I go and get Eddie?' she asked.

'Yes, if you wouldn't mind. It's probably time I was on my way.'

He followed Amy outside, clutching the satchel that flopped loosely now that it held nothing but a photograph. Amy shielded her eyes to look in the direction Eddie had set off, and saw him coming up the hill, swaying somewhat under his load.

'He's got Daisy with him,' she said, smiling at the sight. 'She's my other son's little girl—Eddie's cousin.'

'A little girl,' Sid echoed. 'Milly's baby was a girl, too.' He fidgeted with his satchel. Amy could see that he would rather have taken himself off before the children arrived. But he stood his ground, and watched as Eddie struggled up the slope to them.

Amy relieved Eddie of his wriggling burden as soon as he was close. She slipped an arm around his shoulders and led him over to where Sid Carter waited. 'This is Eddie,' she said. 'Eddie, this is Mr Carter.'

''lo,' said Eddie. He thrust out his hand, and Sid Carter shook it solemnly. He crouched down to Eddie's height, placing his hands on his thighs to steady himself.

'How are you, Eddie?' he asked.

'Good,' said Eddie.

'And do you like school?' It was almost painful to watch Sid's stilted attempt at conversing with a small boy.

'I don't go to school. I do lessons with Granny. I can read, and I can write things, and I can do sums.'

'You teach him at home?' Sid asked, looking up at Amy.

Amy gave Eddie's shoulders a squeeze. 'I enjoy it. He's doing very well, too.'

Sid stood up and patted Eddie on the head in an awkward gesture. 'You be a good boy for your grandmother, then.'

'I am!' Eddie said indignantly.

'Shh, Eddie. Yes, he's a good boy. I'm lucky to have him.'

Sid studied Eddie's face; Amy guessed that he was trying without success to find some trace of Milly there. He turned to Amy and nodded. 'He's a fine boy. Thank you for letting me meet him.'

Eddie held the horse's bridle while Sid mounted. He went back to stand beside Amy as Mr Carter rode off. 'Bye, Mister!' Eddie called after him.

Sid turned in the saddle and waved, then Amy watched him dwindle. Milly's husband. The man who had given her a home; who would have welcomed Eddie for her sake. Milly's best chance of a settled, comfortable life, and one she had clearly taken hold of with both hands. Milly, who had lost family and lover and child, and had had life snatched from her just when it had seemed on the verge of making good some of those losses. Wednesday's child, full of woe. Made for sorrow. No wonder she and Malcolm had found each other.

Amy balanced Daisy on one hip, and with her free arm drew Eddie close. Milly's child. Mal's child. And now Amy's own child. 'Come and sit on the verandah with me,' she said. 'We'll have a little talk.'

Amy set Daisy down on the verandah, and sat on the steps with Eddie at her side. Daisy pulled herself upright against a post, then cautiously moved from one post to the next, clinging to the verandah railings for support. It was a task that took all her concentration, and left Amy free to give Eddie her attention.

'Climb on my lap.' She spread her arms in invitation, and Eddie clambered on readily. She smoothed down the hair at the back of his head that insisted on sticking out in all directions; a pointless exercise, as the hair immediately returned to its previous angle, but one Amy found soothing. She kissed one particularly unruly tuft.

'Do you remember I told you how Mama was very tired, and she wasn't feeling well?' she began. Eddie nodded, his eyes fixed on hers.

'She got really sick, Eddie. That's what Mr Carter—the man who was just here—that's what he came to tell me about. He's been very kind to Mama, looking after her. But she got worse and worse, and then she… she passed away.' Those pale blue eyes stared at her uncomprehendingly; "passed away" meant nothing to him. 'She died, Eddie. Mama died.'

He looked more thoughtful than upset. His face took on the same expression it did when she set him a particularly difficult piece of arithmetic. 'Isn't she coming back?'

'No, she's not. I'm sorry, Eddie.'

He still looked as if he were working through a puzzle. 'Has she gone to Heaven?'

'Yes,' Amy said, snatching gratefully at the suggestion. 'Yes, Mama's in Heaven now. So she won't feel sick any more, or sad, or anything like that.'

Eddie tilted his head to one side, still thoughtful. 'Is she with my dad now?'

'Oh, yes,' Amy said, rather more certain of this than of her previous answer. 'Yes, I'm sure they're together.'

'Do they have horses in Heaven?'

Amy laughed softly. 'Do you know, I've never thought about that. Perhaps they do, for the people who really want them.'

Eddie nodded solemnly. 'They do have horses,' he pronounced. He put a hand on Amy's arm. 'Are you going to die, Granny?'

'One day, yes. But not for a long time, I hope. Not till you're grown up, anyway.' She closed her arms around him more tightly. 'I'm not going away, Eddie. I'll look after you.'

30

Amy sat in the April sunlight, Daisy warm and drowsy on her lap, and watched Eddie riding back and forth. He had cajoled her into letting him set up jumps, though Amy had insisted they be so low that the horse barely had to stretch its stride. But Eddie seemed to find it exciting enough. He gave a whoop of delight at every jump, usually followed by a cry of, 'Did you see me, Granny?'

Between assuring him that she had indeed seen, and that it was very good, Amy stole glances at the latest letter from Sarah, spread out beside her on the old log she was using as a seat. It was close to two years now since she had last seen Sarah, and Amy had no idea how much longer it might yet be before they were reunited.

But for the moment she took pleasure in the soft, milky-smelling baby on her lap, and the laughing little boy riding round and round the paddock. Sparks of orange flame flashed from Eddie as the sunlight struck his hair, while Daisy's growing curls peeped from around her bonnet in an echo of darker red.

The sound of hooves smacking against dried earth, quite different from the soft thud of Eddie's unshod mount in the grassy paddock, caught Amy's attention; she looked up and smiled to see Frank approaching. She tucked the letter away and called him over.

He knotted the bridle and left the horse free to graze along the side of the track. 'I was just on my way up to see Bill,' he said as he sank onto the smooth log beside Amy. 'I thought I'd drop in and see my girls.'

'Beth's gone off for a walk with Dave. I'd go and look for them, except... well, I think they might have gone for a swim.' Amy felt a blush creeping over her face. 'The weather won't be warm enough much longer.'

Frank grinned. 'Good for them. That's all right, I've only got a minute. I'll make do with seeing this little one.'

Daisy had woken up properly at her grandfather's approach. She held out her arms, demanding to be picked up by him. Amy passed her across to Frank, who jiggled her on his lap with well-practised ease. 'Gan-gan-gan,' Daisy crowed, an all-purpose word she was currently using for all three of her grandparents.

'She was asleep when Beth and Dave went off, but they hadn't been gone two minutes before she woke up,' Amy said. 'I know I should leave her to go back to sleep on her own, but...' She smiled and shrugged.

Frank nodded knowingly as Daisy nestled against him, gurgling away to herself. 'You hardly want to miss a minute of them when they're this age, eh? It goes by quick enough.'

'Yes, it does.'

Frank declined her offer of a cup of tea, though he seemed in no particular hurry to leave. They sat together watching Eddie and playing with Daisy, who was delighted at the attention. They talked idly, about the weather and the children and the small happenings of the valley, and then they let conversation lapse, easy enough in each other's company to be as comfortable with silence as with speech.

The buttons on one of Eddie's sleeves had come undone, Amy noticed, and he seemed in danger of getting the loose sleeve tangled in the reins. 'Come here a minute, Eddie,' she called. 'Come and say hello to Uncle Frank.'

Eddie wheeled the horse skillfully, slid from its back and clambered over the fence to run the short distance. 'Hello, Uncle Frank,' he said, wriggling with barely suppressed energy as Amy held his arm to straighten his sleeve and fasten the buttons. 'Did you see me jumping?'

'I sure did. That's pretty good, Eddie.'

Amy patted the cuff flat and released Eddie's arm. 'There, that's better.'

'Can I do some more riding now?' Eddie asked, poised to run off.

'All right, just for a bit. Give Granny a kiss first.'

Eddie complied readily, giving her a wet kiss on the lips. He kissed Daisy, too, for good measure, then scampered back to the paddock. He mounted the horse from the top rail of the fence, and was soon off again.

'He's the image of Mal, eh?' Frank said, following her gaze.

'Yes, he is.' Amy touched her fingers against her mouth, where Eddie's had so recently been pressed. 'Mal would never have done that, though,' she murmured.

'He's a good kid.'

'Yes, and I'm very lucky to have him. He's...' She smiled at Frank. 'Lizzie thinks I'm silly when I say this, but it's as if Eddie's my second chance with Mal. I can make a better job of it this time.'

'I don't see that you did anything wrong last time. You've no need to blame yourself over what happened to Mal.'

Amy did not bother to argue. She had done the best she could for Malcolm, and her warm heart had conspired with her strong sense of duty to induce a fervent love for her wayward son. But duty had always upheld the larger part of that love. It was not like that with Eddie. Loving Eddie took no effort of will.

'I've been given a second chance with all of them, really,' she mused.

'Davie coming back after being away all that time. Sarah finding me.' A warm glow crept through her at the wondrous memory. 'And now getting Eddie. I'm so very lucky. It's just that I never thought I'd have to choose between them.' Amy came to herself and felt a rush of embarrassment; Frank's easy company had made her speak more freely than she had intended.

Frank looked up from watching Daisy clutch at his finger. 'What do you mean, choose between them?'

'Oh, it's not like that, really. But Sarah wants me to go back to Auckland—and I'd been all set to last year, once Beth was well enough to manage. But I can't now. Not with Eddie to look after.'

'You could leave him with Beth and Dave, though. They'd do all right.'

Amy shook her head. 'No, I couldn't. They're a bit young to look after a boy Eddie's age. Well, Dave is,' she amended. 'Anyway, I couldn't leave Eddie, not with him losing his mother. I promised I'd look after him. It wouldn't be right to dump him on Beth and Dave, and have him think I didn't want him.'

'Mm,' Frank said, a noncommittal sound that might have conveyed agreement or simply a disinclination to argue. 'Ah, well, Sarah will understand, I'm sure.'

'I haven't exactly told her,' Amy confessed. 'About promising Eddie I wouldn't leave him, I mean. I'd hate him to think he was a... well, a burden. He's not, really he isn't.'

Frank nodded thoughtfully. 'You know what Lizzie would say about that?'

Amy smiled. She could almost hear Lizzie's voice. 'She'd say Sarah wouldn't tell Eddie anything of the sort, and *I'm* not about to, so where's the sense worrying about it? I should just get on and explain it all to Sarah.'

'Yes, that's about it.'

They sat in silence for several moments before Frank spoke again. 'The thing about Lizzie,' he said, 'is that she's usually right.'

Nothing could be simpler, Sarah declared in response to Amy's next letter. Of course Amy could not leave Eddie, and there was no reason in the world for her to do so. She must bring him to Auckland with her.

The thought of Eddie, bursting with all the energy of a healthy five-year-old boy, set loose in Sarah's calm, well-ordered household made Amy wonder if it would be quite such a simple matter as Sarah supposed. But with that small concern set aside, the idea was beguiling.

She wrote back at once, thanking Sarah warmly. She would bring Eddie for a visit, she told Sarah, and they would see how they all got on. That was as much as Amy was willing to let Sarah commit herself to.

That evening, she tucked Eddie in then sat on the edge of his bed. 'Eddie, you're going to Auckland with me soon,' she told him. 'Next month, it'll be. We're going up to stay with your Aunt Sarah. You can take your nice book and show her how well you can read it.'

Eddie considered the matter. 'Can Daisy come, too?'

Amy shook her head. 'No, Daisy's too little to go on a big trip like that. Just you and me. We might take Daisy another time, when she's bigger.'

The answer seemed to satisfy Eddie. 'Has Aunt Sarah got a horse?'

'Yes, she has—she's got a sort of buggy, and she has horses to pull that. I don't know if you could ride them, though,' Amy added, careful to be honest with the little boy. 'Perhaps you could. We'd have to ask. But Aunt Sarah's got a lovely big house, and a nice garden with trees to climb, and you might even be able to go out on a sailing boat.'

'And we could come back here if we got bored?'

'No, not straight away. We'll be staying there a little while. And I know you'll be a good boy for me at Aunt Sarah's, and not go making a fuss if you don't like things. But yes, we'll come back here if you really don't like it in Auckland after you've given it a proper try.' She leaned down to kiss him goodnight, and wondered to herself if Eddie had inherited her own tendency to seasickness.

There was no risk that Amy might find herself dwelling on painful memories during this voyage. She was far too busy seeing that Eddie did not slip overboard, trip up any unsteady passengers, or just get something dropped on him as he darted around the boat, utterly sure-footed and blessedly untouched by nausea.

It was a relief when the boat drew up to the wharf at Auckland, though with the increased activity on deck Amy had to keep a close grip on Eddie. She held grimly to his hand as a human tide carried them along towards the gangplank, and trusted that Sarah would manage to see them through the crowd.

Sarah was there and waiting. She swept up to them, slipped her arm through Amy's, sent the coachman off to collect their luggage, and guided them to one side of the crowd, all within moments.

'Sarah, this is Eddie,' Amy said as soon as they were safely out of the crush.

Sarah moved to stand in front of Eddie, and lowered herself to his level in a graceful motion.

'Hello, Eddie. I'm your Aunt Sarah. I'm very pleased to meet you.' She extended a hand, and Eddie shook it. Amy watched the two of them sizing each other up. There was not the slightest physical resemblance, but something of the same keen observation showed in each pair of eyes.

'Granny said you've got a horse,' said Eddie.

Sarah laughed. 'As it happens, I do. Come and meet the carriage horses.'

She gave Eddie only a few moments to pat the horses before bundling him and Amy into the carriage and taking her own seat at Amy's side. Eddie knelt on the seat to look out at the bustling city. He had been briefly awed by the noise and crowds on the wharf, but now he stared with interest from the safety of the carriage at the tall buildings and the traffic, pedestrian and horse-drawn.

The journey to Sarah's seemed shorter this time. The carriage drew to a halt, and Eddie tumbled out without waiting to be helped down. When Amy took his hand she found that he was gazing up at the house, his mouth open.

'Are we staying here?' he asked in a smaller voice than usual.

'Yes, we are,' Amy said, giving his hand an encouraging squeeze. 'This is Aunt Sarah's house.'

He let her lead him inside, his eyes wide as he stared at his surroundings. Both the maids that Amy remembered from her previous stay were there to greet them, bobbing curtseys from the side of the passage, then disappearing in the direction of the kitchen.

'I'll show you to your rooms,' said Sarah. 'I expect you'll want to freshen up. The luggage will be brought up shortly.'

They followed her up the stairs, Eddie still allowing his hand to be held. Stairs were a novelty to him; he had never tried anything closer to them than the few steps up to the verandah on the farm. Amy saw him casting a speculative look at the banister rail; she tugged at his hand to get his attention, and shook her head firmly.

'You're in your old room, of course, Amy,' Sarah said. 'I've given Eddie the one next to yours. It's small—I believe it may have been intended as a dressing room—but I think it'll do for now.'

The room was somewhat larger than Eddie's bedroom on the farm, but small enough to be cosy. There was a bed with a yellow coverlet against one wall, a set of drawers against the opposite wall, and a wooden chest near the foot of the bed. A connecting door led through to Amy's room, which was just as she remembered it. Fresh flowers had been placed on the dressing table, hot water was ready in the jug, and clean towels had been laid out. And when Sarah opened the wardrobe door, Amy's lovely dresses were all hanging there, just as she had left them.

'You see?' Sarah said, brushing her fingers lightly over the tops of the hangers. 'I knew I'd lure you back if I held these to ransom for long enough.' She parted the dresses to show the red velvet gown. 'I'm determined to persuade you to wear this one before too long.'

Amy smiled at the sight of the lovely things. 'I'll pull them all out later and try some on. Not right now, though,' she added as she watched Eddie, who was showing signs of becoming restive. His uncharacteristically subdued manner had soon passed, and now he was prowling around the room, looking for something more interesting than dresses. This house, unlike the one on the farm, was full of things that might not survive a five-year-old's attention.

'You must be tired after that long trip,' Sarah said. 'Would Eddie like a sleep, do you think?'

Amy did not give Eddie the chance to voice the rebellion she saw in his eyes. 'I shouldn't think so. I think he could do with a run around, if that's all right?'

'Of course,' said Sarah. 'We can go into the garden—I'll have our afternoon tea brought out there. But wouldn't you like to get changed first, Amy? I know how stale one feels after being on the boat all that time.'

Amy looked down at her creased and travel-stained dress, her elegant surroundings making it look all the more drab. The thought of washing away some of the grime of the journey and changing into one of her pretty dresses was tempting. But a glance at Eddie, who was lying on the windowsill and leaning out as far as he could, made her reconsider. She put her arms around his middle and tugged him back inside. 'I'll be all right like this for now,' she said.

Sarah looked at the two of them and appeared to guess Amy's thoughts. 'I think Eddie can come outside with me and leave you to freshen up. Come along, Eddie.'

Eddie went readily, not a trace of shyness as he skipped out of the room ahead of Sarah. A moment later, Amy heard the muffled thump of his footsteps bumping down the carpeted stairs. She quickly slipped out of her cotton dress, washed, and changed into the first tea gown she found in the wardrobe, wondering as she moved about the room just how Sarah and Eddie were getting on.

She went downstairs and out the front door, and found Sarah at the base of the tallest tree in the garden, looking up. Amy followed her gaze, and saw Eddie's legs dangling from a high branch.

'I suppose this is all right?' Sarah asked uncertainly. 'He told me he climbs trees all the time on the farm.'

'Yes, he's like a cat for climbing,' Amy said. 'He's never fallen from very high up.'

'Oh, good,' said Sarah. 'Because I know he has to be kept busy. I took advice, you see—I've never really had a great deal to do with boys before. The general opinion seemed to be that the more one finds for them to do, the happier everyone is. Mr Kendall was particularly strong on the subject—he has two sons, so he ought to know. He told me boys are bursting with energy, and if one doesn't tire them out by channeling it into harmless activities, it will come out in less desirable ways.'

Amy smiled. 'He's right, really. The only way I can get Eddie to settle down for lessons and things is to make sure he does lots of running around.'

She sat with Sarah at a pretty little bamboo table under a gazebo entwined with climbing roses, a few blowsy flowers still clinging on although the season was almost at an end. Nellie, the maid, brought out a tray with tea things, including several kinds of cake.

'Plain cake, and seed cake, and currant buns,' Sarah said, pointing out each in turn. 'Mrs Jenson said boys like that sort of thing.' She looked enquiringly at Amy, clearly seeking approval.

'I'm sure Eddie will like everything. He'll be happy, as long as there's plenty to eat. You really don't have to go to any bother, Sarah.'

'It wasn't a bother,' Sarah said. 'It's not as if I had any involvement in the process, beyond asking Mrs Jenson's opinion. But I want Eddie to be happy here. I want him to feel at home.'

As if he had sensed the arrival of food, Eddie soon appeared, slithering down the trunk of the tree and jumping from the lowest branch. Amy brushed leaves and twigs from his hair and clothes as best she could. She was relieved to see that Sarah seemed unperturbed by his less than pristine appearance.

Eddie sat on the chair next to Amy's, swinging his feet to and fro as he munched on slices of cake and gulped down lemonade. When he had had enough, he was off again, prowling around the garden and looking speculatively at several of the taller trees. He climbed one of them, and found he could scramble from it to the next tree.

'This is a good garden, Granny,' he called from his perch.

'Mind you don't break anything,' Amy called back. 'I meant branches,' she explained to Sarah. 'Everything's so neat and tidy.'

Sarah smiled. 'I doubt if he could do much damage. I'm glad my garden meets with Eddie's approval—I shall have to tell the gardener.'

Eddie clambered down the tree and began exploring the patch of grass that surrounded a small fountain. Amy saw him bend down several times to pick up small objects. He came back to the gazebo, and was about to spread out his finds on the table.

'Not on the nice tablecloth, Eddie,' Amy admonished. 'Put them on the ground, we can see them all right.'

He had found an acorn, some dried-up berries, and the cast-off skin of what they decided was a grasshopper. Sarah managed to appear more impressed by the finds than Amy suspected she actually was, and told him he could have them in his room if he wanted.

'Eddie likes looking for interesting bits and pieces,' Amy said. 'Rocks and things, too.'

'Does he, indeed? Hmm, that suggests some possible outings. I suppose the museum might be too dry for a child his age?'

'I don't know,' said Amy. 'I've never been to one.'

'The butterflies and insects might interest him, though,' Sarah said, while Eddie sat at their feet arranging his finds in several different configurations. 'It's very near here, it wouldn't be at all out of the way. And some of the beaches might be good for rock hunting. I'll look into it. There's the circus, of course, but that won't be back till next year, I expect. We might try a pantomime, though, if you think he'd like that—I believe there's to be a season of "Cinderella" shortly.'

At the sight of Sarah's animated expression, Amy abandoned any attempt to tell her not to worry herself over it. Sarah was clearly enjoying making plans for Eddie.

The maid came out to clear away the remains of their afternoon tea. 'Nellie, tell Walter we're ready for him,' Sarah said. Amy almost thought she saw Sarah and Nellie exchange a conspiratorial look. She wondered idly what the message to the gardener's boy might mean.

Eddie resumed his exploration of the garden, and Sarah watched him for a minute or two. She glanced towards the corner of the house, then stood up.

'Come with me, please, Eddie.'

Eddie looked up from examining an insect crawling on a leaf. 'Why?' he asked.

'Eddie, do as Aunt Sarah says,' Amy admonished gently. She caught Sarah's eye and looked her own question; Sarah merely smiled, and inclined her head in an invitation to follow her.

Amy took Eddie's hand and led him in Sarah's wake. Just before the path disappeared around the corner leading to the back garden, Sarah turned to face them.

'Now, Eddie,' she said, her serious tone belied by the spark of excitement in her eyes, 'I've work for you. While you're living here, you'll need to do this almost every day. It's most important. Come and see.' She slipped her hand through Amy's free arm and guided her around the corner.

Eddie stopped in his tracks, and Amy felt a quiver of excitement run through him. Walter was standing in front of the stables, his hand on the bridle of a chestnut pony.

'This is Rufus,' said Sarah. 'It's your job to look after him.'

Eddie tugged his hand from Amy's and tottered like a sleepwalker up to the pony. He reached out a trembling hand and stroked the glossy flank. The pony sniffed at him, then gave a soft, breathy snort. Eddie turned to Sarah, his eyes wide, and took great gulps of air before he was able to speak. 'Is he… is he for me?' he managed at last.

'Yes, he is. You'll need to exercise him, and groom him, and so forth. You could go out with Walter when he exercises the carriage horses, although you'll need to get up early in the morning for that.'

'I can get up early.' Eddie's voice ended on something like a squeak.

'We shall see,' said Sarah. 'In the meantime, I'm sure you'd like to take Rufus through his paces.'

Eddie nodded vigorously. Amy recovered from her own shock at the extent of Sarah's generosity, and gave Eddie's shoulder a small shake. 'Eddie, say thank you to Aunt Sarah.'

'Thank you,' Eddie said at once. 'Thank you for the pony. Can I go for a ride now?'

Sarah nodded to Walter, who hoisted Eddie bodily on to the pony's back and adjusted the stirrups. He kept a hand on the bridle and began leading Eddie slowly around the area in front of the stables.

'Sarah, that's… that's very good of you,' Amy said as the two of them watched a delighted Eddie.

'Well, from all you'd told me of Eddie, I knew he'd never settle here if he didn't have a horse to ride.' She turned to face Amy. 'And I do want him to settle. I know that's the only way I'm going to be able to keep you here for any length of time.' Sarah smiled. 'Though I must confess I find myself liking Eddie on his own account. I've never had much to do with small children—when I was teaching, I managed to confine myself to the older ones. I thought they weren't very interesting until they got to eleven or twelve. But there's something rather endearing about this little imp.'

'I've got very fond of him.'

'Yes, I can see that.' Sarah glanced over at Eddie, who was trying to persuade Walter to release his grip on the bridle. 'Do you feel up to a walk in the park? I doubt if Eddie's going to be content with the back garden for long, and the park should be fairly quiet this late in the afternoon.'

Amy assured Sarah she was quite capable of such a stroll. Rather than have Amy change from her tea gown into a walking costume, Sarah rang the bell for the maid and had her bring their cloaks. She issued her instructions to Walter, and they all set off on the short walk to the park.

They passed the statue of the young soldier from the Boer War; she would show it to Eddie one day soon, Amy thought to herself. She had taken him to see Malcolm's monument in Ruatane; he would probably find a statue even more impressive.

Sarah and Amy sat on one of the benches, still arm in arm. Amy pressed against her, delighting in the closeness. While they watched Eddie bring Rufus to a trot, then urge the pony into a slow canter, they talked quietly of what had passed during their time apart. There were matters that neither of them felt able to discuss freely in a public place, even one that was almost deserted, but a few careful words were all that was needed for the other to understand.

The sun was getting low, the golden light of late afternoon fading to a cool blue-grey. Walter, patiently standing by one of the trees, was a barely glimpsed shadow, his clothes much the same colour as the bark against which he leaned. Despite her cloak, Amy gave a shiver.

'Do you want to go back now?' Sarah asked.

'Yes,' said Amy. 'I'll have to get Eddie cleaned up before he's fit for dinner.'

When Eddie came past a few moments later, she stood and waved to him. 'Eddie, it's time to go inside now,' she called.

Eddie executed a neat turn and came back towards her, the pony stepping tidily in a well-controlled walk. 'I don't want to yet. I'm going to stay out here.'

'No, you have to come in now,' Amy said. Something in the set of Eddie's mouth made her heart sink a little. She found his occasional bursts of real obstinacy difficult to cope with even on the farm, where she felt herself to have a measure of authority; she did not look forward to having to deal with one so soon after their arrival at Sarah's.

'I won't,' said Eddie, a hint of colour in his cheeks beyond what exercise and excitement had put there. He jerked the reins irritably.

The pony was startled by the sudden movement, but rather than reacting with a burst of speed it planted its four feet firmly on the ground and came to a dead stop.

Sarah stepped past Amy and put a hand on the bridle. 'Hadn't you better do what your grandmother tells you?' Sarah did not raise her voice, or show the least trace of losing her temper, but Amy would have cringed if that reproving tone had been turned on her. 'Rufus will still be here tomorrow, and you can take him out again. Unless, of course, you'd rather I sent him away?' she added, fixing Eddie with a hard stare.

'No!' Eddie said, his eyes wide with alarm. He glared back at Sarah, opened his mouth in what seemed destined to be a disastrous attempt at rebellion, then abruptly shut it. Eddie knew when he had met his match. 'I'll come back now.'

'Good boy.' Sarah released the reins, and at the same time released Eddie from her stern gaze. 'We'll all go back to the house now.'

She walked along at Eddie's side, an arm loosely around Amy's waist. Amy saw Eddie send occasional covert glances in Sarah's direction, and she traced his thoughts in his face. The remnants of indignation quickly faded, as he recalled just who the source of the pony had been. He caught Sarah's eye and grinned at her, to be met by an answering smile.

When they reached the house, Eddie announced that he had to tend Rufus before he could possibly go inside.

'Not much needs doing, just taking off his tack,' Walter said, grinning at Eddie's earnest expression. 'I can do that on my own.'

'No, I have to do it myself. And I have to *groom* him,' Eddie insisted.

Amy could see that the pony, whose coat looked as glossy as ever after his stint in the park, was in no need of imminent grooming. She could also see how eager Eddie was to establish his claim to Rufus. 'Let him, Sarah,' she murmured.

Sarah patted her arm and nodded. 'Eddie's quite right. As I told him earlier, it's his responsibility to look after Rufus. Walter, show him where everything's kept. You might need to reach the odd thing down for him,' she added more quietly.

Eddie went off to the stables at the older boy's side, bristling with self-importance, both at his weighty task and at the chance to associate with a big boy like Walter. Amy smiled after him, happy to see Eddie so confidently making himself at home. She turned, and followed Sarah into the house.

After taking off their cloaks they went straight to Sarah's study, where she was eager to show Amy some of the books she had acquired during Amy's absence. Amy soon found herself with a tall pile of recommended volumes for bedtime reading, and for their quiet evenings in the drawing room.

They were so absorbed in their discussions that it was some time before Amy realised Eddie had been gone for longer than it would reasonably take for him to tend the pony. She left Sarah organising the books, and set out in search of him.

Walter was still in the stables, but he told Amy he had sent Eddie back to the house some time ago. Knowing what tended to drive Eddie's movements, Amy headed for the kitchen.

There she found Eddie ensconced most comfortably, seated on a high stool at the kitchen table with a plate of various tidbits in front of him. He was holding forth to Mrs Jenson and the kitchen maid, as well as Nellie, who had somehow found it necessary to hover about in the kitchen rather than get on with setting the dining table.

Eddie looked up and grinned at Amy. 'I'm telling them about coming up on the big boat.'

'Quite the journey you had, Mrs Stewart,' Mrs Jenson said, her eyes twinkling. 'Pirates and sea monsters and Lord knows what else.'

'He's as good as a play,' said Nellie. The little kitchen maid, Polly, simply stared wide-eyed at Amy, as if wondering how she could have survived such adventures.

'Master Eddie's been good enough to let me know his favourite puddings, too,' said Mrs Jenson. 'We'll have to see what we can do about that. You can leave him with me any evening you and Miss Sarah want to go out—there'd be no risk of a dull time for Mr Jenson and I with this fellow about! And he's already made friends with our Walter, he tells me.'

At Amy's request, Nellie set about organising hot water. Amy retrieved Eddie, ignoring his complaints that he had not finished the story, and steered him upstairs. 'You need a bath before dinner,' she told him.

'But I just had one on Saturday,' he protested.

'We have baths more often at Aunt Sarah's. You'll have to put on your good clothes for dinner, too. No, it's no good making a fuss about it, Eddie, you just have to.'

Eddie grumbled half-heartedly, but he was somewhat mollified by the sight of the huge bath. He splashed away enthusiastically, getting a good deal of water on the floor and on Amy. Even the mouthful of soapy water he got when he decided to talk just as she was emptying a jug over his head led to hiccuping laughs rather than complaints.

Amy persuaded Eddie to leave the bath by the simple expedient of pulling out the plug. 'So, do you like Aunt Sarah?' she asked as she dried him off.

'She's a bit bossy,' Eddie said in a measuring tone. 'But she's nice, too. Yes, I like her.'

'Good,' said Amy. 'I think she likes you, too.'

After a fine dinner, Amy was feeling the first signs of drowsiness, but Eddie still looked bright-eyed and alert.

'It's just about Eddie's bedtime, but I'll keep him up a little while longer,' she told Sarah. 'He's had such a lot of excitement today, I don't think he'd settle yet.'

The three of them went through to the drawing room, where tea had been set for Amy and Sarah, and warm milk for Eddie. Amy was on the point of suggesting that Eddie go and fetch the book Sarah had sent him for Christmas, when Sarah called the little boy over to her. Beside her stood a low table, with a wooden box resting on it.

'I've something you might like to play with,' Sarah said. 'But you must be very careful—they're quite old, and they're... well, they're rather special.'

She raised the lid of the box. Eddie peered in, reached in a hand and pulled out a brightly-painted lead soldier, mounted on a rearing horse. 'What are they?' he asked, turning the toy round and round in his hand and gazing at it in wonder.

'Soldiers and horses—you'll find a cannon or two in there, too. You can line them up and... I don't know, pretend to have a battle, I suppose. Whatever you like, as long as it doesn't involve breaking anything.'

'They could be in a *story*,' Eddie breathed, pulling out another figure with elaborate care.

'I'm sure they could.' Sarah took her seat beside Amy, where the two of them watched Eddie as he lifted the toys out one by one.

Amy tore her gaze from the pleasant sight of Eddie so happily occupied. 'Sarah, are you sure it's all right for him to play with those?' she asked, keeping her voice low so Eddie would not hear. 'You told me your... your father,' she said, the word coming out only after an awkward hesitation, 'didn't want them disturbed.'

'It's perfectly all right. Father wanted to keep them as Maurice had left them, as something for him to remember Maurice by. But I don't think he would have wanted them treated like sacred objects for all time, as if Maurice had been some sort of saint. Father was a sensible man. I'd like to think he'd have been pleased to know another little boy was enjoying the soldiers. Especially when the little boy concerned is my nephew.'

Eddie played with the toys for almost an hour, devising a complicated series of stories that began with a battle (he announced that a rather splendid general mounted on the largest of the horses represented Eddie's own father), but soon owed more to his favourite fairytales. He persuaded Sarah to allow a brass vase to be used as a castle, while one of the more diminutive soldiers had a scrap of lace wrapped around him and was pressed into service as a princess (naturally called Daisy) who needed rescuing from a monster in the guise of a paperweight.

He provided his own commentary to the tales, though quietly enough not to disturb Amy and Sarah's conversation. Occasional glances told Amy that he was content to entertain himself; they also alerted her when Eddie began to show signs of sleepiness. His speech grew slower and his eyelids drooped. Not long afterwards he came over to the sofa where Amy was sitting and plumped himself down. She slipped her arm around him and he snuggled in against her. It was only a minute or two before he was sprawled with his head in her lap, fast asleep.

'Are they all like that?' Sarah asked. 'Small children, I mean—running around as if they don't know what it means to be tired, then falling asleep all in a moment?'

Amy stroked Eddie's hair. She had combed it while it was still damp from the bath, and for a brief period it had been looking almost tamed. Now it was returning to its usual state of wildness. 'Boys generally are, anyway.' She rubbed Eddie's shoulder gently; he wriggled, but showed no sign of waking. 'It's time I put him to bed.'

She cradled Eddie's head in her hands while she extricated herself, then crouched beside the sofa to lift him in her arms.

'May I?' Sarah asked.

'He's quite heavy,' Amy demurred.

'All the more reason I should be the one to carry him.'

Amy moved aside and let Sarah take her place. Sarah scooped Eddie up somewhat awkwardly; when she stood, Amy guided her arms to take a more secure hold.

Eddie stirred a little. He flung one arm around Sarah's neck, and moved his head to nestle against her shoulder. Amy knew the comforting feel of a child in her arms, all softness and trust; to Sarah it was something new and startling. She blinked in surprise, then cautiously traced a finger along the curve of Eddie's cheek, down to the corner of his mouth. He nuzzled against her more closely.

Sarah lifted her eyes to meet Amy's smiling gaze. 'He's so warm,' she said, a trace of wonder in her voice. She shifted Eddie's weight slightly.

'And he *is* heavy,' she added, setting out towards the stairs.

Amy undressed Eddie and put him to bed by the light from the passage, keeping his little room dim so as not to disturb him. She opened the connecting door to her own room so that she would hear him if he woke in the night, then she and Sarah went out into the passage.

'I know it's early, but I think I might go to bed myself,' Amy said, stifling a yawn. 'It's been a big day.'

'An early night's a fine idea—but can I persuade you to stay up just a little longer? There's something I'd like to show you. It'll only take a moment.'

Mildly curious, Amy allowed Sarah to lead her along the passage to its furthest end, till they stood before a closed door. Sarah opened the door and entered ahead of Amy, turned on the light, then beckoned her in.

Amy found herself in a room that was almost square. The walls were painted pale cream, bright and fresh in the electric light, and with a hint of new paint smell. Large windows along the front wall suggested that the room would be light and airy in the daytime. A high shelf ran along two walls, and a blackboard had been mounted on the remaining one. There was a plain table, low enough to be comfortable for a child, but still convenient for an adult, with two wooden chairs pulled up to it. A slate and several pieces of chalk rested on the table, as well as sheets of paper, pens, pencils and inkwells.

'I've made you a schoolroom,' said Sarah. 'Do you think it will do?'

Amy stood in the centre of the room, gazing about her quite lost for words.

'I know it looks bare,' Sarah said. 'But I thought it would be nicer for you to choose what books and so forth you'd like to use. Paints and drawing things, too. And you'll want maps and pictures for the walls—I've had them left plain so you can put whatever you want on them. We can go out shopping tomorrow if you like.'

'You've done this just for me?' Amy said, regaining her voice at last.

'Yes. I knew you'd want to go on teaching Eddie, and I thought you might like to have a real schoolroom of your own. And—this is completely up to you, of course—but if you felt you wanted one or two other pupils, I've had acquaintances with young children remark that they'd dearly love to send them to you for a term or so rather than straight to a big school. Emily's oldest, for one.'

'They want me to teach their children?' Amy asked, scarcely daring to believe it.

'And why shouldn't they? You're obviously doing a fine job with Eddie. He might enjoy the company of other children, too, until you feel you want to send him to school.'

A schoolroom of her own. As many children to teach as she wished. That spark of excitement when a child first made the link between scratches on a page and the words of a story would be hers to share in over and over again. And in the meantime, a proper room to use for teaching Eddie, not a corner of the kitchen table that had to be cleared as soon as it was time to prepare the next meal.

'Thank you,' Amy said, feeling the words to be hopelessly inadequate. She sank onto one of the chairs.

Sarah took the other chair. 'I do realise I can't keep you here all the time. I know I'll have to share you with Dave and Beth, and Daisy, and goodness knows how many more children that might come along.'

'There won't...' Amy hesitated; was it correct to tell anyone else about this? But Sarah was family. In any case, people would notice soon enough that Daisy was not being joined by brothers or sisters. 'Do you remember me telling you we were worried about Beth when Daisy was on the way? She's come right now, more or less, but... well, they think it might be best if she doesn't have any more. So there'll just be Daisy.'

'Oh, I see.' Sarah sounded thoughtful rather than concerned; she must be blissfully unaware of the contrivances and sacrifices the resolution demanded of David and Beth. She gave a small laugh. 'I'll admit I'm selfishly relieved. I think I'm capable of becoming as fond of two small children as an aunt should be, but I wouldn't like to be put to the test if Beth were to follow her mother's example.'

'Daisy's a lovely baby, I'm sure you'd like her.' Amy knew that Sarah was not overly fond of infants, but Daisy, with all her charms, must be an exception.

'Perhaps I would—we shall have to see. I expect you'll want to visit the farm several times a year, and it will no doubt suit Eddie to run wild there as a change from Auckland.'

'He's very fond of Daisy, he'll want to see her again before long. And they seem grow up so quickly, I don't want to miss too much of that. I wouldn't like to be away too long and have her forget me.'

'We'll make sure there's no danger of that. I shall have to manage without you—and I suspect the house is going to seem very quiet when Eddie's away!' Sarah smiled. 'But I think I may invite myself to go with you occasionally—perhaps at Christmas.'

'That would be lovely! As long as you didn't mind sharing with me— they haven't got a lot of room.'

'Oh, I expect I could put up with you for a week or two,' Sarah teased. 'I find myself wanting to make Daisy's acquaintance, although I know she won't be much of a conversationalist as yet. I hope you realise that I fully intend to interfere in the case of Daisy?' A glint of mischief lit Sarah's eyes. 'Once she's exhausted the possibilities of that little school in the valley, I want to see that she goes to High School, at the very least. My interference will, of course, extend as far as insisting that I be allowed to pay for it. But I won't hear any nonsense about girls not needing a proper education.'

'I'd like to see Daisy go to High School—and I don't think Beth would say she couldn't. Beth's not one for saying girls shouldn't be allowed to do things—she goes out on the farm with Dave, and she gets him to help her in the house so she can manage to do both. And if Beth says it's all right about the High School, Dave'll go along with it.'

'Very sensible of him. But I think I can safely delay any interference in Daisy's future for a good few years yet. It's Eddie who's uppermost in my thoughts at the moment.'

'This will be such a lovely room for his lessons.'

'I'm glad it suits. Whatever else you need, you've only to ask.' Sarah stacked the nearest sheets of paper into a tidy pile, and placed several pencils on it. 'So yes, you'll go and visit Dave and Beth, and you'll make sure Eddie's able to spend time with his cousin. But I want you to consider this your home from now on, Amy. You and Eddie both.'

'You've gone to so much trouble. Getting him a pony and everything!'

'Oh, my motives were purely selfish, I assure you. I was simply thinking of what might help Eddie settle in. I knew I wouldn't be able to persuade you to make your home with me if he wasn't happy here. That, of course, was before I met Eddie,' Sarah said meditatively. 'Now I find myself thinking rather further ahead.'

'What do you mean, dear?'

'His education, for one thing. Of course you'll teach him here for as long as you wish, but we'll look into a good school for when the time comes.'

'Not a boarding school,' Amy said quickly.

'Certainly not. I want Eddie to be brought up by you, not a succession of schoolmasters. No, a primary school as close to home as we can find one we like, then whatever we decide is the best grammar school for him—Auckland Grammar's closer, but we might prefer King's College. And university after that.' She saw Amy's dazed expression, and smiled. 'Oh, yes, I have grand ideas for Eddie, though we'll leave him in blissful ignorance of them for now. I'd like him to study enough law to know whether he's being properly advised or not—I see that as a necessary preparation. Beyond that, he can choose whatever subjects take his interest.'

'University?' Amy echoed faintly. 'Preparation? What for?'

Sarah arranged pieces of chalk around the edge of the slate. 'I don't intend to marry. I'd see that as diminishing my own comfort, and probably the comfort of any man foolish enough to take on the challenge. The one thing I might have felt I lacked was companionship.' She put her hand over Amy's. 'I'll never lack it as long as you're here.

'But meeting Eddie has made me realise what else I might be said to lack. Eventually I'll want someone to take a share of my business responsibilities, and… well, I'll need an heir. I don't plan to acquire one in the usual fashion, but I believe you've found a way to fulfill that need, too.'

'You mean Eddie? You'd make him your… heir?' It seemed a grand word for a small boy.

'Yes, I believe I shall. I can't think of a finer choice than a child raised by you who happens to be my own nephew.' Sarah glanced in the direction of Eddie's room and smiled. 'You know, Amy, I've never felt any great desire to share my home with a child, though I was perfectly willing to do so if it was the price of having you come to live with me.' She laughed softly. 'Now I'm beginning to wonder how I've borne the peace and quiet for so long!'

Printed in Great Britain
by Amazon